PRIORITIES OF LOVE

Romance! Courage! Conflict!
Forgiveness! Reconciliation!
Hope! Faith! Love!

An Inspirational Novel by
ROBERT SIMPSON

PRIORITIES OF LOVE

First published in Great Britain in 2022 by
ScriptCraft Publishing
(a division of the Sunpenny Publishing Group)

First Edition

PRINT ISBN: 978-1-912602-08-7
KINDLE ISBN: 978-1-912602-09-4

SCRIPTCRaFT
Professional Writing and Publishing
Services
SUNPENNY PUBLISHING GROUP

Praise for *Priorities of Love*

I was watching a DNA programme recently and was reminded that family traits can have deep roots. In our Simpson ancestral family there are many examples of bookbinders, writers and theologians. My brother Robert has tasted deeply of all three of these – and I am proud of him, especially since his stroke. The perseverance and persistence of the early days of writing as therapy have become a major focus of Rob's daily life as he creates stories and books and explores ideas for his next adventure. Rob's soul relationship with God is threaded through his writing. To Rob, then, this dedication from a proud sister.
– *Rev Heather Simpson, Missionary, Minister & Spiritual Director (semi-retired)*

Over the years, I have been impressed by the way that Robert has overcome the effects of his depression and stroke by taking up writing. He has woven the threads of history, family experiences and his imagination to create an ever-expanding fictional tapestry, which culminates in *Priorities of Love*. His achievement is an admirable example to us all.
– *Trevor Agnew,* **Queen's Service Medal,** *Retired English Teacher*

You have put down amazing things – first clinical depression, then ECT, followed by a severe stroke and yet, you have come out with a completely different freedom.
– *Stuart Simpson, Minister*

Having raced along with a good portion of *Priorities of Love*, I can heartily say "Well done".
– *Matthew Simpson, Teacher*

Having worked with my husband from the start of *Priorities of Love,* it is a pleasure to say that it is well worth reading.
– *Margaret Simpson*

When Robert first came to me, recommended by another author I had worked with, I thought the lilt of his prose was singularly lyrical in many places, with a delightfully classic touch, and I loved it. We worked hard as a team to achieve the best possible result that would appeal to all ages, while keeping to the ethos and voice of the book. In the midst of this, I managed to get myself hospitalised for 6 months, and unable to work; through it all, Rob waited patiently for my recovery, while many others would have taken the work to someone else, and I cannot say enough how honoured I was by his loyalty. I believe that together we have given our best to produce a final outcome that shines, and that a wide range of readers will fully appreciate.
– *Jo Holloway, ScriptCraft*

*To my dear wife Margaret,
whose patient work alongside me
has been my lifeline.*

In memory of the English author
Howard Spring (1899-1965),
whose books have encouraged me to write
so diligently that his novels have become
part of me, as I have become part
of this novel.

Acknowledgements

Grateful thanks to my colleague Charlie Jemmett.
He reads through my errors and mistakes, before I send
the manuscript to the editor, Jo Holloway. She is of high
repute, bringing life to some aspects needing emphasis,
suggesting other matters that I have not thought of, and
of course, deleting unnecessary words, phrases, paragraphs,
even chapters, thus presenting a perfect book! And to Andrew
Holloway, my excellent proofreader.

James 4, vs1-3 is from the Good News Bible,
published by the New Zealand Bible Society.

Sources that have been helpful in preparing
Priorities of Love include a reference to Elizabeth
Goudge's book, *A City of Bells,* published by
Gerald Duckworth, 1936 and by
Hodder Paperbacks Ltd, 1957; also
A Grief Observed, by CS Lewis, published by
Faber and Faber in 1961.

Other material is obtained from extensive reading,
including works of war artists recalling the
Battle of Loos in Belgium, where my
grandfather was killed.

Adam Fraser's Family Tree

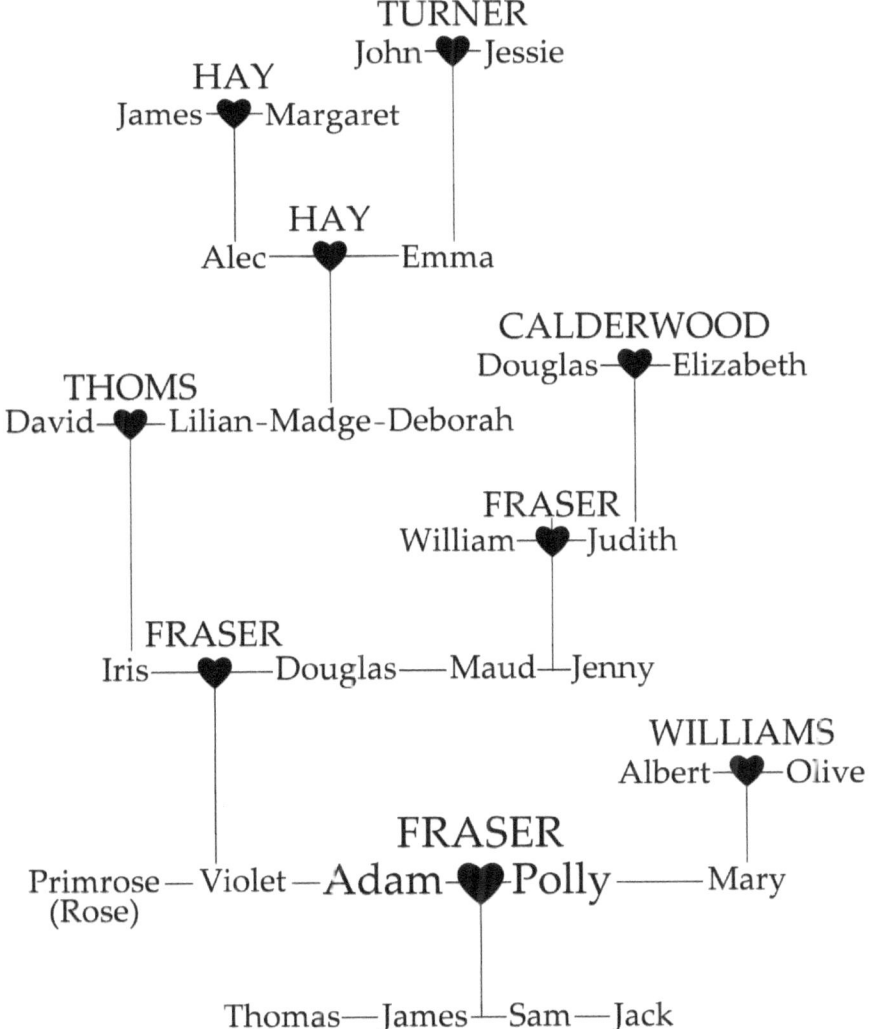

TURNER
John—♥—Jessie

HAY
James—♥—Margaret

HAY
Alec—♥—Emma

CALDERWOOD
Douglas—♥—Elizabeth

THOMS
David—♥—Lilian-Madge-Deborah

FRASER
William—♥—Judith

FRASER
Iris—♥—Douglas—Maud—Jenny

WILLIAMS
Albert—♥—Olive

FRASER
Primrose—Violet—Adam—♥—Polly——Mary
(Rose)

Thomas—James—Sam—Jack

PART ONE

A Tapestry of Love

Preface

OUNG ADAM FRASER and his Great-grandfather, Alec Hay, much enjoyed time spent together. Adam would call at his house most late afternoons to explore with him past family activities and look at possibilities for the future. Because he felt that the words 'Great-grandfather' and 'Great-grandmother' were too much, Adam called them GGF and GGM.

'Very suitable,' said Adam's GGF; 'much more succinct. Here – have a chocolate biscuit.'

Adam liked chocolate biscuits, so having one or two, or maybe three, he settled down to hear what GGF would tell him at this moment.

Oh... I am getting ahead of myself. This doesn't happen for some time. Better to start at the beginning, where all good beginnings start.

Chapter 1

ADAM, ONLY SON of Iris and Douglas Fraser, was born on the 12th of September 1940 in Mosgiel, near the city of Dunedin, in New Zealand. Adam's weight was average, his body firm, his face chubby, and his curly hair auburn. In fact, Iris thought that such a beautiful child would surely catch the eyes of all, so she often pushed him in the pram up and down the town's main street, Gordon Road.

Adam did indeed look quite appealing, with his long auburn ringlets cascading around his face, and it wasn't long before Iris was stopped by a curious woman peeking into the pram, proclaiming, 'What a beautiful baby! How old is she?'

Annoyed, Iris hurriedly returned home and, taking the scissors, cut Adam's hair to make him look more like a boy.

Everyone expected that Adam would be baptised. Talking to Douglas, Iris said laughingly, 'We have my grandparents and my Auntie Madge representing the Presbyterians, and your Glaswegian mother Judith representing the Church of Scotland. I know it is Presbyterian, but it *is* different, isn't it? And my parents represent the Methodists. Adam is going to be baptised in front of them all! I wonder whether the Reverend Andrews knows what he is letting himself in for?'

Walking with bouncy strides, Reverend Andrews was a young man just out of Theological College. He always wore a dog collar that was almost an inch deep, and a very dark suit. This attire tended to make him look older and rather severe, especially with his thin face. Dressed in his black gown and white magisterial bands, he looked rather fierce in the Mosgiel pulpit. It took quite a while for the parishioners to appreciate their new minister.

Before any baptisms, the Reverend Andrews liked to visit parents two or three times on Friday evenings. On this visit, he saw baby Adam before he was put into bed by Iris.

Douglas had some difficulty knowing what to say to the Reverend when Iris was out of the room. Iris returned to hear the minister imperiously utter the words, 'I want you to know that the baptism of a child is a very precious and holy event. The whole congregation will stand with you as you present Adam before God.'

Iris was delighted at this, but Douglas wondered at all the solemnity.

The baptism took place and, with one voice of acclamation, the congregation received Adam into the church. As righteous people do, they vowed that, with Jesus Christ's help, they would give him their encouragement, care and patience, intertwined with their love.

As the Reverend Andrews was showing the now-baptised Adam to his smiling relatives, the child chuckled with delight, his blue eyes darting from one face to another.

Adam's friendly great-grandfather, Alec, waggled his long grey moustache at the child. His great-grandmother Emma made loving eye contact with her own bright blue eyes. Judith, his grandmother, looked over her new spectacles and smiled gently, nodding. Lilian, his other grandmother, adorned with her exquisitely elegant brooch, gracefully bowed her head to Adam in acknowledgement. His grandfather David smiled proudly at all who looked his way. His Great-Auntie Madge blew him a kiss and, surprise, surprise, her tight curls danced to the sounds of the organ music playing softly in the background. Adam's father, Douglas, smiled broadly at him, and Iris looked adoringly at the little boy, softly mouth-

4

ing the words, 'We all love you, Adam!'

Most Sunday afternoons, the great-grandparents, Alec and Emma, welcomed the extended family in the garden at their pleasing Forfar Street home. Alec always took pleasure in his garden. The grass paths he had created were now in a crisscross pattern that made the garden look more decorative. He regularly trimmed the hedges to head height, and the lawn was always freshly mown. He had reluctantly just retired from work, and relaxed on Sundays by wearing his smart brown trousers, open-necked shirt with no tie, and brown buttoned-up cardigan.

Iris, Douglas and baby Adam arrived right at afternoon tea time. When they were settled in the garden seats enjoying their tea and cakes, Alec, who sat next to Iris, said, 'I suppose you want to take a photograph with the child?'

Iris mentioned that Douglas had a brand-new camera, so the photos would be taken on this, but Douglas quickly realised that he would have to get Auntie Madge to take them if he expected to be in the photographs as well.

Of course, Madge was not so keen. Although she didn't need to, she was busy rushing around filling up cups of tea again, and handing out new plates of cream lamingtons. Douglas would have to take the photos himself.

Because she had no warm shawl on, Emma felt the breeze that suddenly whispered into the garden. With a sigh, she asked Madge to take her into her bedroom. All the relatives fussed, telling her how nice it was to see her, but Douglas muttered that he had not yet shown off his photographic skill.

Emma had a chronic complaint which sapped most of her energy, so she needed lots of rest in bed – well, that is what she told Alec – after all, she was in her late seventies, so resting in bed was always her answer, but the other reason was an expectation that her husband would be more attentive and sympathetic.

This expectation did not disappoint. Most mornings,

Alec would be outside early, picking fresh flowers of red, pink or yellow hues from the garden. The fragrance of roses wafted throughout the house, some of which would be placed in Emma's special vase on the small pedestal at the end of her bed.

At exactly half past seven in the morning, Alec would open her bedroom door and swish back the heavy curtains to let the sunshine, in all its glory, in through the window. Emma would slowly sit forward so that he could rearrange her pillows behind her before he gently kissed her. Sitting on the edge of the bed, he would hand her a small plate of porridge with a little bit of milk (but no sugar). He watched as she slowly ate. When finished, Alec gave her some dry toast with either strawberry, apricot or quince jam. There was tea in a fancy pot, with a cup and saucer to match. She always enjoyed her first cup of tea.

When breakfast time was over, Alec always asked her, with a twinkle in his eye, how she had slept during the night. Smiling, Emma always replied that she slept as well as could be expected. They had this short conversation each morning, day after day, month after month – well, until eternity dawned!

Chapter 2

MADGE, DAUGHTER OF Alec and Emma, was kept extremely busy working for *Madge's Millinery*. She had early on arranged for some young acquaintances to distribute leaflets all around town advertising her fledgling business, and the response was so successful that the leaflets were no longer required. Now there was a succession of elegant ladies waiting to try on hats in *her* own style.

Of course, *Madge's Millinery* worked from the Forfar Street house of her parents. She thought that there was no use providing hard-earned cash for a shop in Mosgiel when she knew that these were under the control of greedy commercial rental people. Much better to stay at home, where there was a large bright room at the front of the house that accorded her the exciting opportunity of creating a millinery business, without the overheads.

Upon turning seventeen, Madge had been employed in Dunedin by Mr Edward Wimpole. There, she worked for the certificate that would make her, if she succeeded, a fashion milliner.

Edward Wimpole was an unusual man. He always dressed in the latest fashion, with red as his favourite colour. He frequently wore a bright red waistcoat, offset by a fiery red-striped Edwardian jacket and maroon baggy pants. The long fair hair which adorned his sculpted head made him interesting to members of the feminine sex. His long, tapering fingers and delicate nails, which were cut to perfection, gesticulated as he explained with his hands the milliner's art.

The *unmarried courtier,* as he was described by some swooning students, was in his late thirties. He had been born in Sudbury House, in a village just north of London, where his parents resided in an old, secluded Tudor home. An only child, he was born with a clubfoot, but this did not prevent him from doing all that he wanted to: music, drawing, and skilful artistry.

His army father had wanted Edward to join up with the same regiment he himself had been in, but of course that was impossible because of his son's clubfoot. Edward's overpowering mother encouraged his artistic nature by taking him to tailoring lessons. This skill came to his rescue, for during the Boer War he was, surprisingly, employed by the Royal Engineers on 'special duties' making flying balloons. These were used for observation and reconnoitring in South Africa.

After the Boer War, Edward Wimpole left England for South Africa to find out how effective the balloons had been. Then he travelled on to Australia, where he learnt much but did little. His father and then his mother had died, so that finances arrived regularly for him from the Sudbury House estate. Later he voyaged to New Zealand, settling down in the university city of Dunedin.

Of course, Madge fell head over heels in love with him as soon as she saw him. With eyes always fluttering, and applying rouge to her cheeks, as all the magazines dictated, she wore the red lipstick she had borrowed from her mother's purse, and worked harder than the rest of the students. She completed the sewing certificate with flying colours. 'This is the best in the South Island,' Edward Wimpole enthused in his deep rumbling tones.

Madge made certain that her *loving friend* – though whether he would accept this title fully was debatable – would hear frequently about her excellent work in millinery. The future with Edward Wimpole looked rosy to Madge, so she set out to achieve this with some vigour.

By now they had been 'going out' for quite some time. They both dressed in the latest fashions. They enjoyed looking at the latest catalogues from overseas, and regularly observing other people's clothes while having tea and cakes at various restaurants. Sometimes they visited the cinemas, viewing the most recent movies that revealed the latest American fashions. Although they were often out together, observers would not have taken them as *being* together; however, it was serious enough for Madge.

Shockingly, one day Edward Wimpole was killed in a tragic accident in Dunedin. He began his work early that morning, and the first thing he noticed was that there were slight whiffs of gas percolating from somewhere. He thought it was just residue built up from the night before, so he opened a window to clear it, then five minutes later closed it.

This gas was important. It provided warmth, as well as light, plus boiled his enormous kettle to provide cups of tea, particularly the first welcome one of the day.

After he had enjoyed his steaming drink, he began work on another creation when, all of a sudden, the gas ignited and the building collapsed around him.

'Why did he not smell the gas when he first opened the door?' was one of the coroner's unanswered questions.

The loving nature that had existed between the two *amoureux* was now shattered by his death. There was a massive gap in Madge's life. Anguish overwhelmed her. She had constantly to remind herself that Edward Wimpole was *really* dead!

Over time, she drew into herself more and more. She didn't mention him again. She didn't even have photographs of him displayed at her home with the rest of the family pictures, but she did have a little engraved picture which she wore around her neck under her dress, and lovingly remembered him that way.

Sometimes, when Madge felt overpowered by sadness, she slammed the front door, went down to the Silver Stream and, thus in hiding, she wailed in memory of her Edward.

As excellent as her hat-making business was, she had to force herself to be all smiles to her friendly chatting customers. She wanted to show them that she was very competent and most helpful. She would even hold her hands in the manner of the Dickens character, Uriah Heep, copying his 'humility' by doing a half-curtsy and saying in melodious tones, 'Please come in! What can I do for you?'

The lady's choice might include a hat like the one they had seen Miss So-and-So wearing in Britain, or perhaps they had seen an advertisement in the national newspapers. She would take their hat size and produce the desired creations. *Madge's Millinery* always had satisfied customers!

Chapter 3

VIOLET, ADAM'S YOUNGER sister by three years, was born with a heart murmur. She needed extra care from her parents – certainly time with her father, who had other worries to contend with. However, he took time off his engineering work in Dunedin to be at the large general hospital with little Violet and a worried Iris by her side.

Only that wouldn't be communicated clearly to Adam. Nor would he understand the ramifications of the unravelling situation. So he spent extra time with his grandparents, Lilian and David, where he found all sorts of exciting things were happening in their house.

Adam, now nearly five years of age, enjoyed being with Grandpa David. Holding him closely, Grandpa would run his hand through Adam's curly hair, receiving a happy grin from him in return. The quality time the two spent together meant that they had a first-class relationship.

Adam had been warned about the '*poo*' man coming at night. Wearing his loose gumboots, this man walked silently (yet Adam still heard him), with purpose, around the back of the house to the toilet. A few minutes later, Adam heard him returning along the path with the full slop-bucket.

Wrapped against the wintry blasts in a massive coat and headgear, the *poo-collector* went past the window, where the waning moon threw his shadow onto the bedroom wall. Adam was scared, so he crept into Grandpa's bedroom where, under the bedclothes, David's arm would be waiting to comfort him. He rejoiced that grandpa could hear the poo-man too!

Early one Monday morning, after he had his salty porridge, David biked to his work at the railway station and Adam ran along the footpath to see him off. Turning right at Gordon Road, Grandpa said, 'Goodbye! Go back to Grandma now.'

However, today, instead of returning, Adam made his own lazy way to the station to find out where his father was. On the way he met several agitated men on their bikes, with buttered toast in their mouths, satchels in one hand, handlebar in the other, on their way to catch the Dunedin train. Sometimes, if the men were very late, they would throw their bikes down by the roadside and race to catch the departing train. Later, the patient railway guard – Grandpa David – retrieved their fallen bikes and put them safely away for collection on the travellers' return.

Adam looked but couldn't find his father, who had already departed on a train to Dunedin some time ago. He made his way back slowly to Grandma's house. She hadn't even noticed his absence!

Eighteen months later, Douglas bought a powerful second-hand six-cylinder Chevrolet car. It had lovely wooden panels covering the inner frame inside. Indeed, the whole interior of the car was incredible, with its plush, velvety seats and patterned carpet on the floor. Douglas was familiar with driving because, in earlier years, and fully licensed, he had driven old jalopies around the factory yards where he had been employed. This was completely different.

After purchasing the second-hand sedan four-door car for fifty pounds, the family all climbed in. Adam peered excitedly out of the car's front window at what he could see in the distance. Iris and little Violet reclined majestically on the back seat. Douglas took hold of the steering wheel and put the car into gear. Gordon Road went on a direct line through the town and other short roads branched off on either side, forming a crisscross pattern. With small square-shaped houses arranged in different styles, it made

Mosgiel a neat, snug borough! The family were going out for their first trip in and around the town.

They were all smiles on their return, for the car had performed well. Adam said, still excited as he reluctantly got out, 'Will we go on a car adventure *again?*'

His father smiled. 'Be good and we will see.'

Quietly, he said to Iris, 'I suggest you phone your mother and see if the arrangements are fixed for tomorrow.'

This would be Iris' birthday, and the day would be full of wonderful surprises, starting off with the gifts from the two children and, later, Douglas' gift. Come evening time, celebrations would involve the wider family. On the previous Sunday afternoon, Iris and Douglas, with Violet in the pram and Adam tightly holding onto his father's hand, were walking down Gordon Road. They stopped before Ronald's Emporium and looked at all the wonderful things on show. Iris saw in the corner of the window a small notice: *Delicate Panties from Europe Have Just Arrived*, and said quietly, 'Do you think I could have some of those for my birthday?'

She usually didn't speak of underwear to anyone – not even to her husband – but with the notice there in the window the request had come tumbling out. Showing his surprise, Douglas slowly replied, 'We will see!'

On the due day, presents from the children were practical – a small box of chocolates from Adam with his saved-up money, bought from the newsagents, and a linen tea towel from Violet, bought on her behalf by her father. Douglas had remembered Iris' request and had gone into Ronald's Emporium when he came home early from work one day.

He had only ventured in there twice before – once when he and Iris had been looking for suitable furniture for their new house, and then a few days later, for tools that he needed for doing vital jobs around the place. However, he had never been into the women's underwear department.

He slunk amid those mysterious wonders and he saw what many men had not seen! Written so neatly in front of the headless models were *Fine Bodices Worn by*

Royalty, and *Fashionable Brassiere from America, worn by Hollywood actresses.* There was also a veritable array of *Delicate Panties* and *Strong Knickers from Europe.*

Hesitatingly, Douglas went up to the mature assistant. She looked at him severely. She had short greying hair, a mole on her right cheek, pursed lips, and a strident voice in which she said abruptly, 'Can I help you?'

Douglas' nervousness increased a thousand-fold. Clearing his throat, he said in tones that were not his, 'I would like a pair of satin knickers for my wife,' giving her the size and colour and hoping he had the size right! The assistant proceeded to show him what they had.

By this time, he wished that he hadn't come into this department to be served so superciliously by this snobbish assistant. He said frantically, 'That one please!' He wanted to get out of there as quickly as possible. He had chosen a pair of strong satin pants with stretchy elastic around the waist and legs; not exactly the delicate panties that Iris had requested!

When the time for giving birthday gifts to Iris came, his was produced. Douglas waited anxiously, moving from one foot to the other.

Smiling, Iris unwrapped the lovely paper – she thought that Ronald's Emporium was excellent at wrapping gifts – and the strong, practical, pink satin knickers came out. When she saw them, she was overcome! Her face became angry, her eyes became steely and tears started falling. 'You've got me a pair of bloomers – I hate bloomers, I wanted delicate panties!' she exclaimed. Slamming the lounge door, she ran into the bedroom, crying her heart out.

Douglas was left alone with Adam and Violet, who were both surprised and shocked at their mother's abrupt departure. He said to himself, 'I have done the wrong thing again,' and he smiled wanly at the children.

Neither Iris nor Douglas was happy as they all climbed into the car, setting out for the celebrations of the wider family of her relatives. Silently, Douglas changed gear and backed carefully down the drive. Unfortunately, he drove onto a muddy grass verge that was wet from the rain that had been falling all day, stopping only an hour ago. No matter how he applied the gears or revved up the engine, the two wheels were well and truly stuck.

Iris looked even more upset, and cried out somewhat grumpily, 'We've only just got in! What will the neighbours think?' – as if they had the time or inclination to line up and peer at them through their windows.

Douglas muttered out of the corner of his mouth, 'I should hope one of the them might give me a hand.'

While everyone climbed out, Douglas assured his family that everything would be alright. Iris scowled, tears in her eyes. Violently slamming the car door so loudly that Violet screamed, Iris yelled out in a strident voice, 'I've changed my mind! I won't be going! You can put in my apologies!' She plucked Violet from the car and stalked off toward the house.

With a look of resignation, Douglas called back, 'Yes! Righto, dear!'

Arrangements had been made for the older men in the family to travel together in Douglas' new car to see the final parade of the returning soldiers at Mosgiel's Memorial Gardens. While the men were enjoying these activities, Iris and Violet had intended to remain at the Forfar Street home, where Emma and Lilian would welcome them with cups of tea and cakes. These delicacies were always under Madge's direction, of course. Douglas' talkative mother Judith, with her broad Glaswegian accent, would be there as well. They would enjoy sharing their news as they consumed everything that Madge had made for them. However, now, Iris and baby Violet would stay at home, all alone.

Douglas and Adam hurried to the nearest neighbours to seek their help. Together, they all heaved and struggled until they got the vehicle out of the mud. One helpful neighbour said with a grin, 'Watch that you don't back into the mud again!' and they went on their way.

With a broad smile, Douglas called out, 'I wouldn't dare!'

Speeding over to Lanark Street, he jumped out of the car and, taking the keys with him, went inside. Adam stayed in the car, keen to guard it. The family were waiting patiently for their arrival. Having told them of Iris' decision not to come, Douglas kept quiet about the real reason, pleading a headache for her!

Douglas made sure that Alec and David were comfortably seated in the rear of the car, and given rugs that Iris had supplied. Adam sat in the front. They arrived near the Memorial Gardens just in time to see the approaching soldiers through the car windows. It was a very good spot. The townspeople were celebrating the end of World War Two, and so the soldiers marched proudly together on this last regimental parade. Led by the army brass band, they were looking resplendent. However, young Adam thought, *Why are they still carrying guns when the war is over?*

Iris and Douglas had a long period during which they were not talking to one another. After a lengthy time of reflection on what went wrong, and with Douglas promising not to go into that department of Ronald's Emporium again, Iris reluctantly forgave him.

Chapter 4

LILIAN WAS MOVING out of her Ayr Street house. She had wonderful memories of David, her dear husband, who had since died of a heart attack. Now, after all this time of grieving, it was time to change venue. She was going to live in Iris' and Douglas' two storied house, where Douglas had already changed the ground floor rooms into an attractive flat. Lilian had asked if the painting, *The Quiet Scene,* could be put near the entrance to the flat. Not only did she take pleasure looking at the vista, but visitors could enjoy it also.

Now that Adam and Violet were a little older – eight and five years old – Lilian enjoyed sharing outings with them. She took them to see an ice show that was held in Dunedin. *Exciting and Beautiful,* she had read out from the fancy brochure just before the show started. Not only that, Lilian gave them a lapel pin of ice-boots to put on their coats. They looked like the ones worn by the brilliant dancers of this show!

When she received visitors at the flat, Lilian always offered them freshly made cakes that she had produced in her tiny kitchen. However, when she went to visit her parents, Alec and Emma, she found that Madge was always standing protectively there. She didn't stay long. More often, she travelled by train to Dunedin to do some shopping in the large department stores. She always brought back some small gifts that Adam and Violet liked. She mostly enjoyed coming up the stairs from her flat and having a chat with Iris when they were both alone.

It was obvious to all that her move to this large house

had been a good idea, although the thoughts of David would never go away.

Judith was suffering from severe headaches. She went to her doctor and, when he checked her blood pressure, he found it was very high.

It was when she lay so ill in hospital that her mind recalled many things, like her years in Mosgiel. How pleasant this country was with its lush greenery, compared with living in crowded tenement housing in Glasgow!

Her daughters, four-foot-eleven Jenny and four-ten Maud, had been brought up to be honest and considerate and had taken well to married life. They had made their contribution to the prosperity of the expanding town.

Judith (five foot precisely) also remembered how an exuberant Jenny had reported to the family that she had won the competition for baking sponge cakes. Not only that, one lady who was high up on the committee spoke of the excellent quality and finish of her baking. Thinking there was now no one who could bake sponges as well as *she* did, Jenny had suggested that she start up her own business selling her cakes commercially.

Jenny set to and made a supreme sponge cake for the family. She handed it out on little plates with small cake forks that she had picked up at a church fair, and waited for their verdict.

The cake *was* delicious. It wasn't too floury, nor was it too dry – indeed, it was just right. After they had sung its praises and the cake had disappeared, Jenny remarked, giving a little giggle, 'There are a number of young men who would like to have their faces in the sponges, but just one – Wally, a sturdy, quiet man who is six foot-one – has advanced to the point of asking me to marry him. Of course, I said yes!'

She had taken them all by surprise, for none of them had heard of Wally before. They hurried to congratulate her, and to entreat her to bring him to dinner so they might all meet him.

Her sister, Maud, also bright and breezy, then spoke

up, saying that she had just heard something important.

'Just last week, on Tuesday – or was it Thursday? – this young man... well, I *say* young man, but I couldn't guess at his age – perhaps twenty, or he may have even been thirty – well, you can't tell. As I said, he came to the house. Was it in the morning, or the afternoon? – well, it doesn't matter! He wanted to sell me some house cleaners... or was it gardening products? I could never tell the difference! Anyway, I said that my mother was away but would be returning in the morning.'

Judith found that she was always exhausted by Maud's explanations, but there was more to tell. 'He is arriving tomorrow morning to see if you want to purchase any of them.'

And so it transpired that later the following morning the young man had arrived, and Judith bought some household cleaners from him. Maud promptly fell in love with the chubby twenty-seven-year old Stephen, a friendly and cheerful man.

Judith chuckled now at the memories. Then she thought of her son, Douglas, and her amused chuckling fell silent. She thought him a meticulous student of life. He had always been a follower, and certainly not a leader. She wondered if she should let him read the old letters pertaining to his father, William, who had died in World War One. How would Douglas react to them after so long, especially as she had never spoken to her son about him?

Judith drifted on with her memories – to Glasgow. She could see herself standing at their Henderson Street tenement building looking at the newspaper that boldly stated on the front pages: **THE GREAT WAR!**

However, from its start to its end, it was not the *Great* War, she reflected, but the most atrocious war the world had ever experienced. Many countries took part in it. Millions of people died or were permanently injured. There was a perpetual call for volunteers. General Lord Kitchener glared down from each hoarding displayed throughout the country, stating: *Your Country Needs YOU!!*

William and his good friend, George Moffatt, joined

the machine gun regiment of the Cameron Highlanders in response to this plea. They went to the headquarters of the regiment where, along with other eager young soldiers, they signed up for service. William looked rather smart when he first tried on the uniform. He'd told Judith later quite proudly: 'It is quite stylish with its brown jacket. See how it buttons up to the neck. Look at the kilt,' as he swung it around, admitting that he had never worn one before. He had tried on the leather belt, socks, spats and a tartan cap that he could fold up and put under the small flap on his shoulder.

Judith had already objected quite firmly when William had suggested that he join up. Now he told her about leaving the Clyde shipyards and going to fight the enemy somewhere in Europe.

Responding, she said, 'There is no need to go into the army yet. Your work at the Clyde shipyards is a reserved occupation,' and, pointing her index finger at him, she sputtered, 'There are three kiddies under seven whose name is Fraser. Who is going to look after them? Me, alone?'

William would not budge. Instead, he was full of excitement as he remonstrated, 'Judith, you have to manage our three bairns by yourself. Put them in the care of some neighbours while you go out working. After all, the army called, and the war is supposed to be over by Christmas.' He half-grinned as he gave her his final word, 'We'll be home before we leave!'

William had shown her his resolute side. He was going on an adventure, while she was going nowhere!

So the army had swallowed up William and George, but there were few camps that could accommodate the crowds of these new soldiers and their small pile of equipment. Through those early days of autumn, as the weather became colder, they lived in tents, did army exercises, and used walking sticks instead of rifles to practise with.

After a frustrating day, William said, 'This is a bit too much. We offer to defend this country by flinging ourselves onto the enemy, but the only thing we get from the army is walking sticks!'

William wrote spasmodically to Judith. 'I have peeled spuds and sliced carrots, been on round-and-round route marches, dug deep trenches, fired wobbly rifles, taken machine guns to pieces and put them back again… that is, when we can get them.'

In another letter he wrote, 'This morning, the Cameron Highlanders, including me, refused to come out on parade when we'd had no porridge!'

Judith knew that he had enjoyed his porridge every morning, having set the menu right from the start of their marriage. He not only cleaned up his bowl, but he usually asked if there was any more.

The Fraser family sat on chairs on the pavement when it was sunny, or inside around the fire when it was cold, to read William's amusing anecdotes. Each of the children received a favourite postcard, which was put away in a small scrapbook that their mother provided – Jenny had a ballerina; Maud was given a graceful skater; and baby Douglas, a soldier with a gun – but he'd chewed the card first!

Chapter 5

*J*UDITH'S MEMORY MOVED from her husband
William to his friend, George Moffatt. George,
who went out with the army to deal with the
Germans. He found out that his slight tickle in the chest
was in fact an early symptom of tuberculosis. Perhaps
the original doctor, who was working under extreme
stress, had made a poor decision in sanctioning George
to be accepted. Whatever the cause, this was a serious
infectious disease, and so he was eventually repatriated
from one of the Belgian aid-tents, suffering from weight
loss, increasing fever, and coughing that grew worse with
time.

Before his repatriation, William was given permission
to pay him a quick visit. George said to his friend, 'I want
you to have this little Bible,' laying his hand upon the
Scriptures and pushing it over to him. 'You need it now.
The battles are starting. In here, William, you will find all
you need to know about our Saviour. I have shared all
the facts of how Jesus loves you and died for you, and
now, how He lives for you, too.'

Judith imagined that William had taken the small
Bible from his friend and, giving him a weak grin, said
something like, 'Thanks, George. I will look after it, and
you never know, if the battles we fight are getting tough,
I might believe it too.'

In another letter to Judith, William said:

*We journeyed on trucks to get to the trains and, once
we were in Belgium, we marched on foot through*

22

the battle-scarred hamlets to reach the towns of Mons and Loos. We prepare for battle very soon.

This was written on the 23rd of September, 1915. It was his last letter. After some weeks of anguished frustration waiting on information of William's whereabouts, Judith got her pen and paper out.

She recalled (but didn't write this) William, just before he left on the train to go to the army camp, saying: 'I am not one for fighting but I'm jolly good at running. If I go missing, just look under the hedges.'

What hedges? Judith had heard from somewhere that perhaps William was missing after the Battle of Loos. Judith knew that even though the army had searched diligently for him and the other missing soldiers, they *still* couldn't find his body, after all this time.

'What hedges?' Judith had wondered again. 'If the hedges are there, surely they would be destroyed by the soldiers of both armies who fought, so... what hedges?'

Judith missed William so much that she said to a neighbour, 'I shall think about William's goodness and kindness and all those lovely years that we had together. The first time I met him at the dance at the Caledonian Club, I remember his smile and twinkling eyes. He made me go weak at the knees!' She gave a sad sigh. 'The failure of the army to provide any clues of William's whereabouts makes me think that he is definitely missing, or even possibly dead. If that is true, I'll have to do everything alone now.'

Then Judith's memories focused on the postman. He was pushing a brown letter through the door, marked ON HIS MAJESTY'S SERVICE. She noted the red penny stamp on the right-hand upper corner. Opening the letter slowly, she discovered that it was from the Army. In it she found an official form from the Regimental Paymaster:

I regret to state that information has reached this office that 13659 Private William Fraser of the Cameron Highlanders Regiment has been reported missing.

Suddenly she was very fearful. The official letter was actually *here*, in front of her!

Pulling herself together, she sat down and wrote a letter in response to the same authorities, asking for more information and requesting more than those bald words that she held in her hand.

A month later, Judith had hurriedly opened a second official letter, this time from the War Office in London:

Dear Madam,

I reply to your inquiry. I am commanded by the Army Council to inform you that William Fraser has been missing since 25ᵗʰ September 1915. This is the latest information regarding this soldier which has been received.

I am, madam,

Your obedient Servant

Her aloneness had never felt so real.

Still later, Judith received a small parcel from the army. Inside was a weighty round bronze plaque, depicting *Britannia* holding a wreath of peace and a ferocious lion, declaring that *William Fraser* had *Died for Freedom and Honour*. There was also a brass ornamental tin which, for anyone who wanted to look inside, held three medals wrapped in ordinary tissue paper. The top of the ornamental tin was regally embossed in Latin, which gave it, she supposed, the honoured respect required. There was even a small signed and framed certificate from King George V.

It all meant little to Judith. The only thing she *really* wanted, was William back safe! Those three medals and a plaque, not forgetting the signed article from the King at Buckingham Palace, now in her possession, meant only one thing: that he was truly dead.

If that were so, the only living memory of the children's father was in their small scrapbooks of the strange scenes and peculiar people from around the world. The scrapbooks didn't say much about their father's true nature that they could remember, but they contained enough to tell them that their father had had a hearty way of looking at life. They carried the scrapbooks around for many years.

Although still young – he was coming up to three – Douglas had a faint suspicion that there was something wrong with his mother. He couldn't, of course, know or understand about the war, its repercussions, or the problems in *this* house. Yet another neighbour looked after the children while Judith returned part-time to the woollen mills, where she had worked before her marriage.

'I won't get much,' she told her neighbour sadly. 'Do you know how much pension I get from the Government? A pound for me and three-and-fourpence for the children.'

And now, years and continents later, Judith thought as she lay in her hospital bed that she wanted to pass on all these things to Douglas, who was now a young man.

Chapter 6

WHEN DOUGLAS ARRIVED at the hospital, Judith asked him to sit down with her as she had something important to share with him. 'I'm sorry that I haven't done everything a mother on her own should do,' she said sorrowfully. 'Oh, I have no reason to be sad, for my life has been very rewarding and fulfilling. Through the years you grow older and wiser,' and she looked at him with a sad twinkle in her eyes. 'I have been concerned about your lack of knowledge of your father, his life, his aspirations, and about his becoming a soldier in the Great War, and his death at the Battle of Loos. Nor have I told you about how his loss affected all of our lives. I can't change the fact that I haven't disclosed anything about it. I'm sorry not to have done so sooner. However, I want to put that right now, before it is too late.'

(Readers might ask about a weighty, round bronze plaque, depicting *Britannia* holding a wreath of peace and a ferocious lion, declaring that *William Fraser* had *Died for Freedom and Honour,* and a brass ornamental tin which had three medals wrapped in ordinary tissue paper, regally embossed in Latin – even a small signed and framed certificate from King George. What happened to them? Judith had left them at her home, to be collected by Douglas later.)

Douglas looked troubled.

Judith quickly went on, 'Now it is *your* own future which is important. You will have many questions that I can't answer, so I want to give you these letters that

26

came from the solicitor of an old friend of your father. In these, he will tell you some important things that will, I think, fill in those gaps.'

Taking the letters from her voluminous bag, Judith explained that these had been delivered to her in Glasgow.

Douglas wondered what this correspondence would say about his father that he didn't already know or guess at. Would it give him *all* the answers to his questions? He thought not.

Reluctantly, he took the letters and, placing them in his inner jacket pocket, said goodbye and kissed his mother gently on the forehead. Douglas had an inkling that it would be the last time he would see her alive.

On reaching home, he was immediately caught up in the family excitement. Iris showed him what she had purchased at the Leprosy Mission stall held at the church that day. Then he must show interest in Adam's latest wooden creations that he had made at school. He was delighted to see Violet's dolls, with their lovely formal clothes, taking tea with the British Royal Family.

Judith died the following morning, and he forgot the letters for the moment. Douglas, Jenny and Maud were very busy over the next few days dealing with arranging the funeral. Iris, Wally and Stephen were there to give them valuable support. Many friends attended the ceremony. At the Mosgiel graveside the minister spoke good words about Judith. When the funeral was over, all recalled her kindness, and how she had helped each of them.

It was a long time before Douglas looked at the letters his mother had given him. He went away by himself to be cloistered in his favourite spot beside the Silver Stream. Tall, thick, soft *toi-toi* grasses wrapped around him as he settled down to read the letter from Mr Tweedy, the solicitor's clerk, on behalf of his client in Glasgow.

Following instructions in the top letter, Douglas took out the following correspondence that would explain certain past events. The first one was to his mother from George Moffatt, one of the people who knew his father well, but whom he had not heard of until this day.

This letter comes from the convalescent home in Glasgow, where I am ready to die. I have been ready to die for ages. Jesus Christ has won for me the eternal freedom that I (and you?) needed. Just before I make my way into heaven, I want to inform you that I was employed as a minor clerk in a branch of the Intelligence Service, and was going through some material concerning the Battle of Loos. I was checking how many troops were there, what casualties they had suffered and how many dead men were able to be identified. Many bodies were unrecognisable. Although the authorities never actually found his body, there was the name of William Fraser on one of those lists, detailing his death. This fact was told by another ex-soldier.

Douglas noted that George Moffatt had included a further letter by another soldier, telling of the same episode.

George's letter continued:

I met this soldier at one of those memorial services that the authorities had arranged for the troops who were still alive after the Battle of Loos. There were very few! I can't recall his name but once he'd had a few drinks he began telling me all about William Fraser and his achievements before the sad day at the Battle of Loos on September 25th, 1915. I will leave you now.
>   *Regards,*
>   *George Moffatt*

Looking at his watch, Douglas slowly closed this letter and put it away in the folder with the others, thinking that it had not revealed anything more about his father's death, that he knew of.

Chapter 7

APART FROM AT weekends, Adam went to his great-grandparents' home after school every day. Emma was often resting comfortably in one of the outside garden seats, with two cushions behind her and a colourful quilt over her knees, as she enjoyed the hazy sunlight and the sound of warbling birds. A couple of library books were put on the small table at her side by Madge, but Great-grandmother spoilt everything by complaining about her missing glasses. 'Where are they? I can't do anything until my glasses are found!'

A flustered Madge was instructed to find them but, upon unearthing them, she discovered that Emma had dropped off to sleep.

Now Adam knew he must not upset Great-grandmother if she was sleeping, so, moving silently past the garden seat with big awkward steps, he found his great-grandfather Alec in the lounge, playing his violin.

His playing was not so lively now, as he was getting on a bit; about eighty, or even ninety, Adam thought. Nevertheless, the glorious music wafted through the house and gardens, filling the air and floating over to the sleeping Emma, to unite in a lullaby with the birdsong.

Alec always finished playing with something uplifting and pleasant, which gave him much joy and satisfaction. Adam loved to hear these pieces, so he kept very quiet until the 'concert' was finished. Then he had some lemonade and chocolate biscuits while Alec put his violin away in its case.

Afterwards, his great-grandfather regaled Adam with

long stories from times past. Some of them were funny and some were sad, but all of them were very interesting. Occasionally he talked about the times he had played for a radio station, or how he had chosen an instrument for each of his children when they were born and taught them how to play. He told Adam that even Great-auntie Madge had learned to play the violin. Given Madge's gruff temper, Adam was surprised to hear this!

Madge had just woken Emma up. 'It will be much better sleeping in bed instead of outside,' she had said tightly, as they were journeying through the house to the bedroom. Emma just looked across at her and gave a weak smile.

They entered the bedroom and Madge proceeded to help Emma remove her clothing but, before she had a chance to, Emma decided that she could undress herself, and pushed Madge's hands away.

'Thank you very much,' Madge muttered under her breath. She closed the door behind her with a sudden thump, to make sure that Emma would get the message.

Making her way to the kitchen, she collected a small tureen of prepared soup. Knowing this would be suitable for her father, Madge picked up the hot tureen carefully and entered the dining room, setting it down on the table.

Alec and Adam were still chatting in the lounge next door. Madge left the tureen and came into the room, saying it was time for Adam to go home for his dinner. She guessed that his mother, Iris, would be getting anxious.

Adam balked. 'My father will only just be leaving his work by train, so he won't be home for a while.'

Madge raised her brows; did her father want his tea now, or later? Was Adam staying or leaving? Their silent expressions gave her the same message: Not yet!

She gave a shrug, collected the cooling tureen of soup from the dining room and took it back into the kitchen, then went on her way to do her many other tasks – millinery for instance!

Great-grandfather smiled wanly but he continued with his tale. 'Madge used to go to the front mailbox and faithfully collect the paper each morning to check if the advertisements she had put in were perfect in every way. Unfortunately, the newspaper was often lying on the street. She had a bad back, so it was very difficult and painful to pick it up. If she saw the paper boy, she told him, "You are supposed to put the newspaper in the box attached to the front gate, not on the street!" But the cheeky boy just shrugged his shoulders. He couldn't care less.'

Then Great-grandfather told Adam about the event of two sturdy ships whose passengers had founded the town of Dunedin.

'In early 1848, the ships *John Wickliffe* and *Philip Laing* arrived from England, three weeks apart, sailing through the narrow passage into the beautiful, long Otago harbour. They carried the first settlers from Europe.'

'My teacher told me all about them,' Adam said excitedly. He added, 'Fancy that, I didn't know you were that old!'

Great-grandfather firmly said, 'If you will allow me to get on with the rest of the story, you will be amazed to find that I'm not "that old", or anything like it!'

Adam grinned.

'The gentle wind took them past a Maori settlement, tall forests and bush inlets. These settlers were mainly Scottish, and when they dropped their anchors, they proclaimed the new settlement would be named *Dunedin*, the Gaelic version of Edinburgh. You have been to Dunedin, haven't you?'

Adam nodded vigorously.

'Did you know that part of Bell Hill, on Princes Street, was carved out of solid rock? Well, Princes Street joins George Street, the main thoroughfare, and is then divided halfway by the eight-sided, grassy Octagon. The statue of Robbie Burns stands on its outer edges, looking down to the grandiose railway station. The settlers constructed magnificent churches, giving Dunedin a class that the original settlers would not have dreamed of.

'When my parents, James Hay and Margaret Dix, arrived from Halifax in Northern England in 1860, they found Dunedin to be already a bustling town.

'Margaret Dix worked as a governess for the daughter

of a wealthy passenger on her ship. Unfortunately, the young girl and her mother died soon after their arrival, leaving her a bleak future without income. James Hay, who was employed by the Dunedin Woollen Mills as a dyer, had befriended her on the ship and now looked after her concerns. They fell in love and, a few months later, were married in one of the splendid churches.

'They bought land by a rippling stream and built their own well-constructed house. After settling down, they had a son – whom they named Alec.'

'That's you, Great-grandfather!'

Alec smiled warmly. 'Indeed! They told me I was a bright child and, on top of my basic education, I learned to play the piano, trumpet and violin.

'My father often told the story of how some of their ancestors had gone over to Britain from Europe. Standing tall, with his thumbs gripping the outer edges of his waistcoat, he eagerly addressed the imaginary crowd, which was really only comprised of his patient wife sitting in her special chair, and eager me, who sat cross-legged before him, listening to his enthralling words.'

'"In past days", my father would announce, "Protestant refugees, known as the Huguenots, fled for their very lives from persecution for their faith. Many came over to England from France. Some of them were from our family."

'Thus this tale was passed on to me, and I have told it to my children and then my grandchildren, and now I have told it to you, young scamp.'

Adam smiled, and said, 'I think you have a lot more to tell.'

Remembering the soup tureen, Great-grandfather said, 'Sorry, lad, my stories will have to wait,' as he went hurriedly to have his sparse, slightly colder meal.

Chapter 8

THE NEXT DAY there was a loud bang from the front of the house. Alec discovered that young Adam had entered the front gate and was eagerly approaching, calling out, 'Hello Great-grandfather! You got any more tales to tell me?'

'What, no "how am I"? No "how is Great-grandmother"? No greeting to Auntie Madge? You get right to it, just like a steam-train, ready to be off.'

Adam was so overcome with shame that he reversed his walk, went out of the gate, closed it, turned around, quietly opened the gate and came back at a reasonable pace to Great-grandfather, inquiring after the welfare of the household.

Both laughed and, sitting down on the garden seat, Great-grandfather proceeded to tell Adam what was next in the long tale.

'When I had finished my schooling, I became apprenticed to a Dunedin bootmaker, after which I was a fully-fledged craftsman.

'I was twenty-two when one day, in the hot summer sun, I walked from Dunedin along gravel roads, in my sturdy boots and with a full knapsack on my back. I saw the bush-clad surroundings and heard the magnificent thrushes and bellbirds. At the edge of Mosgiel, I saw the gravel Gordon Road going in a direct line before me, right through town. When I shaded my eyes from the sun just a little bit more, I could make out Factory Road, where the Mosgiel Woollen Mills had been established.

'In the haze of the surrounding large farms and extensive countryside, I could just see the Silver Stream, a tributary of the much larger Taieri River. Adjusting my eyesight, I gave a sudden shout: "Mosgiel is going to have a footwear repairing business!" and, throwing my arms out, "It's all mine!"'

Great-grandfather showed Adam how to wave his arms in a swaying action, but nearly had an accident himself by falling half out of his garden seat.

'My business was near the meeting of the main road and Gordon Road, close to the railway station. The rail lines ran between Dunedin to the north and Invercargill to the south. There was also a new Central Otago line running west, so it was the best position I could imagine.

'My three-roomed home and shop were very functional. The first room had a small counter and till. The repaired shoes were put onto shelves on the wall – each pair with a coloured label with the customer's details written on it. The second room was a workroom. I had bought a giant second-hand repair machine from Dunedin, and this took centre stage. The room had a small window through which I could see what was going on outside. Around the walls were shelves piled high with spare leather of various colours, shoelaces, different sized pots and strengths of glue, and dubbing in order to polish up the shoes when the repairs were done.

'The third room was my private accommodation. Located to the right of the shop, it had a wood stove where I made my meals. The fire was kept going through the colder months to give the whole building some precious warmth. There was a small table where I sat to eat my food and read the newspaper, and an armchair beside the fire. It was made homely by the small windows with their mottled blinds and muslin curtains, giving it an air of individuality. I had an iron bed and a straw mattress, a tallboy, a mirror, and a chest of drawers for my clothes. Outside was the toilet and washhouse. All in all, the building was very comfortable.

'I put, on the window and door, two notices that read: *A G HAY,* and *ORDERS and REPAIRS.* I did more than that. Very early each morning I would stand outside on the gravel path collecting shoes that needed repairing from those hurrying to catch their trains. The owners' names, and what was wrong with the shoes, would be hurriedly written down on a little pad. The repairs would be finished at the end of the following day, ready to be picked up on their owners' return journey.

'The people of Mosgiel and the outlying towns soon became aware of my expertise. They knew that I was the only shoe repairer for them, unless they wanted to go all the way into Dunedin.

'I was a happy type of fellow, of average height and build. I would look at myself in the mirror, smile at my reflection and, only then, open the door to the public. I had short, wavy auburn hair, slicked down. A pity that, because the bowler hat was the norm and the fashion was to wear it constantly. Right under my patrician nose was a firm, neat moustache that I trimmed with very small scissors. I kept my hair neat with a steel comb that was always in my back trouser pocket.

'On Saturday and Sunday afternoons, I would replace my working clothes and bowler hat with my smart three-piece, brown suit. A coloured handkerchief peeked out just over the top pocket of my coat. If I was playing my cornet or trumpet in the Mosgiel Brass Band, the braided uniform made me look trimmer and smarter, well suited to be out showing myself off to the interested public!'

Great-grandfather smiled. 'Yes, Adam, I know what you are thinking: that I was very taken with myself. You seem amazed at what I can remember of all these years ago. If I cannot tell them to you, then who else is there? My wife can't stand my constant memories. Madge only thinks of her millinery business. The local business people will think I'm a bit odd, always talking about the past... But that's enough for today.'

Getting up, he took Adam inside to the kitchen, telling him that he'd bought a second-hand radio from a Dunedin shop. There it stood, a massive Bakelite green/grey monstrosity, both in length and height. The radio was extremely weighty. Inside it had eight large vacuum valves that took some time to be fully operational after turning the radio on. Slowly turning the dial, he found some of the world's countries, speaking strange languages.

Great-grandfather said, 'I think that the quality of music that comes from this radio is much better than from the modern radios we listen to.' He was unaware that all music, classical or not, was purely the presenters' own choice, not the radio's. He knew that classical music had changed, but surely not for music lovers like himself?

Then he said most generously to Adam, 'When I die, you can have my radio.'

Adam was pleased, then told him that he was learning to play the clarinet and cornet at school, and enjoying it. Alec pricked up his ears. Did Adam have musical talent after all, he asked himself? If so, he could play for Alec on his birthday.

And sure enough, on this great day, Adam took out his cornet, hoping to blow a simple melody or two, but such was the crowd of relatives and friends, including Great-auntie Madge being protective and vying for Great-grand-father's attention, that Adam suddenly declined to play.

Chapter 9

DAM, FED UP with the long terms he had to call his great-grandparents, came up with abbreviations – GGF and GGM.

'Good names, pithy, to the point,' said the new GGF.

Though disappointed at Adam's refusal to play the cornet for his birthday, Great-grandfather was ready to relate the story of Great-grandma's history.

Adam, sitting on the seat in the rose garden with GGF, listened to his memories of GGM.

'It all started when she was a little child.'

'Where was this?' Adam demanded.

'Mosgiel,' said GGF.

'Carry on.'

'Thank you! It all started when she was a little child. *LOURISTON LODGE* was written in large letters on the wooden outer gate of this somewhat mysterious property. It was a white, two-storey house standing at the end of a very long driveway, which was lined with poplars and guarded by tall yew trees. Occupied by a London solicitor, John Turner and his wife Jessie, the house was called this to remind the Turners of their life in a leafy suburb beside the Thames.

'Any visitors were treated to a whole host of exciting features. A small humped bridge went over the Silver Stream and a walkway brought them to a smaller inner gate, leading them to a winding path. Proceeding around the final corner, they beheld a sheltered area drawing them in to a magnificent house, with two large basement rooms that were part of the building. The wide doors welcomed them. The open windows allowed quiet, perfumed breezes to filter around the rooms.

'A private staircase rose from the ground floor of the main house, to the long, wide hall where there were numerous bedrooms on one side. On the other side, were a large lounge, living room, kitchen, bathroom, and a back door which gave access to a verandah and vast grassy lawns.'

Then GGF said, 'I want to give a goodly description, because later *Louriston Lodge* was pulled down. After all, you've never seen it, have you? No! So then, let me continue.

'Just inside the entrance and taking pride of place was a splendid work, done by an unknown artist. Quite often, John Turner came through the open doors and stopped before this painting. He saw how the artist had captured the wonder of the quiet, dry riverbed in the foreground with tall spindly grass growing on the many large rocks. In the far distance were the marvellous Southern Alps covered with radiant snow, which gave the painting its peaceful tranquillity. It was thrilling to John Turner's heart, too. Every time he saw it, his chest would swell up as he considered its name, *The Quiet Scene*.'

'Yes, I've seen the same painting in your front passage,' said an excited Adam. 'I'll look at it again and see if it does to me what it did to John Turner.'

GGF continued: 'He could be thought of as a strange man. Every time he used his name it was the full name: not just *John* or *Turner* but *John Turner*. With his greying hair, neat black moustache and full figure, he felt that the extended title gave him added importance.

'One cloudy morning, a new day dawned – a daughter was born to the Turners. Jessie, her rather frightened mother, was assisted by the very able midwife, Nurse Hickson. Of course, John Turner didn't see the child's birth, but after the nurse had come down the stairs telling him that he had a daughter, he decided to call her Emma.

'Walking slowly from the painting up the stairs to see how Jessie had coped with the birth of his new daughter, he knocked on the bedroom door to make certain that he could see them both. However, Jessie was exhausted from bringing Emma into the world and, as soon as she had fed the child, both had fallen sound asleep. John Turner had to wait for another time.

'At mid-day, Molly, the kind girl who lived with them, took some food up to her tired mistress. Jessie woke and sampled the food, while Molly gave a curtsy and left the bedroom.

'Jessie's complaint was not about Molly's meal, for though it was bland, it was very nutritious. Nor did she complain about the doctor, who was excellent, or the baby – who was perfect! But whispering to Nurse Hickson, who had just come bustling in, she said, "I'm having trouble down below!"

'With a wicked grin, Nurse Hickson proclaimed in her Cockney accent, "I'm not surprised. You were pushing for a long time before we ever saw the child. It'll be right in a day – or three!"

'Again, hearing their mumbling conversations, John Turner went in to see his wife and told her that the name of the child he had chosen was Emma. He wanted to cuddle the baby, but she was fast asleep. When he asked if he could take his daughter out of the cot, the midwife quickly told him, "Later, later on!" without specifying when, which frustrated him no end!

'Jessie got lots of rest over the next few days. She changed Emma, bathed her and sprinkled on lots of baby powder. After she had finished, she took her to the window for a moment to let Emma hear the trees gently moving in the breeze, and the distant, delightful rippling stream. And, as Nurse Hickson had promised, Jessie's troubles "down below" were better after three days, much to her relief.'

Adam was puzzled, not by this strange talk about 'down there' – he still didn't know what that was about – but he said, 'Seeing as you weren't there, how did you know all this?'

'Good detective work!' said GGF superciliously.

'Tell me another!' Adam smirked.

'Your GGM told me.'

'How did she know all the secret bits that concerned her as a baby?'

'Molly told her later. They became very good friends. Ah well, time for a mug of tea, a drink of lemonade, and lots of chocolate biscuits. Here Madge is, struggling with the afternoon tea paraphernalia.'

Madge had come out of the house with her hands grasping the tray, which was covered with a pretty cloth and held a pot of tea, two ornate cups with saucers, a jug of milk, a sugar bowl, and two spoons. She had not provided them with chocolate biscuits, nor Adam with lemonade. Setting the tray down on the adjacent table, Madge left them without a word.

'Well, we won't give Madge any chance of reacting. Will your pour the tea?' said GGF. 'After that, we will continue.'

When they had taken their nourishment, GGF said, 'Emma took her first wobbly steps with her mother's help. Later, her father showed her the picture, *The Quiet Scene,* and she made appropriate noises as she wriggled in his arms. In her posh pram, Emma's father pushed her around the garden, and across the small bridge over the rippling stream. He spoke seriously to her, not using baby-talk as other men used for their children.

'By the time Emma had reached her fifth birthday, she had received many elaborate gifts and outgrown many beautiful clothes given to her on these important occasions. Her mother, Jessie, always looked very elegant with her slim shape, long hair, blue eyes, and fashionable clothing that were the latest creations from London, so she didn't want to ruin her figure by having any more children. Emma was to be her first and last child. She was quickly passed into the care of Molly, who would be paid well for her increasing responsibilities.

'We've been concentrating on Emma, but now I will tell you about Mr Gladstone, her friendly and outgoing dog. He went everywhere with Emma and Molly. Many conversations were had between Emma and the dog. All that Mr Gladstone could do in reply was to give loud barks, and whisk his tail back and forth, but Emma understood.

'At the garden parties Jessie held, the important visitors would shoo Mr Gladstone away, complaining to Emma, who was done up in her best clothes with Molly standing beside her: "I wish you would keep the dog away from me – these are new clothes!"

'Still slurping and forever barking, Mr Gladstone, who could do no wrong in Emma's eyes, would go off to excitedly examine myriad other fascinating things instead.

'John Turner had bought the friendly pup for his daughter when Emma was small. He had visited the local farmer, who had advertised puppies for sale. He chose the smallest of the litter, and when he brought the dog home, Emma was overjoyed. Her father playfully pulled the dog's ears saying, "This is Mr Gladstone. Look at his face. It reminds me of Mr Gladstone, a politician in England."

'Emma's mother was much more practical, saying that Mr Gladstone should sleep outside in a corner of the verandah. "We can put a blanket and a bowl of water there for his comfort," she said. Emma was sad, but she obeyed.

'On the first night, she listened to Mr Gladstone's loud whining. The dog was very lonely on the verandah, and was frightened of the dark quietness of this strange place. He wanted company. Emma crept down and rescued him, taking him back up to her bedroom where he was immediately silent, settling down to sleep at the foot of her bed. The following day she explained to her parents what she had done. "If I had not rescued Mr Gladstone then you would have been disturbed in the night by his whining."

'So right from the start Mr Gladstone took centre stage. There was nothing better for him to do than to rush helter-skelter through the neat, prize plants placed around the lawns or among the trees. The flowers and the birds encouraged him to charge from one to the other, and he did what all dogs would do in that heavenly place – he peed constantly!

'Emma had grown well into her teens before she

noticed how old and tired Mr Gladstone was becoming. She and Molly took the dog to the vet and he told them that their pet had developed a fatal liver complaint, and would die very soon. Her reluctant parents and her good friends all came to see Mr Gladstone to say their final goodbyes. The old gardener buried him in a small grave round the back of the property. Emma read a simple verse she had written, and Molly put a sturdy card on the graveside: *Mr Gladstone – Extraordinary Friend.*'

Adam was saddened at the thought of this loving dog dying like that, so he asked, 'Do you like dogs?'

'No,' GGF said shortly. 'I like dogs, but at a distance. They always take you by surprise, get around your feet, particularly when you get to my age. Shall I carry on with my story?'

'Yes please!'

And GGF told of another event, this time about John Turner, solicitor in Mosgiel.

'John Turner came from London and knew the ways of the legal system in England. Renting a building midway up – or down – Gordon Road, he put up a sign: *John Turner: Solicitor.*

'Jessie Turner was thrilled about her husband's position, making sure that no one would stand in his way. How did she do this? By regularly arranging garden parties. In turn, this meant that Jessie would be given an invitation to accompany John Turner to many other occasions in Mosgiel, and beyond. This gave her great pleasure. When a guest asked, purely out of interest, "How is your lovely daughter, Emma?" then, giving a wave of her hand, Jessie would say, "Oh! Emma is fine! Her companion, Molly looks after her! Oh, and the dog, Mr Gladstone, fills her with excitement!" Then she continued waxing lyrically about her excellent husband who had just won yet another Alberty in court.

'To their dismay, John Turner found out that a distant male cousin of his also lived in the vicinity. Wattie Turner worked as a clerk in the Mosgiel Woollen Mills, and after finishing work each day drank far too much whisky at the Crossroads Hotel, a prime spot at the junction of four important roads.'

Adam said proudly, 'My parents have said not to be seen outside any pubs "You might not like what you see," they said.'

'Very wise,' said GGF, and then, 'Shall I continue?'

Grinning, Adam nodded.

'Well, the men of Mosgiel would gather at the hotel to talk over drinks, smoke quiet pipes, settle things peaceably without any rancour, and many deals and quiet transactions took place there between the local farmers and Mosgiel's businessmen – important select men like solicitor John Turner. In fact, John Turner often had important conversations with regional council members, so he certainly didn't want Wattie to annoy him, or anyone else.

'The large friendly publican leant over the counter and said to the assembled drinking crowd, "Oh, you are talking about Wattie Turner. I don't know how he does it. He comes in here and drinks a full bottle of whisky, then goes home to sleep it off and is at his job the following day, completely sober!"

'One day, Wattie became exceptionally noisy and inebriated. Stumbling out into the middle of the junction, he began to direct the sparse horse traffic. Ten-year old Emma, accompanied by Molly, had just left home to walk to where Emma had her piano lessons, at the opposite end of Mosgiel. This meant going past the Crossroads Hotel at the same time as Wattie was exiting.

'Standing still behind some bushes, they watched what Wattie was doing, fearful that he knew that Emma was a relation of his and so may take a few steps towards her and plant a sloppy kiss on her cheek.

'Emma saw a lone policeman slowly approach the drunken man. Standing tall and far too strong for Wattie, he arrested him without difficulty. She then understood the dangers of drink as she continued on for her piano lesson.'

Then GGF told Adam that Wattie had had an interesting change in his life. 'He didn't go to prison for *Directing Traffic in Unusual Circumstances* – that's what the charge sheet said when he was taken before the magistrate. Instead, he was let off with a warning.

'Going to Dunedin, he met an ardent Christian who changed Wattie's life. He became a travelling preacher and never drank again. Many years later, he came back to Mosgiel for a Christian Celebration. But more about that later. I'm quite exhausted. I will tell you about the next thrilling adventures of GGM next time!' And he loped away to the outside toilet.

Adam supposed that that was the end of story time, so he went out of the gate – very quietly.

Chapter 10

A 'BUNDLE OF JOY!' was what Iris called her new-born daughter, Primrose. At the time of her birth there had been carpets of bright primroses in the Mosgiel gardens, so she was named after these.

Extending all along the rear of the house was a verandah that was well protected from the wind and the rain. It was a veritable sun-trap, so was used for many purposes, including the latest stories that Douglas told on Saturday mornings.

Adam and Violet sat on the very old but still substantial sofa. With Primrose sitting on her lap, Iris reclined in a garden chair, ready for Douglas to commence.

All through the week, at suitable times, Douglas had composed on his small Remington typewriter some amazing events – 'Adam's Stupendous Meals' or 'Violet's Exciting Dolls' or 'Gardens of Primrose', or the playful one, 'Restful Iris.' If Grandma Lilian was there, the next piece of 'Grandma's Shopping Expedition' was told.

When Primrose was about three months old, she suddenly began to cry excessively, disrupting these tales. It was her developing teeth, so she would let out mighty wails. This went on intermittently for about a year. Her temperament, Iris felt, should be called a bundle of frustration, not joy!

Lilian tentatively asked whether she could help, but Iris said no. She thought that if her mother had been able to cope with her family, she should be able to cope with Primrose.

However, it got to the stage where Iris became very stressed and found herself opening one of the upper windows, intending to throw her crying daughter down to the ground. Recognising that some urgent help was needed, Douglas went to the new Mosgiel Nursing Clinic – Nurse Hickson's ongoing legacy – and arranged for a night-time babysitter. This would allow Iris to get some much-needed sleep. With the Clinic providing help, over time Iris became able to cope with Primrose.

Douglas was not let off the hook so easily – not so far as Iris was concerned. Take the episode of the rotary clothesline. It stood at the top edge of a small indent, so that the wind could dry the wet clothing quickly. When there were no clothes on the line, Adam enjoyed swinging on it. It was exciting being out in the fresh air, away from the noise of the family.

One particular day the clothesline pole suddenly bent over, carrying Adam with it. He had 'experienced' it too far! From the open kitchen window, Iris caught sight of this, and she called out rather sharply, 'Look out when your father comes home – there will be punishment for you!'

Violet had watched her mother tell Adam off. She was looking forward to seeing him punished – although she was not yet sure of the word's meaning.

When Douglas did come home from work, Iris expected him to deal with Adam immediately. However, he needed his normal three kisses and a rich cup of tea first. So it was after Violet had gone to bed when Iris tore strips off her husband.

'What did you do? You just quietly told Adam off and then sent him to his bedroom. I imagine he is still looking at his comics, not a bit punished!'

Douglas was not out of trouble yet, for Iris said the next day, a Saturday: 'I expected you and Adam to fix the pole together, but you have fixed it by yourself. This means you haven't given him the opportunity to learn how to repair it and to realise his wrongdoing.'

Douglas gave Iris a half-grin and told her that having

been brought up with *no* father and certainly *no* brothers he preferred to take a more friendly and kinder approach. He shrugged his shoulders and thought, *Oh, well! He is only a boy!*

Throughout the next days, which went into weeks, then months, then years, Douglas found himself up and down emotionally. Not only because of Iris, but from his memories of his dead father.

Secretly watching his father putting things into the small high up cupboard at the end of the verandah one day, Adam thought, *Ah! A treasure trove!*

Waiting for an opportunity, he finally crept along to find the answer. The cupboard was locked but soon he discovered the key hidden in a groove at the top. Opening the door, he didn't find any treasure, but some old letters and an ornate box in which lay three medals, a heavy bronze medallion and a small plaque from King George V. The letters Adam didn't look at, but he examined the rest.

What were they for?

Then he remembered that his grandfather William had been in and had died in Belgium in the First World War. Maybe they were about him?

Closing the box with its war things and old letters placed alongside, Adam locked the cupboard and put the key where no one could find it – back in the groove at the top of cupboard! Then he slunk away, thinking that his father was making considerable changes to their lives.

It wasn't long before Douglas gave up working at the engineering shop at the Hillside Railways, where he toiled mainly on giant locomotives. Changing his occupation entirely, he become the quality inspector of cooking ovens at a Mosgiel factory.

Chapter 11

ITTING IN HIS garden seat, GGF gave young Adam a playful ruffle to his auburn hair, and then continued the story of his wife, Emma.

'She was about twelve when she first attended the Methodist Church in Gordon Road without her parents. On Sundays she went to the church service in the morning, then to Sunday School in the afternoon, and sometimes to church again in the evening.

'Emma went with others to Mosgiel's Majestic Theatre for an Evangelistic Gathering. The preacher delivered an exciting message, and they were invited to decide for Jesus.

'Later, she told Molly that she had made her decision only for her parents' sake, and not for her own. John and Jessie Turner were most impressed at her decision, thinking that she would behave a lot better.

'It wasn't to be. Emma went on to be a Sunday Christian, mouthing holy words in Church and obeying the little regulations on Sunday, but living the rest of the week as before.

'At nineteen, Emma caught sight of a strange man coming out of a Mosgiel bank, and was instantly smitten. Discreetly, she asked around for information. The answers came back that he was unmarried – a single man – me!

'One of Emma's many friends said that she had seen me banking my takings from my week's business. Of course, Emma wanted to get to know me better. She wondered how she was going to achieve this. She must tread very, very carefully.'

GGF, remembering the days when Emma was young and pretty, and what came out of their fortuitous meeting, continued:

'Emma had a beauty that outshone other young women in Mosgiel, and maybe further afield. Her long black hair reached down to her waist. I supposed that in the morning she brushed it many times before stepping outside her room, so that her adoring public could admire the shining results. Her eyes sparkled, taking you into her confidence right away. Her infectious grin enveloped everyone who saw her. She often wore a pearl or sparkly necklace, ornate brooch, and stitched gloves which, when combined with lovely hats, showed that she was ready for any and every occasion!

'Emma had decided that she would enter my repair shop wearing her best clothes. One Thursday, after the morning rush hour was over and people had departed on various trains and country buses, she walked smartly along Gordon Road to my shop, carrying a wrapped parcel of shoes tied with a piece of coloured string. Opening the door, she came inside and placed the parcel on the small counter. Removing her gloves, she told me in her clear voice, "My father, Mr John Turner, is indisposed with influenza and my mother, Jessie Turner is busy looking after him. I had to bring his shoes along for repairs myself. Look," she said, turning them over, "their soles are well worn."

'She was clearly thinking that I would be so entranced at this that I would be speechless! I smiled to myself, for I had seen her in Mosgiel and liked what I saw!

'Taking off the string and putting the paper to one side, I held up the shoes. Having examined them closely, I cleared my throat while thinking fast how I could keep her a little longer in my shop. I said slowly, "I think it would take me three days to repair them. Would you come back next Monday?"

'She nodded, and I presented her with a little chit so that I would recognise her shoes (as if I would forget)

49

when she returned on the due date to pick them up. I then asked her whether she wanted to take the brown paper and string away with her, or did she want me to put them away for when the shoes were finally repaired?

'She said demurely, "The latter please", and went out of the shop very pleased with herself. I saw her skipping along the road, but then she realised that she ought to walk more gracefully, so she did so.

'The days went fast, and Emma picked up the shoes and paid the due amount. She had another set of shoes done up in another parcel – this time a lady's pair. "Do you think that you could repair these, too?" she asked.

'So that became a regular pattern. Your great-grand-mother would bring me another pair of shoes to mend each time she collected the previously repaired ones.

'She continued this way until the wardrobe of Turner shoes ran out. Her parents were surprised to see all the newly repaired shoes appearing in their home!

'At my shoe shop great conversations took place about the style, texture, finish, or how each shoe was to be repaired, and for what reason. Emma had a little seat that I brought out for her to sit on. We talked about a whole host of interesting things.

'I had been telling her about my dreams for expand-ing the business. "Just think," I said, "the towns around here all need shoe and boot repairs. If I set up a kiosk in each town where the public passes by constantly, then I'll increase my business. They would be under my name, but other people would do the work. *A G Hay* would be everywhere there are shoes!" And I started the business that moment – well, shortly after Emma had left.'

Adam was flabbergasted at all of this. 'I guess you were really in love.'

'Was I in love? I was head over heels in love,' GGF proclaimed, 'but I went very slowly. I eventually asked her if she was interested in hearing the brass band playing on Sunday afternoon at the Mosgiel Gardens. If so, would she be ready at one o'clock beneath the big oak tree, just near the band rotunda? "I will be there. If you like, bring a companion with you, of course."

'I was there at the prescribed hour, but I had changed out of my working clothes into the smart uniform of the Mosgiel Municipal Band. Emma and her friend Molly were very surprised. Smiling, I said, "I told you I would surprise you!"

'That wasn't the end of the surprise, for at my side I carried a trumpet to play in the concert. Having seated the two ladies on the chairs that the Council put out each Sunday for the listening audience, before climbing up the steps to the rotunda I called out, "It will be an hour's entertainment and then I will be free to walk in these lovely gardens with you. I'm going to take you to see the roses. They are wonderful!"

'As time progressed, we talked about the musical arts and what was going on in Mosgiel and Dunedin. I spoke about the successful brass band and classical music, while Emma talked about the famous pieces on the piano-forte. Of course, Molly would take herself off to the ice cream vendor as soon as we started discussing the more interesting things!

'Emma's many friends were starting to get concerned about this man – me. Some of them thought that I was not of the same class as her. "Do you think this romance is getting out of hand? Do your parents know what is happening? You must think of them! What will they say?"

'She was not a person to be swayed by outside influ-ences, and certainly not by her parents, so she said righteously, "No! I don't think my parents will have *any* say. If Alec points to the future, and speaks words of great wisdom, then I'll believe and trust him. He *is* such a wise and yet a gentle man."

'It wasn't very long before I asked her to marry me, and she said yes!'

Chapter 12

WISE GGF CONTINUED: 'Emma wasn't yet twenty-one. She had not reached the age of consent, but she said confidently, "Yes!" breathlessly, countless times to me. We had entered the land of happiness!

'The Turners were easily convinced that our intended marriage was absolutely worthy, so they gave it their blessing. Of course, it gave John Turner an excuse to tell all his colleagues about the forthcoming event, where he not only provided for the wedding reception at their grand house, but even put some money into a new bank account for Emma's expected children.

'I arranged to have a house built on the vacant corner of Lanark Street – this wonderful place,' GGF said, looking around at his property. 'You can see that it is constructed of fashioned wood with a painted corrugated iron roof, many ornate windows, and two distinctive chimneys.

'I put my footwear business there on sale. It went to a fish shop and then later to the Taieri Hotel. I had lots of cash to invest. Moving my footwear business into the new Agricultural Hall in Gordon Road, I found it was a much more central location and the new shops going up around me were important to my trade.

'Over the many happy but exhausting years, Emma produced, with the help of Nurse Hickson and my enthusiastic participation, three daughters – Lilian, Deborah and Madge, so that John Turner's gifted bank account became very handy. The family's good fortunes and increasing prosperity were also due to my skill and expertise in the footwear.'

Adam thought admiringly: *What a successful business man GGF is!*

'We brought up a strong, close family. Emma concentrated on making clothes for the children. She was skilled on the Singer sewing-machine, so the children were always smartly dressed. John and Jessie Turner gave us *The Quiet Scene* as a wedding present. As you know, it has prime position in our passageway.

'While our children were still young, their grandfather John Turner died. Top solicitor and member of the Mosgiel Council, he was talking to a local Member of Parliament at the Crossroads Hotel when he suddenly had a massive heart attack.

'Jessie was most distressed at her husband's death. The thought of having to look after their large house and its extensive gardens that used to fill her with pleasure, now filled her with dread. She sold their property and moved into one of the small houses, where Emma could keep an eye on her. Jessie never got over John Turner's death and she too soon died, a lonely and a very sad woman, with a heart which was truly broken.' He shook his head sadly at the memory.

'In Dunedin, my mother Margaret developed some insidious disease, and her death was very sudden. My father James was so heartbroken that he died a short time later with heart complications. I mourned for them. I never found out whether the story my father used to tell about the Huguenots coming over to Britain from France was true or not.'

GGF questioned Adam, saying, 'I hope all this detail is okay for you? Not too boring? Not too much?'

Adam thought, then said, 'No, go ahead with the rest.'

So GGF went ahead. 'Every time my wife produced another child, I gave her a rose, a kiss on her cheek and always asked how she was. When the children were a little older, I gave them an instrument to play – a viola for Lilian and one violin each for Deborah and Madge. With me on the cornet or the violin, and Emma on the piano, we had the family practice each day. Each one had a piece from a favourite composer. When it was fine, we might have the window open for the passing public to hear the wonderful music emanating from within.

'On top of the upright piano were the most amazing coloured Albertian vases. With everyone gathered around, there was a danger that these large vases might break, as the piano often shook with the enthusiasm of the pianist, so we would move them to a safer place before their mother sat down to play. Standing by my own tall chair, I held my beloved violin, waiting to play, as Emma pulled out a musical surprise from her music case – maybe the latest pieces that she had just bought at Briggs Music Shop in Dunedin.

'One Sunday, Emma returned from the Methodist morning service, bursting with news. "The old organist has died, and the church has no one else to take his place. The Reverend Randle said he wondered whether the Hay family orchestra would be interested in helping out."

'I saw that this might be a way to increase public appreciation of our small orchestra, so I said enthusiastically, "Yes. I'm interested," but I didn't ask my daughters first! Instead of them resting in bed on Sunday mornings, the whole family would have to dress in their finest clothes and carry their instruments to the Methodist church.

'Each Sunday, word would come back to me after their playing was finished: "Well done on the little *Fauré* that you used for the offering," or "I appreciated the *Haydn* you used as the voluntary," or "The way the orchestra played the first hymn was absolutely perfect."

'However, the Reverend Randle encouraged the congregation to hear and inwardly digest the sermons that were coming from his lips. The messages that he delivered were enthusiastic, interesting and mostly informative. At times my family were more engrossed with how the orchestra was playing, or more enthusiastic about the music than matching the music with the theme of the services.

'The minister grew somewhat peeved. In fact, he nearly stopped giving some of his sermons because, out of the corner of his eye, he could see that we weren't paying the slightest bit of attention to his preaching.

'He went to the church elders and spoke of his concern. "Alec Hay is putting the orchestra on a higher level," he graciously said. "To give him his due, he is raising an appreciation of music amongst the congregation. The orchestra does contribute pleasant harmonies to the hymns. However, I think they are providing us with a musical concert, and my sermons are taking second place."

'With the elders' permission, the minister asked if he could see me and Mrs Hay at four o'clock that Sunday afternoon in the vestry. We thought that he was going to say, "Well done!" for the "concert" played on the previous Sunday.

'Once we were seated, the Reverend Randle kindly said, "The orchestra played excellently." Emma and I puffed up with gratitude and pride. "But you are taking away from the Word of God, and my sermon time too. Couldn't you tone it down a bit? Could you play shorter pieces instead?" he suggested.

'I was stunned. Emma took umbrage and retorted, "It was *you,* minister, who invited the Hay orchestra in the first place. If you don't like it," getting more upset, "we will – we will go elsewhere!"'

Adam grinned. He had no idea that GGM was as feisty as that!

'Immediately, Emma got up and with a haughty look in the minister's direction, said to me, "Coming?" and swept out of the room, with me dutifully following.

'Reverend Randle was shocked. Now the small orchestra had gone! Emma and I decided it would be better to practice our art away from the Methodist Church, so we immediately transferred our allegiance to the local Presbyterian church. However, there was no room for our orchestra there – the organist was still in control.

'That is enough now,' murmured an exhausted GGF. 'Hurry home and do your homework.'

Adam ran home, not to do his homework but to tell of

the way that his great-grandparents had changed from being Methodists to Presbyterians, over such a silly thing as their orchestra!

Chapter 13

OST DAYS, ADAM still enjoyed visiting the house of his great-grandparents, but was one day shocked to see an ambulance outside, and Emma being carried on a stretcher towards the vehicle. It struck Adam that as his great-grandmother passed by, she hadn't raised her hand to him in any sort of welcome. Then came the realisation that perhaps she was unconscious... or even dead...

Old Dr Jamieson was coming out too, supporting Alec, who looked worried and upset. He kept undoing and redoing the buttons on his new cardigan, saying, 'What do I do now?'

The doctor replied calmly, 'It's all over. You and I have nursed Emma over many years – you with your lovely roses and cheery manner and I with the latest medical expertise, but I'm afraid that the cancer has won.'

Adam looked at his great-grandfather in fear. He had heard of cancer – but he didn't know what it meant. Great-grandfather's expression displayed a new emotion to Adam; something new. His eyes were filled with tears! Adam had never seen his great-grandfather cry. He didn't seem to see Adam, or acknowledge him. This experience was entirely new to the child; he reluctantly held back from putting his arms around GGF, though he desperately wanted to offer comfort.

Great-auntie Madge agitatedly pulled at his clothes as she demanded silence from Adam. She wrote a short note to take to his home telling them the sad news, and sent him on his way.

Having seen the ambulance speed away, and with his beloved GGF being taken indoors by Great-auntie Madge, Adam raced home full of the news of the death of his great-grandmother.

He was devastated; nothing would ever be the same again.

Over the next few days, many people visited Alec in his home, sharing the sadness as well as all the good things about Emma. Now Madge was in her element! Whether it was looking after her father, serving teas and handing out freshly made cakes, receiving enormous bunches of flowers, or answering the phone with the callers not knowing what to say, she wasn't worried. In fact, Madge revelled in all the attention. Her sisters, Lilian and Deborah, kept a watch on Madge, feeling that she was becoming too self-important.

The family buried Emma at the Mosgiel Cemetery and everything quietened down. Madge became even more protective of her father. She fussed over him terribly, but a few years later, he too died. Emma's death had left a great gap in his life which Alec couldn't fill.

Madge decided that her dead father, who had always had a lively interest in the latest news, should be one of the first to be cremated in Dunedin, and not buried in Mosgiel. Apart from travelling that distance to Dunedin, it didn't really matter what arrangements were in place; their father *had* died, and being cremated or buried didn't take away their memories.

At their father's funeral, Madge thought that her two sisters, Lilian and Deborah, were talking about her. They weren't. They had more compassionate things to say to the sorrowing people attending Alec Hay's committal.

However, sensitive Madge thought that some remarks made at his funeral service by her two sisters were unkind, ungrateful and demeaning. She took further umbrage with them and became even more isolated from her siblings.

Although he was now in his early teens, Adam was not allowed to attend the funeral service of his beloved GGF.

It was considered that a funeral was not for children of any age. This deeply saddened him, as he thought about his GGF constantly.

When Douglas used his car to collect Alec's massive radio, Adam remembered all the conversations through the years, including the radio. Whether GGF knew all the foreign languages or not, it made him more interested in the world 'out there.' Maybe that would be his way of remembering GGF, by using his 'out there' radio. Adam hoped so.

Two months later, Lilian died of a heart attack, and all the extended family were brought together again. The funeral took place at the Presbyterian Church, where they recalled her past life and sang their solemn hymns. Then they buried her in the Mosgiel Cemetery, and as they stood silently the minister said the words of final committal and the coffin made its journey into the grave.

Although he shouldn't have done this, Douglas let his thoughts wander. *There have been a lot of deaths in the families recently.* He totted them up in his mind. *There was not only my mother-in-law Lilian, but also my own mother, Judith. Emma, who died from cancer. Alec, having nearly outlived them all; and David, my friendly father-in-law, also died recently.*

Douglas' racing thoughts reached an outstanding conclusion. In all these deaths, he was yet not a member of any church. Oh, he had been to the various churches when something grand was being held, like the baptisms of Adam, Violet and Primrose, but to be a member of one particular church and giving his all...

Quickly he looked up to see if anyone had noted his furrowed brow. No one had; they were too sad at the passing of Lilian. In fact, they were waiting with heads bowed for the minister to give the final words, and then it was all over.

While a group of mourners murmured how sorry they were, and how much Lilian would be missed, Douglas grabbed hold of Iris' arm and hurriedly told her of his sudden change of direction.

Surprisingly, Iris looked earnestly at him, and a few seconds later, she agreed. 'Such a change as that,' she said, 'will be tremendous.'

Admittedly she did think, *Is it really Douglas having this change in direction? Or has my mother's funeral shocked him into making this alteration? After all, he has no one senior to him, no one in the family that he could call 'his' – perhaps he is looking for the church as a consolation.*

Before she could say anything, Douglas announced, 'We will go to The Rialto this evening and talk about it.'

They asked a friendly neighbour to look after the children and, seated in the dining room of The Rialto, with the staff looking after them royally, they ate pumpkin soup, then roast lamb and potatoes with all the trimmings, followed by banana splits with flavoured ice-cream. Then they had coffee and Douglas shared his thoughts with Iris.

'God has given me such a long time to reach this crucial point of changing my life,' Douglas began. 'Do you remember when I arrived in Mosgiel?'

'Of course,' Iris said, 'You were eight. The first time that I met you was down at the Silver Stream. I had been warned by my parents not to go near the water, so I never did. I preferred the peaceful grandeur, taking in the ebb and flow of the water or the sounds of the wind and the smell of the gorgeous grasses, blossoming flowers and tall trees!'

Douglas laughed and said, 'Well, all that may be true, but I had just moved here with my family, from Scotland. My mother had just purchased a house with a large section on Glasgow Street. I liked building smaller monstrosities in the backyard. Occasionally you walked by on your way to the Silver Stream and peered through the open gate to see what I was up to. I was making a wooden trolley, though I daresay it didn't look much like one. I hammered bent nails. I used an ancient saw that gave me bruised thumbs and small saw cuts. I cut off scraps of wood to be an approximate size and was working so hard that I didn't really notice you there.

'The next morning, I went on to build a helicopter to go on top of the trolley. It was powered by four large car springs underneath the machine. However, the tall, gangly, awkward structure was now a topsy-turvy affair. When I attempted to take it along the narrow path beside the Silver Stream it fell, quite naturally, into the water. I attempted to rescue the machine by heaving it out of the stream. My mother had just purchased for me, from Hannah's shoe shop in town, some very flash boots, but they and the bottom of my trousers got soaking wet.

'Emerging from your hidden vantage point, you came to help me rescue the helicopter. We took it along to my backyard for repairs, and so we chattered away. You said that you recognised me from being at school but in a different class. With a nervous look, I whispered to you not to say anything about the trolley falling into the water to my mother.

'Parking the awkward machine by the back door, we went inside into the kitchen. My mother wasn't home yet but, after looking at the clock on the kitchen mantelpiece, I knew she would be home shortly and proceeded to put the kettle on. "I had better change out of my wet trousers and put newspapers in my boots," I said, and grabbing yesterday's newspapers, I quickly disappeared into my bedroom.

'Meantime, my mother came into the kitchen to find a strange girl – you, all alone, making tea. You introduced yourself but made no mention of the water or the trolley. Then mum said that it was nice to have some of my school friends to the house.

'You shyly replied, "My mother taught me to make tea", giving her a big smile. Meanwhile, I quickly put on dry trousers and with bare feet, rushed back into the kitchen. I was surprised to find the tea made. We all had a cup. An old biscuit jar piled high with the latest from the store provided our treats.'

Iris wondered where this tale, delightful as it was, was taking them, but he looked as if he was thoroughly enjoying the tale, so she let him go on. She had just finished her coffee, and wondered if she should order another cup, then thought, *better not.*

Douglas continued. 'Take it a few years forward and I was a proud fourteen. From the back yard of my house I was building, not a trolley this time, but a magnificent motorbike. Every week or so I went sifting through the Mosgiel rubbish tip and had seen this old motorbike with motor attached. I was so excited. I got the machine home with some difficulty, and used strong tape on a split seat that had foam coming out. Very uncomfortable! The two wheels were alright, but it had bald tyres. Returning to the rubbish tip, I was excited to find another set of tyres in reasonable condition that were the right size for the wheels. I claimed them! Finally, I nicked some bright orange paint from the council rooms refurbishment that had been left round the back, that no one wanted.

'The motorbike was a veritable wonder! Getting a small container of free benzine from the friendly mechanic at the corner of Gordon and Factory Roads, I revved the powerful engine, driving around and around my large yard. I wondered if you would see me on the bike when you came past towards the Silver Stream.'

By this time, Iris had called the waiter to fill up both cups with this 'delightful coffee'. While she was waiting for it to cool down, she asked Douglas if there was much more – and what did this tale have to do with the church across the road?

Douglas said, 'There's more, but it still has you and God as its main interest. I want to tell you about the news-agent's shop. I had become more interested in exciting books rather than the comic books that I used to read. My mother got me some work at the newsagent's, where I could now read all the books on display in the bookshop. Delving into titles such as *Kidnapped, Tom Brown's School Days* and *Coral Island,* I even attempted ploughing through the heavy but fascinating *Oxford Dictionary!* This would only be when the customers had disappeared, of course.

'On Saturdays, I parcelled up early editions of Dunedin's *Evening Star* newspaper for the afternoon train trip to Central Otago. Taking them to the station by news-agent's trolley, I had them ready for the train that was stopping for a ten-minute rest. I had the romantic job of going through each carriage calling out, "Paper! Get your newspaper here!" in a piping treble voice! My only snag was absolute terror when the train was just straining to move on. There would always be someone who was still fumbling for his money, muttering, "Where have I put it?" and "I know it's here somewhere", but I survived.

'Sometimes my thoughts would race off in quite another direction from the literature which surrounded me in the bookshop. I felt absolute joy when I saw you coming brightly and regularly into the store, and on occasions with girlfriends. Of course, now I was a little older, my face reddened with embarrassment. I wasn't sure how to contain the rush of blood on these occasions. I didn't quite know where to put myself.

'On this particular day, to my dismay I found that you were not alone – you had brought a bevy of girl-friends who were hidden in different parts of the shop, watching quietly. I didn't know what to say to this clutch of giggling girls. If I did say "hello", I found out that I produced the wrong words. I thought that life would be a lot more interesting if they'd leave me alone in the shop... with lovely Iris!'

Then Iris caught sight of Douglas' eyes filling with tears. *This was the reason that he was telling me this long tale,* she said to herself.

She slipped her hand into his, gave him a bright smile and said softly, 'I love you... let's go home and we can discuss this... *ah...* something more.'

Chapter 14

'**S**OMETHING MORE' WAS Iris cuddling up to Douglas and listening to more of his distant memories. She didn't mind; it was rather lovely re-living the past this way.

'It was just before Christmas 1921, and our family were embarking on a great journey. Our destination was the South Island of New Zealand. My grandfather, Douglas Calderwood (for whom I am named), clothed in an enormous overcoat, thick scarf and leather gloves, and lots of relatives and friends, saw us off at Glasgow's railway station. I was a spindly seven-year-old, and more interested in reading comics than in waving goodbye to those people who I would never see again. My nice but rather finicky mother, Judith, kept an eye on me as we went south in the train.'

'I had the habit of asking her very awkward questions at odd times, like, "What *really* happened to my father?" Sometimes I became most upset, "Why don't *I* have a father?" or even, "What happened to *mine*?"'

'Of course, she wanted me to feel settled and comfortable in New Zealand. This would be a new country, where fresh circumstances would take precedence over my father's identity. So my honest questions were left unanswered, and even though I couldn't articulate it, I felt bereft.

'The train chuffed its long way down to London and then to the Southampton docks. Someone had supplied us with pillows just in case we dropped off to sleep, but we didn't need them because of the exciting journey. At

the docks, we were very tired, but the officious authorities were not finished yet. Our names were called in
alphabetical order and we were given numbered berths
on the ship.'

Douglas smiled, saying, 'I thought that we were being
drafted on like sheep. In fact, I nearly gave a *baa* to the
worried official, but I didn't.

'When it was nearly dark, another lot of officious
officers told us which gangplank to walk up. Wearily
we climbed up with our luggage to find our numbered
cabin. The cabin was deep in the ship's hold, with four
berths. It had little space. Once the luggage had been
stowed inside, the atmosphere got hotter and stuffier,
with precious little fresh air.

'The SS *Pakeha* steamship smelled strongly of fresh
paint. She had recently been converted from a cargo to
a passenger ship. I had seen that on the official notice
posted by the ship's entrance, and read that she was
capable of 13 knots, was twin screwed, launched in 1910,
nearly 8000 tons and could carry about 300 passengers.

'My mother found that she was inundated with other
immigrants, some with noisy children. Watching some of
the girls laughing and having great fun, she muttered, "I
hope we can get a decent night's sleep!"

'Many other people were seasick, but my mother was
the only one in our family to suffer in this way. There
were three sittings for each meal, but we were too shy to
go on our own, so my mother with her queasy stomach
had to struggle up the stairs with us. She would get us
started on the meal and then dash back down to the
cabin to be violently sick again.

'We soon got our bearings and began to enjoy the
deck games that the ship put on for us, in the hot but
breezy sunshine. However, I was not interested in games
like quoits, races and exercises; instead I liked walking
around the outside of the deck and stopping at various
points of interest. When it was raining, we sat inside on
wooden forms at long tables with dozens of other children, to play quiet games. I had the ship's library books
to keep me satisfied. We enjoyed refreshing lime juice

each day and, on Sundays, bananas and oranges to guard against scurvy.

'During the six-week voyage, the *SS Pakeha* had two stops – one at Cólon at the northern end of the Panama Canal, and the other at Pitcairn Island in the Pacific. Sisters Maud and Jenny, with me half-listening, sat outside the steward's office talking about our arrival at Cólon. Maud sniggered, "*Cólon* sounds like a nasty bit of your body." Jenny said, "No, I think that *Cólon* is a punctuation requirement when writing."

'The steward, the same one who poured out the lime juice at mealtimes, looked at us and said, "It is pronounced *CO-lohn*" and, breaking into laughter, added, "it certainly doesn't mean either of those that you have suggested!"

'Whatever the correct way of pronouncing Cólon, it still lay at the northern end of the Panama Canal. This was where the ship lay anchored.

'My mother had found her sea legs, so we were free to get off the ship and walk up and down the dock, marching quickly behind her. Mother warned us, "Don't touch this" or "Watch out for that". The town was full of ongoing excitement, but she didn't want to be too excited!

'The people of Cólon wore brightly coloured clothing. She thought the language was a strange Spanish. Whenever she asked in her Glasgow accent about the price of some exotic bananas, a few vendors answered her in a complicated lingo that sounded to her like English, but from Glasgow's infant schools. After a half hour of walking, which she thought had been invigorating for us, my mother called out, "We will go back to the ship now," and we hurried after her as she strode quickly up the gangplank.

'I relished the adventure of going through the Panama Canal. I watched carefully the various locks, the channels of different lengths and, would you believe it, artificial lakes. An inquisitive boy by nature, I looked out for anything mechanical. I had grown used to the working seamen, asking anyone, "What does that mean?" or "What is this for?" and "What do you really do with this type of equipment?" They responded with facts I found fascinating.

'We slowly travelled along the Panama Canal to the Pacific Ocean. I asked the same steward questions about our next stop, Pitcairn Island. He was most impressed at my interest, so he sat down beside me to explain. "In 1914 they opened the Panama Canal which, in turn, placed this island on a direct route to New Zealand. Do you remember the mutineers on the good ship *Bounty*? Captain Bligh, and all that?"

'I nodded, although I wasn't too sure.

'"Well, that's the same island, Pitcairn Island. It's very small, both in population and area. There is no port as such. Many travellers are eager to have mementos, so the ship will lie off-shore and the islanders will come in their canoes and sell their wares. Selling their produce and ornaments to a ship each week changes the pattern of life for them."

'When we had reached Pitcairn Island, I found that the steward was right. However, our mother looked after her money extremely well, so when we asked her if we could buy Pitcairn mementos, her reply was, "I don't know how much cash I will have when we get to New Zealand. You can see the items but not touch them."

'We were disappointed, but the thought of New Zealand was sufficient to stop us from asking any more. I thought I might ask the steward for information on New Zealand, but he was not there at the relevant moment. However, my mother told us much about Mosgiel.

'Early one morning we saw the outline of South Island shores. The ship arrived at the docks in Lyttelton, which lay over steep hills from the city of Christchurch. The twinkling lights in the houses scattered about were just being turned off as the ship's crew made fast the ropes between the ship and the docks.

'Some of the crowd, including us, stood with their luggage on the deck ready to disembark as soon as possible onto dry land. The sights and sounds were now of a new and different life. I was looking forward to staying at Mosgiel.

'My mother's distant cousin was a bald, stocky man

from the "old country" of Scotland. He had journeyed up from Mosgiel to meet the ship. How glad she was to see his face among the crowd. What joy as this man yelled out, "Welcome to your new home!" By now the trip had made her exhausted, so she looked forward gladly to him taking over responsibility for a while.

'We boarded the steaming passenger train that was waiting at the railed wharf. We sat in allocated red plush seats in the comfortable carriage. "Gosh," I said, "we have each got a pillow, look, in every seat! And notice how the seats can be reversed!" I demonstrated how it was done so my mother would take notice. The friend had bought me the latest comics; for the rest, the latest magazines. He also bought pieces of fruit cake that were distributed by the smartly dressed vendor, who shouted out the virtues of the cake while walking through the carriages. The carriage posters told us we would travel *through rural Ashburton – Summer Amusements to be enjoyed at Timaru – see Seals and Penguins at Oamaru – going through the Long Tunnel before coming to the Magnificent Station at Dunedin.*

"'All those stops," her cousin told our mother, with his comfortable braces extending over his stomach, "are where the passengers can get *more* cups of tea and *more* giant portions of cake." He had the refreshments down to a tee. However, in spite of all these further delicacies on offer, our mother was sincerely hoping that we would soon be getting off at our final stop – Mosgiel.

'The train picked up speed. At times, eager me listened to the sounds of the wheels whisking along until I exclaimed, "Listen!" They all listened. "Listen to the sounds. They are repeating themselves: *Mosgiel is next! – Mosgiel is next! – Mosgiel is next!*" They listened again, and they were!

'Just as the sun was going down the train drew up finally at Mosgiel Station. Having come through two long tunnels, the giant steam engine was glad to take a rest, puffing out large congratulatory clouds of steam. The long line of carriages had a rest as well. We had arrived.'

Iris changed her position. 'This is a long tale. Much

more?' she asked Douglas.

'Not much more. Before we got off, my mother told Maud, Jenny and me to carry one suitcase each. We weren't sure where to put the numerous empty cups and residual cake papers that were wrapped into a ball and placed neatly under the seat. We reckoned they could stay where they were. After all, they would be collected by attendants when the train got into the southern city of Invercargill.

'We disembarked onto the crowded platform. It wasn't that the platform didn't stretch along the train's length, but it was the small building and narrow exit that was causing the difficulty. The station's old but nimble guard – your father – had a lot to be concerned about. He wove in and out of the crowd, checking on someone who had mislaid a coat, or taking down the facts of a missing suit-case, or trying to keep people from falling into the gap between the train and the platform, onto the rails.

'I decided that I would take a closer look at the engine. There it stood, with steam pouring through the giant wheels as one of the drivers bent down to check them. One of the train guards blew hard on his whistle to hurry the crowd up – it was all too much for me, so I slipped inside the waiting room until the train had gone.

'My mother was frightened that I might still be on the train. Leaving the two girls with the luggage, and her cousin in charge of it all, she rushed to the guard – your father – to get help, shouting out at the top of her Glaswegian voice, "You must help me. I've lost my son!"

'When your father realised that I wasn't lost but in the waiting room, my mother, followed by the guard, came in to find me sitting forlornly in a corner. She told me off right in front of the concerned guard. He might have thought I would be well and truly chastised, but then she smiled and comforted me with a big hug.

'The train finally departed on its way south. The passengers gradually left with relatives or friends. Mother's cousin had previously arranged transport, and – there they were! So my mother said goodbye to the friendly guard, then remarked, "What a nice man. I wonder if we will see him again?"

'And we have seen him again!' Douglas said emphatically, saying to Iris that her father *was* a good man, who looked after the welfare of everybody. "As far as I was concerned," I thoughtfully said, "he was always a *comfortable* man – is that the right word? I think it is. He offered quiet advice with a generous spirit – yes, comfortable."

'When I was much older, your father and I walked slowly and quietly along the road by Wingatui racecourse, chatting about many things. I recalled how he drew me out with how I coped with no father of my own. I told him about those distant memories of my childhood that had been stored away in a dark corner with no one with whom to discuss them. Then I told him how my father, William, had died at the Battle of Loos in Belgium, and how my mother had been silent about it all this time.

'When we stopped to sit down, I picked a piece of long, wispy grass and, turning it upside down, I put it in the corner of my mouth, explaining to your father how it helped me to concentrate. He raised one eyebrow slightly but made no comment. We viewed the tall grass that needed cutting. We looked at the trees surrounding Wingatui grounds, coming to life in the gentle breeze. The atmosphere was still and peaceful. Then I gave a large sigh, saying that I was so frustrated and, clenching my hands, I added that I wasn't sure where I could direct it, or even what I was really frustrated about! Was it my mother? I often thought that one day she would suddenly reveal all the facts. She had given me those letters about him, the three medals, the heavy plinth and the signed picture of the King – but as for the facts, she had given me nothing.

'Your father smiled and enquired, "What will you do?" As he had listened, he'd realised that I needed to talk to someone – perhaps a minister from the local church, he told me later. I suppose that he was testing the waters when he said, "Romance with Iris might relieve some of your frustration."

'However, this did not seem to help me at all. Standing up quickly, I replied somewhat testily, "This is *my* problem and no one else's. I will sort it out by myself. I certainly won't let it get in the way of my relationship with Iris!"

'I let go of the spindly grass and, pulling myself together, I asked him, "Do you want to go any further?"

'Smiling and possibly relieved, your father then got up and quipped, "We had better discuss matters of religion and faith instead."

'We walked on with long strides, and after much talking, we both decided that, "Faith is the space given to God so that He can live and move and create in us mercy, love and kindness".

'Don't you see?' Douglas literally cried out as he stood up. 'Faith is the *space* given by God so that I am now a man with God's mercy, love and peace, leaving me satisfied!'

Chapter 15

T WAS THE end of Adam's final year in the church's youth group, and he was chosen as top student. At the appropriate moment, he rushed to the front of the church to collect his new Bible from the maturing minister, Reverend Andrews.

Amused, the congregation watched this young man, who had done so well in the church's national exams. Looking at the Bible's inscription, Adam read these words: *... in the hope that he will use it well and become a student and teacher of the Bible, and that it will assist him in all walks of life.*

Because Adam was so excited, he called in at the Lanark Street house to see Great-auntie Madge, wanting to show her his new Bible. She had inherited the house after the death of her parents. What a dispute there was with other relatives...! But we won't go into that. There she had continued her millinery business. With her white hair still done in tight curls, gruff old Madge, or rather *Mademoiselle Madge* in accordance to the notice she had placed on the front gate, opened the door.

Madge said to come in if he wanted to. Adam did want to, and did so.

As Great-auntie Madge closed the front door all was quiet. The chiming clock that his GGF had always kept to the minute was now rundown. There were no fresh flowers in the hall. She supplied Adam with a drink of water and two measly, rather dry biscuits. She wasn't too impressed with the crisp new Bible. She sniffed and said that buying it with well-earned cash was much better than having it given to you, even if the church had endowed the well-earned title – top student.

'You had better take notice of what it says,' Great-auntie Madge said, as if she was the only one to have read the scriptures. Then she marched Adam to the lounge, where there were no fresh flowers either, but she showed him many photographs of the Turner family. She was immensely proud of them, so she insisted that Adam take notice of all that *they* had done.

Then he noticed a very small photograph in a large frame on the wall, which stood out from the rest. Going closer, he enquired about it.

Great-auntie Madge looked flustered. She was concerned that the person in the photo would become more widely known so, grabbing hold of Adam's arm, she said grumpily that it was, 'Edward Wimpole, my dear friend who died a long time ago,' then propelled Adam away from the small photo to look at others.

He came to Wattie Turner, the one who had transformed from being a drunk to an ardent gospel preacher, so Adam cheekily enquired, 'Was Wattie Turner *really* directing Mosgiel traffic in the old days?'

Great-auntie Madge double-sniffed. 'Where did you hear that?'

He answered, 'Great-grandfather told me.'

Retorting, 'Well I never!' she hurriedly removed him from the lounge. All the Turner photographs and the one of Edward Wimpole were seen no more. The chariot wheels of conversation between the two ground to a halt. Adam never saw Great-auntie Madge again.

When summer time came, Adam went to a seaside Christian camp, taking his new Bible with him.

Douglas knew from the camp information that he was welcome to go along. The whole family could even go as a group. He decided not to – that he would be a father looking over Adam's shoulder all the time, even if he tried not to be. Douglas thought that Adam might share his thoughts and possibly his ideas with him, so waited wisely to be told his son's future direction.

When Adam returned home, he was very excited. 'I met well-known Christian people. I also met two lecturers from Bible College. There was a bookstall as well. We sang some wonderful songs. I've learned so much. I believe God is calling me to be an overseas missionary!'

Now Douglas was in a bit of a bind. He ought to be encouraging his son in this overseas missionary venture, but if he did so Adam would disappear. What should he do?

On Adam's bedroom wall, there was a giant map of the world's countries. This was partly the result of Great-grandfather's radio that he was listening to, although Adam had no idea of the languages being spoken.

He stood before the map placing capital cities alongside their respective countries. He also read mission articles detailing the hard and dangerous work performed by missionaries around the world. Thinking that he knew the world now, he wrote to one mission expressing his interest. He was declined, not because of his enthusiasm, but because he was still but a young man, and therefore had no theological training.

Wisely, Iris noticed his disappointment and scoured the newspapers, marking anything that looked like interesting work that might start Adam on the way.

Of course, this might mean working outside of Mosgiel, maybe in Dunedin? And Dunedin it was!

Chapter 16

WITH IRIS PLAYING 'Patience' on the kitchen table, the quiet sound of the melodious clock ticking its time away, and Douglas sitting so peacefully at the other end of the room reading his evening newspaper, Iris suddenly remembered the days when Mosgiel was abuzz with excitement – the blind preacher Wattie Turner was coming to town.

It was her mother who had told her about the troubles that Wattie had had with his drinking, and of his directing traffic outside the Crossroads Hotel; they wondered how he would cope with returning to preach the good news in his hometown.

When her mother added that Wattie was a distant relative of hers, the sixteen-year-old Iris wanted to go and see him. There was an excited crowd queueing to get in, so she ended up sitting at the front seat of the church.

The outstanding orator spoke for over an hour, giving a thrilling expedition through the scriptures, and yes, he referred to his sorrowful days; then finally he gave an invitation – 'If there is anyone here who wants to know Jesus Christ, there will be an opportunity during the singing of the next hymn for you to come forward, so we can introduce Him to you.'

The crowd stood to lustily sing *Just as I Am, Without One Plea*, but no one came to the front. Then, at the last verse, at the last phrase, Iris alone made the important choice to become a Christian. Rising and moving forward a little, she thought about many things, particularly her purposeless life. Oh, her parents were the best of parents, comforting her when she had problems, supporting her various successes, and generally seeing that the way forward was always the right way. Yet this guidance seemed superficial. She now wanted the inner peace that had been spoken of, so she made her commitment to God.

Wattie Turner shook Iris' hand and then gave her a copy of John's Gospel and a few scripture verses to learn, saying, 'Well done. You have started on your journey with Christ!'

As good upright parents do, David and Lilian were waiting up for her. Iris related all that had gone on that night, the preaching and the going up alone to the front at his invitation. Then she said that some of the congregation had told her that they were very proud of her decision.

David thought his daughter was becoming too involved in Christian aspects between right and wrong, so he just rattled the newspaper pages and gave small grunts.

Lilian took the same view as David. Her ageing parents Alec and Emma were Christian, though with a small 'c', but she said, 'That's nice, dear,' pouring a cup of tea for Iris, adding, 'What do you have on this week?'

Over time, both parents noticed some subtle changes in Iris' life that were good and wholesome.

Iris called them 'Jesus ways'. Now these Jesus ways were being somewhat tested by Adam's disappearance to Dunedin. What say he disappeared to other cities, perhaps even overseas? There was the possibility of that happening. While she may be worried, she thought of leaving it up to God to look after him – that would be the best way. She would put seventeen-year old Adam in God's care.

Adam was bursting to tell them certain things that he found were interesting; old things which were brought to life by a young man with a new fresh outlook.

'Dunedin,' he said, 'the university city with its ornate mansions and ordinary houses built on its majestic hills of many different suburbs. At the city centre is the eight-sided Octagon. Among the wonderful buildings and gardens full of radiant flowers and shady trees, surrounding a large divided lawn where people can sit on garden seats and have meaningful conversations, is the Religious Book Centre.'

Both his parents knew this, but let their enthusiastic son carry on about it.

'This first morning I marched excitedly and confidently from the railway station to begin my literature career. On three levels, the building is a sturdy constructed shop. On entering, customers find a spacious and inviting interior. The shelves are filled with delightful and interesting general books. Whether or not people were intending to buy, they nearly always plucked some books off the welcoming shelves and brought them to the busy counter for purchase.'

Adam drew in a breath. 'Downstairs is the religious section, which was buzzing with excited students from the University or Concord Bible College, who wanted to explore the shelves for the latest theological books.'

Adam was working at a different part of the bookshop and told his parents a week later that it had a lower, third section which was his concern. 'It has a back door where the postman delivers mail from all over the world – the van is always well laden. It involves numerous tasks for me, including unpacking large sacks of post and calculating the prices for publications from abroad. Storing excess titles and special orders for valued country customers is also part of the business.

'The students get to know the staff well and eagerly share their news. They rejoice in their exam results, or share about a fresh parish, or speak of an overseas missionary posting when they have graduated.'

Adam was so excited! The next evening, the same excitement was paraded. 'Among the customers today was Sir Timothy Walters, a retired publisher who had something to do with the university. Aged about eighty and therefore very wise, his thin, stooped figure came into the shop's theological section, and with great enthusiasm he found more treasures for his expanding home library.

'Sir Timothy was very kind to me. I had been working

on my first attempt at writing, so I asked him if he would mind reading it. When he had finished, he wisely said to the manager, "I am reading what this budding young author has written." Although he didn't make any comment about my writing at the end, he did advise me about publishing the work.

"'Irrespective of the subject matter", Sir Timothy said, "you must present the manuscript in a formal manner. The typed pages must be done in double-spacing. The title of the book must be given at the very beginning. Some publishers insist that it be on top of each page. The pages must be numbered. On two or three pages, you must outline the theme to the publishers, and once you've done that, leave it up to them to do their thing. They might take a few months to answer you!"

'Sir Timothy gave me a smile and left me to reflect on his words.'

Everything was falling into place for Adam. He had gained a strengthening of his faith and literary knowledge. The next step was to do some theological training, so he became a student at Concord Bible College, and later the nearby university.

At Concord College, Adam found the central offices on the left and the rather cramped library on the right. Inside was a small courtyard that faced the dining room and numerous lecture rooms. The students' library was on one side and all the staff offices were on the other. There were a few bedrooms for married students, but the rest of the two hundred or so individual students' rooms were divided up – men from women, and ne'er the twain shall meet – well, they only saw each other when they were in lectures or having their meals. Strict rules applied to everything, and the matron's room was situated so that she could survey all!

At twenty-one (the age of maturity at that time), Adam had just barely begun his college studies when he received an official letter from a government agency that would stop all of this! Taking it to his bedroom, he read the short letter.

Under the National Military Service Act, it required Adam

to have a medical examination at the Army Drill Hall.

This one letter from the army developed into a whole lot of other official correspondence. Over a month of serious thinking, Adam decided to become a Conscientious Objector. On conveying this to the army, they instructed him to put his objections to *Performing Combatant Duties* in writing. Adam should also provide the name of a witness who could *Vouch for his sincerity.*

Thankfully, the army authorities decided that the objection should be put on hold until Adam had completed his studies.

Adam made friends at the college right away. This was going to be an exciting, if arduous, six years – three in Concord College and three at the university – but he rarely wrote to his family in Mosgiel. This one he did send:

> *We always enjoy theological discussions and sit examination papers on various subjects; we take devotions and have study time in the library... prepare meals and sometimes serve them... we take part in great singing performances in the College Hall, my singing with the melodious baritone that does wonders for the rest. We do extensive pastoral work in Dunedin as well.*
>
> *There is one mission that has already acknowledged my interest, the* Christian Bookshop *in Port Moresby. Just in case you don't know, or the memory escapes you* (he reminded his father), *this is in Papua New Guinea!*
>
> *One missionary who has just returned from that country says: 'Papua New Guinean children, who had never seen an atlas before, were amazed to see the shape and size of the country. It looked like a strange bird, with a fixed eye and open mouth ready to devour those staring at it. Below its large belly, they saw its scrawny feet, the capital, Port Moresby.'*
>
> *My experience in the Religious Bookshop, my time at Concord Bible College and the university and hopefully as a trained minister, will enable me*

to serve them with the gospel.

Chapter 17

*T*HE UNIVERSITY PROVIDED a great variety of academic teaching staff. Once a year these highly qualified teachers chose one student to present a speech entitled: *What is Vital to Me*. Now twenty-six, Adam was chosen to speak in his final year. The auditorium was packed with students. Seated on the platform were the college hierarchy wearing a wonderful array of multi-coloured gowns and unusual but stylishly shaped caps. They all fell silent as Adam stood up and approached the lectern.

Looking nervously around at everyone, he started to speak, but then he made the mistake of looking down at his notes. Recalling the words of one of the lecturers at Concord College who had said on *Good Communication*: 'Speak to your audience and not to your notes', he quickly lifted his head and spoke clearly and distinctly about an interest that was very important to him.

'Once there was a boy who held his parents' hands as they all watched the annual parade of returned soldiers wending their way through the streets of the town.

'Groups of soldierly men marched tightly between brass or pipe bands. The boys' faint cheers could barely be heard through the noise of the crowds on the footpaths. The lusty shouts, combined with the discordant sound of music being blown from a tuba or pipes, and drowned out by cymbals and drums, created a chaotic cacophony.

'Such excitement each Memorial Day – for that was

what it was – would always end exhaustedly for those both marching and watching. The marchers would inevitably go to have a beer with their mates, and the watchers returned to their homes to celebrate with a good hearty meal.'

Putting his hands firmly on both sides of the lectern, Adam lowered his voice and said quietly, 'As the boy went past the cenotaph, he stared at the names chiselled on stone and at the wreaths all around its base. He had just recognised one name, which came from *his* family! As the boy grew to be a young man, he learned and understood a little bit more about the reasons for this special day.'

Adam now lifted his voice and spoke with greater emotion.

'This young man took special pride in the fact that one of his grandfathers had joined the Cameron Highlanders in Scotland, but had died fighting the Germans at the Battle of Loos in Belgium. One year, he had even worn his grandfather's medals as he stood watching the other medalled men march smartly before him.

'The years went by and he noticed more changes in the way the soldiers marched. The older men, the retired soldiers, who held memories going right back to the earliest wars, were now taking things more slowly, with many obviously struggling to keep up. There were also other soldiers who had been involved in the Korean War and the Malayan Emergency.

'He noticed changes in the attitudes of the crowds on the footpaths, as well. They came now from a community where there was a diminishing perception of heroism and of the glory of conflict, if there can ever be glory in any situation of war.'

Adam's eyes went slowly around the audience before he went on to give the high point of his speech.

'Then came the war in Vietnam, starting in 1955. Just prior to New Zealand's involvement in that conflict, this young man was called up and caught in the conscription raffle that was supposedly the fairest way to ensure his country offered the most effective defence that it could.

'A Christian, with high ideals and clear-cut ethical standards, he was forced to make a choice that would effectively decide whether he too would or would not parade along the streets of any of our cities.

'This studious man – yes, it's me' – acknowledging it with a smile, 'came to study the Bible and theology in preparation for missionary service. However, I had received a letter which told me I had been selected for Compulsory Service.' And, waving his army letter, he made his final point: 'I chose to be a Conscientious Objector!'

Then, very slowly, Adam said, 'I am in a quandary as to what may be the answers to going to war, or if there are any answers at all. Perhaps it could be summed up by saying that pacifism is my ideal – though I would have doubts as to whether I could stand by those ideals when the need arose, but,' raising his voice, '*I will try!*'

Adam gathered his notes together and sat down. His fellow students and most of the Concord College academics rose to their feet, applauding him. Over the years some had known of the conflict within him. Now he had expressed it skilfully in this speech.

A number of older university academics who were seated on the stage shook his hand and said something like, 'If only I had had the same gumption as you.'

Only Sir Timothy Walters expressed his sad surprise. Gripping Adam's arm tightly, he put his face close to Adam's and spoke with great passion.

'Well, you've spelled out your reasons very succinctly as to *why* you're a conscientious objector. I bet that when you have to face actual contact with the enemy, the *real* situation is completely different. We must *fight* with all our strength and determination. We must *defend* ourselves for peace and justice – all that we *believe in.* We cannot *walk away.* We cannot *celebrate* until the conflict is over!'

Sir Timothy then released his steady grip and, wrapping his gown around himself, he strode away from the scene, a lonely figure, trembling and upset.

Adam was shocked at this, but guessed that Sir Timothy had in the past been involved in a war. Perhaps he had been a prisoner somewhere. Maybe he had seen mates die. Obviously, he carried many secret scars within. If asked, Adam would offer an explanation to him, but not a backing down of what he felt was right.

Graduation was the following day. The university auditorium was becoming very full, but Adam found a place for his family down near the front, then sat down with other graduating students on the stage. All the staff paraded in and took their seats, and the Chancellor of the University spoke. After he had finished his oration, Adam listened carefully for his name as a graduate. He was so proud! Receiving the two degrees from both institutions, he imagined – no, he *knew* – that he was ready for the tasks that God had before him.

Being a conscientious objector, the army provided him with the opportunity to present his case as to why he would expect some leeway from them. Earnestly Adam explained that he wished to work as a Christian missionary overseas, and had been accepted by worldwide *Christian Bookshop* in Port Moresby. The army authorities had then allowed his conscientious objection to stand, while he was carrying out this work.

Chapter 18

AT PORT MORESBY'S hot and humid airport, Adam was met by his missionary colleagues, leaders Connor and Thelma Holmes. They came from England and would be returning home at a later date. They took the now sweaty Adam to the mission house, where he had a quick, cooling shower which made him feel far more comfortable. He changed into more suitable clothing for a hot climate – a bright open-necked shirt, checked shorts, long socks and sneakers. After a long cooling drink and some delicious pawpaw to eat, he was taken to the mission bookshop in the middle of town.

Standing in the large shop, Adam turned slowly around and noted how the shelves were crammed full of interesting books of various sizes, languages and value. A young man from Hula, a village some distance along the East Coast from Port Moresby, was very busy dusting the books. This chocolate-coloured man with an enormous hairstyle was Tau Rebu, who gave him a cheery smile and a handshake.

Behind the glass counter was an entrance to the adequate back room, where the staff were involved in the day-to-day tasks. One by one they welcomed him – Mary, a large friendly woman from Manila, and an Australian married couple, Jill and Peter, who were expecting their first child.

Adam next had a quick look through the open doors to the large property outside, which was filled with tropical plants. He could see a small house that he supposed was for Tau and his wife.

Going outside to the front of the shop, he saw that it was a two-storey building on a wide sealed road. Up and down the street were several Chinese trading stores catering for many of the local customers. Further up, restaurants provided secluded places under palm trees for wealthier clientèle.

The main street, which ran parallel to the one that the *Christian Bookshop* was on, was always busy with local and tribal people from various parts of the country. Often, they sat in small groups on the path offering goods for sale, including betel nut, which unfortunately when chewed turned the saliva in the mouth a red colour. They often spat onto the pavement. At the busy intersection was a centre podium, where a smart uniformed policeman directed disorderly traffic and inebriated pedestrians alike. Adam felt that he had come to a town with exciting possibilities!

Connor and Thelma had been in Port Moresby for some time, opening up a Christian bookshop. This was one in a succession of similar stores operated by faithful people and placed in strategic positions all around the world. Connor and Thelma's vision included searching all over the country for area agents who would begin their own literature ministries in towns, villages and more isolated areas of Papua New Guinea.

Every day the shop bustled with activity. Each had their own responsibilities. Peter sold books in the shop. Mary ordered books from publishers overseas. Jill dealt with the accounts and banking. In the sticky heat, relieved only by a large roof fan in the middle of the building that tried hard to circulate the air, Adam quickly learnt to pack parcels in response to orders from people, both missionaries and lay folk, from all over the country.

Most Saturday mornings, Adam served in a bookstall at the local market. He loaded up the large estate car with a variety of Bibles in the local languages for customers to browse and buy. Small scripture portions or other simple Bible leaflets were freely available. Adam made great efforts to shout out in *Pidgin English* or *Police Motu*, two languages which he was yet to master fully, hoping that those books which he brought would capture some attention.

Adam often went down to the docks to collect new stock. Parcels came from all over the world containing Christian books, religious cards and other stationery, paintings and, sometimes, beautiful jewellery. However, finding the boxes and packages was difficult. He usually found that they were in various customs warehouses, and sheaves of official papers were required before they could be released into his care.

At that time, Port Moresby had both local and international airports. Jumbo jets had just begun to fly into the capital. However, many single or twin-engine planes, some amphibious with floats, flew throughout the country calling in to towns, villages and hidden valleys high in the mountains, low in the jungle swampland, or landing on rivers, taking goods and people back and forth. The daring pilots landed and took off sometimes in tricky weather or situations, occasionally greatly alarming their frightened passengers. Adam regularly kept the area agents well supplied with Christian books and other materials that winged their way to a wide variety of destinations.

Every Monday, the staff shared their weekend adventures over morning tea. Adam talked about the trouble at the Koki market. 'Every week someone creates a fight or has an argument. One local Hanuabada woman deliberately spat some red betel nut onto a passing girl of a different tribe. There was such a fight!'

Describing some of the people that he had seen at the market, he added, 'There are so many different skin colours, unusual dress codes and strange languages.'

Thelma's voice sang out from the crowded shop, 'There are about seven hundred languages!'

Adam smiled. 'Thank goodness we don't have to learn them all,' he mumbled. He had been working to grow a thick auburn beard, hoping that it made him look more self-assured, but sometimes the staff had difficulty in understanding his words through his whiskers.

'God loves all these people, however they dress, act,

smell or talk,' clean-shaven Connor said, munching on a tough gingernut biscuit and spraying crumbs.

One day, Connor took Adam to one side and said very quietly that he was aware of his conscientious objector status, but there was one thing that troubled him. 'You might take this to extremes and, instead of being a missionary, hold another purpose than the one which we stand for. You won't do that, will you?'

Adam grinned. 'No, I won't. You have my guarantee.'

Connor spoke again. 'If you ever get the chance, go to the Reverend Colin Grey. He lives east, in Alotau in the Milne Bay District. You will find a person who is not only a very gracious and most holy servant but who, through the years, has become a scholar of conscientious objection.'

Six months later Adam received an invitation to fly to Alotau to stay with the Reverend Colin Grey for three weeks. Single all his life, he was an energetic servant of God at seventy-four years. He fulfilled the task of area agent for the *Christian Bookshop* in Port Moresby.

Alotau was made up of a rather scattered group of villages lying halfway along the northern shore of Milne Bay. Beginning as a small grass-covered stream, then widening and growing much deeper until it became a giant trough, the bay disbursed its waters to the open sea many miles away. Part of the land area had been used as a military airfield during World War Two battles against the Japanese; it was now a civilian airfield.

The single-engined Missionary Aviation plane landed on Bubuletta airfield, with Adam the only passenger. As he unloaded his luggage, the missionary pilot gunned his plane's motor for departure. Leaving Milne Bay, its noise reverberated and bounced in waves off both sides of the jungle. Adam watched as it disappeared into the distance.

The sun shone relentlessly from the cloudless sky and the breeze blew gently. He heard sounds now of a lone grass cutter working with a large bush knife. Apart from this noise, it was very still and quiet. He sat down in the 'airport' – a small tin shed surrounded by palm trees – and was glad to have some shelter. He read a book, ate some watermelon, and drank coconut milk which the grass cutter gave him. This was most agreeable. Thus he passed the time as he waited three hours for the missionary to collect him.

The putt-putt of a 50cc motorcycle signalled Colin Grey's arrival. Adam heard the cry, 'Hop on!' He did so, perching on the back and holding his gear as they sped along the jungle dirt road. The motorcycle negotiated tortuous paths and rocky streams, making detours to avoid the women returning from their gardens loaded with enormous hands of bananas on their heads.

They eventually arrived at their destination, covered in dust and dirt. Adam climbed awkwardly off the bike and walked into the house. His host provided a drink and something to eat before showing him to his room to have a sleep. Drifting off, he smiled at the thought of the narrow escapes they had had from the large rocks that 'snapped' at them on the muddy track!

The next day, some of the local men laughed and nodded their heads when Adam told them about the rough landing of the Cessna plane. 'It was dreadfully bumpy – it made my head and stomach drop!'

One said, 'It's the Marston Matting put down by soldiers in the last war. You can still see it hidden in the grass. From the air the surface looks very muddy. It's only the matting which holds it together.'

Another raised his voice. 'It helped the large planes loaded with heavy equipment to land here.'

A third and more technical Papuan, attached to an air company, said languidly, 'Made from long pieces of highly-strung steel arranged together to form hundreds of thousands of small, metal clips. You can put them into whatever shape is needed, giving the planes traction on the muddy ground. Very useful here! One of the great American triumphs of the war, the Marston Matting.'

The well-constructed wooden house was one of the early mission stations in Papua. Built on a slight incline, the large, elegant home was surrounded by lush gardens and a sweeping gravel road. There was a small boat-making business right by the quiet waters of Milne Bay.

The Reverend Colin Grey had been visited by all sorts

of people – rich and famous, theological bigwigs, government administrators and ordinary folks, like Adam. The Reverend enjoyed the old style of living in the spacious residence. From a comfortable chair he could see most things, including watching cricket matches played on the well-manicured oval. This day, he observed that the play was taking place between vigorous Europeans and friendly Papuans.

Dressed in creamy whites and wearing striped caps at slight angles on their heads, these gentlemen were piling up runs, at the same time offering, 'Oh, well done!' or 'You're out!' Then the tinkling of lemonade-filled glasses interrupted the game; it was time to stop for refreshments.

In the late afternoon, Adam had a 'bucket shower'. It was an ordinary bucket with a screwed-on shower rose at the bottom. It was filled with warm water, pulled up on a rope, and when the rose was turned it acted as a shower for the recipient. It didn't allow much time to enjoy it, but it was refreshing.

Putting on his clothes, a white shirt, summer-weight white trousers and grey sandals, he was now ready to look forward to drinks at six and dinner at seven. No doubt Colin Grey and the other guests staying there would join him.

In the dining room, someone had already hung the bright 'zapping' kerosene pressure lamps high up so that any insects were neatly dispatched.

Adam soon learnt about the local wartime history – particularly the major battles with the Japanese that had taken place in this area. *Even here,* he thought, *you can experience war on your doorstep.*

An old wizened pastor who sat opposite Adam spoke softly, sharing the details of what had happened. 'On the night of August 25th, 1942,' he explained, 'advancing Australian soldiers killed four Japanese soldiers. They were scouts and were going back to their ships which lay a little offshore, but the Japanese presence had been revealed. It didn't take long before many of *our* soldiers arrived by air, landing on the Marston Matting strip – the one that you landed on – and marched quickly to defeat the enemy. However, the battles took a long time.'

The pastor had said, 'Look around and see the results of war.' So, the next day, wandering around the closer villages, Adam could see the remains of military paraphernalia rusting in the jungle beneath the encroaching vegetation. He could even 'hear and feel' with his mind's eye all the soldiers of both sides who had strenuously engaged in battle here.

When Adam had a conversation with the Reverend Colin Grey, he said what he was really thinking. 'War starts because of human thoughts and greed, but then it finishes in a pretty foul, unimaginable sort of way. We are always ending wars – but never winning peace.'

Adam poured himself a glass of freshly made lemonade before continuing, 'The scriptures tell us that war is unthinkable if Christianity is to be taken seriously.'

His wise companion was sitting comfortably in his chair. He put his hands together, as if he was about to impart some valuable insight from a sermon. 'Not bearing arms is ideal, but we can still have niggling doubts as to whether we should fight if the need arose.'

Adam thought back to the time when he had spoken at Concord College, and how Sir Timothy Walters, the old retired publisher, had challenged him about his thinking.

Then Colin Grey went on: 'Just because all the answers are not available to us, we shouldn't use this as an excuse for doing nothing. Jesus calls us where we are to do what we can, but peace-making should be our primary aim. *Blessed are the peacemakers*, not *peace lovers*. What we do personally *will* have an effect on peace, throughout the world.'

The smiling man continued in gentle wisdom: 'We can never take a portion of the Bible as a clue event in our searching, or use the Bible as a quarry from which we mine biblical bases for our inner convictions. In my opinion, Jesus is the answer, for He always leads us to see God's point of view every time!'

Chapter 19

AT OROKOLO, IN the Gulf District, Polly Williams, nurse, midwife and missionary, excitedly stood in the humid heat waiting for the small plane from Port Moresby to arrive.

Now Polly could hear its approaching drone, and shaded her eyes to watch it swoop down and taxi along the grass airstrip. While all the passengers looked out to see who was waiting for them, Adam remained settled in his seat, calm, serene and taking in the scenery. Then he went through the door and escaped from the air-conditioned plane into a wall of humid heat. Hurrying towards Polly with a broad smile on his face, he no longer cared about his now-crumpled clothing, for he had seen *her* waiting for *him*.

Adam remembered what Polly had told him in Port Moresby: 'You must not kiss me or even hold my hand in a romantic way. The people here have strict rules about behaviour between a man and a woman. There must be no hanky-panky!'

Immensely disappointed, he nevertheless had promised to behave when he made the journey to see her. 'You will know how to act,' Polly encouraged him.

So now they smiled at each other and shook hands – frequently!

Some years before, Polly, with a petite figure and a beautiful face, set out from London's Heathrow Airport on the long journey to Papua New Guinea. She was determined to be God's person. Arriving at Port Moresby, she quickly became aware of *new* sounds, *new* people, *new* animals and *new* birds. Flying west to Orokolo on the noisy Catalina plane was a *new* experience for her. She saw scattered villages with people milling around, bush roads connecting them, wide curving rivers and, just down on a wide grassed area, the *new* hospital buildings which stood by the sea.

This, then, was to be her place of work.

At the hospital there were many new things to experience. The bite of the mosquitos and sand-flies, geckos on the bedroom wall gently clicking to each other, and a praying mantis staring with enormous eyes while rocking on its hind legs, watching all the goings-on.

When Polly paid a visit to the toilet, friendly croaking frogs sometimes made their presence known by sitting on top of the cistern. They were very interested in the goings-on!

At night, sleeping hens perched on the trees outside, clucking as they dreamed of daytime adventures, or squawking if disturbed.

High up in the rafters were the sounds of scampering rats, or the cunning hospital cat singing her jubilant song with a dead rat in her mouth.

The presence of enormous cockroaches and other insects became part of a normal way of life.

The Orokolo people were the main reason for Polly being here. For a while she spoke very awkwardly in the Orokolo language, learning short medical phrases like, 'Where is your pain?' and 'What is your name?'

The people encouraged Polly and there was much raucous laughter at her mistakes! Language was an absolute requirement, so she studied hard. Some weeks went by before she reported, 'I took my first hospital service and I used the story of *Jesus and the Storm,* but I could only express one example to explain the story. It was only a small start, but a good experience.'

Each week at the Sunday service, Polly sat on the floor with the other women and tried to understand the language. Her confidence and language skills improved with perseverance and eventually she spoke enough Orokolo to communicate with the people.

The general hospital buzzed with patients who came in with malaria, tuberculosis, pneumonia, injuries and other conditions, including leprosy. At the day clinic a number of injuries were treated, like falls, burns, broken bones, as well as snake bite and, occasionally, crocodile attacks.

Pregnant mothers came for antenatal care, assessment and delivery. There were always children needing attention.

Often there was an indifference to certain health problems. Regular village patrols took place each week for TB and leprosy treatment, and villages were visited monthly providing clinics to check on all the children and give vaccinations.

Well-packed with medical supplies, nurses and medical orderlies travelled by foot, bicycle or motorbike on most tracks. However, when Polly visited more isolated villages, the nurse-aid was instructed to find the children. Sometimes they took off into the bush when she brought out the needle!

Occasionally a mother would have birth complications. Babies were not usually born in hospital. They tended to be delivered in houses with local women in attendance, or occasionally in the bush *en route* to hospital.

Babies in the hospital were greeted with wide smiles, especially following a difficult delivery. Family members would quickly produce a large dish of cooked green leaves after the births, which provided a good source of iron for the mother. They were given all the help they needed by the hospital staff. Polly enjoyed seeing babies from all over Orokolo growing up to become heathy children.

Occasionally a celebration took place for the local staff and their families. It was always an amazing sight to see the enormous amounts of rice that the children could eat. They expanded visibly until they could consume no more. When they listened to the stories of Jesus their eyes were wide open with wonder!

For some time, Polly had been excited about her engagement to Adam, the astute bookseller in Port Moresby. Unable to keep it to herself any longer, she told one of the other staff members, Sister Liz Hearty.

'Adam said he had just finished serving customers, looked up and noticed my exquisite knees as I came in the door of the bookshop,' Polly explained. 'A few seconds later, he noticed the rest of me. Of course, he also remembered what I looked like and what I was wearing. He said that I had given him an enormous smile and his knees wobbled like jelly! He was really lost. Since then we met a few times when I visited Port Moresby for Nursing Council business. We began to write letters to each other.'

A relieved Liz laughed. 'Oh, that's the reason that you were in the toilet so often. You were reading the letters from *him*. I was beginning to think that there was something wrong with you.'

Polly smiled and, shaking her head vigorously, she said, 'On my last visit, when the bookshop had closed, we went up to the flat to enjoy supper and listen to some gentle music, but it went on and on. It was getting very late, so I was starting to get anxious. Then Adam plucked up courage, fell on one knee and asked if I would marry him. Of course, I agreed! Then, with a "don't go away" sort of look, he ran back down the passage and brought from his room a diamond ring that he had bought from the jewellers that week.'

Polly held it up to the light, admiring the diamonds. 'He fell on his knee again, took my hand and put it on my finger. It was so-o-o-o romantic! You can imagine what happened then. We kissed rather madly but our noses got in the way and we collapsed laughing. We were engaged!'

Meanwhile, Adam had been telling the rest of the missionaries in the bookshop how wonderful Polly Williams was.

'She is on the National Nursing Council in Port Moresby, which requires her to call once a month. While she was visiting her friend's house to buy some dress material, this friend very cunningly brought us together for an evening meal. The conversation between us developed into something more meaningful. The next day I phoned Polly to ask her out, but she let out a sigh and said, "I'm going back to Orokolo tomorrow", but she quickly added, "I'll be back next month! I suppose we could write to each other while we are waiting."

'Which we did, and so romance began!'

Chapter 20

*A*DAM KNEW THAT the central post office would be very busy, delivering their letters between Orokolo and Port Moresby; between the bush hospital and the bookshop.

Their letters had been rather stilted at first.

Adam not only read Christian books, he read just about everything, so he said, 'I've just been down at the second-hand bookshop and picked up a copy of one of Howard Spring's novels. His description of his English characters is excellent. I think I'll get more of his books.'

Polly loved music and, when she had the chance, played the piano. 'One of my favourite pieces is Bach's Toccata and Fugue, which I play on the tape-recorder,' she wrote. Both enjoyed this type of music.

Polly also enjoyed Howard Spring's books, as she was regularly supplied with the latest from his bookshelf.

Adam planned to visit Polly at Christmas time. 'I've made my bookings for the 23rd of December,' he wrote.

A couple of weeks after Christmas and after his joyous visit, she wrote to him, 'I can't get over the short stay you had here. It almost seems like a dream.'

Adam replied, 'How wonderful it is to love someone as lovely as you!'

So, the feeling of interest grew into companionship and then into true love.

Tau Rebu was a mischievous character. His sixteen-year-old wife, Para, had just given birth to a daughter, Ari, so he was doubly mischievous! It was Tau's responsibility at the bookshop each day to dust the stock and work his way around each section until eventually he started again. He didn't just wipe the dust off. He took the books out, one by one and banged them, then gently wiped the outside covers of each book that had become dusty from the road outside. Sometimes tiny weevils, which enjoyed eating the glue between some of the book covers, were dislodged. He had saved a lot of stock from damage, so this was a very important job. However, Tau had another task – to organise morning and afternoon teas for everyone.

The cups were placed upside down so that the large cockroaches couldn't get into them. Once, when Adam was given a full, fresh cup of coffee, he'd enjoyed it until he found an enormous dead cockroach resting upside down in the bottom of the cup. After this he didn't trust Tau when he made the coffee.

Tau was the one who went to the post office twice a day to collect the mail, including Polly's letters. As he returned, he examined each Orokolo envelope. Once, he hid her correspondence from Adam who always asked Tau when he returned, 'Have you got Polly's letter?' This time he was told 'no'.

Adam was very disappointed, and throughout the day he was miserable, still thinking about the lack of a letter and despondently added a second spoonful of coffee to an already pleasant cup that was cockroach free. On seeing this, Tau realised that the hidden letter had better be handed over. He produced it with a wicked smile and said, 'Oh! I must have forgotten this...'

Adam was so delighted with Polly's letter that he forgot to tell Tau off!

Over Christmas time, visiting Polly at Orokolo was one of the most exciting periods of Adam's life. However, he had been told to stay in another house on the mission station and *not* at the nurses' accommodation. Between the nurses and the mission house was a tidal creek with a rickety bridge, thus removing all temptation!

Due to the very high rainfall in the area, the mission house was built on high piles, with steps leading up to a wide verandah cooled by welcomed sea breezes. Underneath, there was a bathroom and toilet standing on a concrete floor. Pigs, chickens and dogs always roamed outside. A novelty for Adam!

Nearby was the local church where the Orokolo people gathered for worship. Adam thought that he and Polly would be together. He was very disappointed, for he discovered that he had to sit with the men, cross-legged on the floor, while his betrothed sat with the women, singing hymns beautifully written in their own language and listening intently to the Pastor preaching from the local language Bible.

Adam described this in another short letter to his parents. 'My beloved was sitting surrounded by a whole bevy of melodious songsters, enjoying themselves with forceful, eloquent singing. But the worship went on and on and my bottom got numb, while I became considerably fed up! When the songs were over, and the prayers were finished, Polly and I were reunited. Polly looked at me and, laughing, she said, *"Ae e karia le va ka!"*

'"What does that mean?" I questioned.

'"For ever and ever!" she humorously replied.'

Polly and Adam went for a romantic walk on the black sandy beach, keeping their hands apart, but only occasionally just touching fingertips. Unfortunately, there was no kissing allowed, not even a small peck. They shied away from other folk on the beach when a member of staff, or even a sickly patient, would wander from this place to the next.

After a short while they went inside to sit on sturdy, comfortable chairs, talking at length of their experiences that had brought them to this tender moment.

Bravo Albert, the hospital cat named after the radio call sign of the hospital, interrupted her rat catching to sit quietly underneath Adam's chair, listening to their conversation and acting as chaperone.

For this occasion, Adam was now dressed in baggy shorts and a sports shirt that was slightly open – 'because it's too hot,' was his explanation to Polly.

Polly laughed. She was still in her white nurse's uniform. She reminisced about the Christmas family gatherings that had taken place during her childhood at

Willowdene, her grandfather's home.

Adam tucked his feet away under the chair and placed the cushions around him as he listened. Bravo Albert now moved under Polly's chair to listen closer. 'On Christmas Day, we children climbed into Dad and Mum's bed and opened our Santa Claus stockings together. There was usually a colouring or quiz book, coloured pencils, and an orange at the toe of the stocking. After breakfast, we played with the gifts.'

Adam interrupted. 'So did we!'

Polly didn't mind the interruptions. Because they were off the beach and inside the nurses' house, she reached over and gave him a kiss or two. Unfortunately, this made the temperature rise! Polly straightened her crumpled dress, for she had allowed him to see *those knees* again!

'The uncles kept the fires going because the weather was cold and nasty,' she continued.

Adam shook his head. 'Just the opposite at our house.'

'We didn't go to church because there were no services on Christmas Day, due to the weather I suppose.'

Adam was surprised and said almost vainly, 'We *always* had a short Christmas service. Most women were wanting to get back and prepare the dinner. We children always wanted to open our Christmas presents.'

Polly smiled. 'After our fantastic dinner, the uncles would put on their aprons to wash up the dishes while the aunties cleared the table.'

Adam interrupted again. 'Do you know, that's what *our* season was like at our house. One uncle had this thing about doing the dishes right after we'd finished eating! The trouble was that the rest of the men felt guilty when they saw him standing there with the dishes piled high, wearing an apron and with dish cloth at the ready!'

Their tall glasses, the ones Adam had purchased from the large store in Port Moresby to give to Polly on Christmas Day, were empty. He refilled them, and they sipped their drinks slowly, quietly enjoying each other's company.

Adam took Polly's hand, wrapping it gently in his,

deciding that he would tell her something that might sound a bit risqué.

Polly looked puzzled. Adam said, 'Last year, I went up to Banz on the wide plateau of the Southern Highlands. They hold the annual Bible convention at the teachers' college there. Have you been there?'

She shook her head.

'I took another man from the bookshop with me. We loaded the books onto the mission plane that was going to fly us all the way from Port Moresby. It was quite thrilling, flying high over the country at unimaginable heights. The pilot enjoyed pointing out places of interest. He drew our attention to the flat jungle, and to various mission stations. We passed over rivers snaking their way from the cloud-covered mountains towards the coast.

'The flight was two hours. Unfortunately, I forgot to go to the toilet before leaving. The pilot was unable to land because the plane was going over thick jungle and there were no landing strips nearby. Instead, he handed me an empty Coke bottle and he cheerily said, "Fill her up!" I was embarrassed, but I filled the bottle up. Only it was too small, and the overflow saturated my trousers. There was nothing I could do except sit there awkwardly until we landed at our destination.

'On our arrival, we shifted the boxes of books onto the Land Rover. The tribal people looked askance at my condition! The local driver was amused at my embarrassment but made no comment as he drove us to the convention. The trousers soon dried in the tropical heat, but I changed them all the same. They were definitely going in for a good wash!'

Polly laughed. She wasn't sure whether he was being risqué or not.

Adam continued: 'The local people at the convention, including missionaries, came from all over the country, not just from the local villages. I saw how the attitude of war-like tribal people was completely transformed by Jesus Christ. The missionaries were all book-hungry, hardly letting us get the books unpacked before they swooped in to buy. After being so isolated in places hidden away in the wop-wops, the arrival of new books was an annual feast indeed.

'The convention went on for a week, and then we travelled back by air with a lighter load and this time, I had dry trousers!'

Adam refilled their glasses with lemonade from the enormous jug left on the table. Smiling, he went on.

'On a different adventure, I wanted to explore Lae and Mount Hagen, and ask the business people if they would like a Christian bookshop in their town, rather than seeing agents in their homes.

'Of course, I was able to manage a visit to the Wycliffe Bible Translators' base at Ukarumpa, and the Independence Celebrations in Mount Hagen that the Australian government had arranged. It was good that Australia was just about to grant independence to the whole country.

'I boarded a small bus with other passengers and left the lush greenery of the coast, travelling on a magnificent but twisting bumpy road into the Highlands.'

He asked Polly if she had ever travelled on that road, but again, she shook her head.

'The gravel road wound its way over narrow passes, across bridged rivers and around the lips of gorges, until it got through to the extensive Markham Valley. On reaching the top the driver stopped so we could all view the second largest rift valley in the world. It was an amazing sight and we quickly took wonderful photos. We looked down at the Kassam Pass, which the bus had just struggled up. "What a change in terrain", said one. "And temperature", said another, and we all put on our jerseys.

'The road went on for a considerable distance until I was let off the bus at Ukarumpa. It was a small village buzzing with activity. Some skilled Europeans had combined with local translators to do exciting and exacting work on the Bible. Do you know how long translating the scriptures can take? From twelve to fifteen years! It begins with the arrival of a translator at the target village; a lonely and sometimes frightening place to be.

'Starting from scratch to learn a completely new

language requires patience, skill and lots of faith. Translation is impossible to achieve without knowing the customs, culture, and the local language, so the work is painstaking.'

Polly got up to move around the room a couple of times, while smiling at Adam. After ruffling up her chair cushions, and noting the cat's continued interest, she sat down again and softly said, 'You can carry on.'

'As I sat there with the translator, the local informant and the linguistic checker, the text was minutely examined until all three agreed on the accuracy and meaning. Then, very slowly, would come the final translation. With God's help, they had completed one of the books of the Bible in yet another language.

'However, when that was done, there was the printing, distribution and the selling of the books, and,' Adam added proudly, 'this was where the *Christian Bookshop* came in.'

Adam took a deep breath and then a final drink from his glass of lemonade. 'Shall I leave it there?' he asked.

Reaching over, Polly gave her permission for him to continue, giving his hand a gentle squeeze.

Chapter 21

THRILLED AT HER touch, Adam gulped and then said, 'I travelled on a bus to the next town of Mount Hagen. Someone at Ukarumpa had suggested that just after leaving Goroka I might like to stop, and walk to a remote village some distance away. He said that one of their native translators, who came from that village, was going back there on the bus, and so perhaps we could go together. He told me that the whole tribe had changed completely, purely because their difficult language had been translated by one of the Bible translators there – him. I did as he suggested. The bus driver stopped at a lonely place and my new companion and I set off.'

Adam smiled in recollection. 'The lively breeze made swishing sounds as we went along the narrow, winding, sunburnt track bordered by dense undergrowth. We were then confronted by a dangerously steep and more difficult slope, so I had to be more careful where I put my sandalled feet. The translator was agile, so he carried on and didn't worry where his bare feet stepped.

'Eventually we reached a dark semi-forested area, and I suddenly found myself thinking – I don't know why – about all these Highlanders coming to Port Moresby in droves. I reminded myself that the use of planes had made a huge difference for many people living in the remote parts of the country, especially in the Highlands.

'Many spent their money on airfares and flew into the cities, where they looked for work. On finding our *Christian Bookshop*, a few hoped for a job, rather than books. This presented a difficulty for me. I wanted to be generous, but was informed by Connor, our leader, that providing work for one would mean indirectly the whole tribe would follow as well. These out-of-towners gathered together, creating little enclaves that eventually became small suburbs.

'Then I thought of a proud, fierce man who came from the Highlands wearing Bird of Paradise feathers in his hair, his body smeared with rank pig fat. He came up to me asking for work in Pidgin English. I was unable to give him any, but the man's darting eyes could see my weekly shopping on the bench behind, so he obviously thought I was exceedingly wealthy. However, he was more intent on getting work than raiding my goods.'

Adam glanced at Polly, then said quietly, 'Maybe the warrior came from this village. Anyway, we went around a sharp bend and I found myself at my destination. In the centre were circular houses made from bush materials. On the periphery, I was greeted by someone who I guessed was the chief. He had all his warriors around him. They looked strong and muscular, with fierce expressions on their faces, and they held long spears or bows and arrows in their hands. They wore a bark frontispiece to hide their genitals, and displayed glorious Bird of Paradise feathers on their heads, which gave them a certain panache! With their noses pierced with bones, and bodies vividly painted, they presented an amazing and frightening sight. I could feel their excitement. Some men with bearded faces had an even more ferocious appearance. They stared at me in surprise at the amazing colour of my *red* hair and beard.

'As they stood, silent and somewhat threatening, the only sound that could be heard came from under the shrubs and trees. It was the tribe's "wealth" in the form of large pigs that were snuffling around looking for sustenance.

'I imagine that most of the village people weren't too sure how to greet this strange European with flaming red hair and beard! So I smiled at them, saying confidently to the chief in what was my limited and rather stunted Pidgin English, "I have a letter to explain why I am here," as I handed it over to him.

'This letter was given to me by one of the staff members at Ukarumpa and was written in the tribe's language. It said that I was a Christian bookseller from Port Moresby, selling Bibles written in all sorts of tribal languages, including that of their village.

'As the chief read the letter I looked around at the neat community. I saw a collection of yams and bananas beside the recently constructed small church, perhaps as a gift to the new pastor. The translator stood away from the warriors, with what I supposed were his family.

'Now the chief knew that I was alright, and smilingly told the rest of the tribe. True fellowship developed. After spending a period with the now-amiable warriors, and sharing their friendly meal, I soon discovered that the tribe was going to the Mount Hagen Show. That was the reason for them all appearing so warrior-like!

'Regrettably, the time raced forward, and it was time to meet the bus. I gathered my luggage and said goodbye to everyone. The friendly translator said he would come to the bus stop, so together we slowly made our way back on the long, upward track. Arriving at the stop, we smiled and shook hands as I caught the last bus into Mount Hagen. The "warrior tribe" would later walk to the main road to be picked up by large trucks and would be transported to Mount Hagen in that manner.

'Many vehicles travelled together, filled with excited warriors singing and chanting their tribal songs, shouting and calling out loudly to friends, or sometimes rude things to their enemies! On disembarking by some enormous pavilions, they joined up with warriors from other tribes. The Mekeo men had multi-coloured painted faces. The Asaro Mud-Men wore finely crafted masks over their heads, looking very fierce. Even the jet-black Bougainvillean people from the far eastern islands were there.

'Hour after hour, no, day after day, they exhibited their wildly strenuous dances. Some would often sing a line, and the rest would reply with rhythmical chants. The temperature was always hot and steamy, so sweat poured down their costumed bodies. Various competitions took place between the tribes. The organisers, very wisely, gave prizes to everyone. If Papua New Guinea sought independence from Australia, they had to be on their best behaviour!

'I eagerly joined the thousands of watchers in the stadium. They had come from all over the country. Everyone waited for the more formal dignitaries to conclude their speeches. Then, very symbolically, the spears, bows and arrows were all laid down.

'An eager reporter from the Mount Hagen newspaper published his first article the next morning: "All tribes of the nation have a new flag with the diagonal line dividing the colours – red and black. It features the stars of the Southern Cross and a yellow Bird of Paradise. This belongs to all of us."'

Adam then fell silent. 'I feel as if I've been talking for ages. Sorry! I had better tell you that the two possible Christian bookshops that I was investigating in Lae and Mount Hagen, were non-starters, at least for a year or so.'

Then he asked Polly whether *she* had any interesting stories to tell. Giving another yawn (for she had been working hard during the day) she sleepily said, 'I'm too tired now, but I will tell you all my own news tomorrow night...'

Chapter 22

'I WAS INVOLVED with a kerosene-filled fridge that caught fire,' Polly began.

She looked at Adam's startled face and laughed. 'Did I shock you? It turned out alright though. The burns to my legs were serious so they spoke to the doctor on the radio. He travelled from Kapuna hospital by canoe, some distance away, crossing several rivers. He stayed for a fortnight to look after me, as well as the hospital patients.

'It was very dramatic! I was filling up the fridge with kerosene fuel when all of a sudden, it blew up. I had burns on both arms and legs. On the tip of my nose was a large blister and my hands were bandaged up. Not a pretty sight!'

She changed her position on the chair to make herself more comfortable.

'I think it was an unfortunate accident. There must have been benzine in the drum as well as kerosene. Thank God for getting away from the flames like that. The house wasn't burnt down so there was no real damage to property. *Acriflavine* was put on my burns – the stuff applied for healing, so my damaged legs and arms were now transformed to a vile yellow! The only thing left was the blister right at the end of my nose, a difficult place to put *Acriflavine*. It's a wonder I didn't end up cross-eyed! Later, I tried walking and the nurse, Liz Hearty, said I looked like an old witch hobbling along!' She giggled infectiously, taking the fear from Adam's face.

'When I was able to write a letter a week later to my

parents, I said: "My skin doesn't look so piggish now. I seem to be peeling and itching all over. I went down to the hospital and received a joyous welcome. There was much *ikihero-ing* in the Orokolo language, which means roughly: *my liver goes out to your liver!*"'

Adam looked for her nasty burns. 'When did this happen?'

'Oh, about a year ago. They have just about healed up. Look at my nose. It is pristine clean.'

Laughing, he gave her a kiss on her perfect nose. 'They must have been quite painful,' he said in reflection.

Polly replied, 'Only my leg causes me discomfort now.'

Adam offered her some sympathy by humbly saying, 'What a horrifying event,' and, reaching over to take her delicate hands, he gave her a gentle kiss on each finger.

The following night the nursing staff mysteriously disappeared, and Adam and Polly were now able to sit comfortably on inside chairs and look out to a moonlit sea.

Adam said, 'I want to tell you of my adventure with the New Zealand Navy. My grandmother Lilian died just before I took the journey to Auckland. She was a kind, gracious lady, who dressed well in lovely clothes and wore her necklaces whenever she went out. She was in her seventies when she died from a heart attack. I remember Dad being distraught by first the death of his father-in-law, and then shortly after, his own mother. Now my grandmother had died. He had been left with no older members in the family.

'Dad didn't say anything to me about my joining the Navy, but I felt some resistance from the vibes that I was getting. In spite of all this, I left home and travelled by train from Mosgiel to Christchurch, then an overnight steamer to Wellington, where I caught another overnight train to Auckland. When I got off the train near the railway station there was a small Navy boat with two sailors ready to take me and other recruits to the training facility, HMNZS Philomel, the Navy base across the busy harbour.

'Another recruit had travelled with me from Dunedin.

He was free of the social restraints of that time – more than I had been used to anyway. I asked myself, *What about the other recruits coming from all over the country? Will they all be the same as this slightly drunk, sex-starved man?*

'I had been planning to join the Navy for some time. I went into the recruiting office in my lunch hour and brought home material that might make my parents more amenable to my going. My worried mother had said, "You can't join up until you're nearly eighteen," but that time soon came around and she had no reason for refusing to let me go.

'My dad? Although he was very interested in my well-being, he kept out of my way. I suppose he had memories of what had happened to his own father, rushing off to war. He couldn't come up with a suitable argument against this mad Navy venture. Of course, Dad and the rest of the family saw me off at the railway station, but even then, he didn't say anything except, "Goodbye and good luck."'

Polly said, 'That must have been sad for you, leaving everybody, particularly your father.'

Adam thought about this. 'Well, as I was a recruit going into the Navy, I barely thought about the relationship being strained like that. At the Navy base, the first thing we did was move from this room to that, from one test to the next, stripping off our clothes and then putting on a new uniform. There was an opportunity to talk with others about their chosen career and, to my surprise, I could only find a few who were really happy.

'In the evening I stood in line with the other men waiting to be sworn in for eight years. Down the line came the officer. To each one he asked, "Do you swear to serve Queen and country? Put your hand on this Bible and swear after me that you will." Then it seemed that God was whispering in my ear: *I called you to be an overseas missionary from that same Bible.* Could I do it? No!

'I stepped from the line and said to the officer, "Sir, I don't feel that this is the life God wants me to live. I wish to withdraw."

'The officer looked surprised, but with his permission I made my way to the back and sat down to watch the rest of the proceedings. As soon as he finished the swearing in, his whole manner changed. Instead of being an understanding man he became an abrupt man, shouting out, "Where do you think you're going? Get in line! You're wearing the Queen's uniform now!"'

Adam filled his lemonade glass again. He was quite thirsty now, but he wanted to tell his tale right to the end.

'The next day the Navy vessel took me back into Auckland, providing me with limited funds to catch the two trains and the night ferry to my home. I phoned Mum first, saying in a rather subdued voice, "I'm coming home". She let out a relieved sigh and said, "I thought you might. I've been praying for you."

'On arriving home, I discovered that Mum had already been scouring the local newspaper and pencilled in jobs that I could do, or ones that she thought I must apply for. Mum looked at me, and said with a loving smile, "I hope this is the last adventure that you are going on!"'

Polly exclaimed, 'That is wonderful! But what about your father? Did you make any headway with him?'

Very sadly, Adam replied, 'I'm afraid I didn't. Dad was being very elusive, as if I wasn't around. We were like two strangers, both at home and in public. Through my mother's influence I got work in Dunedin's religious bookshop the following week. That led me on to Concord College, university, and then to Port Moresby, where I met – lovely you,' and he gave Polly another very passionate kiss!

Chapter 23

AS THE GLORIOUS sun was sinking, the slightly odorous kerosene lamp was lit and placed at the far end of the large room of the nurses' house. This attracted stink beetles and clouds of tiny night insects, which by morning would be dead on the floor, or piled up high on the table.

Polly was looking at Adam, who was very handsome, but she resisted the temptation to kiss him, and continued their conversation.

'One of the earliest memories I had when about three or four, was of dressing up in a nurse's uniform. I had a doll who was done up as a patient, so nursing became my passion. While I was still at high school, a nurse who lived next door offered to give me a reference for an application to University College Hospital, in London. I duly applied when I was seventeen.

'The return letter granting me an interview arrived. I got out the maps and train timetable and with Mum's help we worked out how to get there. We walked up the front steps of the hospital and sat in a waiting room before being shown into the matron's office. She was a very tall woman, clothed in Navy uniform dress, with starched cuffs and a stiff, frilly cap. There was no difficulty in standing to attention! Although very nervous, I gave the right answers to her questions. A week later I received a letter to say that I had been accepted for training. The time came to say my goodbyes, and I set off by myself into a new world.

'I arrived at the nurses' home and joined the fifty new

girls at the Preliminary Training School. Each of us had a room that was small but quite adequate. We were given time to unpack, find our uniforms and make a cup of tea. We were told that we were to always be in the home by ten o'clock at night or we would be locked out, and in big trouble.'

Polly laughed. 'Now I see that the trouble has changed – you're here! That's trouble enough for me!'

The evening became rather stormy. As the atmosphere grew heavier and more humid by the minute, Polly felt very languid. 'I wish the thunderstorm would come,' she said. Then she gave a yawn, smiled lazily and said, 'Getting fed up?'

Adam was a gentleman. His shirt, which he had just washed, was now saturated with streams of perspiration running down to his shorts, making him very uncomfortable. However, he said in a low voice, 'No, I'm alright. You're telling me the events of *your* life!'

Polly smiled and gave another yawn. Her legs, which had been folded up beneath her, had become numb, so she stretched and waggled her feet to bring them back into circulation. Then she said very quietly, 'I think we had better go to bed. No!! *Separate* beds,' for she saw his face light up. *Surely, he didn't think that!* She gave him another yawn as a clue. 'We have a busy day ahead!'

Adam smiled broadly! Being a very proper gentleman, although wishing he didn't have to, he got up, ready to go over to the other house. He gave Polly a last kiss before going down the steps of the nurses' home. Seeing that the massive thunderstorm had already chased through the big ugly clouds, leaving the outside area with fresh globules of moisture, and the air clean but still humid, he rejoiced as he went over the rickety bridge and up the wide steps to his temporary home.

Even though they had been brought up at opposite ends of the world, they both had amazing experiences to recount. Some were similar, others quite different, but they were woven together in the jungle at the Orokolo hospital. They became more devoted than ever to each other. Now he would get a decent sleep, dreaming of being together with Polly for the rest of their lives.

Very early the next morning, Adam joined Polly and the Hewitt teenagers, children of Doctors Gordon and Agnes Hewitt. They would travel to Kapuna Hospital together. This was a six-hour journey. Carrying their belongings, they walked a considerable distance from the hospital to the village nearest to the Purari river mouth, where a large outboard canoe waited for them.

The tall forest trees *topped with umbrellas* (said one of the Hewitts) shaded them from the hot sun above. Reaching the wide creek which led to the river, the hot sun, which had *hidden its hat* (again the Hewitts), suddenly broke through the canopy and burned down with an intense heat.

They climbed into the canoe, and its movement across the water generated some relief with a small breeze. Making their way slowly through small channels between the mangrove swamps, they were attacked by large numbers of mosquitoes and sand-flies, despite being well protected with insect repellent.

The small islands of mud and mangrove, with their tangled roots and dismembered branches, made it a scary adventure. They could see scraggy trees that hid river snakes sliding silently into the dark tidal waters. Occasionally, strong weeds caught in the propeller of the outboard motor. Apart from the sounds of the water lapping against the sides of the boat, it was very quiet when stopped. One of the team dived into the water to free the propeller while the others looked out for crocodiles and snakes. It was a great relief when all was well, and the journey could continue.

Finally, the canoe emerged from the *traps of danger* (Hewitts) to face the strong currents of the river mouth, where they turned inland and headed towards the distant Kapuna Hospital. They began to rock up and down on the passing waves. Adam felt quite queasy. Polly sat still, holding on to the vessel. The three teenagers, however, were comfortably seated. One was at the bow, navigating; another was steering, and the third peered over the side for any dangerous branches that might damage the outboard motor. They were old hands at this.

Time was getting on and everyone's stomachs were beginning to rumble. The navigator said they were stopping at one of the larger islands for a short while; it was time to eat. Drawn up under the shade of some gnarled trees, they enjoyed a feast of freshly made Orokolo bread and sun-melted cheese, followed by delicious juicy pawpaws and plenty of thirst-quenching drink.

Adam was wearing his large 'personally-made' hat – so called by the Highlands hat-seller. This hat became a vital protection for his face and neck, particularly in a situation like this. His legs and knees were already getting burnt by the reflection of the sun on the water. Again, he rubbed on his sun-cream.

Polly called out to him, 'You can pile the cream on but I'm afraid you can't change your light skin!'

He applied it anyway, plus to his face. When he put his hat on again, Polly looked at him and laughed, saying, 'Now you look even more unfamiliar!'

Later, the adventurers arrived at a sizeable village. Built high, and near the edge of the river, the toilet could be seen by everyone. It was a tall, spindly affair with a ramp going up to two areas separated by a flax wall. The wall had holes in it, so it was easy to see what your companions were doing. It was only for visitors, of course. There was no paper, only coconut husk. The hefty pigs snuffled below, eating the people's residue!

Polly said, when they had been up and down the rickety ladder, 'Pretty basic isn't it? Kapuna is not far now.'

Adam flashed her a quick grin.

The canoe and all its passengers ventured on, and before they knew it, they had reached Kapuna Hospital. This was a busy central building, providing loving medical care to many in need. Most of the teaching staff and some of the more agile patients welcomed them.

Although very tired, Polly and Adam soon perked up when they were shown their separate bedrooms in the mission house, where they could change out of their sticky clothes into fresher ones.

Ever smiling, Dr Gordon, in his white shirt and shorts, said to Adam, 'Look at your red legs. I don't think your sunscreen has done the trick. I'd better get some calamine lotion from the hospital and you can apply it after you've had a shower,' and so he did.

After a ready shower, and calamine lotion applied, Adam was ushered into the dining room. A slim Agnes welcomed him again and, removing her apron, she served dinner.

After her shower, Polly looked a new person. Wearing her soft flowing dress and seated next to Adam, gorgeous whiffs of perfume floated by, delighting him.

The teenagers too changed out of their sweaty clothes and put on decent apparel for dinner.

Dr Gordon sliced the tender pork as they all parked themselves around the table. They gave thanks to God, then started to demolish the meal of delicious meat, cooked bananas, sweet potato, and manioc cooked in coconut milk, followed by homemade ice cream and freshly picked fruit.

Adam said afterwards as he patted his stomach, 'That was a *lovely* meal.' Agnes was pleased. Laughingly, he continued, 'It was well worth the walk of all those miles, then putting the canoe through its paces on the choppy river among mangrove islands, and a visit to the village toilet, to get this reward!'

The next morning Polly had a tummy upset. 'Not from yesterday's meal,' she quickly said to Agnes, but nevertheless she stayed in bed to recover for the day.

The night time window shutters were now removed, so Polly could see the comings and goings of the staff as they went about their work. Many students came from other parts of Papua to do their nurse training here. She could also see distant patients arriving in their canoes, and people from the jungle visiting relatives.

Polly was dressed now in a flimsy nightie that was anchored down under the sheet. Adam still had the most loving thoughts towards her, but was slightly disappointed that she had kept certain things hidden. And to make sure that he wouldn't catch the same stomach bug, he gave Polly only a light a kiss on her forehead.

Adam sat down on a sturdy chair. Polly was instructed by Agnes, her bed-supervisor, to remain in bed while she had the chance.

Polly nibbled a piece of pawpaw, as she told Adam how she had become involved in the work of her missionary society.

'I arrived at Carey Hall Theological College in Birmingham. It was quite a mix of students from various churches. The college community was friendly, although the Principal, Miss Thrill, was very good at winding people up; making outrageous theological statements at the meal table to encourage everyone to think about what they really believed.'

Polly's stomach was still queasy, but eating another piece of pawpaw settled her well, and she went on with her tale.

'Before leaving England, there was a special service of commission in the Westminster Chapel in London. The building seated a thousand people and it was full for the service. One of us had to give a testimony about becoming a missionary, and then we were all commissioned. People were so kind and supportive, and have continued to be so throughout my time in Orokolo. It was a humbling and amazing experience. The singing was fantastic and there was such praise for a loving God!'

Adam asked, 'How did you travel? By air or by ship?'

Polly gave her reply in a roundabout way. 'My mother didn't come to Heathrow Airport. Just before I left, I caught sight of her sitting in her bedroom pretending to read her book, which she couldn't do as her eyes were full of tears. And the book was upside down. Yet despite her sadness, my going away brought many good things for her. She sent me parcels and regular letters. We now keep in touch a bit more than we previously did. More than that, it gave her contact with other people and increased her confidence and sense of her own worth.'

'And what about your father?'

'He always said that I wouldn't be strong enough to

be a missionary and pooh-poohed the idea. But the fact that I had gone gave him a sense of pride and purpose.'

Agnes poked her head around the door and said, 'I don't want to be a nuisance, but I think you've had enough time, Adam. Why don't you allow Polly to have a sleep?'

And he did. He knew that Polly was tired and looking rather flushed, so reluctantly he left her alone, to sleep.

Chapter 24

IME WENT BY and the great day dawned. Doctor Gordon Hewitt was going to be an honorary 'father' for Polly at her Orokolo wedding. Albert Williams, her own father, couldn't make the long journey from England. In fact, only her Australian friend, Myrtle, flew out that day from Port Moresby, along with Tau Rebu, who was travelling to the wedding at Adam's invitation.

Myrtle was to be bridesmaid for Polly. Tau was a companion to Adam. As much as Adam's family wanted to come to the wedding, it was too far away for the Frasers to travel from Mosgiel.

Adam and Polly planned to be married in the late morning at Orokolo, and after the reception to fly back to Port Moresby, where a Service of Blessing was to be held in the church in the evening. This would enable their friends to join in the celebration as well.

Everyone at the Orokolo mission station was putting the final touches to the wedding. Many local families from the surrounding villages were planning to come and join in with the festivities. One of the hospital patients had been making blue grass skirts for the four shy, young local bridesmaids – bemused as they tried them on.

On the night before the wedding, Adam was staring through the window at the damage that the extreme wind, and the three inches of rain that saturated everything, had done. He muttered, 'I bet the rain will be turning these tracks into quagmires!'

He was right – it came down in buckets. In the

morning, some distance from the church, the borrowed Land Rover became bogged down in the mud.

Dressed in his old clothes, and as a passenger on his way to his own wedding, Adam climbed down to help the driver, the local European Catholic priest, who was trying to extricate the vehicle from the quagmire. It was well and truly stuck.

Putting his wrapped wedding suit on top of his head, he left the priest and the vehicle and walked the rest of the way, arriving at the church hot and muddy but still smiling!

The worried priest managed to get some local men to help him free the Land Rover, ready to later transport Adam and Polly.

Meanwhile, water had been gathering on the floor of the palm-covered church shelter where the wedding was to take place. Some energetic young schoolchildren joined Adam and Tau to sweep the water away with their hardy bush-brooms. This left puddles that rapidly turned into sun-baked mud so, renewing their efforts, they energetically swept them away too.

An hour later, in a nearby schoolroom, Adam and Tau quickly changed their muddy attire for wedding clothes. Tau, who was rather nervous because he hadn't a clue what he was to do, was positioned with Adam under the freshly swept, leafy shelter at the front of the church.

Behind them, there was a buzz of conversation as the people awaited the bride. Adam stood thinking about all the things that had led to this moment.

Polly had some firm ideas about the wedding, but Adam remembered all the frustrations when planning the whole affair, she in Orokolo and he in Port Moresby. He had been worried about the heavy rain that could have stopped everything. He thought of Polly's friend, Myrtle, and his companion, Tau, who was standing beside him.

He wondered what would happen if the wedding party were to be stranded by rain in Orokolo and unable to return to Port Moresby for the second church service. More importantly, he wondered about Polly and whether he was worthy of marrying her.

Looking lovely, Polly held the doctor's arm tightly as they left the mission house. She was barefoot, walking gracefully through the short grass and then down the aisle between rows of smiling Oroloko and European people. Wearing a dress of white voile, sleeves and veil of lace, and carrying a streamer of pink and white frangipani flowers, Polly was followed by four wide-eyed Papuan children in blue grass skirts, wearing pink frangipani garlands around their necks.

The people sang in Orokolo and English. The balding, smiling Bishop spoke the majestic words of the Christian wedding.

Near the ocean, by the Orokolo jungle, in front of two witnesses and many guests, Adam and Polly exchanged rings, and made their holy vows to become man and wife.

When the wedding party paraded out, there were photos galore. The relieved priest smiled and waited in the now extricated Land Rover, taking the happy couple on a circuitous route to the hospital, where the reception was to take place under a shelter on the lawn, beneath tall, swaying palm trees.

All the rest clambered over the rickety log-bridge to greet the bride and groom when they arrived in style!

Food had been prepared and was placed under some woven palm leaves for protection from the hot sun. Myrtle and Tau, who were more relaxed now, were amazed at the smoothness of the arrangements.

Telegrams from various parts of the world were read, and then the wedding cake was cut and eaten.

Afterwards, Adam said: 'Friends, there are many different types of attractions at Orokolo. There are the beautiful sandy beaches and the broad expanse of the sea. There are the brilliant sunsets. There is a spirit of dedication to service amongst the staff. There are the attractive villages, schools and gardens, and the people who look after them. There are so many friends who have been so kind to us today. But the best one of all is someone very special – who has just become my wife!'

Adam and all the guests lifted their glasses to Polly. She thanked them all, saying, 'If you come to Port

Moresby, come and visit me and my husband!'

Adam half-heartedly said, 'We will be glad to sell you some books!'

The hospital staff and patients were sad that Polly was leaving them, so they gave many gifts to her and Adam; six grass skirts, a string bag for their first child, table mats, a sugar bowl, a small Bible dictionary, numerous handmade bags and baskets, a pineapple, and a water-melon. Oh, and a live chicken trussed up. Adam decided that this would go for Tau and his family to dine on later.

When it was time to depart, the wedding party was driven in the Land Rover by the tired priest to the airstrip a little distance away.

Sister Liz Hearty wanted to take one last photo of them, so she clambered onto the outside of the plane's cockpit, revealing her pink knickers to everyone inside! She took the photo and alighted.

'Thank goodness!' exclaimed an embarrassed Polly aloud. 'I thought we were going to have the image of a pair of pink knickers permanently before us.'

The plane started its engine and they winged their way to Port Moresby. On their arrival, the rather tired yet cheerful couple enjoyed a short rest in their new, old home – the apartment above the shop.

The second service started at six-thirty. Everyone who was invited came along. The married couple joyously swept to the front of the church, where the university chaplain and close friend was waiting to bless them.

Chapter 25

PROUD DOUGLAS, LOVELY Iris, bespectacled Violet, and hopelessly curious Primrose, were celebrating the wedding at a posh restaurant in Dunedin's centre, the magnificent Grange Restaurant.

Although the small orchestra was just beginning to play quietly, at six o'clock the upstairs restaurant was still peaceful. Douglas ordered a bottle of wine, thinking that it would go nicely with the meal. The waiter recommended *Cold Duck,* which quickly arrived. The meal was delayed. The management said this was due to a sudden influx of other guests.

The wine was quickly consumed, so Douglas foolishly ordered another one. Finally, when he couldn't get the waiter's attention, he stood up and said rather unsteadily, 'I ordered a meal forty minutes ago. It should be coming by now.' The apologetic waiter went away to enquire.

After another frustrating twenty minutes the substantial meal finally appeared, and they started to eat. The two bottles of wine had made them all woozy. At the end of the meal, they departed with fiery cheeks, having trouble in negotiating the stairs to the main street below. Emerging from the restaurant doors, they trippled down towards the picture theatre, giggling as they went.

Going past the Exchange Building and the magnificent seven-storey Post Office, Douglas decided that he had to go to the toilet before going inside the picture theatre. He turned back but couldn't remember the location. He stopped a stern policeman, who told him that the nearest one – at the Octagon – was closed for repairs.

Slightly tipsy, Iris whispered, 'You can go at the theatre!' So, bidding farewell with great enthusiasm to the policeman, Douglas hastened along with the others, still giggling, to the theatre. He rushed to the toilet while Iris purchased their tickets.

Having seen the film highlights on giant posters, Violet laughed and said, 'I think we'll be watching a comedy.' Indeed, their general humour grew when they sat down in the seats that the usher directed them to – right in the front row. Cricked necks were required to get the only possible view.

But they'd all had a lovely time celebrating Adam and Polly's wedding!

In England, at their house in Galleyend, Albert and Olive Williams wanted to celebrate the wedding too. They invited a few members of the family: Mary, Polly's young sister; Bill, who was married to Mary; and their immediate neighbours, to come to their house for a glass of sherry and a piece of special wedding cake. Thus they remembered Polly and Adam's great occasion held in Orokolo, so far away.

Adam and Polly spent their relaxing honeymoon near Hombrom's Bluff, a high mountain promontory well behind Port Moresby. Through the haze, they turned a corner and could see the narrow, twisting dirt road behind them travelling away into the distance. The views were stunning. They journeyed a few more miles inland and found that their motel was quiet and peaceful, just as the advertisement had said – or that's what they thought at first.

In the morning, they enjoyed eating their quiet breakfast outside. As they sat on the large patio, they narrowly missed being attacked by a Papuan Black, one of the deadliest snakes in the land. Out of the corner of his eye Adam saw the danger they were in. Quietly, urgently, he warned Polly and very slowly they removed themselves to the safety of inside the lobby. On informing the manageress, she very neatly shot the snake with her double-barrelled shotgun!

The second night, they were confined to their room because the manageress's estranged husband was running amok and threatening the guests with a loaded gun.

On the third night, there was also tribal unrest in the locality. They could hear the constant drums being beaten in the villages for conflict.

However, each evening, they dressed for dinner. Polly wore her long, soft-flowing green dress, which displayed her narrow waist and perfect curves; in addition her mother's pearl necklace, a hibiscus flower behind her left ear, and her beautiful smile; all totally captured Adam. He was well and truly in love!

The energetic cook made a mouth-watering sizzling baked half-chicken with lots of local vegetables every night. Their motel was not far from the Kokoda Trail. This trail was made famous by the Australian soldiers and the "Fuzzy Wuzzy Angels" – the name for the local Papuans who fought for their land in the Second World War. The injured Australians were supporting them over the mountainous range, as they escaped the terrible conflict with the Japanese soldiers.

Polly and Adam drove through sparse undergrowth to the entrance of the trail. There they found a wire statue of a soldier that had been placed as an everlasting memorial. With a helmet on the statue's head and a rifle in its hand, he stared down towards the jungle – a rain-driven, steamy terrain, far below.

Adam imagined how this statue soldier listened for the distant heartfelt cries of the wounded men who were carried on stretchers up those impossible tracks, or who stumbled through the jungle towards some sort of safety. Pointing downwards Adam remarked, 'It must have been horrendous for those soldiers.'

Gazing at the terrain, Polly said, 'They didn't see the beauty here that we have seen. To them it was a hot, humid hell-hole.'

Adam got up to wander around the picnic area. He

was troubled not only by this historical war, but by recent wars occurring everywhere, worldwide, wrecking the lives of ordinary people who just wanted to live in peace.

Sighing, he said to Polly, 'I guess you know I was and still am a conscientious objector. I'm afraid I couldn't be a soldier like that,' pointing to the wire statue.

Adam looked at Polly. 'It doesn't mean that I'm against the army as such, but more against killing and the types of armaments used.'

The breeze rumpled his hair and cooled his shirt before he continued.

'I remember giving a speech at the university in Dunedin. People were coming to congratulate me for my courage in speaking out to tell them of my conscientious objection. Then I was trapped by an older academic man, Sir Timothy Waters, a publisher. He took hold of my hand fiercely, with strength. I could feel his bony fingers as he said very quietly, his face close to my own: "You've spelled out your reasons so clearly why you're a conscientious objector. I bet that when you have to face the real situation you will end up like most of us, looking at the enemy face to face!" He was right, of course. Sir Timothy paused, then expressed what he was really feeling. "Often, we must fight the enemy before we can safely walk away."'

Adam sadly said then that this old man disappeared from sight. He hesitated. 'Now the Kokoda Trail brings home to me Sir Timothy's words,' he said softly as he pointed to the jungle with all its hidden memories. 'I hope you don't choke on your sandwiches, but it was only because I was a student at Concord College and the university that they put a hold on my call-up. I was allowed to leave New Zealand by the army authorities.'

Polly asked hesitantly, 'Does that still apply or have things changed in New Zealand now?'

'If I go back home and the law hasn't changed, I could be standing again before the army authorities and telling them I couldn't bear arms. However,' Adam added laughing, 'if I told them I had married a lovely wife who came from the English village of Galleyend and is a trained nurse and a great midwife, they might change their minds!'

Standing there, they looked at the wire soldier and listened to the sounds of the jungle below them. Polly snuggled up to Adam. He put his arm around her as she said in a very low voice, 'I love you!'

He said proudly, 'I know,' and finding her lips, he lovingly kissed her. The honeymoon was certainly one they would never forget.

Returning, they settled down quickly and happily into married life. However, they received a letter from Adam's parents complaining that they hadn't heard from him for some weeks. They went on to say that they had received a hurried note accompanying the film of their wedding, but after that, nothing. Inside the letter was a mock sympathy card saying, *In memory of your pen.*

Adam was highly amused, but still didn't do much about the letter except show it to Polly, saying 'I will answer it, some time.'

However, underneath Douglas' disappointment of no letter lay a much deeper meaning than words unspoken by Adam. He was now not too concerned about him being an overseas missionary. In fact, he was quite proud of him, having achieved the degrees, and becoming married to Polly.

However, having missed out on the company of *his* own father, Douglas was now missing the company of his son Adam. They often used to discuss important matters and share stories with a quick wit and intelligent repartee. He felt frustrated and almost hurt, but what could he do?

A few months later, Violet and Primrose came up with a plan to have an Australian bush safari holiday. Douglas suggested that they might also like to include a visit to Port Moresby to see Adam and meet Polly. The girls agreed.

The sisters journeyed to Brisbane, but unfortunately the airport baggage handlers were on strike and their flight was delayed. Adam and Polly waited in anticipation at Port Moresby airport for their arrival, but when the plane didn't arrive they returned home. No sooner had they entered the flat than the phone rang, and Violet's familiar voice said they were waiting to be collected, and Adam and his bride turned right around!

Once they were settled into the flat, and in accordance with their mother's instructions, the girls soon got to know and to like their new sister-in-law. Writing back home to their parents, they said that Adam had made an excellent choice.

Violet and Primrose soon learned to cope with the high humidity and hot temperatures. Wearing loose summer dresses, colourful hats, and flip-flops on their feet, they ventured outside to explore the city. They discovered a mix of people from all parts of the country, varying in skin colour, exotic dress and strange languages.

In the *Christian Bookshop* they met some European customers. A very tall older English missionary and his smaller, patient mother from Popondetta on the northern coast of Papua, wanting communion glasses, spoke in earnest Anglican terms. Two American Pentecostal women from an isolated part of the distant Highlands, having a break in the city, were next. Two Australian university lecturers from Rabaul came later, wanting their new books to be published, enquiring about the price and how long it would take.

Adam answered each one with pleasurable alacrity!

To get a greater feel for the country, Polly suggested that the two travellers stay at an isolated mission station on the east coast, near the populated island of Samarai. When they got back, Adam suggested that they go by plane to visit the Ukarumpa village, saying, 'This is where people from all over the world come to study and learn the local languages for translation.' They would be experiencing several different aspects of Papua New Guinea. They would have lots of interesting stories to tell their parents and friends when they arrived home.

They would certainly speak of Polly's suspicion that she was carrying twins, for during their Port Moresby visit her pregnancy had become much more evident.

Chapter 26

POLLY WAS WORKING as a midwife tutor at the local government hospital. Adam took her to work early each morning and collected her in the late afternoon. She prepared the evening meal while he returned to the shop. He didn't have far to return home from his work – just out of the shop's front door, making sure it was locked, and climbing the stairs to the apartment.

This evening, everything was quiet. There were no sounds of rattling tins or crockery, no smells of cooking in progress – in fact, no sign of any preparation of their evening meal. He put his face around the door – all was peaceful, except for the sounds of gentle breathing. Adam crept into the lounge and found Polly fast asleep on the couch. She woke up to his gentle touch and said, 'I feel horrible.' Adam gave her a hand up and sent her to bed. He made the evening meal of baked beans on toast. This was rejected by her.

The next day Polly went to the doctor and asked him about the baby, if everything was normal. 'Yes,' he said. 'Nothing to worry about. All is well.' As an after-thought he added, 'You may need to rest more!'

However, Polly complained, 'I keep dropping off to sleep at odd times. It isn't very convenient!' Putting her loose dress on again and doing up the buttons, she asked the doctor, 'Am I expecting twins?'

The friendly doctor didn't say a definitive yes or no, just a maybe. So, with this 'maybe' pregnancy, Polly and Adam discussed what they would do next.

It didn't take them long to make up their minds. Polly would finish her work at the hospital immediately and Adam would continue to work at the bookshop until the beginning of December. He would inform the *Christian Bookshop's* head office that they needed to provide another person, because he and Polly were going south. He told his parents that they would be home in Mosgiel in time for Christmas.

Just before they left, Adam found in the second-hand bookshop a copy of *A City of Bells*, written by Elizabeth Goudge, and these words stood out:

A bookseller is the link between Mind and Mind; the feeder of the Hungry; very often the Binder up of wounds. There he sits, your bookseller, surrounded by a thousand minds all done up neatly in card-board cases – beautiful minds, courageous minds, strong minds, wise minds, all sorts and conditions. And there come to him other Minds, hungry for beauty, for knowledge, for truth and for love. To the best of his ability he satisfies them all.

'Do you know,' Adam said, 'I've been involved in books right from when I was young. My mother often bought me simple rag books when I couldn't read. When I went to school, I spent most of the spare time in the library. When I was seven, I used to call at the city library regularly, spending two or three hours each Saturday morning pouring over many exciting books. As I took my return journey on the bus, those who saw me also saw the many books that would last me all week. I wouldn't be seen without a book. Now I'm involved in the trade from the reverse side of the counter, and that is satisfaction itself.'

Polly, who was sitting on an easy chair most uncomfortably, kept a lookout for more customers. 'The whole scene has changed. You don't get *ye olde-world* bookshops portrayed in the novels of Elizabeth Goudge now. Today's bookshops are big business!'

'But we can still influence people for God, sharing and

giving books of excellence – maybe in England?' replied Adam. He was referring to missionary Connor Hughes, who had gone back to Britain with Thelma his wife some time ago. Connor had recently written a short letter to Adam: 'I have just heard of a wonderful opportunity for work in an English legal publishing company that might suit you.' So they began directing their thoughts to the other side of the world.

Just before Christmas, it was time to say *bamahuta* (farewell) to Papua New Guinea. One Saturday afternoon, when the bookshop usually closed for business, Polly and Adam went to the airport accompanied by the wonderful missionary staff – Jill and Peter and their growing son, and a rather sad Tau, with shy Para his wife, and bubbling baby Ari. They sadly said their goodbyes for the last time.

Pregnant Polly was looking enormous, so Adam was always fussing, scared that the situation would go wrong. Going up the Jumbo jet stairway, just before entering the aircraft they gave a wave to their friends, then hurriedly took their seats. They were going on a long journey to New Zealand and Polly would have the best care that he, and the airline could provide.

After flying over the Tasman Sea and touching down in Christchurch for an hour or so, the couple flew into Mosgiel aerodrome late in the afternoon.

Adam's family gave them both a wonderful welcome with broad smiles and lots of loving kisses. On the way to their home Polly looked with pleasure at the town's green lawns and all the different budding flowers. As Polly put it, 'They were beautiful to see, in the sense that they fed my soul and I immediately felt at peace.'

One of the first things that Adam did was to go into Dunedin to see the army authorities and ask about his status as a conscientious objector. He was informed that the new government had altered the rules and, to his relief, the military authorities were no longer interested in recruiting him. Adam and Polly celebrated with a quiet restaurant meal.

Polly paid a visit to the hospital to book in for the birth

of their first child. The doctor who was examining her, like the previous doctor in Port Moresby, told her that all was well. He was rather surprised when she asked, 'Do you think I'm having twins?' Having explained her own self-examination and the Port Moresby doctor's 'maybe', the doctor examined her again, sending her for an X-ray that did indeed reveal twins. She had been right all along!

Polly waddled slowly along the corridor, smiling widely, and informed Adam with a joyful hug that he was going to be the father of *two* babies! They phoned Iris and Douglas with the good news, and then they also sent a telegram to Polly's English parents.

Adam was aware that his two sisters, Violet and Primrose, had become much wiser. The time that they had spent in Papua New Guinea and the camping trip through Australia had matured them greatly.

Violet's employment in the haberdashery department of Ronald's Emporium was now just a memory; nursing was her new profession. While demanding on her time and energy, it was very rewarding because she met the eager and bluff giant, Gregg McKenzie. With much joy, they became engaged and were later married.

Primrose had worked in the microbiology department at the hospital for some time. However, she decided to leave and attend the same Concord College that Adam had been to many years before. She also shortened her name to the much simpler 'Rose'.

Now in their early fifties, Iris and Douglas made their home comfortable for Adam and Polly.

Over the years, they too had changed in many ways. Iris still had bright blue eyes, and a merry but chubbier face. Douglas was starting to lose his hair, but managed the thinner parts by gently combing it over to make it more presentable. His glasses made him look quite professional and, as he was a quiet person who considered each point before speaking, that was important to his listeners, and of course himself.

Douglas had hoped that Adam would become a parish minister in a New Zealand church, maybe even in Mosgiel.

However, he would have to relinquish this idea, again. Although he was still the same delightful intellectual son, Adam was more interested now in his experiences in Papua New Guinea, the anticipated arrival of the twins, and his new career with the English legal publishers, *Judicial Books*.

One still evening, Adam and his father sat together watching the sun as it set gracefully in the low sky. He told his father all about his plans. He explained how Connor and Thelma had worked at the Port Moresby bookshop for a long time and then returned to England. Bearing in mind his interest in publishing companies in Britain, they had got in touch with the managing director of a large legal firm in London.

'They asked this director if there were any suitable positions for me,' Adam explained. 'The director's reply was a tentative: "I'll have to check further", and before proceeding, he asked for more personal details. Later, there was another letter from Connor to say that there was a strong probability of professional and business training for me in *Judicial Books*. It meant that the editorial, production, sales, publicity and distribution departments would, over time, provide excellent training for a management position. That situation is to start in three months' time.'

Douglas was sad that their visit to their home was only temporary, and that Adam and the delightful Polly, plus his new expected grandchildren, would not be staying long.

He reluctantly decided to offer his help to Violet and her Gregg. They could do with his skills, certainly when they were building their first house. Maybe any children they had would enable him to practise his grandfatherly ways. 'And you never know,' he said to Iris, while they were getting ready for bed, 'there is the possibility of Primrose (he still didn't get her shorter name right) going overseas. We can keep in touch with her wherever she might end up.'

Meanwhile, the thought of grandchildren made them quite proud. They were all a-twitter, as they told anyone who would listen, about the forthcoming presence of twins in their midst!

Polly was instructed to go into the hospital right away, as the doctors wanted to keep a close eye on her and the twins. They were premature, born five weeks early. Adam reported to his parents from the hospital that, 'After a lot of hard work by Polly and a lot of back rubbing by me, Thomas and James (delightful names), were born without any trouble.'

Iris wondered if Polly saw it in the same light!

It was a long time since Iris had cared for newborn babies. She described looking after them as 'a work of art' as she attempted to feed the crying twins with bottles of milk. She faithfully supported Polly with the nappy changes and the ceaseless rounds of washing. Iris rocked the twins with both her feet while they lay in their individual bouncinettes. No wonder she was tired after helping Polly do all this!

Douglas said, 'I wake up at night and hear her feeding the twins, gurgle, gurgle. I can also hear Adam being woken up as well and, I guess, assisting her with the other twin. I think he falls asleep. She is quite cross with him in the morning.'

One morning Polly wandered out from the bedroom looking rather dishevelled in her nightwear. Yawning, she said that she had missed out on a lot of sleep that night, for Adam had fallen asleep – yet again. One baby had been trying to find the teat of the bottle that he was supposed to be holding, but the teat was in the baby's ear!

The home nurse had said that she would come each Thursday to weigh the twins and check that everything was alright. It was! So, later, Adam and Polly left the twins with their grandparents and took a tour in Douglas' car.

Visiting the Early Settlers Museum in Dunedin, they found a photograph of his great-great-grandparents, James and Margaret Hay, high up on the display walls.

Another day, they visited Mosgiel's little-used railway station, where the Fraser family had disembarked from the Christchurch train to start a new life. Now the station

stood alone and aloof. There were wide cracks in the platform. Clumps of weeds had taken root as well. The posters
of exciting places to visit overseas looked forlorn now.

Calling into the Taieri Hotel for lunch, Adam excitedly
told Polly the reason for their visit there. 'This hotel was
built on the actual site of Mosgiel's first shoe repair business, started by my great-grandfather, Alec Hay.'

Then they viewed the houses where his recent relatives used to live – Lilian and David Thoms in Ayr Street;
Judith Fraser in Glasgow Street; Alec and Emma Hay
in Lanark Street – so they stopped there for a moment.
Adam told Polly a plethora of exciting and amusing facts
about GGF and GGM. Then he gave a wave to great-auntie
Madge, who was still alive and possibly living at the same
place. 'She may have been looking out of the window's
lace curtains at the sound of our car, thinking there are
burglars around!' said Adam.

Polly was impressed with all of this but needed to get
back home. She had given Iris some milk in bottles, but
her breasts were getting uncomfortable now.

One Sunday a few weeks later, on a glorious day, they all
went across the road to the Presbyterian Church for the
twins' baptism.

Iris and Douglas recalled the baptism of their own
children. Many of the relatives who had attended Adam's
baptism had now died – Alec and Emma, Lilian and
David, as well as Judith. And although she had been
invited to the twins' baptism, upset older Madge wouldn't
come near the church – any church. Even today, Madge
wouldn't come for any occasion that included her distant
relatives.

Now, the minister stood near the baptismal font and
said these crucial words to Adam and Polly: *Though
these little children do not understand these things yet
the promise is also to them...*

Now much older and considerably wiser, he thought,
Adam was about to give the sermon from the pulpit after
the children's baptism. If the twins began to cry (they
didn't) then Polly and proud Iris would slip out with them.

Adam thanked the minister for his kindness. He said how proud he was to be father of the twins, Thomas and James. He also spoke about his wife, wonderful Polly, whom he had met in Papua. He spoke about his parents, who had a lot to put up with, having the boys in the house. With conviction, he finally said, 'We can all be God's faithful messengers, wherever we are and whatever we are doing!'

Iris gave a sigh. She thought that they would never see the boys again after they left for England. Wrapped in bright blue romper-suits, happy Thomas and James were being taken to England shortly by their parents. As they came out of the church, Douglas' voice trembled with emotion as he slowly said to Iris, 'We will see them again, won't we?'

Then his wife had a brilliant idea, and as they were crossing the road, she said excitedly, 'We will do more than that! We will go and visit them in a couple of years' time, in that rather strangely named place, Galleyend. I wonder what it's like?'

Chapter 27

ITTLE THROSTLE WAS the medieval name for a thrush. It was also the quaint name of a Tudor house in the village of Galleyend, where Adam, Polly, Thomas and James now lived. Near to Chelmsford, the house stood at the top of one of the gentle hills overlooking the surrounding Essex countryside.

The setting was beautiful. In early spring, large wisterias decorated the front of their house, with their cascading blooms of blue and purple perfuming the air. Daffodil, bluebell, jonquil, poppy and crocus danced in the breeze along the neat cobbled path to the front door.

The back of the house looked quite different, with a large open area of green land sloping away to tall trees in the distance. The scent of newly mown grass pervaded the warm atmosphere and the air was full of birdsong.

Adam and Polly often liked to lean on their back fence and look beyond their land. The neighbouring houses were interspersed with tall, magnificently shaped hedges that made them appear mysterious. The railway line was just visible from where they stood; hearing faint whispers of a train's whistle told them which way it was travelling.

The Common, with its sweeping vistas, was an area of natural beauty with trees of oak, elm and ash. For their spring flowering, the family looked in wonder at the carpet of bluebells, the air infused with their perfume. However, certain parts of the bracken were out of bounds, for the snakes hatched there.

On hot summer days the twins liked exploring. When

the autumn showers came, they wrapped themselves up in raincoats and gumboots and stumbled through wet undergrowth. In winter, they saw its trees looking bare and lonely, amidst muddy grass and grey, stagnant ponds.

Two local ancient pubs, one at each end of the Common, plied their trade there. Adam spent an evening or two at these taverns and, over a glass of red wine, listened to the local gossip given in a flat Essex burr.

Even though they had not been in England long, Adam was not as robust as he had been in Port Moresby. 'Because it's cooler here,' he explained to anyone, 'I eat more and move less. I sit on trains or at an office desk, instead of lifting books in extreme heat. My mother-in-law also feeds me very well, so I put on more weight.'

Polly's parents, Olive and Albert, lived along the same hedge-protected road as they did. A tall man with a rosy face and receding grey hair, Albert had had an important job in local government, but was now retired. He worked around the house, still wearing his suit and tie and with a lit cigarette perpetually hanging from the corner of his lips.

When it was very cold, or the rain or snow kept him inside, Albert enjoyed the warmth of the under-floor electric heating. He washed the dishes and often peered out of the kitchen window, taking regular puffs on his cigarette. When some ash fell on the floor he said, 'Well, it keeps the moths away,' as he rubbed it into the carpet with his foot. Albert usually said this with a broad smile, and loud enough for Olive to hear. From the lounge Olive quickly remonstrated, 'Bert! Clean it up!' He must have cleaned it because, at the weekends, the Fraser family came along for tea, and Olive always made two first courses and a choice of two desserts. So, it was very easy for Adam to gain weight!

Adam had still not learned the skill of writing regularly to his parents. When he did so, it was very long:

Little Throstle *is two storeys, with four bedrooms, a big lounge, dining room and kitchen, and a wide entrance-way leading to a double garage. Behind* the garage is a fairly big section for the twins to play. We have also been busy buying furniture and all the etceteras necessary. Now this centrally-heated home is our cosy wee hoose.

We have bought a second-hand car, a bright blue 1300 Triumph Herald that we take out each weekend for a speedy run. I don't mind the travel to London. I leave home for the train early, at 6.45am in the morning, and arrive home at 7.45pm at night. The first thing I do is kiss Polly. Remember Dad, the first thing you did was to give Mum your three kisses? Then I go upstairs to settle the twins, who are waiting on my return with lovely laughter or sorrowful tears, in which case I don't get my evening meal until later.

I managed to get British Rail sorted out before I started work in London with Judicial Books. When I went first to the Chelmsford station, I spotted a small cubicle where all the tickets were being distributed. I was supposed to give my request through the little screen in front of me. The man would put my ticket on his side of a circular disc while I put money on my side. This was rotated so that I received my ticket and he received my cash. Any change was given the same way.

Of course, I didn't know this and both of us were getting frustrated. My face was becoming redder and his voice was getting louder. The people behind me were getting annoyed but then they realised my predicament, and explained how this brilliant piece of British machinery worked!

Well, having accomplished this, I took up my position on the train that arrived in London in just over an hour, providing there were no delays. I had had a look at Judicial Books, from across the very busy road. Traffic is chaotic! The building is a seven-storey structure. This is set right over the Underground and very convenient for travelling to and from Little Throstle.

Did you know that the road going alongside

Judicial Books, *the wide, bleak, and uninteresting Kingsway, was constructed in 1905? This is the route to the lower Aldwych, which in medieval times was a densely built-up area – 'Via de Aldwych'. Then it joins with northern Strand and, following that direction, Fleet Street, and further still, the magnificent St. Paul's Cathedral.*

Think how many houses and small businesses must have been destroyed and how many people displaced simply because Kingsway was required!

The various Barristers' Inns (rooms) are tucked away in the nearby secluded courtyards and quiet lawns. A legal person's paradise! Charles Dickens composed some stories in one of them. Many famous legal minds have worked there.

For a while, I travelled First Class on British Rail. One day there was only one other person in my carriage – a trim and narrow man with a small monocle that he would put onto his eye and, the next moment, would take it off. We read our newspapers in peace. Maybe that was the reason for taking his monocle in and out – the Financial Times newspaper's pink-coloured print wasn't right for him. However, as we turned over our pages, to my surprise, this man spoke.

The railways have a very strict rule, or at least this is what I've found, of no talking to your fellow passengers, but he was most agitated and said, 'I see in today's paper there is an article about train journeys becoming more and more dangerous. London stations could be used as places to plant bombs. We have been warned by the authorities not to leave briefcases, bags or parcels unattended. A bomber can exchange them and, a few minutes later, a bomb goes off! Or the parcel is considered suspicious, and the police and military are called to detonate it, if necessary.'

I shuddered and asked him why these criminals don't do their thing in their own countries? The gent replied in his cultured tone that they will go wherever there is a means to create untold havoc!

The following day, late in the afternoon, at 5:30pm, when lots of other passengers and I had just climbed wearily onto our trains at the station, an urgent notice came over the loudspeakers: 'Please disperse quickly and calmly! There is a suspected bomb in the area.'

I had been settling very happily into my comfortable first class seat, but the urgency of this information made me get smartly out of the train. With the rest of the frightened crowd, I was directed by a scared official to go down to the Underground. Unfortunately, there were lots of other people who were just coming off the tubes, wanting to go to the station above. Absolute confusion reigned. We were thrown together like sardines!

I was wearing my thick winter coat, but it had enormous, chunky buttons that got caught in a young woman's coat. We were joined for a moment at the waist. I was still carrying my briefcase, and this frightened her even more. She stared at me with huge, fearful eyes. Luckily the surging maelstrom parted us.

When the voice of British Rail finally gave the all clear and we got back onto our individual trains, I found myself amazed that the scared girl had thought that I was an actual bomber, ready to do untold damage! I also thought about the different forms of cruelty and sometimes death perpetrated by evil people in various places, for whatever cause! It is always innocent people who are thrown into absolute misery and confusion.

Now, let me turn to a totally different subject – the Underground itself. What a revelation! I listened to the sounds of the wheels grinding underneath me. In the carriage, I noted the newspapers and magazines being turned over at regular intervals by glassy-eyed people. I concentrated on London maps that were displayed above our heads, showing a fascinating variety of tube lines in different colours.

However, they didn't tell you if a station had a lift or an escalator, or both!

I exited at one of these old stations where they had a creaking lift as well as stairs. I chose the lift. This had a folding grille gate that made me feel I was back in an old department store in Dunedin, where the wire doors clanged shut. Woe to your fingers if you didn't watch out!

When the lift suddenly stopped at what should have been the ground level I was confronted by a blank wall. There was blackness all around except for the lonely lift light. I naturally thought that I was trapped in between the station and my freedom above. As I stood there facing what I presumed was a disaster, I heard a voice behind me: 'Turn around! Turn around!'

On turning around, I saw a ticket collector with an open gate, welcoming me to my freedom, on the opposite side from where I had entered. The man was chortling at my stupidity, for I hadn't seen the exit sign in the lift.

Then Adam wrote a cheery,

Goodbye, till next time, whenever that will be.

Douglas and Iris enjoyed this letter so much that they forgave him for taking so long to write. Douglas smiled to himself, thinking that he would like to join Adam on one of his London adventures. Then he realised he was half a world away.

Chapter 28

ADAM WAS DRESSED in his new navy-blue three-piece suit and a polka dot bow tie; with his briefcase held securely in his right hand, he was the first to get off the tube at Holborn Station. Weaving in and out of the other slower passengers, he strode his way up the two steep escalators and came out at one of the city's busiest street corners. Passing through the solid doors into the very substantial entrance of *Judicial Books,* Adam greeted other legal men and women on the way to their busy departments.

Adam had been doing this trip for six months now, so he was becoming used to the journey. While waiting for the lift he always read the notice on the wall about the history of the company, and remembered the first time he had entered the vestibule.

Then, people waiting for the lift had serious faces and carried bulging briefcases. They were surprised when they heard his New Zealand accent speaking so eagerly, but they did have some idea about this man who had been taken under the wing of the managing director.

Occasionally, Adam said something like, 'This company is so big – editorial, production, sales, publicity and distribution departments...'

No one said anything. One or two had a slight grin, but the rest were looking at the ground until the lift stopped and the doors slowly opened. They all crowded in.

Adam quietly laughed when he noted how each one indicated his or her floor to the old lift-man, who sat in a corner seat where he could work the controls.

As several people got off at the third floor, he thought to himself that they must be some of the editorial staff.

Only a young woman remained. She worked in the publicity department on the fourth floor. Some days they got talking. Adam explained that he had visited some of the Magistrate's Courts in their ancient chambers. Another day he had taken messages into the Royal Courts of Justice. 'I even had crucial appointments with the Secretary of the Privy Council...' and, lowering his voice to a mock whisper, he continued, '... in Number 11, Downing Street! Although, the Secretary wasn't there to greet me, so I had to give my piece to a steward.' Grinning, he concluded, 'It has been very interesting.'

The young woman gave a hesitant smile and left the lift, clearly relieved!

The lift trundled up to the seventh floor. The operator came to life. He had been listening and made the remark, 'Have you visited our legal bookshop, associated with this company? It's tucked in behind one of the lawned courts. It has lots of material there that I think would interest you!'

As Adam approached the door of his office, he replied, 'Yes, I have been to the shop. It made me think of being back in Charles Dickens' time. Some of the characters in the bookshop even wore Dickens-style clothing!'

Knowing what he meant, the man chuckled as he took the lift down.

The Holburn area was extremely busy, with many cars, vans and trucks that travelled at a slow pace, unloading their valuable articles, or having materials loaded by equally slow-moving brown-coated men. Red double-decker buses struggled to pass. Hurrying pedestrians treated each other to dour faces.

In *Judicial Books* however, Adam stood by the open corner office window and, looking out, saw busy pigeons and hopping sparrows that swooped to the ground. Following the birds' flight, he saw that they were eating the sandwich remains left on the footpath. Rather disgusting, but very pleasing to the hungry pigeons and hopping sparrows!

If Adam turned his head to the right, he could see the Tudor buildings that provided a curious fragment of medieval London. Staple Inn was nearby and used for the training of barristers. This was also part of Lincoln's Inn inner complex. Looking ahead, he could see that Old Oxford Street merged to upmarket Oxford Street, where there were many opulent department stores. If he wanted to go further (he didn't) then expensive Bond Street and Marble Arch – without gallows – stood in the distance.

Returning to his neat desk, Adam looked at the manuscript before him. A biannual academic legal periodical that *Judicial Books* published on behalf of and for the organisation *Law and Justice*.

Coming from a Christian perspective of the law, with an emphasis on religious freedom, ethics and morality, this journal was now in proof form. Adam had an excellent understanding of what the pre-publishing proofs were all about – however, he still needed to go through all of the pages of this journal with a fine toothcomb, correcting grammar, spelling and syntax, and implementing throughout the style of *Judicial Books*.

There was very little that he had to alter so, putting it aside for now, he worked on his titled *Statutory Instruments* – the never-ending proclamations from parliament that were presented to all legal publishing companies for the exacting examination of each individual point of law. His work involved checking carefully through the written law and altering each *jot and tittle* on the most recent laws to put in the ongoing supplements that they sent to customers.

After each Friday's work, Adam was ready to join a few lawyer friends from *Judicial Books* at a quiet pub, almost hidden down a lane that led to a walled and grassed square lawn, all designed by Inigo Jones many years ago. Over drinks, they had pleasant conversation regarding the events of the week before going home for a relaxing weekend.

Adam purchased a red wine, took a sip and, putting the glass down on the table, told them about spending a couple of weeks at a small hotel at Beccles in East

Anglia. He was studying the ins-and-outs of printing at a large company in that town. Unfortunately, it was during the winter so much of his free time had been spent in the quiet hotel. He was the only guest, so he ate scrumptious meals and delicious desserts.

'By this time, I had put on so much weight,' he complained to his interested listeners, 'that my only decent pair of trousers split at the seam. I had to ring for the housekeeper's help and a repair was quickly made. The mishap, of course, was soon around the hotel. Given the size of the town and the interest of various people, I had to walk as if I didn't have a care in the world!'

On yet another Friday, Adam spoke about a recent visit to the local art exhibition in his home village of Galleyend. 'On view was a selection of war paintings from the First World War. One stood out. It was of Scottish soldiers in army uniform and wearing kilts, who charged with their rifles held high to attack the Germans. Apparently, the painting depicts the Battle of Loos in Belgium. It also shows a 150-foot double-structure of what the British soldiers called the "Two Towers".'

The lawyers listened. They also had memories of that war, having heard of the experiences of various older relatives.

Adam said, 'My grandfather, William Fraser from Glasgow, fought in the Battle of Loos. He was working at the Clyde River shipyards as a draughtsman, so he had already been told that he didn't need to join up because of his vital job on the ships, so having restricted employment. He still went ahead though, joining the machine gun regiment of the Cameron Highlanders. To one side of this painting there was a little notice saying: *Two Scottish regiments joined the 75,000 soldiers in that first Battle of Loos.* Maybe my grandfather was in that mayhem of the soldiers' battle.'

Perceptive Jacob Hallenstein reached over and put his hand gently on Adam's, and enquired kindly, 'Did he survive the war?'

'No, he didn't. When the battle was over, nearly 20,000 men had been killed. As with so many missing men, they didn't find his body, even though the authorities searched for him. Judith, his wife, my grandmother, eventually received a parcel from the army containing three ordinary medals, a heavy round plaque, a certificate from King George V and an ornate copper box to put them in. A poor return for the active William. I reckon that having him working at the shipyards would have been much better than those things! Shortly after, the rest of the family, including a son called Douglas – my father – went to New Zealand to settle in Mosgiel.'

Adam was mindful that the telling of this tale was not the normal story that was shared on Friday nights, but the canny lawyers understood and sympathised with him. He finished by saying, 'I've inherited the little box, his three medals, the heavy round plaque, and the certificate from the King.'

Adam and the lawyers emptied their wine glasses, put on their Saville Row coats and Homburgs and, saying goodbye to each other, went out into the milling crowd.

Chapter 29

AFTER TWO EXCITING and demanding years in *Judicial Books*, Adam was now invited to go with the top people of various departments in the company to the marvellous Astoria Restaurant for a celebratory meal. He sat quietly down with the others at a central table. This was beautifully set, as if they were the most important people there.

A waiter circulated with the wine list, but unfortunately the names of the French wines were unfamiliar to Adam. Vivian Rutherford, the managing director, kindly came to his rescue. He had been a regular patron of the restaurant for years so knew all the French wines, and anticipated what Adam would like.

After they had ordered from the menu and their wine glasses were full, it was time to celebrate. Congratulations echoed around the table, for *Judicial Books* had just published a new set of Hall's Law volumes, with never-ending supplements. This was why they were there.

Short and tubby Venerable Lord Hall, who had overseen the project, was embarrassed at all the fuss. However, he drank his wine and replied to the effusive accolades.

The *Judicial Books* building had six ordinary uncarpeted floors. However, on the fifth floor all the individual directors' rooms and the hallway leading into them were carpeted. Adam quickly found this out when he exited the lift, for he had received an urgent call from Vivian Rutherford to see him. Tall and debonair, he had been very kind to Adam, taking the time to see that he had settled in and was happy with his work.

The managing director got to the point right away, without mentioning the enjoyable function the previous night. Standing very erect, he said, 'I'm sorry to tell you this, but *Judicial Books* is being taken over by another large company. I'm not sure where you are going to be. There is the possibility of redundancies. There is even talk of disposing of the current Board. I just wanted to tell you so that you are prepared.' Pondering for a moment he then continued, 'I will be retiring.' Then he shook Adam's hand, saying, 'I wish you well.'

Of course, Adam had no idea what had been going on. Why would he? He was just thankful that the managing director had warned him. However, this warning didn't mean that he was going to lose his position just yet.

Judicial Books was taken over within the month. Vivian Rutherford retired, and the Board resigned. This meant that the old English establishment had far less of the face-to-face interaction with individual barristers and lawyers which he had enjoyed. He was told the vision of this new company was dealing with scientific and medical books, as well as the legal literature – but the name *Judicial Books* would continue.

For the past 100 years or so, *Judicial Books* had been publishing legal books of high quality for British law practitioners. However, the new management had started to look for innovative and progressive directions to bring it back to its former standard. It was going to take a long time, so a Pilot Team was established to help guide the process, and Adam was on it.

All through this last year, Polly was still very busy but continued her happy life at *Little Throstle*. It was a far cry from the needs of the patients at Orokolo Hospital or the teaching of trainee nurses in Port Moresby. Her sister Mary had two young children born a year apart, named Bill and Fred. (Mary's husband's name was Bill and his own father's name was Fred, so they were named after them – simple, if not confusing). Without her husband,

Mary's family often came over to Polly's place, either to walk on the Common with Polly, Thomas and James, or, when the weather was bad, to relax in Polly's home. One day, while walking on the Common with the children, Polly said, 'I have had a brilliant idea about starting up a "twins club". Many mothers around here are tied to their homes because of the extra requirements for their children.'

Mary thought it would be excellent idea, but she said, 'Where will we have it?'

'In our large lounge,' Polly said.

'How often will we have it?'

'Once a week, on Thursdays, starting at ten for about an hour and a half,' was her reply.

They duly started the twins club and, before they knew it, it was too crowded, with the lounge full of happy women, and many little children vying for the same toy. A few weeks forward, Polly decided to approach the local Anglican church nearby, asking if they would be so kind as to allow them to use the large, comfortable hall on Thursday mornings from ten to eleven-thirty.

Soon the staid and mostly older church ladies became interested, and a goodly proportion volunteered to be helpers, offering their time and expertise. Those women with small children and babies who hadn't been inside a church hall before, were pleased to be made so welcome. They told their husbands and some of them began to attend the regular church services with their families.

All because Polly had heard and observed the voice of God. Her missionary days were not over!

About this time, eager Douglas and ever-ready-to-fly Iris sent a message to Adam that they would be arriving soon from Mosgiel. They would arrive during Adam's holiday. They had sold their car, let out their Mosgiel house, Douglas had resigned from his employment, said a farewell to the church, and they were ready to be off on the aircraft.

Thomas and James were very excited. With their merry eyes, busy hands and mischievous laughter, they would be soon entertained by *everyone!*

When Douglas and Iris arrived, they were agog to see what had been planned for them. Douglas recalled his difficult days with his mother and sisters in Glasgow and the trip from that city to Southampton docks when he was seven, but he didn't go there on a journey of remembrance. England in the summertime meant that he and Iris could be outdoors in the lovely sweet-smelling fresh air – unless it rained, of course!

Having had their breakfast, the excited twins had just been told that they were going out to Galleyend Common and they, the grandparents, were to take them. Polly had already said that there might be nasty snakes in the wild grass, so they were to put on their little wellies to protect them, just in case.

Firmly, their grandparents took both their hands and they went out exploring. It wasn't long before Thomas and James were captivated by Douglas who, taking a piece of misshapen wood from the ground, created a fantastic story that the boys lapped up.

Douglas also remembered the happy times when young Adam would listen so avidly to him telling tales, so he looked around the Common to create another story.

Catching sight of a robin bringing a worm back for the noisy baby birds, he told them a tale of a recently injured robin who now couldn't manage to fly to her starving offspring. What was the robin to do? I know! Mr Robin was nearby, watching his family, and he came to the rescue.

One evening, Iris and Douglas looked after Thomas and James while their parents were at last dining out alone at a local restaurant. The boys had been safely put to bed, but the pitter-patter of feet could be heard in their upstairs bedroom. Douglas hurried up the stairs and found that these soccer stars had a large round ball that they were practising with between the bed-leg 'goalposts'. Hiding his smile behind a frown, he told them sternly not to get out of bed again until their mother woke them in the morning!

With both thumbs in their mouths, Thomas and James stared at him, dumbfounded. They weren't used to having grandfather in their bedroom telling them off for practising goals. Nevertheless, they reluctantly settled down and within a very short time all was peaceful.

When Polly and Adam returned home and sat with them around the kitchen table, they heard the whole amusing story from Douglas.

Iris also reported what had happened to the rest of their relatives in New Zealand. Violet was still without a child but working as a senior nurse in the general hospital. Her husband Gregg was now associated with the national Young Christian Association. Rose had settled down in Fiji at the medical branch of Concord College, taking up the position of looking after the female students' needs.

Adam then asked about his great-auntie Madge.

Smiling, Iris said, 'I am sure you know that she liked to be called *Mademoiselle Madge?*'

Adam remembered the faded Mosgiel scroll on the front gate.

She continued. 'On Madge's eighty-ninth birthday, she got rid of the little car which she had been driving for years. Of course, she still carried on with her millinery business in the same house. However, when she died her house was a tip, full of yesterday's fashion hats and old crumbling catalogues. The Turner photographs were still displayed on the wall of both the lounge and the dining room, including the small photo of Edward Wimpole. We took them to the council, where they were gratefully received. They said they would give them to the museum, except the one of Edward Wimpole, which they returned.

'Later we found out that Madge left instructions that upon her death the portrait of this man was to be buried with her. Her funeral had already taken place, so we had a small ceremony where we burned it. It seemed the best way.'

Hours after, Iris made a comment. 'Do you know that apart from the minister, Dad and I were the only two mourners at the graveside service? Other relatives didn't or wouldn't come to the service. Pity,' and looking at Adam, she added, 'I guess you can tell a few personal stories about your Great-auntie Madge.'

Adam nodded. He could! He could even tell them a few facts that they didn't know about Edward Wimpole from the distant past, but Adam remained quiet.

Chapter 30

THE GALLEYEND CHURCH was situated at the corner of two narrow hedge-lined paths. Having solid oak doors, through which many friendly and influential people entered; visitors were overwhelmed at the peaceful beauty of the old place of worship. Wide aisles gave an impression of space, enhanced by the sunlight filtering through the stained-glass windows.

The vicar was the Reverend Bartholomew Cuthbertson. A small, rotund, bald-headed man with thick glasses, he was a childless widower. A group of Anglican women looked after all his practical needs. A gentle and righteous man, he had lived in the parish for nearly forty years, during which time he got to know most of the parishioners' foibles, both lovely and unfortunate.

The Reverend lived in a neat house adjacent to the church. If any visitors went to his home and found it empty, they tried the church. There, they would often discover him sitting peacefully in the front pew, mulling over what he would say in the next sermon. Sometimes he stood contemplating again all the wonderful stained-glass windows, to receive inspiration from them. Sometimes he would simply stand in front of the great painting of Christ, in sheer amazement at the beauty of his Saviour and at the wonder of His Lord.

The first time that Iris and Douglas visited the church it was empty. They were just writing in the visitors' book when they were suddenly confronted by the vicar in his service finery, clutching to his chest a handful of mail.

He had entered through another door near the front of the nave, used rarely and only by him.

They all looked at one another in surprise, but he didn't stop, disappearing again through the main entrance. He quickly returned and, giving a laugh, the priest explained that he was trying to catch the local postman, and not escaping the devil! He was saving time by going through the church interior.

Entering into conversation, Douglas said he thought that this church had a special appeal.

Eagerly, the priest told them some of the history of the parish, including how Kings Charles II and George III had bought numerous racehorses, and raced them around the large oval shaped Common. This was in between the elms and oak trees. Though they were before his time, he proudly said, 'They must have been quite exciting races.'

Iris told the priest that they would come with the rest of the family on Sunday (the next day) to hear more of his wonderful stories and, of course, to listen to his sermon.

On Sunday the church's inner doors were open for morning worship. Iris entered, followed by Douglas and the rest of the family. The ancient pews made loud creaking sounds as the weightier members of the congregation sat down. The family sat in a back pew.

When the service was over (the priest had mentioned a few of Douglas and Iris' adventures in his sermon), Polly explained to Iris that the smell in the church was the result of years of people gathering for baptisms, weddings, funerals and harvest festivals, as well as a succession of flower-filled vases, the aroma of oil lamps and lots of polish.

Of course, Thomas and James were going to this church now. Seeing that they had another set of grandparents, they might receive more lollies, if they behaved themselves!

Sitting in church, Adam quietly studied Douglas out of the corner of his eye. His father was becoming more restless and unsure of himself. What Douglas was really thinking about was a desire to visit Loos in Belgium, where his father had died so long ago.

Douglas didn't think that he would be back in England again, so if there was a time to go, this was it. He could see with his own eyes *the dying field of his father* in the wonderful coloured glass window of the church. Adam had seen the glorious glass painting when he had first entered the church, and it drew him back time after time.

Douglas also knew that he would have to leave it to other people if the practical things, like the arranging of the ferry across the Channel, hiring the rental car, driving on the wrong side of the road, booking the hotel rooms, and coping with other languages while travelling around Loos, were to be achieved.

Douglas had George Moffatt's fragile letters tucked away in his old satchel in a plastic folder. Many years before, Iris had taken them out to read the contents. She had wisely said, 'I think that you will have these letters for a long time before you decide what you will do with them.'

On this occasion, Iris repeated herself, saying, 'Maybe you will take the same steps that your father took during the war, and end up at Loos. Remember though, because there was no trace of your father, the only way that you may find out anything about him is by writing to the British or the Belgian authorities for information.'

Douglas made up his mind to go anyway, and asked Adam if he would go with him to see the battlefield of Loos.

Adam responded quickly. 'I'm glad that you asked me, Dad. There are lots of questions in my own mind about the First World War, and particularly about my grandfather.'

He also thought it was an opportunity to do something special for his father that was both enjoyable and long-lasting; something that would provide answers to all those unanswered questions and give his father some peace of mind. So, he generously said, 'I'll be pleased to arrange the ferry, the car and accommodation for us as well.'

Explaining to the local travel company their urgency and that they would only have five days to go to Belgium to visit the old battleground at Loos, they were booked into a quiet Ypres hotel and hired a small car from a rental company near *Little Throstle*.

As they were getting into the car, Polly whispered to Adam, 'I'll be missing you. I hope you have a good time with your dad,' before kissing him tenderly.

The eager twins wanted to get in on the act, so they accorded Adam some tears mixed with sloppy kisses.

Iris gave Douglas a gentle hug, saying, 'I hope you find what you are looking for,' and then choked up. She didn't know what else to say.

They journeyed to Dover, crossed over the smooth channel, and ventured through part of France to arrive in Belgium, where they ended up in a quiet Ypres hotel. The weather was fine, the countryside looked peaceful, and an atmosphere of hope and prosperity now prevailed.

After enjoying their first evening meal that the hotel provided, they sat down in comfortable chairs in the lounge. Douglas reached into his worn satchel and pulled out the bundle of George Moffatt's valuable letters. 'When my mother died in hospital, they came to me. Now, I want to give them to you to read.'

As Adam began to read the letters, the efficient Belgian headwaiter came over to them, enquiring in excellent English, 'Would you like a lunch prepared for tomorrow, and someone who speaks English to act as a guide on your trip to the Loos war graves?'

They were surprised by this, wondering how anyone knew where they wanted to go, not knowing that the travel agents had let the hotel know the urgent reason for their trip. They were most grateful at the mention of a very good lunch. The waiter said it would be ready for collection after breakfast the next day.

As for visiting Loos, they hadn't made any definite plans. The waiter then explained that it would be wise to have a guide because the countryside where the battles of the two wars took place had altered very much over the years. 'The guide that I have in mind is an older colleague, who understands why some places may be disturbing for you. He understands when to be saying something and when to be silent.'

With those points of excellence, they agreed.

'Anselm Pirard will meet you inside the visitors' centre in Loos,' the headwaiter said. 'Just ask for him at the counter.'

Douglas and Adam were ready bright and early the next morning. They collected their lunch from the hotel and journeyed the short distance to Loos.

Anselm Pirard was completely different to what they had imagined him to be. They thought the headwaiter had let them down. Coming through the door into the bright sunlight, they saw that he had a thin face, long black hair secured by a rubber-band, and a rather scruffy beard of indiscriminate colour.

Adam questioned him about the possible mix-up. Speaking in school-boy English, he said, 'I'm afraid my father, Anselm Pirard, died last week.'

Adam looked at his father as if to say, 'Do we trust him?'

Douglas gave a half-shrug as if to say, 'I don't know.'

Adam was now sitting behind the steering wheel. Quickly Anselm opened the door to the front passenger's seat, so that Douglas had to take the back seat. He felt rather cross – *How dare he take my seat like that!* – but he kept silent.

Adam looked in the mirror at his father and humor-ously said, 'Are you sitting comfortably?' When he got the answer that all was as well as could be expected, Adam asked the guide what they should call him.

'Anselm,' said the guide. 'Anselm.' He was now smiling nervously. 'Pirard can be forgotten.' Straight away he referred to his maps on the First World War and inter-esting newspaper articles from that period. Turning to Adam, he said, 'The Loos Battlefield lies this way,' showing him with his extended arm.

Adam started the car and they set off, while Anselm excitedly described the passing scenery. 'Look, all the ground around here is flat. You can still see the coal-mining slag heaps standing like mountains. In 1915 they presented a big challenge for the enemy.'

Anselm didn't say what enemy he was referring to – perhaps both. 'It is little changed today, except that the coal industry is nearly finished,' he continued, and pointed out the railway lines dotted around the battle area. He showed them unusual trenches of white chalk surrounded by barren grass. However, he didn't need to point out the two towers structure. It stood proud in front of them.

Adam slammed on the brakes, stopping the car (luckily, there wasn't any traffic behind him). Where had he heard of the two towers before? From the written material, Anselm went on to tell them that the complicated 150-foot tall structure of two individual towers, placed in a very solid building, was a set of lifting gear for the main coal pit.

As they restarted the car, Adam again wondered where he had heard of the two towers.

Douglas was thinking about his lunch so, naturally, was looking out for a picnic place. Eventually, Adam found a grassy area and stopped the car. Anselm had no food, so they shared with him what the hotel had provided.

While eating (hadn't Anselm realised that he was not to talk while eating food?) he read out: 'In the First World War the army stretched out over twenty miles. It had seventeen infantry divisions, supported by 420 heavy guns. Can you imagine the noise!' and lowering his voice he said, '*four – days – of – continuous – bombardment!*'

Douglas shuddered. He supposed that his own father must have been among them.

'About the 20th of September in 1915, the infantry units began moving.' Here Anselm emphasised, '*Seventy-five thousand men!*'

Adam noticed the effect of these words on his father, so he said quickly, 'Please stop. You are upsetting my father!'

Anselm fell silent.

Douglas and Adam thought about the horror that lay behind his words. After paying a quick visit to the Soldiers

Memorial cemetery, they understood that Anselm had finished all his explanations, and he showed it by throwing up both his hands – most difficult in the car!

Adam took him back to the Loos visitors' centre. On giving him his money, Adam said that they were most grateful to him for informing them something of the history and effects of the Loos battle. Anselm was pleased that the first venture since his father's death had been a success.

Douglas gave him a weak smile.

Douglas and Adam stepped into the surrounds of the Loos battleground. It was so quiet and peaceful, set in very beautiful surroundings. Long vistas stretched out before them, with numerous yew trees interspersed with quiet seats. They saw that the garden was blanketed with tall, wispy, red poppies. Then they realised the true significance of the flowers' presence was to express the red terribleness of death *and* the energising redness of life.

The authorities had built a high wall at the back, commemorating the lives of soldiers who had fallen in this area. Douglas noted that all those commemorated were without names. However, they were still surrounded by hedges of remembrance. He sighed and, wiping his eyes, blew his nose, put his hanky away in his trouser pocket and murmured quietly, 'Oh, Dad!'

Taking a breath, Douglas still wanted to tell Adam about the way his father had affected his life, so he said, 'Because I was two years old, I didn't really know him. He wasn't there, as a father ought to be. As I grew up, I knew that I was missing out on all those practical – and I suppose spiritual – things that I would have learned from him. The experience of this garden has been very fulfilling. I now have some understanding of my father, even though I know there is no actual body.'

Then Douglas said, 'Just a moment.' Going back to the car and reaching inside, he got the worn satchel containing another letter from George Moffatt. Although Adam had seen the letters that Douglas had given him to read at the hotel, he had never seen this one.

'I didn't want to let you see it until I'd seen the memorial of the Loos battleground,' his father said.

Adam started to read it while his father sipped the remains of warm tea from the thermos.

This ex-soldier, a proud man, who knew where he was going, was at the Reunion. He said to me (George Moffatt) that the Scottish division was the first British offensive on the western front. They had started moving forward. A few of us who were manning the machine guns were shot or wounded. It was like a picture of hell.

Then George made his own personal comment:

The memory of this man was so chillingly factual. He spoke in such a concise manner that a stranger listening to his comments may have thought that this was about an earlier period of history, instead of some valid facts just a few years ago.

The letter went on:

Just as the battle on the 25th of September had started, William Fraser took out the small pocket Bible, the one given to him by me just before I was taken to England so ill, and he read it to the men who were around him: 'I read from the Psalms, "To God, my defender, I say: Why have you forsaken me? But I will put my hope in God, and once again I will praise him, my Saviour and my God."'

Putting the Bible away in his tunic he prayed somewhat earnestly: 'Lord, we put our trust in You.' What William was seeing was what was obvious to us all – a ghastly scene! We looked for landmarks on the German lines to guide us to the right spot. With increasing smoke whirling around, amid the stench from the men dying, we suddenly and without reason put aside the machine guns, and took up our rifles to confront the enemy. This was near the edifice, the Two Towers. We knew if we were not actively fighting the enemy, we would be lost, so William quickly chivvied the men to fire that one last time.

I wouldn't be here at this reunion if he had not done this! It defeated the enemy only temporarily, firing again, for they were on slightly higher ground now. William was slain. He was killed as other soldiers met their own doom.

You might be wondering why I have been so meticulous. Thinking of the verse that William had just read: I will put MY hope in God – I was the only one saved!

What will I do with this salvation? Before the war, I was an artist. Now I will paint these battle scenes.

Adam put down this letter. He now remembered where he had heard of these Two Towers. It was at the art exhibition at Galleyend.

His father looked at him and said, 'What's wrong?'

'I don't believe it!' Adam said very emotionally. 'Some time ago, Polly and I went to an art exhibition of the First World War, and there we saw a painting of the Battle of Loos, showing the Cameron Highlanders being involved in a battle – just like this one,' and Adam pointed to George Moffatt's letter. 'I thought it was just an imaginary painting of the battle scenes, but I didn't expect the wonderful explanation in this piece of correspondence.'

Adam took up the letter and read it out loud again.

... without reason, we threw down our machine guns, took up our rifles and confronted the enemy. This was near the edifice, the Two Towers. We knew if we were not actively fighting the enemy, we would be lost, so William quickly chivvied the men to fire that one last time.

Douglas was overcome with sadness, and then joy at his father William's last sacrifice. He wept.

Chapter 31

*A*DAM LOOKED AGAIN at the letters and found, on a last separate page, that here was what George Moffatt had laughingly called 'The glorious facts of war at Loos'. There was an old article which read:

Frenchman General Joffre said that he had chosen Loos as a suitable spot on the map, even though it meant attacking across coalfields and through a wilderness of miners' cottages.

But that wasn't enough!

In the three weeks from the 25th September to the 16th October, there were 15,800 killed, and 34,580 missing and wounded, at the battle of Loos. Yet we have heard from others that Joffre was still a confident man, irrespective of whether he had defeated the enemy or not. He still believed he was wearing them down!

Adam slowly handed the letters back to his father and said very quietly, 'There's a Bible verse which explains the situation so clearly.'

Douglas had now recovered his equilibrium, so he burst into laughter. 'You could say there are many Bible verses that can be quoted to suit any situation,' he said.

Adam grinned. 'The Bible verse is in the New Testament letter of James. *Where do all the fights and quarrels come from? You want things, but you can't have them, so you are ready to kill; you strongly desire things, so you quarrel and fight to get them. Your motives are bad; you ask for your own pleasures, not God's.'*

Douglas remained silent, refusing to comment or argue on any verses of the Bible. Instead, he sat down on one of the rather uncomfortable seats and said, 'Let's see if I've got all my personal history right. My father William joined the Cameron Highlanders in World War One. He was married to my mother and had three children, one of them being me. He was sent to Loos, where he fought with a machine gun and a rifle. He died in battle. My mother and the wider family didn't want to say anything about the war, so I was brought up not having any clear idea about my father. The Second World War saw my family in New Zealand. I tried to join up, but I had restricted employment, so I didn't go to war, seeing out my service repairing training planes.

'I found that through my father-in-law David Thoms, and of course good wise Alec Hay, I could now discuss these things that had bothered me for ages. When my mother lay at death's door, she gave me the letters from George Moffatt, a good friend of my father, telling me just a bit of my father's life. A few years further down the track, you were called up but registered as a conscientious objector. You went to Papua New Guinea as a literature missionary instead.'

Now sitting down, Adam agreed with all of this. However, he said softly, 'In those letters from George Moffatt, the ex-soldier said that my grandfather William read from the Psalms. That is the first time I know of him reading the scriptures. Then, when the soldiers were too scared, he chivvied them up with his rifle. Thirdly, he had been instrumental in saving one of the men from death, namely this ex-soldier. Tremendous activities in the most atrocious circumstances.'

Douglas thought for a moment, then agreed. He thought that although the First World War was ghastly, there had also been many acts of kindness and compassion. He could look at it from a different angle. His face slowly broke into a smile.

After a moment, he asked, 'When you were called up by the army, why couldn't you have explored other options? You could have done... ambulance driving, or some other thing.'

Adam slowly came to the realisation that he really hadn't explored *all* the options, and so he gave his father a rather weak grin, but no further explanation.

It was now getting chilly, so Douglas sent Adam to go to the car and bring back a large blanket to put around himself. As he was waiting, he thought of something that had been troubling him off and on and for some time.

As Adam sat down and Douglas wrapped the blanket around his shoulders, he gave a little cough and spoke these words hesitatingly: 'Do you remember the time when you were leaving for the Navy all those years ago?'

Adam gave a frown and then a grin, not knowing what was to come next. He noted that his father had curled his lower lip a smidgen, which meant that he was going to say something really significant.

'I was at the railway station with your mother and your sisters, saying goodbye to you, but I said nothing about your choice of joining the Navy. Although there was a whole host of things going through my mind, I want to say that I am sorry if the impression I gave you was wrong.'

Adam let out a long sigh and then said very understandingly, 'I know, Dad. I know!'

Chapter 32

AVING TOUCHED ON these important issues, Douglas and Adam didn't quite know what to do next. Douglas looked intently at all the inscriptions of the dead soldiers again and Adam, looking down at the ground, gave it two or three gentle kicks of his foot.

With a start, Adam noticed a whole network of glistening lines spreading out across the lawn. Bending down, he was amazed to see that it was a spider's web. Grabbing hold of his father's arm Adam said in wonder, 'God is showing us something special!'

They both looked at the intricacy of the spider's web in silence. Adam said excitedly, 'Look at the complexity of the design; the strength of the weaving; the tenacious resistance to the breeze that blows everything else about. It would only be us who could damage this web. However, if we did so, and we examined the same web tomorrow, we would see no sign of any damage, because the clever spider would have restored it.'

He went on thoughtfully, 'It is a reminder that God is in the repair and restoration business. He will restore what has been damaged and bring healing and wholeness.'

Douglas was confused. However, this matter was very important to Adam, so he suggested that he put it another way.

Adam smiled. 'Think of wars and think of conscientious objectors. Through the years, we have received a lot of misinformed anger from others. Having had all

165

these experiences, I have been forced to see everything from grandfather William's point of view. Look, he had a soldier's number – Private 12345. So did the rest of the soldiers. Wearing their numbers declared that they belonged to the army. They had no say within the army but had to obey the orders given, regardless of the outcome.

'However, Grandfather had the guts to do three things. In the midst of battle, he made a personal stand. He had the gumption to be different – just like the spider. He chivvied the men to fight with all their might.'

Adam smiled again as he continued, 'We have come all this way to find out about grandfather's bravery. Has this enabled us to sort out our own difficulties and disagreements? After all, we have found God's answer in the simple spider and its web!'

Douglas snapped off one of the red poppies as a reminder of this important day and, with a firm and lasting handshake, they went back to the hotel in Ypres. He placed the poppy inside his Bible.

The next morning, they set out on their return journey to *Little Throstle*. Adam sang his favourite hymns on the way and Douglas cheerfully joined in.

Douglas and Iris had one last thing to do before they departed for home. A large, flat, heavy parcel that had been shipped out from Mosgiel was their thanks for their stay at *Little Throstle*. It had arrived on the day before their return.

Adam and Polly, Thomas and James stood around this parcel wondering what it contained.

Douglas said with a grin, 'Can you remember the picture that has come down to us from all the relatives, *The Quiet Scene*?'

Adam nodded.

'Well, here it is!' said Douglas.

Douglas got out the small pocket knife that he always had with him and proceeded to remove all the shipping details, sticky tape and layered brown paper that wrapped the parcel. He commented, 'You wrapped this well, Iris!'

His wife smiled and gave a shrug. Eventually the wrapping was disposed of and the painting was revealed.

Iris recounted all those who had previously owned the picture. 'John Turner bought this for himself long ago. Then it was passed on to Emma and Alec Hay. Then it was my parents, Lilian and David Thoms. After that it was our turn. Now it's passed on to you.'

Adam was completely taken by surprise. Polly, standing next to him, gave a beautiful smile.

Iris went on. 'The painting did not look right in the lounge or the passage of our house, so it has sat in the garage all this time. Then I wrote secretly to ask Polly if you would like it, and she wrote back, "Of course we would!" So – here it is!'

The Quiet Scene was hung above the fireplace in their large lounge. Standing before it, Adam noted how the artist had captured the wonder of the quiet, dry riverbed; the tall, spindly grass growing on the large rocks and, in the distance, marvellous mountains covered with radiant snow – all giving the painting its peaceful tranquillity. The artist had seen all that in his mind and painted it so well that the picture was always vibrantly alive.

Douglas said to Adam, as he took his hand gratefully again, 'You have blessed me with peace. My whole attitude has changed.'

Adam gave a wry grin. 'And I wonder if my conscientious objection will need to be changed.'

Iris and Polly looked on with delight, for not only had William's bravery been recognised, but any animosity or disagreement between Douglas and Adam had been healed in the poppy garden at the Loos war memorial gardens.

PART TWO

An Attitude of Love

Chapter 33

ADAM FRASER WAS perplexed. A worldwide legal expert and a knowledgeable man who had a wide grasp of litigation matters, he looked at the possible names that he might use one day for his own business – *Judicial and Religious Action, Morality in Judicial Circles, Christian Legal Issues,* or even *Legal Affairs.* But in practical terms, he still did not know what steps he needed to take in order to bring this into fruition.

Sighing, Adam thought about his career so far. Introduced to bookselling at sixteen years old, he became a student when he was twenty at Concord Bible College, then the nearby university in Dunedin, New Zealand.

Completing his studies at twenty-seven, Adam's faith adventures as a missionary bookseller in Papua New Guinea were both exciting and fulfilling.

Four years later, Adam was employed by a London legal publishing company, *Judicial Books.* It was having its internal troubles, and the company hoped that Adam and six other chosen experts would bring it to modern standards. They named it the *Project Team.*

A soon-to-retire and possibly wiser man, Geoffrey Chalfont, whose temper was extremely volatile, had the responsibility of being in charge of the group.

Clive London was an outside-the-square adviser; a short dapper fellow in his late forties with a thin face made more funereal by his thick glasses and bushy black eyebrows, he had all the facts in the worldwide computer business.

The young secretary to the Managing Director, Carol

Finch, was always dressed in a smart tailored suit, brilliant pearls and matching earrings. She had an understanding of what the computer costs were.

A short, portly, balding Irishman from Dublin, by the name of Patrick Flinn, dealt with all the computer complications. He managed to get to the core of any problem, no matter how difficult.

Then there was Penelope Winters, an articulate and well-groomed older woman, who never revealed her age, and was employed for her knowledge of not only legal, but medical and scientific books.

Tall, slim, neat and older than them all, Colonel Henry Ivanov came next. He had a large nose, deep brown eyes and a cultured voice. A Scottish law-examiner had said earlier that the Colonel was "a skilful, exacting, canny man, so that anyone asking him a question on any legal matter was quickly and correctly answered". Certainly his manner, his standing with other people concerned with the judiciary, and his general outlook on life, meant that no one dared call him by any other title than *The Colonel*.

With a start, Adam looked at his watch to find it was long after midnight – too late for his brain to be working so hard! And too late for disturbing his wife Polly.

Scratching his receding auburn hair and stroking his greying beard, he took off his pink striped tie and, opening his gaudy waistcoat, revealed startling red braces.

A little later, while sleeping in his bed, Adam had a dream – God told him to go to Christchurch.

Chapter 34

THE CRICKETERS' ARMS pub was tucked away in a tree-lined street near the cricket ground, just a gentle walk from the opulent buildings of *Judicial Books*. There were no sounds of noisy cars racing along the roads, but occasionally the Pilot Team saw crowded double-decker buses making their slow sonorous way to the sleepy outlying villages, letting off its weary passengers at the most inconvenient places.

Covering the walls of the Cricketers' Arms was an elaborate photographic display of outstanding cricket matches throughout the years. Old stalwarts, who were more interested in drinking, occasionally raised their heads to exclaim the great day when so-and-so got a century or had been out for a duck. Then their lips would revert to taking in another long sip.

Passing these stalwarts, the Pilot Team went to the rear of the pub, where they could sit comfortably, away from the rest of the crowd.

Beside one of the solid tables, the keen manager waited on them. The main reason for them being there was very important to his trade, so he instructed the staff that only he would serve them with their substantial drinks and various nibbles.

They never stayed past half-past seven, when the pub started to get noisy and sometimes boisterous, but the manager never let any revealing computer information that came from their lips go any further.

Therefore, they were able to talk quite openly about the new system being installed. The large but cumbersome computers that *Judicial Books* had just bought, and the software programmes that were being hurriedly written, were not of any interest to outside listeners.

The Pilot Team had had plenty of failures. One day of importance, the typists in their large room were waiting eagerly to get started on the first computer programme. Each one knew that the written information was to be correctly typed onto various forms. In the late afternoon, with these instruction forms, the packing department would then send the valuable law books and their invoices to influential legal customers all over the country.

However, once they started their computer processes, the Pilot Team found out that the typed forms were saying one thing and the wall of computers was saying another.

They had failed miserably! In fact, the effects were catastrophic. Frustrated legal clerks made urgent and angry phone calls. They wrote stern letters, or even visited the company, saying they were "most upset", or other words of similar effect.

Equally upset barristers, lawyers, and solicitors working for the local authorities, having been satisfied with the old written system, learned the reason why the situation had suddenly changed – those airy-fairy computers!

The Pilot Team went all out with their urgent discussions during several extra nights at the Cricketers' Arms. Eventually, they came up with a more suitable answer – the whole computer process would have to start again. It took them ages to sort out this problem, until the day when the Pilot Team was disbanded.

Geoffrey Chalfont, his hair now snowy white and wiry, retired to the south of Spain. There he would rest on the beach, well imbued with never-ending alcoholic drinks. Clive London now had an exciting position far away with a Canadian company. Patrick Flinn took his family back to Dublin for more exciting computer prospects. The vivacious Miss Carol Finch had been promoted by the company, taking charge of all things relating to the computers. Penelope Winters had resigned due to a pleasant surprise – she had won a fortune on some TV programme, and left very suddenly to cruise around the world.

The Colonel wanted to contribute all his legal knowledge, but found that he had constant disputes with the leader of the Pilot Team. These disputes were not so much about small legalities but in response to this man's own rude and gruff manner.

For three months they argued back and forth, causing the Colonel to have a minor breakdown. After resting quietly in his home for some time, he decided to go somewhere overseas. Looking at the job advertisements in The Times, he found the perfect one – legal work for a Papua New Guinea mining company on Bougainville Island.

Chapter 35

ARLY ONE SATURDAY morning, Polly woke with a start and quickly got out of bed. Putting on her clothes, she was ready to go downstairs to see about breakfast for their four sons. *Oh, how they have grown and are therefore always hungry,* she thought.

Polly knew that today the boys were going out early on an adventure with their schoolmates and two other brave parents. This meant she didn't have much of a lie-in. Looking at Adam sleeping so righteously, if not peacefully, she sighed and thought, *I wish I could be like him!*

Suddenly Adam woke up and invitingly said softly, 'Won't you come back to bed?' When Polly told him the reason why not, he began to get dressed too. As he put on his T-shirt, he suddenly mentioned God's startling word from his dream. 'You know how I've been mulling over our next step?'

'Yes,' muttered Polly. 'You have been mulling over it for ages!' Her friendliness began to change as she suspected what was going to come next. Saying pertinently, imitating his deep voice: '"I've got a new position!" or, "I want to move again!" or, "Oh, I know, we'll move right out of the country!"'

Adam didn't say any of that. Instead, with his scruffy corduroy trousers on, he followed her down to the kitchen, still wanting to give her his explanation.

Taking two pieces of thick, brown bread and putting them into the toaster, he said, 'Last night, God firmly told me, *Christchurch*. What do you think of that?'

Adam waited for his toast to be ready – he enjoyed almost burnt toast. When both slices were very well done, he took them gingerly from the toaster and, with a blunt knife from the pile of cutlery left permanently on the table, applied delicious thick butter, followed by thickly spread marmalade. The result was extremely messy. Using his tongue, he wiped the residue from the toast's edge before eating the almost fractured pieces.

There was no further reaction from Polly. Pausing in his crunching, he mumbled to her again, 'I think God has revealed what the next step is.'

However, Polly clammed up even more! Perhaps it was from farewelling the boys out of the house, well prepared with their breakfast under their belts, or for another more direct reason; but clamming up was Polly's thing – she was becoming well practiced in the art.

So Adam now asked a question. 'You know Colonel Henry Ivanov, the one who used to work in the Pilot Team with me? He went out to Papua New Guinea. Later he left that country and is now in Christchurch, in New Zealand. I'll write to him and see what the work situation is like there.'

Polly now turned her full attention to Adam. 'Oh no! Are you talking about Christchurch in New Zealand? I thought you meant Christchurch in Dorset, on the South Coast.'

Stamping her foot, she went on. 'Listen to me! We've got comfortably settled. The boys are enjoying school,' her voice becoming more brittle, 'and now that I've got a little bit of freedom – well! Do you love and respect the boys and me?'

'Yes,' Adam smoothly affirmed. 'I love and respect you all!'

'So why do you upset me like this?' She stamped her foot again, which unfortunately met the sharp edge at the bottom of the stove, making it very sore. She was not a happy person!

In spite of Polly's rather terse manner, Adam gave her a gentle smile and, taking hold of both her hands, gave her a kiss on both sides of her troubled face. 'God is in this somewhere,' he said.

Throwing off Adam's hands, she strutted out from the kitchen into the dining room. The boys had finished their breakfast and had hurriedly left with their friends to pursue more manly pursuits, leaving the table mimicking a pigsty.

Polly collected the half-empty honey and marmalade jars, still muttering and declaring under her breath, 'I'm not worried about God being somewhere.'

Growing even more agitated, she tried putting the lids on the wrong jars, ending up by shouting in a shrill voice, 'Everyone knows that God is everywhere!'

She had another go at the lids, successfully this time. 'But I'm concerned about your state of health – *it's* nowhere!'

Giving him a *daggerish* look, she went back into the kitchen and, plonking the dirty dishes plus other washable implements into the frothy hot water, she said, 'I will do them another time. Now I've got a terrible headache,' and, showing Adam what a headache looked like, she went upstairs for a rest on the unmade bed.

Chapter 36

CAROL FINCH, THE highly efficient secretary who was on the Pilot Team of *Judicial Books,* found the old personal records of the Colonel and his latest address in Christchurch, New Zealand. Adam wrote to the Colonel, who quickly replied:

My dear Adam,

This comes from Christchurch down under, 12,000 miles away. Yes, I can remember us talking when were together in the Pilot Team, about its successes and about our many failures. I simply want to forget the experience! However, here is my up-to-date story that will, I hope, leave you some-what surprised – my religious faith!

When I came back from Papua New Guinea, and after my different experiences in that disturb-ing land, I lived in Chipping Ongar, a pretty village north of London. There was a period in my life when I became quite downcast and lonely, so I went along to church – purely for the company of other decent people. Through many conversations, the latest religious books, and a few sermons hitting the mark, I slowly came to realise that, under-neath, I was a very needy man who had to face my past before conquering the future. It has been quite an effort to do this! Perhaps, in his mercy, Jesus Christ understands.

The church where I went showed very little interest in any visitors such as myself. I told myself that I would try it out until Christmas, two months away. The service started with an ancient sage clothed in his ministerial finery, climbing very slowly and standing in his high pulpit, looking down at us from afar. He commenced the worship, singing in religious tones, 'Oh, Holy, Mighty, Magnificent and Marvellous God, we worship you.'

Over time I came to see that the people here were not stuffy or overly religious, even the old sage. Since then, I have married a perfect wife, Sophie Pretty. She is eighteen years my junior, a member of the same congregation, and is also a barrister. When I declared my faith in Jesus Christ – well, I have good news for you – Sophie, dear lady, had been waiting until I had made this decision before she made any sign of affection for me!

It is good that you and Polly, plus your four boys, have plans about coming to New Zealand. Write to me again and I will tell you of the possibilities of legal work in Christchurch. I have the feeling that we will meet some time in the near future.

Yours,
Colonel Henry and Sophie Ivanov

Adam was grateful for this letter, more grateful that the Colonel had married Sophie, and extra grateful for his change of heart. The thing that he was most grateful for was the work possibilities in down-under Christchurch. However, after Polly's agitated reaction to his news, he decided he would take the move slowly, even if it be over a number of years.

The following spring, when the birds were training their voices to sing detailed trills and amazing cadenzas, the small furry animals were concentrating on building fresh beds for their young, the leaves were budding on the trees, and the temperatures were altering quite dramatically, Adam and Polly, wrapped up well, walked slowly hand-in-hand from the garden seat to the house. The twilight evening had disappeared and now the sounds of night were taking over as the stars came out.

On the little table just inside the front door lay the telephone, and it rang just as they entered. It was Albert Williams, Polly's father, who sadly informed her that her mother Olive had just died.

Olive had been ill with tuberculosis, but her health had been slowly improving, so her death was unexpected. The whole family gathered at the crematorium for her funeral. Albert looked haggard and alone, in spite of the consolation that was offered to him. The local priest led the funeral service for a very loving wife, keen mother, and stalwart of the community.

When Olive was nineteen, she had worked in the Chelmsford Town Hall typing pool. Albert was involved in the same place but in local government. All the young typists were kept busy doing their work, but occasionally, in those in-between minutes when the work ran out, a few of them larked about, including Olive.

Once she lost her balance and ended up sitting in the waste-paper basket! With a red face, getting redder by the minute, Olive tried to pull down her 1920s dress that had become dangerously high. Arranging her dark hair and hiding what was to become her ridiculous mirth, she made awkward crying sounds, 'Can someone help me?'

Albert quickly came to her aid and rescued this damsel in distress! He had noticed Olive before and thought it would be nice to ask her out – but without the wastepaper basket.

Six months later they were married in the Galley-end village church. Apart from eagerly attending their services, Olive's main regular outing was to the Women's Institute monthly meeting. Amongst other things of a practical nature, like *How to turn Vegetables into Various Sauces* and *How to Repair Furniture when you are Unsure of How to Go About It*, she would enjoy listening to her friends singing *Jerusalem* at the end of the meeting. She didn't sing a note.

Olive was dead now, but the old priest had picked up on this theme. 'We are thankful that she has now reached eternal Jerusalem,' he said.

After the funeral, Albert had a lonely time, so when he couldn't sleep at night he wrote simple poems, or short, pithy stories. Polly would call at his house most days, usually about morning teatime. Albert would take his time preparing the cups and saucers, pot of tea and the biscuits that were necessary for her visit. Adam popped in during the evenings.

However, a weekend session when grandfather told his favourite tales was something that his grandsons, Thomas, James, Sam and Jack, delighted in – particularly when they were treated with yummy chocolate biscuits!

On arrival, the boys would give four or five sharp knocks on the back door before entering the house and collecting their chocolate treats from the kitchen. Then they would go into the lounge and find him sitting in his chair, his thick glasses sliding down to the end of his nose. He was very anxious to start. As soon as they sat down and exchanged friendly pleasantries, Grandfather Albert started to read.

'Good poem!' or 'Fantastic story!' the boys said when he had finished. They then said their goodbyes until next weekend came. This continued until he died.

At his death, the boys were deeply upset and decided that it would be a good idea to collect those wonderful poems and pithy stories and put them into a book. When he heard of this idea, Adam proudly encouraged them. 'It can be called: *Grandfather's Stories and Pithy Poems,*' he said.

The family had definitely made up their minds to move to New Zealand. Well, Adam had. Polly had some reservations about returning to the opposite side of the world, but knew that her parents' deaths had removed the barrier that prevented her experiencing a new life so far away. Before getting married, Polly had been a missionary nurse and midwife in the village of Orokolo in Papua New Guinea. There she met and married Adam, who worked in a Port Moresby Christian bookshop. So eventually she said to herself, 'Why not take this step, and go to Christchurch?'

And so, they did.

Chapter 37

HE DC10 CHARGED down the runway at Gatwick airport. All the family were set to go to sunny California in the USA!

The flight took ten hours, passing over Greenland and down the Western States. They saw some fantastic sights, magnificent mountains, wonderful lakes and sparkling cities far below.

Arriving in mist-shrouded Los Angeles early in the morning, they settled into a nearby airport hotel. On examining all the tourist brochures, Adam discovered Disneyland, amongst all the other experiences on offer.

Issued with their entrance tickets, *Passport for Many Adventures*, they delighted in most activities including Fantasyland, where they visited 'Small World – the Children of All Nations' three times.

Two days later, they left America at midnight, and they soon all fell into a deep sleep on their flight to Hawaii. When Adam woke up, he caught a glimpse of a stupendous sunrise that made him think God must have worked overtime on this heavenly presentation!

After landing and collecting their mountain of luggage, Sam began to feel the uncomfortable effects of prickly heat affecting his body. Adam explained that the air-conditioned plane was quite different to the temperatures of Hawaii. Sam's body was now perspiring to help keep him cool, hence his reaction. His troubled frown changed into a grateful smile, but he continued to scratch all the way to the hotel, where they stayed in a complex of rooms on the beachfront.

After a long cool shower, Sam felt comfortable again. The family changed into more suitable clothing for the Hawaiian climate – casual shorts and colourful open-necked shirts for Adam and the boys, and a more comfortable cotton summer dress for Polly. They all wore sunglasses and large hats to ward off the brilliant sunshine.

They enjoyed a variety of luscious pawpaw, passion fruit, pineapple, mango, guava, star fruit, and fresh bananas each morning at the hotel's restaurant. During the evening, they were captivated by men's wild dances, and the slower, flowing movements of the beautiful women.

After a week of Hawaiian bliss, they got on another plane to take them on to hot and humid Port Moresby. This is where Adam and Polly first met, so they smiled fondly when they recalled all those events of yesteryear.

Just before the plane was about to land at the airport, the boys excitedly looked out of the oval windows, wondering what was before them.

'I know that some of the Papua New Guinea girls have very little on,' said teenager Thomas, demonstrating with his hands.

'Breasts are free from bras?' questioned James.

'Blowing in the breeze!' said Thomas proudly.

Sam and Jack just grinned!

Hearing them, Adam sighed. They were exhibiting Western culture. Now that they were in this tropical country, they would see many women's breasts. The excitement at the sight of them usually lasted for a day or two, after which the breast situation – and possibly the memory – would become ho-hum. Well, he hoped so!

All the airline passengers were welcomed into the large, very modern, air-conditioned building. Adam looked around, remembering the last time he had been there. Port Moresby airport had been very different then, when only a glass divide separated the overseas and local destination areas. Small passenger planes would weigh the ticket-holder as well as the luggage.

A mixture of aromas pervaded the area; aircraft fuel from parked planes waiting to take off, and unique pig-fat smells from Highland people, who used it on their skin to cope with the cold temperatures in the Highlands, greeted the travellers!

After the family had gone through the customs' check surrounded by the loud voices of people speaking many local dialects mixed in among overseas languages, they grabbed their luggage and escaped into the humid tropical air.

'Sam would be used to the clammy temperatures now,' Adam muttered.

Sam looked up, with some idea that what he said was true.

A large Papuan man quickly drove them in an ancient taxi into town. He was willing to answer any questions that the boys had.

Along the waterfront, surrounded by tall palm trees waving in the calming breeze, stood their opulent hotel. As they entered it, they noticed the shaped swimming-pool, and a few happy children enjoying leisure time. There was a large restaurant, with inside and outside dining.

After they had been shown to their rooms and started to unpack their luggage, the boys asked Polly if they could go for a swim and have their mid-day meal later. She told them, 'Yes, but don't get into any trouble!'

They all looked surprised. Trouble was not their thing! 'Half an hour is long enough,' Polly continued, 'then you can get changed and join us for lunch.'

Changing into their swimming togs, the boys rushed to the pool. This allowed Adam and Polly time to have a discussion. They hadn't told anyone of their visit, except for the English travel agent and, of course, Adam's parents. They didn't know how many of their old friends and acquaintances were still in Port Moresby.

'I will go tomorrow to the Church office where I worked, and make my presence known', said Polly. As she sat down on the bed, she recalled her first flight into Port Moresby. Of course, Adam knew all about some of her past memories but kept quiet – better not to disturb Polly's unfolding thoughts!

'It was eight o'clock on a beautiful sunny morning

when the plane made its final descent,' Polly recalled. 'I could see Gemo Island in the harbour. Only a short distance away were the village houses of Hanuabada, perching on stilts over the lapping water. Then, with a few bumps, we landed at the airport.

'A few days later, Gemo Island was my first adventure. Travelling on a small boat with an outboard motor, I arrived at the jetty to be welcomed by a group of smiling young leprosy patients. After a cup of tea, the nursing sister showed me around the hospital. I learned about the patients' treatments with medication and the care of their damaged limbs. They were able to go fishing, cook their own meals and were also able to earn an income by learning how to do beadwork, making brightly coloured belts, necklaces and wristbands.'

Polly went on to say how she had written her first letter to her parents:

I have found that this country is a good place, full of colour but very hot and humid. I feel rather inadequate, so I asked God to help me.

'God must have helped me, because I was a competent nurse, a careful midwife, and did leprosy work for the seven years that I was there. Then I met a handsome bookseller – you!'

Adam smiled, and Polly continued. 'Do you remember *our* exciting adventures when you visited me in Orokolo? The one that took us six hours across the treacherous Purari River in a large propelled canoe, to a humid inland Kapuna hospital? Our Orokolo wedding in a large shelter made out of pandanus leaves, with the Bishop conducting the ceremony? What about our delightful honeymoon in a secluded hotel in the mountains behind Port Moresby? And do you recall the dangerous snake that advanced on us at breakfast time? Or the distant drumming and war-cries of the warriors? Do you remember all that? Do you?'

Adam laughed. After gently kissing her on the lips he said, 'I remember! First, though, we must find our boys.'

Chapter 38

T HE NEXT DAY, Adam set off to the *Christian Bookshop*, thinking about the enlightened pastors, local teachers, dedicated nurses, and missionaries, all of whom had been his past customers.

He also remembered taking Christian literature to the recently established university and other tertiary institutions, as well as to the churches in the local villages. He had travelled in small planes to religious conventions and lonely mission stations. Now he was going excitedly to his old bookshop.

In the past, Adam had placed a large printed sign on the top of the shop verandah to catch people's attention, declaring what the Christian bookshop stood for, but when he looked for the notice it wasn't there. However, on the front window a small notice declared, *CHRISTIAN BOOKSHOP.*

Adam recalled how he used to have the shelves stocked for the religious Christian everybody. In his day, there were about fifty different missionary centres all over Papua New Guinea, ranging from High Anglican, Catholic, Lutheran, Seventh Day Adventist, the Uniting Church, and other keen individuals who made their way to the Port Moresby bookshop.

Going inside the shop, Adam took from the shelves a very expensive book. He found dust not only on the cover but all along the edges of the outer book rim. Thinking that the rest of the stock was the same, and that they hadn't been dusted for a while, he came to the conclusion that there was no shop assistant as efficient as Papuan

Tau Rebu, who had worked in the bookshop with him.

Tau's task had been to 'bang' all the books to remove any of the swirling dust from the road outside, gently wiping the outside covers of each book. Sometimes tiny weevils enjoyed eating the glue between some of the book covers. These were dislodged by the banging, and his work saved a lot of stock from damage.

Polly went to the Uniting Church mission office. She was surprised to meet a few old acquaintances, some from Australia, some from England, or local Papuan people who came from distant places, calling in for urgent advice or maybe for greater funds.

They were pleased to see her but said reluctantly they were too busy to chat. Perhaps another time would be better, and they got out their diaries. Polly said she was only staying for four days and her family must have precedence. Saying goodbye to them, she despondently returned to the hotel and, going into the quiet café, found Adam sadly sipping his coffee. Sitting down beside him, Polly said, 'You look as despondent as I feel.'

There was just a smattering of conversation from the hotel desk, so, ordering an orange drink, they talked about what they had found.

Meanwhile Thomas, James, Sam and Jack were walking eagerly along the wharves. They saw the large American ocean liner that had come into the harbour overnight. They were confronted by a succession of corpulent men with cameras slung about them, chatting to shrill women with tinted hair as they trooped down to the end of the gangplank. Bypassing the expensive bunting and pennant flags of welcome, as well as the friendly local people displaying their wares of colourful indigenous masks or valuable delicate beadwork, they carried on chatting amongst themselves, as they hurriedly headed to the European gift shops. There they were greeted by eager shopkeepers selling them similar articles that could have been bought for much less on the jetty.

Oh well! The boys quickly headed for the busy main street, where they saw a large policeman doing his best to sort out the traffic while standing on a slightly raised platform. He looked as if he was doing a difficult dance as he controlled the dangerous traffic coming from four different directions. A few inebriated people added to the danger.

'Breathtaking,' the boys said as they walked along to the large stalls at Koki market. Some large palm trees provided a little shelter as they moved among the stalls. They saw ripe bananas, fresh paw-paws and delicious mangoes. Of unusual shapes, sizes and colours were loads of fresh fish caught that morning. Oval-shaped green betel nut, a stimulant drug, whose contents when chewed made the mouth go distinctly red, were also available. The lively, noisy market had an air of business as deals were made.

However, the boys were far more interested in the young topless girls, wondering if they would be at Koki market. They had already noticed some old, scrawny women wearing grass skirts and nothing else. James chuckled, 'I overheard Mum tell Dad that some of the older Orokolo women tucked a breast under each arm when chasing naughty children, cackling with the effort!'

Most of the girls that they saw were adequately dressed. A hulking Papuan man, angry at some strangers who ventured into the market but bought nothing, got to his feet and indicated that he would spit red betel nut juice over them. They gave the girls shy smiles and quickly went on through the market to explore other interesting sights.

Meandering their way back to the hotel about midday, the boys were ready to eat their substantial smorgasbord lunch. They listened to what their parents had discovered on their outings, and how disappointed they had been.

'The situation is this,' Adam said, putting his empty plate to one side and wiping his mouth with a large hotel-embossed serviette. 'We only have three more days here. We can either get on a small plane to visit distant towns – but that would be a rush, or we can get an atmosphere of the whole country by going to the National Fair.'

He waited for their response.

Wise James said, 'I think it better that you make the decisions, Dad.'

Adam, filled with pride at his son's great perception, replied, 'I think it will be the National Fair.' Being diplomatic, and remembering his words about moving to New Zealand, he quickly said to Polly, 'What do you think, dear?'

Polly just half-smiled her agreement. Anything would be alright with her, so the next day they went to see the National Fair.

Chapter 39

PORT MORESBY STADIUM was full of local people and interested visitors from all over the world – a vibrant tapestry of languages, accents, shades of colour, light and dark, and outstanding cultures.

The Fraser family slowly shuffled along to reach their seats, but were trapped by another more voluble group coming out from the previous show, and the two clusters had to struggle to get past each other.

A rotund Papuan man, with wiry brown hair in a bushy halo, was waiting for the crowds to disperse. He gave a start as if he suddenly recognised someone in the family group. Sporting a cheeky grin, he rudely shouted across the now interested people, 'Are you Adam Fraser?'

Surprised, Adam shouted back, 'Yes. I am. Who wants to know?'

The rotund man said, still smiling, pointed to himself. 'Well, look at me more closely and you will see who I am.'

Adam stared hard at him. He thought to himself, *If I allow for many years to go by, yes... this could be...*

He broke into a broad smile, and asked, 'Are you Tau?'

Tau roared with laughter. Struggling through the crowd, he took hold of Adam's hands, shaking them up and down vigorously in the strong Papuan way. He eagerly said, 'It's been a long time since we were at the bookshop. I thought I was seeing things but when I saw your fading red hair and neat beard, then I knew that you were in town again!'

They went on shaking hands until they were forced to

get out of the way, for the crowd was still struggling to get by.

Adam remembered his manners and quickly said, 'Do you remember Polly?' drawing her close and putting his arm affectionately around her.

Tau looked at her. Polly looked back at him, then in mock anger she raised her hand as if she wanted to slap Tau. 'Fancy hiding my letters from Adam!'

Tau remembered that one of his jobs at the bookshop was collecting the mail from the post office. One time he had told Adam that there was no letter from Polly, his unmarried sweetheart, when there were three! They laughed at the occasion.

Waiting by the fence, the boys came over when they heard this. 'Naughty Tau had hidden the letters for a joke when he was collecting the mail,' their mother explained. 'Your father was very miserable.'

Adam drew his sons into the conversation. 'Let me introduce you to my four boys. The twins, Thomas and James, and Sam and Jack.' He turned to the boys, and smiling said, 'Tau worked at the bookshop at the same time as I did.'

Smiling, Tau shook hands with them all.

Thomas was getting anxious and said, 'Time is getting on. Shouldn't we go inside?'

Adam quickly said to Polly, 'I wonder if you and the boys can go into the show while I stay and catch up with Tau. It's on for an hour. We can go to the café over the road. I'll see you when you all come out.'

'Of course,' she said, and off they all went.

Reaching the café, Adam and Tau settled themselves at a small table decorated with a red cloth and an empty wine bottle holding a large candle, which would only be lit when it got dark at about 6pm. A canopy protected them from the sun. They were served by a large, harried Italian man wearing a tight linen apron around his large waist. His gentle side was revealed when he whispered to customers that his argumentative nature came from *the missus, she who was inside*, and not from valuable guests like them!

Smiling, they made their orders and a minute or so later, two enormous cups of freshly made coffee arrived, prepared by *The Missus*.

Tau started to tell some of his story. 'Do you remember taking my wife Para and me to the hospital when my little girl Ari was about to be born? Well, we left the bookshop shortly after you did, and returned to our village of Hula, which as you know is some fifty miles away. Some of my brothers and I started a lorry business, taking passengers and livestock to and from Port Moresby. Of course, we had seats arranged on the back of the truck.'

Adam thought of several truck journeys just like this. In the middle of the vehicle the livestock gathered – noisy, tied-up scrawny chickens or small goats that munched away at anything available. Usually the numerous humans, including happy children, crammed around the sides on rickety seats.

Tau continued. 'We carry gifts like woven tapa cloths made in the Hula district, and sell them at a considerable profit at the National Fair. In fact, I've just delivered some and was coming out when I saw you.'

Then Adam told him about his life in England and the unique house, *Little Throstle*. He explained the legal business and the family's decision to return to New Zealand, and how he intended to start up a similar business in Christchurch.

Tau told Adam of how his family had grown. Para had produced three more children, and Ari was now married with a child of her own on the way.

Adam told Tau of some of the frustrations of travel. 'Most days I went to London by electric train. There were thousands of people from various parts of the country all arriving in the city. When I got off the overground train, I had to continue my journey by underground trains to get to my office.'

As they slurped more coffee, Adam said that he had been to the Christian bookshop the previous day and was very disappointed at the number of changes that had taken place. 'Have you ever been back?' he asked.

Tau shook his head and smilingly said, 'I can remember how we celebrated your wedding day at Orokolo. You gave me a live chicken which squawked all the way on the plane to Port Moresby. When cooked, it was firm and juicy and enabled Para and me to have a good feast.'

The rest of the family came out of the stadium and, crossing over the rather hectic road, they found the two old friends still reminiscing. The boys wanted some cold drinks and Adam ordered coffee for Polly. As the still-harried waiter was writing down their orders, Tau gave a sign that he was leaving. He remarked, 'The rest of the men will think I've deserted them. I have kept an eye on them though. They're just over the road.' He was looking at a lorry that was well hidden under some trees. There, two men were sitting in the cab, snoozing.

Still laughing, Tau said, 'I've enjoyed meeting you all,' and, crossing over to the lorry, he opened the door, told the other men that he'd been side-tracked, started up the noisy motor, and gave the family a final wave before leaving the scene. The truck's exhaust spewed forth black smoke while moving away. Soon it could no longer be seen, although heard for quite a while.

Polly enquired, 'Had a good time?'

Adam thought how he would have missed seeing Tau if he hadn't gone to the National Fair, so, putting his coffee cup to one side and wiping his beard, he said, 'Yes, we talked about many things. How did you get on?'

James excitedly cried, 'Dad, there were men from *Mekeo* who had amazing multi-coloured painted faces!'

Thomas joined in. 'And there were Mud Men from the Highlands who wore mud plastered all over their faces and upper chests. They looked quite frightening, coming out of their dark hiding place as though they were about to attack us!'

Sam put on his ghostly face in an attempt to scare his mother, but Polly had seen more disturbing sights, including Sam, who still occasionally walked in his sleep.

Jack said that he had taken off his Hawaiian sunhat and bought a brand new cap from a New Guinea seller. He sat with his range of hats on display, yelling out, 'The latest from the Highlands! You won't get any better.'

Of course, Jack had bought one right away! However, just as they were sitting down, he looked at his new hat and discovered that it had bright feathers sewn roughly on either side. On further inspection, he also discovered that it was made somewhere in Asia, and not deep in the jungles of Papua New Guinea. He was disappointed.

As they were leaving the fair, Jack mischievously said to his brothers, raising his voice just loud enough to be heard by the hat-seller, who was still sitting in the blazing sun: 'I liked the men with the Birds of Paradise feathers in their hair. They must have taken ages to arrange them and fit them on their heads like that,' alluding to his own hat on which he'd found three measly feathers of indiscriminate colours.

Adam laughed when he heard this. 'Nothing has changed! Many years ago, when I was paying a visit to the Highlands, I was sold an enormous hat and the seller gave me all that rigmarole. It wasn't until I had been everywhere from the eastern Milne Bay to Wapenamanda high up in the Western Highlands – playing tennis, would you believe! – I found out that these hats were manufactured in the factories of Asia.'

Still laughing, Adam stood up and enquired, 'But are you satisfied with what you have seen?'

Again, James wisely uttered, 'It's been a great festival, and exciting to see all the people, particularly Tau.'

Adam put his arm around Polly and, smiling at his four well-educated sons, they strolled back to the hotel, satisfied with what they had found in Port Moresby.

The boys never mentioned bare breasts!

Chapter 40

*T*HE FAMILY LEFT Port Moresby by Jumbo jet, on their journey to Christchurch. By now all the young travellers considered their flights rather old hat, so they didn't look out through the windows but settled down to read.

However, Adam and Polly did show their interest. They flew over Queensland's countryside, with riverbeds giving way to lush green bush and purple-hazed towns. Then it was the Tasman Sea, where there was not much to see except the pale blue choppy expanse of ocean. Eventually, they saw rugged snow-covered mountains – the Southern Alps, marching in splendour up the west coast of the South Island.

Adam immediately recognised Christchurch as it came into sight; he saw the colourful roofs of the houses trapped between the strongly braided northern Waimakariri river and the more sedately braided Rakaia River to the south. He marvelled at the wonderful variety of greenery below – tall trees and tidy shelter hedges that made up the large farms on the extensive Canterbury Plains. Adam could see the towering city buildings, where he imagined people going about their business with enthusiasm.

Douglas and Iris, Adam's parents, would be waiting eagerly to see the family. He wondered if his sister Violet and her husband, Gregg McKenzie, would be there on one of their regular visits from Dunedin.

Violet was still working as a nurse in a Dunedin hospital. She had become the youngest *Matron who knows everything*, well, almost everything that the other nurses would want to know!

Gregg had been a great sportsman who had travelled from Canada to New Zealand with only a backpack on his shoulders. He was now thirty years old and had thought that he must do something regarding his career. He did so by commencing study at the university in order to gain his Degree in Biblical Studies. He then took a senior position with the Young People's Association (YPA), an organisation involved with sports.

Adam thought further. He remembered a collision between Gregg and Violet. Coming out of *Arthur Barnett's* wonderful store and loaded up with expensive purchases, Violet tripped over and found herself and the expensive shopping on the footpath. Immediately, Gregg went to help, kneeling down to take a closer look at her to see if there was any damage. Seeing that there was none except perhaps to her pride, Gregg put the shopping awkwardly back into their exclusive bags. As they were adjusting themselves, they made their introductions, picked up the purchases, and went into a nearby restaurant to enjoy afternoon tea together.

One thing led to another and six months later Gregg proposed marriage. Violet was thrilled, and accepted his offer. Violet's parents, Iris and Douglas, Gregg's parents from Canada, and many good friends came to the wonderful church wedding. Afterwards, they gathered at the Grange Restaurant with some of the nurses and all the YPA staff, who celebrated and wished long life to the happy, married couple.

Ever since, Violet and Gregg took regular breaks, including this one to Christchurch. Eagerly they said to Iris and Douglas, 'We can meet Adam and Polly and family,' then adding, 'if you like.'

However, Iris did not want anybody to take away the thrill of welcoming the weary travellers, so she quickly suggested an alternative. 'Why don't you go to the airport hotel, where we have booked them in, to make sure everything is ready?' Reluctantly, they followed her instructions.

Adam and his family collected their luggage and

passed through customs. Iris didn't shake their hands, she just slipped through the barrier to give them lots of hugs and kisses. Oh, the excitement as she welcomed them to Christchurch!

Douglas looked worried at the sight of so much luggage. Adam told him not to be so concerned. His sons would do everything! And so they did, lifting the heavy sixteen pieces of luggage with ease, as they made their way to the hotel without any help. Douglas was impressed – and somewhat surprised – at their ability now.

Waiting patiently inside the hotel lobby were Violet and Gregg, and they assured Iris that all was well.

Rose, Adam's youngest sister, was also there. She was soon to depart yet again to Fiji, where her work involved the welfare of unmarried women. She understood her mother would not want anybody else to welcome Adam and Polly and their family, so had come to the hotel instead.

Adam gave them a great big welcoming smile, sloppy kisses to Rose and Violet, and to Gregg a friendly handshake. They, and all their luggage, rose in lifts to the top floor. There they found themselves in a very quiet passageway, no doubt thanks to the hotel's excellent double-glazing that blocked the noise of planes.

Adam opened the suite door, to discover on the table two bottles of excellent bubbly and fresh jugged orange juice, supplied by the hotel management. There were numerous glasses too, so striding over to the table he poured out what was required. When they had all had drinks, Adam exclaimed, 'What a reunion!'

After their trip to England, Douglas found that the whole experience had been marvellously cleansing. He discovered that he no longer worried about his soldier father William. Douglas now saw his father in a new light.

Iris saw Douglas slightly differently. He had a new spirit and was much happier with life. Without really knowing what happened in Belgium between Douglas and their son, Adam, Iris realised she no longer needed to worry about her husband.

Together then, Douglas and Iris set out to find themselves a small cottage in the Christchurch suburb of Sea View. They had been staying in a quiet seafront motel, and after their morning teas they had taken long walks up and down the streets looking out for 'For Sale' properties. While walking around one of the cul-de-sacs, Iris saw out of the corner of her eye a delightful cottage, standing back from all the rest. Tall hedges on either side were generously covered with honeysuckle and different types of colourful roses, all entwined in togetherness and covering the delighted Iris in their wonderful aromas.

When Douglas opened the gate, they followed the path to the back of the house. More floral perfumes accompanied them, with blossoms bright, right up to the back door. It took them only a few minutes of peering through the windows before they made up their minds that this cottage was the one that they had been searching for – their hidden gem!

Noting the estate agent's address was in the middle of Sea View village, they quickly walked as fast as their legs would take them to the office. They were taken to view the interior of the property, and decided to buy it – subject of course, to their solicitor arranging all the necessary checks on the house. They were so excited!

Eventually, they received the keys. Violet and Gregg came up from Dunedin to help with their move. Gregg gave Douglas a hand with the interior of the house. Together they painted the walls in pale green and replaced the fallen-down wood stove with a modern gas fire. They replaced the cracked toilet. The old bath that delivered cold water only was replaced with a modern shower with hot and cold water. Violet and Iris made brightly coloured linen curtains to put in the cottage windows. Before they knew it, they had settled into their new home.

Now, Douglas wondered where Adam's family would live. The family couldn't stay long in the hotel, could they? It would cost them a fortune! What would Adam and Polly do in the future? What education would the grandsons have? Or had the twins finished studying and were now perhaps looking for work? Sam and Jack, what sort of schooling would *they* have?

Adam hadn't told them much at all.

Two days later, Iris invited Adam and Polly to dine at *Sweethearts Restaurant,* just on the edge of the city. She and Douglas came to this favourite quite often to enjoy a hearty lunch, or the delightful morning or afternoon teas, relishing the view of the mountains, as they were seated in this *home from home.*

They enjoyed the simplicity of the restaurant. Standing in a magnificent setting, its surroundings were restful, the structured grounds ornate, the menu excellent, the wines exquisite, the seating comfortable, the music mostly classical, and the staff attentive. The name *Sweethearts* was perfect!

Having heard all of this glory from Iris, Adam and Polly were keen to try it out. After they had finished their first course, Douglas reached into his jacket pocket and drew out a poem that he had just written for Adam:

Adam Fraser – may his sons excel –
Awoke today, having slumbered well.
He saw among the regular disorder,
An angel whispering to a tape-recorder.
What say you? said Adam, all a-flutter.
The angel raised his eyes, and with
A look of kind intent, replied,
The names of those who spread the word.
And is mine one? he was heard to utter.
Nay, not so, saith the angel. Adam
Dropped his eyes, but cheerily said,
*Record my name, then, along with those
who've earned their daily bread.*
The angel spoke not, but vanished.
Next day he came again, and gave
A great exultant call:
Adam's name now surpassed them all!

Adam was speechless as his father passed the poem to him. His father explained that he was exultant to have Adam, Polly and family in the city and, leaning forward, he said kindly, 'Would you please tell us, seeing that *your name surpasses them all*, what your plans are?'

Laughing, Adam told them of the wonderful opportunities involving legal companies in Christchurch.

This was what Douglas wanted to hear! The conversation continued about important matters until it got to the actual place where this budding business might be situated. Adam said that it would have to be quite a large property.

Douglas immediately told Adam about some real estate that he had seen advertised in the *Property Gazette*. 'It has recently come onto the market and it is near the airport. Maybe this will be suitable for all your needs.'

Adam smiled at his father's persuasive voice and asked, 'Do you have the agent's name?'

'Yes, I do,' Douglas smugly said. 'I have brought the *Property Gazette* with me.' Reaching again into his bulging coat pocket, he brought it out and handed it over.

After a cursory glance at the advertisement, perceiving that this house and property might indeed be *the one*, Adam said, 'I will contact the agent when I've had a chat with Colonel Henry Ivanov.'

Polly quickly explained to them, 'Colonel Ivanov has had a great influence on Adam. Tell them, my dear.'

Adam was still reticent to reveal the whole story. He had said to Polly that morning that the instruction from God was very succinct: *Christchurch*, so all he did was to give the parents a grateful smile and, lifting his cup, he offered instead, 'Excellent coffee!'

Chapter 41

ADAM MET COLONEL Henry Ivanov the next day in the Avon Conservative Club in Christchurch. Overlooking the meandering Avon River, the old three-storey establishment had points of excellence, such as single suites for members staying for short periods of time. It also had a quiet library and a small but excellent restaurant that served only members and their guests.

The Colonel was a member, and Adam his welcome guest.

They shook hands and, observing each other, liked what they saw. Adam still thought of the Colonel as a no-nonsense type of man, but someone who could be a very lasting and good friend.

The Colonel saw that Adam had changed quite a lot. Instead of a bombastic young man at *Judicial Books* with all publishing legalities at his fingertips, he was now more cautious, not willing to jump without some reason for doing so.

Soon they were comfortable in leathery seats in the quiet library. They looked out of the window at a small-hedged garden with a neat lawn rolling down to the river below, knowing that they wouldn't be disturbed there as they discussed the vision for the future.

The Colonel called out to an elderly limping waiter, who came over to the glass table and attended to their orders. 'I will have my usual red wine,' he said. Turning to Adam he asked, 'What will you have? Tea? Coffee? There are various spirits, wines and beers. Or something

202

else?'

Adam said, 'Red wine please,' and that soldier from somewhere slowly went to get the drinks.

'When I read your reply to my letter,' Adam explained, 'I could foresee that one day we would be sitting in Christchurch having a conversation about the great days of the past, and then peering into the future – as we are now.'

Then Adam broke off. What more could he say? He told himself that the vision God had given him was one word – *Christchurch*. He didn't have anything else to be going on with so, smiling, he said, 'You had better go first. I will concur if God's vision to me matches up with yours.'

The drinks were set down on the table. The waiter had a final task. Pulling out a small pad of paper from his side pocket he gave it to the Colonel for signing, then disappeared.

The Colonel said, 'As I only gave you a small part of my history while we were at *Judicial Books*, I will now give you a greater picture. Then we will see whether you can take me on as a partner in this legal venture or not.'

Taking a sip of the excellent wine, the Colonel started to tell his story.

'Many years ago, I lived near George Town in Malaysia on our estate, *Grace Chateau*. My mother's name was Hyan Grace Hough. She was thirty-nine and married to my Russian father, Petya Ivanov, who was fifty-nine. A jeweller of some repute, he died suddenly from natural causes. Knowing that her husband was expecting some important visitors next week, my mother stirred herself and began to organise the servants to prepare the chateau and its extensive grounds.

'With the cook's help, my mother had checked on the food that was in the large larder. Noting what was missing, she placed an order with George Town's main supplier. Next, she instructed the gardeners to tidy up the extensive flower gardens and rake all the gravel paths. There was a prominent brass plate inviting visitors to enter the chateau property, so this was also polished. Other servants cleared the gutters and washed the windows.

'Well, that visit was a complete success. When all the crowd had gone, my mother reclined in an armchair on the quiet verandah, enjoying a glass of lemonade put down by one of the servants. Catching sight of a photograph of her husband on the little table just inside the open door, she noticed that Petya was examining some sparkling jewels he had just had made to place around *her* neck. *Yes, he was always interested in things of beauty,* she thought.'

Adam interrupted. 'Where and when and how did your parents meet?'

Smiling, the Colonel replied, 'Thailand. In the spring of 1913 at a select jewellers' meeting. My mother was a very clever young woman of nineteen, but she had not yet ventured into Thai society. On this important occasion, her parents – they were in the jewellery profession too – decided she was ready to meet some top jewellers.

'Proudly they brought her into the spacious room where everyone had gathered; all conversation stopped, stunned into silence by her demure grace and beauty. She had been introduced to many people that night, but she would never forget meeting the gracious Petya Ivanov. Gently taking Hyan's hand, he kissed it and murmured in a clear Russian accent that he was very pleased to meet her. Her heart responded to this man's charm and kindness. Other jewel giants faded away, but these two had *clicked* and they were never separated again.'

The Colonel went on: 'Growing up in Vladivostok as a poor boy, my father was dependent on food and shelter from wherever it could be found. As he walked past fashionable shop displays, he caught a glimpse of scintillating coloured jewellery that sparkled and shone. Stopping in amazement at the glorious sight, he was noticed by an old craftsman on the opposite side of the road. Calling my father inside for food, warmth and shelter, he thought that this boy could help him clean up the back room, where the jeweller created beautiful jewellery out of precious stones. Asking him his name, the reply was Petya – meaning stone or gem!

'Every day my father watched closely and learned more from the old craftsman. To him the nature of each gem was exquisite. By the time the old man died he was able to take his place. Creating works of great beauty, he took on more staff and eventually became celebrated as a jeweller of note.

'At about thirty, my father started to travel. Taking with him a lot of expensive and exquisite pieces of his outstanding jewellery, he was employed by rather important craftsmen of the same trade in Eastern China, and then in Thailand. Later, he set up a small jewellery business for Bangkok's select clients. He was invited to come to this grand occasion by a jeweller friend, and there, he had the pleasure of meeting my mother. They fell head over heels in love and married as soon as they were able.'

Laughing at his remembrance, the Colonel said that his father once told him, when he was about eight, 'I saw this petite, graceful figure, Hyan Grace Hough, who filled my dreams and cared for my every need!'

Adam clapped his hands. 'I enjoy stories that have a happy ending!'

The Colonel wryly smiled and gave a sign that he had not yet finished.

'My mother had a mixed-race parenthood. Her tiny mother was from an out-of-the-way place somewhere in northern Thailand. Her name was *Manee,* which too means precious stone! She had converted to Christianity at an early age. Her future fiancé, Andrew Hough, was from Edinburgh, a travelling jeweller looking out for precious objects that were unknown back in Scotland. They were married in Bangkok. He was a cheery, neat man and adopted a saying: *Strong in faith. Pure in truth. Graceful in action.*

'He had often told his daughter – my mother – that God loved her, saying in scriptural words: *God's mercy is so abundant and His love for us is so great that while we were spiritually dead, it is by God's grace that we have been saved by Christ.* That was the reason that your mother and I chose the second name, Grace, for you, in the hope that you will take God's Grace to everyone that you meet!'

The Colonel toyed with the thought of ordering more red wine, but changed his mind. There was still a little wine left in each glass that would tide them over. He continued: 'Then the situation changed dramatically. When Grandmother Manee died in Bangkok, Grandfather Hough returned to Edinburgh. Petya and Hyan Grace moved to Malaya, to the small town of George Town. They lived at *Grace Chateau*.'

Adam queried, 'Is George Town the capital of Penang?'

The Colonel nodded.

Adam pursued his thought. 'This *Grace Chateau* – was it in the centre of the island?'

'Yes!'

'Up in the mountains?'

'You've got it!' Laughing, the Colonel continued. 'As well as the exquisite pieces that he had created in Vladivostok, my father added to his wonderful array the jewellery that he had made in Thailand. He also worked long hours to produce even more beautiful jewellery for wealthy Malaysian clients. Indeed, *Grace Chateau* was known far and wide.

'My mother looked after running the whole property, the inside staff and the outside gardeners. I was born a year later. Growing up, I played to my heart's content around the chateau.

'My mother wondered what she should do next. One day she had an idea. Christians were always looking for a venue for quiet solitude, a silent retreat, or somewhere for a small conference centre. She thought about it for a while, then had notices drawn up, to be placed wherever Christians gathered.

'Her first bookings came from an organisation that arranged Silent Retreats in Asia. When the first guests arrived, they relaxed in the comfortable seating around the grounds, enjoying the quiet stillness. Marvelling at the Creator's beauty of flowers and the soft sound of wind sighing through the singing trees, they wandered where they liked and communed with God.

'Now my mother, this demure lady Hyan Grace Hough, had a purpose in life. She had also been graced by God for others, too!'

However, the Colonel sadly remembered that the story didn't have a happy ending.

'When I was nine, my mother and I travelled by ship to Southampton. We were going to Edinburgh to visit my Scottish grandfather, who was poorly. Aunt Matilda Hough, Grandfather's unmarried sister, looked after him, constantly saying, "He is very ill, so don't make any noise!"

'However, in Southampton my mother had caught a serious infection and it was *she* that died, and not my grandfather. Taking me to their home, the ship's First Officer and his wife looked after me. After contacting my grandfather with the sad news of Mother's death, he quickly came to life and rescued me.

'My mother's casket was put on the train to Edinburgh, but we travelled the long distance in Grandfather's luxurious car. A few days later, the funeral was held in a Scottish church.

'After this, and before *Grace Chateau* was sold, my grandfather asked me if I remembered anything about the house that might be relevant. The only thing that I could say was that one day I had seen my father put the collected jewellery away in a big trunk. It was hidden, but I couldn't remember where.

'My grandfather instructed my older cousin to go with urgent haste to find the exquisite jewellery that my father had accrued. On finding it, he was to return and deposit it in the Bank of Scotland vaults. Grandfather had contact with one of the managers. He then put me into a private school in Edinburgh, where he could keep his eagle eye on me.

'When I was eighteen, my grandfather *did* die. Aunt Matilda suddenly slipped with alacrity into her new position of looking after the jewellery business.'

Taking his last sip of wine, the Colonel carried on: 'Remember Adam, apart from my Thai grandmother, the Hough family from generations back were all gifted jewellers, working to the highest standard in silver and gold.

'I sat for my degree of Scottish law and passed it with

flying colours but, because of the impending war, I went immediately into the army. There was a requirement for soldiers trained in the law to become army barristers.

'Now I told you in my letter about my many years of diligent legal work during the war, in the English law-courts and much later at *Judicial Books*. I held such a *wonderful record that anyone there who had questions about legal matters was quickly and correctly answered.*'

Chuckling, he said, 'That was a comment from one of my earliest examiners. However, I had many differences of opinion with the Pilot Team's leader.'

Adam smiled, telling the Colonel that they had all heard the constant arguments between the two combatants!

Giving another chuckle, the Colonel said, 'Well, I wanted a complete change, and a complete change presented itself – I went to Papua New Guinea.'

Chapter 42

'FOR SOME TIME,' said the Colonel, 'I was employed by the large mining company in Bougainville, but mainly worked and lived in Port Moresby, where I made sure the legal niceties were being observed. Of course, I went out to the Island of Bougainville quite often. There I saw the local people coming from their villages to one large centre, *Panguna*, where copper, gold and silver were mined. I wore long shorts, partly open tropical shirts, comfortable sandals and a wide hat, and made friends with the local indigenous people as well as Australian mates!'

Laughing, he said, 'I soon learned that I was too feeble and much too old for those adventurous adventurers! The amount of beer and spirits that disappeared down parched throats took me out of my comfort zone. As well as these things, the buzzing flies and annoying mosquitoes were all over me for my tasty blood. The increasing warring conflicts and ineptitude of society eventually made me resign my position.

'I next went to the Southern Highlands, where I was involved with the legal side of growing coffee beans and, later, the distribution of pure coffee. The earthquakes,' (living in New Zealand, Adam too had experienced earthquakes, frequently occurring in multitudinous places) 'dangerous snakes slithering around, and untold creatures lurking in the long grass caused me to walk circumspectly! In all of this, I missed the things that I could so easily obtain in Britain, so I went home and settled as a quiet solicitor in Chipping Ongar, north of London.

'Writing to my Great-aunt Matilda, I learned that she had been a faithful watcher of the jewellery business since my grandfather died, and still was accruing considerable interest at the Bank of Scotland. I was a wealthy man, but I was becoming quite lonely. One autumn day I went along to the local church, purely for the company of others, you understand. Through many heartfelt conversations and lots of messages that hit the mark, I knew that I must make some decisions about all the mistakes made through my life.'

Adam looked at the Colonel – a man at peace. He certainly had no worries or concerns. However, he was not finished yet.

'Having received the old priest's permission, I wrote a piece for the church weekly newsletter: *Help available to anyone in their new legal business. Contact Colonel Henry Ivanov.* I received only one reply, from a Miss Sophie Pretty. In her early thirties, she was a bright, pretty woman who went well with her name.

'Wisely, the priest had suggested that we meet in a public place, saying that one of the front offices would be free at 3pm.

'Miss Sophie Pretty said, "I have become very frustrated when the written law is often misinterpreted and misrepresented by people. You know it has been said, *Much law, poor justice?* – That is something that I want to change."

'Our conversation was animated. I interjected when some points needed clarification and listened to her lengthy replies. She leaned forward with much excitement and said, "We could call the new company *Legality Incorporated.* We would need three rooms – one each for the manager, a staff member working on the law, and one for the secretary. We'll also need a small waiting area and a room to meet with the clients. It would be good to be able to offer refreshments to them as well," she finished with a brilliant smile.

'I smiled back. She had thought of everything! I was silent for a moment, then gently inquired: "Where do you think I would fit in?"

'She responded in an excited voice, "Oh, you're the manager of the business!"

'With another friendly smile, I accepted!

'She got up and gave me a gentle kiss on my cheek, saying, "Thank you." I was a little embarrassed.'

The Colonel was thoughtful for a moment, then said to Adam, 'I had been saved by God and then shown a way to make up for my past mistakes.' He added, 'Of course, Miss Pretty and I wanted to start in a small way, but life at *Legality Incorporated* became so good that I felt free to propose marriage to her the following year.'

Adam broke into this long but interesting tale, 'I can guess what you did next! Once you were married, you came to Christchurch, where you would have a completely new start of life in the legal business – right?'

'In October, 1979,' the Colonel said precisely, 'we commenced our new life together. I have enough money in the bank for Sophie and myself to live comfortably in Christchurch. We haven't made a terrible mistake in coming all this way. Instead, we took this step as God's way for our future.'

He paused for a long time, then said confidently, 'Do you recall my saying to you, "We will meet again?" Well, we have met, on this day, in Christchurch, so maybe this is the start of our new venture together.'

Adam smiled, then asked him, 'Well, what's next?'

The Colonel replied, 'Well, I have tentatively made arrangements with the estate agent for you to go and see the sprawling *Honeysuckle House* estate tomorrow,' and, putting his hand in his pocket, he brought out the description of the house.

Adam felt a thrilling sense of anticipation. 'My father told me that there is a property available that is just like this. Fancy that! A sign from God?'

The Colonel gave only a wry smile. He wasn't surprised any longer that the next direction was actually God's way. Then he said, 'The property is on the edge of town, close to the airport and near to *Sweethearts Restaurant*, where guests can be taken. It also has easy access for the city's legal fraternity.'

Smiling, he further explained, 'The large estate has five offices – that would suit me, you and Polly and, of course, Sophie and Miss Marchant, whom you haven't met yet.

'Adjacent to the five rooms I've just described, there is a separate suite of three other rooms. They are a short distance away, having a sturdy walkway providing protection from the weather.'

Then he said, 'I suppose the name can be something other than the English one, *Legality Incorporated*. Any ideas?'

Adam succinctly said: '*Legal Affairs*.'

The Colonel thought that this name could be looked on with some suspicion.

Adam said that the word *Legal* took in everything imaginable and the word *Affairs* made it open to all good possibilities!

The Colonel paused but couldn't think of anything else to say about the name. He continued with more details about the *Honeysuckle House* from the agent's document. 'It is a massive three-storey house. There is plenty of room for two families – maybe yours? Maybe mine? I will stay away while you take your first look at the property, but the agent can go with you to give you advice.'

Adam said, 'I'm amazed! Not only have you been aware of my hesitancy at the single word, *Christchurch*, that God gave me so long ago, but you have been at work to find a building suitable for the start of setting up our new business and to meet all our needs!'

Taking the smartly creased red handkerchief from his top pocket, the Colonel wiped the corner of his eyes and said, 'Get away with you,' and went quickly upstairs to his room.

Departing through the Avon Club's large doors, Adam was suddenly assaulted by the sounds of the city. That didn't upset him though. This was a new day with new opportunities for new legal work!

Chapter 43

ADAM AND POLLY, their sons Thomas, James, Sam and Jack, along with Adam's parents Douglas and Iris, as well as a very keen agent, were all viewing the sprawling *Honeysuckle House*.

They were all, apart from the agent, inspired! They saw the long, sweeping drive with its variety of ornate shrubs on either side. They saw the colourful gardens with bright red poppies, yellow daffodils, and white snowdrops that bowed their heads in regal recognition. Behind them, tall hydrangea bushes, camellias and rhododendrons danced a slow waltz in the lazy breeze.

The air was full of sound and movement as noble blackbirds, cheeky sparrows and speckled thrushes swooped to the ground for worms. Then they saw the sprawling white wooden house, standing alone like a gracious sentinel. Trees, some native, some imported, surrounded it.

At a distance, standing on top of a slight ridge, stood two large oak trees that were magnificently mature. Their extended boughs provided shade on hot summer days.

A much stronger breeze caused them to look up. They saw the heavens thick with cumulus clouds, that stayed for a while before being blown elsewhere.

There was also a small oval lake fed by a gentle stream from somewhere. There, graceful silent swans were preening their feathers. Rude, quacking, exuberant ducks moved amongst them, all doing their necessary business.

Adam moved on to the undulated lawns. He was aware

of the smell of freshly mown grass. He ought to congratulate the agent for having arranged this. Perhaps it could become a permanent arrangement. Actually, he thought that he could hear the sounds of the ride-on lawnmower getting louder. Yes, there it was, coming into view near the far tennis court, adjacent to the bowling green where dandelions, buttercups and clover were prolific. Adam noticed that this man had cut the lawns so well that if he missed a piece, he would go back over it until it was done.

Though it was obvious, Adam told the family and the agent that he was excited at the whole scene! They came closer and, getting into the outdoors theme, he waxed on: 'We can use this area for picnics. There could be garden seats here, and perhaps over there,' pointing in various directions.

As they approached the two oak trees, Adam pointed to what he thought was the perfect spot. 'One can relax here and talk over drinks,' and putting an imaginary glass to his lips, he showed them how it was done.

Polly looked very disturbed at her husband's behaviour. Noticing this, he then said something yet more outrageous.

'We could have a grand affair where people from town would have a chance to parade themselves in their finery.' Rushing over to another newly cut piece of lawn, he continued. 'We might have to provide the guests with entertainment – an exclusive band – the latest opera singer – some reputable speakers who would talk on various subjects – audiences seated in sturdy chairs, listening to...' Then Adam changed tack. 'Look at those two tall oak trees!' They looked. 'We could put strong wooden seats around them!' he said.

Then Adam thought over other possibilities for the small croquet lawn and tennis court. Neither of them had been used for some time. In fact, on closer inspection he saw that the net on the tennis court was all bunched up. It was dirty and had collected spiders' webs and other nasty things. The croquet lawn was not up to standard, not the velvet grass that top players would want.

If they bought the property, Adam would have to bring in some experts to improve both settings, buying at least two fresh nets as well as small mallets and iron hoops. He could change these facilities into something worthwhile.

Sharing his ideas, for his mind was full of them, Adam excitedly said, 'On Saturdays, the teams could play both games with pleasurable enthusiasm, as long as it isn't raining. If it is, they could go inside to enjoy chatting over cups of tea, or eating lots of sandwiches or small cream cakes.'

Douglas had been having trouble with his hearing. However, when he heard of this wonderful plan that included those delicacies, he laughed and said, 'I'll reserve my seat, as I always love cups of tea and small cream cakes!'

Accompanied by more chatter about the possibilities, they made their way to the house. They noted that it was a large Edwardian house, designed as a French Chateau, with honeysuckle and wisteria on the front wall. Climbing roses also made their presence known, but were not yet in flower. A variety of daffodils, bluebells and pansies danced demurely in front.

Walking along the slightly elongated and well-built verandah, the visitors came to the open front doors. With encouragement from the agent, they walked through the entranceway into a magnificent open area. They looked up to see glazed windows on both sides of the enormous doors that they had just come through. The interior, with its rich décor, promised greatness and majesty beyond the powers of anticipation!

The agent told them that the downstairs area to the left was completely taken up by five airy office rooms. They looked at these and Adam thought that they could be used for the business of *Legal Affairs*. He could see the Colonel, Miss Sophie Pretty, Polly, himself and the unacquainted Miss Marchant, all sitting behind their desks, taking desperate telephone calls, or seeing friendly clients and doing the tasks that *Legal Affairs* was called upon to do.

The agent next took them through to the three adja-cent rooms, which could house the law workers and the secretary, Adam thought. The agent told them further that the doors on the right hand side led into a substan-tial kitchen with a large pantry behind it. Whispering, he said, 'There is a toilet and washroom tucked away just next to the kitchen. Beyond that is a small wine cellar.'

Returning to the front hall, they saw a magnificent staircase covered in a thick rose-patterned carpet. The staircase also had solid oak handrails.

In a flurry of eagerness, they energetically climbed to the first floor. On either side was a corridor leading to six large bedrooms. Each had a casement window and an individual balcony firmly attached to the wall outside. There was a large lounge, a tucked-away kitchen and a small room for necessities. Adam thought that over the giant fireplace would be a good position to hang the beloved painting, *The Quiet Scene.*

They then climbed up another well-trodden thinly carpeted staircase to view three smaller rooms. The agent told them that some of the staff used to live there long ago. Adam thought that the rooms might be useful for a computer, a sewing room for Polly and a junk room that could be used for anything.

There were other parts of the house that they had not yet seen. The agent told them that on the other side of the lounge was a well-prepared, two-bedroom flat. A lockable door separated them and the flat, which had its own access from outside, and was currently occupied by a night watchman who, through the ongoing absence of owners of the property, was looking after the place. It would be ideal for the Colonel and Sophie, Adam thought.

They went downstairs to a large, magnificent conser-vatory. A short distance away was a big garden shed containing garden tools and a single working mower.

Perhaps he didn't want to say anything to interrupt Adam's enthusiasm for the house, but now the agent commented that the whole house had been strengthened throughout against earthquakes, tornadoes and strong nor'westers.

Polly thanked him and then proceeded to look at the bedrooms again. Noting that they were extremely dusty, she discovered that the tall, dowdy ceilings of great grandeur and difficult creaking doors required much work. She asked the agent, 'Where do we find staff to do all the cleaning?'

He replied, 'I'm glad that you asked. Behind the house stands a two-bedroomed cottage that has been used by a middle-aged husband and wife team. They are on holiday at present. Known as Mr Charlie, who is tall, and Mrs Mable, who is short, or as they prefer to be called, Mr C and Mrs M, they are still happy to do the inside work if the prospective owners require it. Mrs M also knows the previous daily who lives in the village. She used to prepare lovely meals for the last owner, so if wanted Mrs Mulligan would come. (She expects her full title to be used.) The new owners would only have to let her know.'

The next day Adam contacted the Colonel, remarking what a good time they had had exploring the house and property. He reckoned that this was it!

On receiving these words, the Colonel commenced all the financial work. He withdrew the money placed in the Bank of Scotland and finalised negotiations with the current owner, who went away satisfied. The land agent was thrilled that the property had been sold in such a short time, and was well rewarded by the Colonel.

Sophie, too, took a journey from the city to see what the actual buildings were like. She was overjoyed when she was confronted by *Honeysuckle House* in all its glory. She was also introduced to Adam, who was just coming back from the oval lake.

At the Avon Conservative Club, the Colonel met a Methodist lay-preacher, Alfred P Stroud. A recently retired accountant and an ardent croquet player, he was a narrow man with narrow forehead, narrow eyebrows, narrow nose, chin, and his whole body narrow down to his pin-legs. After a time, the Colonel asked him to be an auditor of *Legal Affairs*. He jumped at the chance.

After explaining that *Honeysuckle House* had already

been purchased outright by the Colonel, he was told that, if he wished to, he could be a director. Agreeing to that position, the first time they had a board meeting, the rest of the company directors – the Colonel and Sophie Ivanov, Miss Marchant, Adam and Polly – gave Alfred P Stroud a hearty welcome.

Apart from attending those monthly meetings, Alfred P Stroud drove out from the city once a month on Tuesday afternoons to meet with the Colonel. Over drinks – he liked iced tea – they worked together through any problems and rejoiced at the success of the expanding business.

Polly was also glad that the estate agent had informed her of the inestimable Mrs Mulligan. She was short and dumpy and a very cheerful woman. Polly found out later that when she spoke, a sharp clacking noise issued from her dentures to accompany her crisp words. Still, she thought, if the agent's description is true, then we won't have much to worry about – except for her teeth; they might fall into something that she was making!

After their first meal, Adam's positive reaction to Mrs Mulligan meant that she became known as the best cook in the whole of Christchurch! He had tasted the enormous glazed chicken plus ornate trimmings, followed by a rich chocolate cake with thick icing in between and chocolate niceties on top – it was terrific. *The Mistress of Eating* – that is what Adam called her.

Although it was January, they dressed according to the variable climate, spring one day, summer the next, and cold winds or intermittent rain for the rest of the time. It wasn't until proper summer came in February that trousers were changed for shorts, open-necked tops took the place of jerseys, and practical sandals replaced shoes.

Working with the Colonel's steady supervision, Thomas and James used strong scaffolding to paint the lower half of the house off-white. Sam and Jack moved the scaffold along while Thomas and James opened the fresh tins to swirl the paint with large spatulas. Professional painters were brought in to deal with the places nobody else could reach.

Douglas helped Adam by holding the tall ladder as he put up all the art works inside. This included the painting of *The Quiet Scene* that they put in the lounge, just above the mantelpiece.

Iris helped Polly with choosing and then putting up the new curtains. Sophie concentrated on the furniture bought from the city's fashionable retailers. Then she had the job of placing new cushions, choosing what style would go with each different room's décor.

The husband and wife team, the exuberant Mr C and Mrs M, were happy to be re-employed when they came back from overseas. One of their first tasks was working on the pale green 'inner sanctum' – as they called the conservatory – using soft cleaners and stiff brushes to clean awkward places.

Alfred P Stroud performed the necessary miracles to the croquet lawn. The gardener, Francis Delgado – the man who was cutting lawns when Adam first saw him – worked on the tennis court.

Mrs Mulligan provided them all with a continuous flow of delicious food, giving them enough energy to complete their work. It was gratefully received.

Eventually the extensive property was made shipshape. Adam, Polly and their family moved into their own part of the house. The Colonel and Sophie settled in a few weeks later, moving into the two-bedroomed flat.

The ragged tennis court and sparse croquet green became first class venues for exciting and exacting sports. Competing visitors began coming from far and wide. When it rained, they enjoyed playing table tennis or indoor bowls inside the conservatory.

Adam commenced a monthly venue where reputable speakers talked on a variety of different subjects. Occasionally, select musicians played charming melodies and small choirs entertained appreciative audiences.

Mrs Mulligan warbled her Gilbert and Sullivan ditties as she cooked her favourite dishes in the kitchen. A difficult task, particularly when she had her dentures somewhat awry! Thankfully, she usually took them out when she sang along with the distant voices of the sopranos and tenors.

In the conservatory, Adam also arranged an occasional conference and classic films. On these occasions extra staff were employed to assist the exuberant Mr C and Mrs M.

Extra transport was arranged by a close friend of the Colonel, Gentleman Steve (Hamilton). He had been in prison for a short time but, due to the Colonel's forceful argument, he had been released without charge. He was very grateful to become the Colonel's 'man' instead.

Thomas and James, maybe Sam, and possibly Jack, loved the oak trees. They brought home their young girl-friends and would sit on the ground in the shade and talk about all manner of things.

Adam kept an eye on them, occasionally walking by to check on the boys. They had been given strict boundaries which, if crossed, would reap serious consequences. Better for the adults to keep an eye at a distance and allow the young some freedom.

The growing surrounding suburb was made up of older farming properties, now interspersed with the latest large modern houses, wide streets and lovely parks.

Down the road, at the tar-sealed village end, was, at that stage, a friendly inter-denominational church whose people worshipped God and provided acts of kindness and friendship.

A few weeks later Polly was persuaded to play the organ on alternate weeks with another organist. The music they made encouraged the joyful singing of the congregation, to the delight of all.

They became part of the wider Christian family that nurtured them in faith and supported them in their struggles.

Chapter 44

STILL AN EXPERT on worldwide legal matters, Adam was working on the ground rules for outlining *Reconciliation between Prisoners on Parole and Victims of Crime*. He realised that he needed to have a competent secretary to work alongside him – one who would have the nous to ask questions and suggest changes to the far away court case. Adam thought of the efficient secretary Miss Marchant, but she was involved in collecting all the needed material for the Colonel and Sophie, who were having such a difficult court case in the city.

However, when they met in his office for an evening chat, the Colonel offered to Adam, 'I think I've got the answer to your problem – a secretary. She is not so efficient as you were expecting. In fact, she has just come out of secretarial college, but she is exceptionally bright and would quickly learn all the requirements regarding legal matters. Her name is Alison Green, and I think that she is nineteen years of age.'

So, with the Colonel's endorsement, Adam arranged to see Alison.

Arriving early, Alison went into the gardens and sat down on the seat under one of the oak trees. Adam had seen her, so he left his office and wandered across the lawn.

Giving a little cough, he said, 'My name is Adam Fraser of *Legal Affairs*. Isn't this a wonderful garden? Would you like to have your interview here?' And he sat down beside her.

Alison was surprised. The secretarial college didn't have any rules about outside interviews! Taking a breath, she soon began to relate some of her story. Her demure conversational words were relevant to the occasion. She finished with, 'I have found that God delights in me much more than I can ever know. That means I am confident that if I get the job here, and I hope I will, I will give it plenty of care and attention. You see, I want to do things in God's way, as well as mine.'

Naturally, Alison got the work!

Adam was all enthused. *Legal Affairs* was going places. Yet over time, and in spite of Alison's ready help, the effects of this exacting work left him feeling surprisingly despondent, both in spirit and in body.

It got to the stage where Polly always greeted him with a smile, saying, 'Let's go into our dining room and have something good to eat,' or 'Mrs Mulligan has baked roast beef for us.' – Or it was lovely lamb, or braised chicken or something equally wonderful.

She expected smiles and perhaps hugs, but Adam was giving large sighs and weary words. 'I don't want anything, just a glass of red wine will be sufficient.' And, taking his wine, he went down into his office, where he would read crucial legal literature far into the night.

Polly never received cuddles when at last he came to bed; he just turned over, exhausted, trying for sleep.

After months of this, Polly poured out her troubles to the Colonel and, one blustery autumn day, he marched into Adam's office to have what he called *an intense talk*. Staring directly into Adam's face with his penetrating eyes, he asked him some pertinent questions about his health. Having a reputation for being a man who took no nonsense, he was quite short with his friend.

'You have been over-stressed for months,' he rattled. 'The legal work that is supposed to be for the other staff members, you insist on doing yourself! I hear that you have just about taken over some of the church respon-sibilities, too. I imagine it's only the minister and the organist whose jobs you haven't stolen!'

Adam admitted to himself that going to the village church didn't do anything to relieve the pressure. Rather than being uplifted by the worship and various church social activities, he felt removed from all spiritual reality. He felt that it was all becoming a waste of time.

The Colonel rattled on: 'No wonder you are stressed!' Bending down he briskly demanded, 'What are you going to do about it?'

Adam was put on the spot. He hadn't thought about his health. The Colonel called it stress. What if other people had noticed and were wondering about his health?

Adam slowly said to the Colonel, 'Yes, I *am* going through a period of melancholy. There *are* times when I want to drive away by myself, somewhere where no one knows me. Then I think about Polly, of my sons, my work, even about the church, and realise that the consequences are too large. My reasoning then suddenly snaps back into place and I carry on as normal – as you can see.' He gave a weak but honest smile to his answer.

The Colonel listened carefully, but he wasn't convinced. He waited a moment, then strode to the office door and opened it, saying, 'Come with me into the conservatory and tell me what you see.'

At this time of the year, particularly in the morning, the conservatory was a chilly place. The sun didn't make its full appearance until shortly before midday, and when it did it would only reflect weak rays for a short time before disappearing behind the trees. In the dark surroundings the Colonel said again, 'Tell me what you see,' directing Adam's attention outside.

'I can see places of great beauty. I can see the gurgling stream going down into the lake. I can see the green foliage surrounding it.'

'Look further.'

Adam raised his eyes. 'I see the varying colours of the hills.'

'Further still.'

'In the distance I can see snow-capped mountains.'

'Now take what you have just seen and project it forward, say to the midst of deep winter. What can you see then?'

Adam thought for a moment before finally saying, 'Early in the morning, or just before the sun has set, those places would become stark, where cold air is trapped, where ice crackles underfoot and the whispering trees are standing bare of leaves in strange and frightening forms.'

The Colonel gave a gentle half-smile. 'Yes! Apart from your wonderful poetry, the place of beauty becomes now a shadowland, what I call the *Glen of Gloom.*' Then he forcefully added, 'That is what you've got.'

He placed his hand firmly on Adam's right shoulder as they made their way back to the warm offices. He then said, 'Anyone who has suffered from stress but doesn't take adequate breaks becomes too brittle and extremely fragile. You are working too long and too hard and are becoming brittle and fragile!'

The Colonel went on: 'Sophie and I have a small cottage near the mountains which you can use anytime. Take yourself there when you're feeling down. Take Polly too, if you like. The cottage is looked after by someone next door. Oh, that next door is some distance away, so no worries about any disturbing noise. Apart from collecting and returning the key, you won't know that they are there.'

Adam thought he would like to go to the Colonel's cottage, but only when he was feeling a bit less despondent.

Chapter 45

SOPHIE WAS EXPECTING her first child. When the Colonel heard that she was pregnant he sent her home to take plenty of rest. He was determined she wasn't going to suffer stress, as Adam was. There, the distance that she had to walk was minimal, just up the outside staircase to enjoy the flat's tranquil surroundings.

However, what did she do when she got there? Twiddle her thumbs? Sophie had a short, sharp argument with her husband that she would stay there only as long as he provided her with some legal work to do. 'Remember,' she argued forcefully, 'the whole concept of *Legal Affairs,* or rather, the original *Legality Incorporated,* was mine!'

Of course, Sophie was right. The Colonel started bringing legal work upstairs. Gratefully, she arranged files that had been standing forlorn and unsorted for some time. She approved air-miles chits for staff flying to various cities in Australia or Pacific regions; even cast her eyes over some women's legal problems. However, her fulltime work was taking care of her pregnancy. Because of her age – forty – the family doctor was very cautious.

Through the doors that separated their respective lounges, midwife Polly kept a close watch on Sophie's pregnancy. She also heard some of Sophie's past history.

'Living up to my maiden name, Pretty, my life was a happy one. My parents lived quite well in a village north of London, called Chipping Ongar. Father was a tall man with receding hair, a small moustache and kind eyes, and,' she laughed, 'he also had an enormous Adam's Apple.

When I was a young girl and he spoke, I used to watch it move up and down, wondering how he got on at work with such a fascinating appendage! He was a professor lecturing in the London School of Economics. I used to imagine that the students would be amazed at the size of his Adam's Apple as they watched it going up and down, like a lift on rocket fuel!

'My mother was a small woman, rather mousy but with a cheerful outlook. She stayed at home to look after everything. Every week she cleaned through the two-bedroomed two-storey house making it spotless. She wore a fashionable ensemble with a bright polka dot scarf around her head. If there was any piece of what she called "steady furniture" she cleaned around it furiously but left the rest as it was. So, you would get half the house done to perfection and the other half, not!'

They both giggled, and then Sophie continued.

'After finishing at the local school, I commenced law studies at the university. This would enable me to become a solicitor. Later, when working at Epping's solicitors *Mudge and Andrews*, I continued to further my legal education to become a barrister. I also met the man of my dreams at church, Colonel Henry Ivanov.'

She gave a long sigh as she remembered those days of outstanding significance. 'Later, we were married and my parents came to the wedding. They were thrilled. After all this time – I was in my thirties and still living at home – I had actually found someone I loved enough to marry! Not like many young people who just live together.'

On other occasions, when nurse Polly was checking Sophie's blood pressure and taking regard to the position of the baby in utero, she thought that this woman had great personality. Apart from being a successful barrister, Sophie also had a multitude of other strings to her bow. Classical music came to Polly's mind. When the windows were open, anyone might hear the piano being played. In the evening, Sophie's husband often listened willingly to her romantic playing.

Sophie also wrote a column for a young children's newspaper, about fanciful things taken from her own experiences at *Honeysuckle House*. Stories of snails and creepy-crawlies under the earth, dogs chasing birds, and cats sleeping in the sun, butterflies flying from one petalled perfumed flower to another, swans swimming sedately in the gentle lake, swooping birds passing by, and two massive oak trees full of acorn nuts surrounded by flowering shrubs. These were a few of the many glimpses from Auntie Sophie.

She also wrote for a legal journal that had, on the back page, a short scriptural column called 'QUESTIONS?' Her job was to provide an answer to them. One questioner queried:

> *I heard recently of a conversation between a Christian woman and her unbelieving colleague who asked whether there were many others like her who had the same system of belief?*

Sophie's reply was:

> *The line between distinctive Christianity and the modern mishmash of religions has been lost. Our belief is in Jesus Christ, not in doing to others the same as we would have them do to us, but as the Saviour would do. He sets people free from the shackles of a noun to share the adventures of a verb.*

Then Adam's secretary Alison's life was suddenly altered. Her parents were killed in Australia, having fallen over a dangerous cliff edge while they were trekking through the Blue Mountains National Park. Her close high school friend, Rebekah More, invited her to stay at her friendly home near to *Honeysuckle House*. There she would be looked after in her grief.

From the time of leaving school, the young women looked very similar – same height of five feet three inches, neatly cut brown hair, startling blue eyes and smiling mouths. They wore loose tops, comfortable dresses or sometimes, in winter months, warm slacks. Their dresses were often light blue, pale brown or sometimes poppy-red, or all three in a colourful confusion. Flat unadorned shoes elegantly encompassed their feet.

Orphaned as a baby, Rebekah had grown up in an Anglican Home. She married at an early age to her army boyfriend, Hugh. They brought forth a daughter, Penny, now six years old. Unfortunately, Hugh was often away on overseas army duty, so Rebekah and Penny kept very close company.

Born with Down Syndrome, Penny was a precious and slightly pernickety child. She had a button nose, wore glasses, and had a speaking impediment. When Alison was despondent, Penny helped her to cope, in a remarkably adult way. She would put her arms around her mother tightly, asking, 'Would you like my fresh hanky?'

Sometimes she burst into singing simple songs that she had learned from the children's TV programmes. It made such a difference to Alison to see Penny act in such a happy, friendly, sometimes hilarious manner. Within a few minutes, broad smiles and noisy laughter would break out, not only from Penny but her mother as well.

One day, in the cold of winter, when Alison prepared to take a walk, Penny mumbled to her, 'Push out the old air and breathe in to bursting point. Then all this sparkly frosty air will come into your body!'

Penny always made sure that before Alison went out, she was wearing her warm voluminous coat, her hat with a strap under the chin, thick gloves and fur boots. She explained in her serious voice, 'The weather is alright now, but it may be different when you come back.'

Hugh was due home for one of his leaves when he was killed with other soldiers by an explosive device while out on patrol. The New Zealand Army Officer weaved his way back and forth around the front room furniture as he told Rebekah the sad news. 'Many deaths! Numerous tragedies! Sad outcome!' he pompously said.

After a long period of waiting, Rebekah received her husband's body in the provided coffin. The heartbreak continued during the funeral at the nearby *Honeysuckle*

Cemetery. Many attended; Penny and Alison stood one on each side and comforted sorrowful Rebekah.

After the funeral, Rebekah told Alison that her dead husband had bought their property and willed it to her. 'If anything should go wrong, the family will have a home,' he had said. It also meant that she would now hear *new sweet sounds*, after some healing from her grief. That is why she named the place *SweetSounds*.

Rebekah and Alison now forged a firm, everlasting friendship, greater than they had known when they were at school. They looked after each other in a kindly way. They shared words of support and encouragement. Although sometimes they didn't see eye to eye, they were very thankful to have young Penny by their side to keep them in order!

Alison now found that her daily work at *Legal Affairs* was a godsend. It meant walking a short distance across the road, which allowed her to collect her thoughts. Climbing the outside stairs first, she visited pregnant Sophie, who always gave her a hug. Sophie's laughter cheered her up. Alison certainly appreciated her playing on the piano, or listening to her reading the latest from her pen. Whatever form they took, there were many helpful factors, so that Alison was now able to focus on her secretarial work.

Having relinquished her *Legal Affairs* position as a full-time director, Polly opened a Christian bookshop on site. She was a missionary, yes; a competent nurse, yes; an adroit midwife, yes; an adept mother of four sons, yes; now a knowledgeable part-time director, yes; so why couldn't she be a bookseller like her husband, Adam? After all, she thought to herself, when we were first married, the times that I spent in the Port Moresby bookshop serving customers when I was pregnant means that I have the qualities to manage this small bookshop.

Looking at *Honeysuckle House* from the front, this bookshop was adjacent to the right side of the conservatory. However, this was a rather untidy room, so Polly set to and had a good clear out and clean up – a dirty and dusty job. The tatty curtains around the large windows were replaced with brightly coloured new ones. The shelves were lacquered with clear varnish which, when dried, provided a good place to arrange some of the latest attractive Christian books. The circular glass display cabinet in the centre of the room provided an excellent place for a display of greeting cards. She placed a notice at the outside entrance:

BOOKSHOP. THIS WAY. WELCOME.

Polly sometimes visited various church groups and, after giving one of her short talks to the People of St. Whatever, she offered her Christian books, children's material, a few Bibles, and loads of greeting cards, all with a warm, encouraging smile!

Chapter 46

THOMAS WAS LEAVING home to pursue more exciting things. At twenty-two, he had been halfway through his third year of an art course. One of the female lecturers, who was in her thirties, had a very beautiful oval face and long curly golden locks. Thomas rather liked her, so looked in any available mirror to detect any imperfections in his appearance.

However, the amount of time he spent considering what action he would take, if any, affected his concentration. He certainly missed out on the generous marks that he had expected. Completing the course by the narrowest of margins, he found work with a well-established printing company, and continued his training to become a fully-fledged printer.

Thomas thus met Jo, who was working as a secretary for the same printers. Her name was short for Joanna, but nobody called her that. Her father's name was a simple Joe and her mother's name was Jo, short for Josephine. The question was, what name did they use when they were all together?

Jo dressed smartly in the latest fashionable clothing. Thomas discarded his starry-eyed infatuation for the beautiful lecturer, as his passion was now stirred for another. He fell deeply in love with Jo. After many smooching kisses, Jo murmured in his ear that she enjoyed being his starry-eyed girl. Thomas was delighted, and they began life madly in love, but not yet married, at least not at this stage.

Unfortunately, the chemicals used in the printing trade began to affect Thomas' health, and he had to give up work a few months later. Though they had minimal funds, he and Jo decided to go on an extensive trip to Britain and then wander around Europe, just stopping to get work when necessary. While they were in London, they met up with his twin brother, James.

James had been working as an English teacher in Christchurch. He had left this position, opting instead for a year-long mission training course in outer London. Even though his parents had been through the same missionary adventures some years before, in Papua New Guinea, they were a bit unsure of his decision.

James had told them about the official letter accepting him, saying that there were twelve Christian students aged from twenty to thirty years, coming from various countries, all getting to know the ins-and-outs of mission life.

On arriving in London, he was taken to a mission house in Stepney Green, from where James sent them a London postcard. He explained to them his first impressions of the other students. 'Everyone can understand English,' he wrote, 'but our colour, culture and social backgrounds are completely different!'

Today, James, Thomas and Jo were adventuring together on a long free day available to them. Clambering up to the top of a double-decker tourist bus, they viewed some of the fantastic sights of London, like Buckingham Palace, the tree-lined Mall, Houses of Parliament, Downing Street, Fleet Street, and St Paul's Cathedral.

They turned their heads leftwards as they realised that the wide, rather bland Kingsway was leading to the office of *Judicial Books* – the place where their father had worked. They didn't attempt going there.

While travelling, they had bought some food to share. Because of the noisy traffic, they had to raise their voices. Thomas remembered their father's wise words and reminded James to 'speak clearly and distinctly!'

James smiled. He shouted how he was getting on with the mission course, following this with, 'Please don't say anything to Mum and Dad about this yet, but I think I'm falling in love with an amazing girl from Queensland who is on the same course!'

Thomas and Jo were impressed. They said 'Congratulations!' and 'Well done!' and 'Let us know how you proceed!', indicating their pleasure. Not having tied the marriage knot themselves, they were still itching to tell their own tales of what they had been up to.

Thomas shouted out, 'We've been living in the old Combi van. Shopping is done locally and we stop at various large towns to do portrait painting...'

Jo intervened, 'Or my secretarial work when we had no cash or people to paint...'

Then Thomas broke in, 'We explored most of England, a few bits of Wales and the whole of Cornwall!'

And Jo added, 'Now we're going to France to adventure there!'

At the end of the exhausting but pleasurable day, James returned to his missionary studies thankful that not only did he enjoy his work, but he would continue to increase his affections towards the young Australian lady. It wasn't long before this lady was returning his affections.

Thomas and Jo returned to collect the Combi van and, on boarding the ferry, they set sail for France.

Back at *Honeysuckle House*, Polly and Adam were somewhat disappointed. Not because Thomas and Jo were taking the trip of a lifetime through Britain and France, and certainly not because James was interested in the year-long mission course in London – no, they were upset because they had all disappeared within a few weeks of each other!

Then Sam decided to leave home as well; however, flatting with Christchurch friends in a suburb that was not too far away meant that he could come for meals, or even for some cash from his parents when needed.

Finding employment at Wardell's Food Emporium, Sam learned that he was to cook the hams early in the morning for the Christmas rush. After eating his porridge at the flat, and after extending his greetings to his fellow-workers, Sam went down into the basement to find, in the large fridge, unadorned hams that hung on massive hooks. He had to clean out inches of fat from the cooking vats that had accrued from the previous day's cooking. This work called for a healthy stomach, not one that was filled with gurgling porridge!

Sam told himself that after Christmas he would gladly find some other employment.

Near the end of Christchurch's long Colombo Street stood a long, narrow, dowdy footwear shop. After an interview, the elderly manager said that Sam could now be employed as a junior salesman. This meant that he presented the latest fashionable shoe styles to interested customers, while extolling their virtues and hoping for sales. On accomplishing this, he was also supposed to remember to suggest that they might like to purchase a second pair of shoes at half-price. If they did, then extra shoelaces were provided and a special shoe cleaner from a well-known manufacturer was recommended. Presented in a plastic container, a shoe-duster was also offered at a small price.

To complete the cunning, calculated, but friendly work of Sam, he always had to give a gracious smile. He worked there for ages, so was obviously pleasing to the customers and his boss!

Sam's interest was really in cars. He partly indulged this with the old vehicles that he had bought – a disreputable Austin 7, followed by a large oil-guzzling Holden, and then a snazzy blue Triumph Herald. However one day, while travelling on a difficult, narrow, twisting, dusty mountain road, another car smashed into the Triumph, causing extensive damage. Sam wasn't hurt, but for the remainder of the year he saved up his money, then bought an open-top large American sports car as a reward!

Later, having reached the slightly more mature age of twenty, Sam realised that the direction in which he was travelling was achieving nothing. Applying for, and getting, an apprenticeship at a reputable garage, over time he gained his mechanic's certificate. There he learned a lot about sensible cars, but he enjoyed filling the vacant seat with lovely girls beside him.

What about eighteen-year old Jack? He and a friend went for a countryside drive, but wrapped the car around a tree. Jack was slightly injured, but because his friend hadn't been wearing a seatbelt, he was killed. Jack withdrew into himself and was unable to talk to his parents or close *Honeysuckle House* friends about how he was feeling.

One day Jack quietly said to his father that he was feeling so miserable that if he didn't do anything soon, then he didn't know how he could continue to cope with life. Father and son started searching for an indoor archery facility that wasn't too large, but big enough to give the competitors some freedom.

On the outskirts of the city was a large steel building used for such activities, with four clear targets on which to practice. Jack was soon coping better with all his frustrations as his straight, graceful arrows shot towards the distant target. The moment they struck the centre mark, he discovered that some of his anger would be dissipated.

The archery instructor was a professor from the university's accounting department. He became a friend to Jack, introducing him to business computers.

Jack cleaned out one of the upper rooms at *Honeysuckle House*, making it into his office. He became a regular worker for the university professor and for clients of the Polytechnic. In this way Jack spread his horizons while maintaining his interest in archery.

Chapter 47

ALTHOUGH ADAM SHOULD have known this, it wasn't in his mind that the mowing of lawns, done by the Spanish man Francis Delgado, was only temporary.

'All his work is excellent,' the Colonel explained when they were discussing the property, 'but Francis' hours are not long enough to take care of the whole area, like the grass around the lake. Perhaps you can offer him full-time work?'

The next day Adam put the offer to Francis. His eyes lit up and he replied 'Yes!' almost without thinking. He told Adam what he would like to do with the whole property now that he was to be fully employed. Francis said, 'I have in mind that these gardens will be similar to my home in Southern Spain,' and he started telling Adam about his earlier life.

'My Catholic mother is very tall. A giant, many people call her. She comes from Paris. She speaks not only French but a smattering of Portuguese. My Jewish father is a Moroccan dwarf speaking Arabic and Spanish. Therefore, they have four languages between them. It was decided that I ought to learn another universal tongue, so I learned to speak English.

'In my teens, I was under the care of a dwarf called Old Tom. Old Tom not only taught me my exacting English grammar but also taught me how to look after beautiful flowers, trim hedges, care for vegetables, and sit on the ride-on mower to cut shapely lawns, like these ones!'

Adam stretched his legs as he rested on one of the

circular seats, underneath the old oak trees. Francis went on, with the passion of his native land:

'I was nineteen and had planned a trip around the world for some time. My parents were in tears when I told them about my venture. I said that I would be back some time and told them to never fear, for I was going on an exciting adventure. With reluctance, they let me go. The last time I saw them they were sitting on cushioned seats overlooking the ever-sparkling Mediterranean Sea, remembering, I hoped, all their faith experiences with me. I don't have much time for Catholic holy rigmarole, or the Jewish religion with all its extenuating laws, but I have a faith which is open, so I have some of those same values. Do you get what I mean?'

Adam didn't, but thinking to himself, *He's still a young man. When he comes against some sort of opposition, where will he be then?* 'Carry on,' was all that he could say.

'I went to Athens, where I stayed for two months working at the wonderful summer flower exhibition. Next, I went to Delhi, and found employment taking care of the extensive lawns and gardens of wealthy Indians. Three months later, in Malaysia, I restored the gardens of a sanctuary high up in the mountains near George Town. It was a challenge. Dead and dying bushes had to be cleared, revealing old paths that required serious maintenance. Trees that had fallen over during storms had to be disposed of. I even had to clean the eaves of the buildings, removing spiders and other nasty things. The house was all shut up and there was only one old man who looked after the place. Even the sign on the front gate was covered in years of muck, but as I cleaned its surface, I could read the words, *Grace Chateau.*'

Francis stopped. He noted a change in Adam's demeanour and asked him anxiously, 'What is the matter?'

Adam was staggered at what he had just heard. He spluttered out, 'You just said, *Grace Chateau?*'

Francis said 'Yes,' but had heard nothing to give him a clue as to what Adam was talking about.

Adam said, '*Grace Chateau* is the same place where

the young Colonel lived with his parents, in Malaysia. Yes! The same man who is now at *Honeysuckle House!'*

Francis was amazed. Giving a big smile, he said, 'Well, if I can do a similar work on this property, it could very well be Christchurch's *Grace Chateau!'*

They were both silent for a moment and then Adam asked, 'I don't suppose you know what happened after the Colonel had departed for Britain? How did the place get into this terrible condition?'

'The only way I got to hear about the property was through a worldwide land speculator,' explained Francis. 'He had a lot of old properties in various parts of the world, and he asked me if I wanted the chance to work in the Malaysian mountains. When I said yes, he gave me instructions of how I was to contact the local caretaker – the old man that I just mentioned. I found that it was a long project. While I was there, a very wealthy Malaysian prince arrived, whose intention was to convert it into a hotel for wealthy clients.'

Adam made a mental note to inform the Colonel that Francis had been working at his old home and, that same evening, the Colonel was indeed thrilled to hear the news. He decided that they should later take some time to discuss it, but at present he was more excited about Sophie and his forthcoming child's imminent birth.

Chapter 48

OPHIE HAD BEEN feeling contractions throughout the day and, as evening fell, they became stronger. The Colonel fetched the car and rushed her to the small private hospital nearby. While she was getting awkwardly into the passenger seat, he told her that he had everything under control. Really, he didn't! However, Sophie had her wits about her and as they were driving at an excessively dangerous speed, she told him to slow down immediately! She didn't want the police chasing them on these suburban roads, so he took his foot off the accelerator and they arrived at the hospital safely.

Sophie gave birth during the night. Exhausted but happy, she and the much-relieved Colonel, using a hanky to wipe his brow, named the child Peter Hough Ivanov.

Early the next morning, at the corner shop, the Colonel bought bunches and bunches of beautiful flowers, and an enormous box of chocolates, knowing that his dear wife would thoroughly enjoy them. The rest of the customers, calling in for their morning paper, congratulated him on becoming a father. He was so proud that he nearly forgot his purchases!

Gifts from the rest of the *Legal Affairs* team would be brought later so that they, too, could celebrate the new baby.

Sophie was surprised that the birth of their son had gone so smoothly. Apart from the normal labour pains, she thought that childbearing in her mature years would be difficult. She had not told the doctor about her occasional chest pains, making excuses to herself that they were only small ones, occurring only occasionally. However, the canny doctor knew of her condition and of Sophie's stubbornness. He was keeping a close eye on her during the baby's journey, which went quite smoothly.

Sophie was delighted with her wonderful, amazing son, Peter. From the start mother and son got on well. What expressions of love as they looked intently at each other, especially when she freed him from his smelly garments, delicately bathed and put fresh clothes on him!

When Peter became more adventurous, valuable items of expensive pottery found another, safer place. What joy came to his parents as Peter pulled himself up onto his feet and toddled between them, concentrating on walking without any help. With lots of *oohing and aahing,* they looked in wonder at the amazing achievements of their son.

Young Peter and Sophie were soon at the simple speaking stage. They discussed the pretty flowers as they meandered up to the front gate to collect the post. They had a sense of triumph at their journey's end, for both were given a reward – small ice-creams, made proudly by Mrs Mulligan, awaited their appearance in the kitchen. While waiting she often sang songs from her repertoire of *Gilbert and Sullivan,* but was silent when Sophie, the piano maestro, was there with her son.

As Peter became a little older, they examined insects together in the mulched garden beds. Sophie pointed out the different types of small bushes and trees, giving the Latin names to each one as well. Sometimes they went outside in the spring or autumn rain. In his enormous coat and winter hat, Peter really enjoyed the sound of his welly-boots *sssslurping* in and out of the sloppy puddles.

Marvellous small animals and insects sometimes popped out to see what was going on. They observed him as much as he observed them. Peter gingerly lifted a hedgehog up to his face, checking out the little ball of quivering tips, inquisitive nose and eyes that peered keenly at him. The hedgehog had been searching for a nesting place for her soon-to-be-born babies, and he was rudely impeding her efforts. Sophie would have much more material to submit to the newspaper now that young investigative Peter was around!

As Peter grew up he listened intently to his mother playing the piano. He would look adoringly at his father and say to himself that he was famous.

Approaching his fifth birthday, Peter showed signs of being good at everything (claimed his parents!). He had good manners. He spoke well. He had few friends of his own age, although there was kind Penny More, but she was slightly older and had some strange ailment. The few adults he occasionally met were from the staff at *Legal Affairs.* They were always friendly to him and didn't speak down to him, as grown-up people often do to children.

Peter was also good friends with Jack, who was usually ready to stop his computing work when he climbed up the stairs to knock loudly at his door. Peter would say with a smile, 'Let's play!' – and the two screaming boys would race along the passages, diving into and exiting through open doors and charging into the conservatory when there was no-one there. They never went into the kitchen, for Mrs Mulligan would have been very cross.

Sometimes they went to the *Legal Affairs* offices, but the staff there were too busy and greeted them with annoyed expressions.

Often, Jack would chase Peter through the open front door, where there were some large climbable trees. On numerous occasions Jack seemed to disappear, only to be found hiding behind some hardy fence or wall or bush or hedge, jumping out to frighten Peter with an enormous shout. They would be lost in laughter!

However, Jack had a cunning side, too. The trees on the property had many noisy cicadas that sang with gusto. Jack said to the now-six-year old Peter, 'Their singing is a bit different to clacking Mrs Mulligan's, isn't it? You know how they make those sounds? With tiny violins, that's how!'

'Really?' Peter wondered.

Jack said, 'Their sound is a kind of song, a mating call.'

Jack also enjoyed collecting the dead cicada skins that were shed to accommodate the growth of new skin. He had overheard the Colonel telling a group of clients who were leaving that there was only one thing that frightened him – cicada shells. 'They are horrible!' he had said.

Collecting those same shells, Jack passed them on to Peter, suggesting that he might put them in some place where his father would be surprised at the sight of their delicate membranes, say, on the lounge table. This was the place where the Colonel enjoyed a glass of wine most nights. However, he was not amused when he saw these ghastly dead cicada shells. In fact, he was so scared by them that he quickly summoned Peter and sternly told him off. He didn't enjoy his normally delightful drink that night!

The next year Peter was slightly taller and a little more grown up. He was nearly seven now. His birthday would be the following week. He was keen enough to collect a pile of dead cicada shells by himself, saying under his breath that there was no need for Jack's sneaky instructions. 'I will play this trick on my father again,' he decided.

Sneaking into the Colonel's office, he put his evil contribution under a pile of letters that needed signing.

Again, the Colonel was not amused! He asked Miss Marchant, who was in his office at the time of discovery, if she minded getting rid of them. Smiling, she enquired, 'You mean *these* cicada shells?' – shoving them under his face.

He backed away, and with a nervous grin the poor man replied, 'Yes! I mean those cicada shells!'

Laughing, Miss Marchant went outside to dispose of them in the garden rubbish.

Peter was listening, as he usually did, to the radio, and heard that the weather forecast was for rain later. Looking out of the window, he saw many dark clouds gathering. He told himself that the opportunity for outside celebrations for his seventh birthday was virtually nil. He presumed that they would now have his party in the conservatory. It was on a Friday, which meant it was a school day.

All the legal staff, including his parents, would be

working in their offices early on their important tasks. Peter slowly ate his porridge and wondered what presents his parents had for him. Maybe a pleasing book to go with the others that were taking up space in his bedroom?

Two schoolboys from his class, who shared his interest in space comics, would be coming. Peter hoped they might bring him the newest comics.

Usually Uncle Adam and Auntie Polly presented him with the latest edition of the book, *Facts and More Facts* – maybe they would give him the newest one, again.

Jack was more creative when choosing his gifts. Last year he had given him an outlandish book on Fly Fishing, explaining to Peter that he could do it on the little lake. Jack had forgotten that their lake had no fish to catch, only quacking ducks and regal swans!

Peter went on to Miss Marchant's possible choice. She would buy a gift from the boys' department of the exclusive city shop – like bright coloured socks, or small bow ties. She also would present the gift to him with a ghastly kiss on the lips – horrors!

Alison would probably give him posh writing paper and envelopes. She understood that he would be only seven but, as she told his mother, better start young than not at all.

Alison's friends, Rebekah and young Penny, would also come to his birthday party. Peter guessed that they would ring up his mother and see what he *really* needed. Later Peter would examine the gift and would make up his own mind as to whether he really needed it or not!

Peter's mother, Sophie, had already said to the Colonel that the new parish minister, the Reverend Geoff Silver, might be interested to see *Honeysuckle House*. Wouldn't it be a nice idea to invite him to come to the birthday party? And so an invitation was sent to him, too.

Then the Colonel suggested to Francis that if he was available, he too might like to join in the celebrations.

Francis asked, 'Do I need to change out of my gardening clothes?'

'If you look respectable,' the Colonel commented. 'I don't see any problem. Come a bit later, say about four-thirty. Peter will no doubt be reading from the special book that my wife and I are giving to him. It is a secret so don't say anything to him before the great occasion.'

Peter hoped that Mrs Mulligan would supply white bread-squares spread with Vegemite and hundreds-and-thousands, yummy chocolate lamingtons, and chocolate fish at the party, as well as the lemonade and orange drinks.

He remembered Mrs Mulligan's mock horror when he had suggested to her all these items. 'What?' she had loftily said. 'Vegemite *and* hundreds-and-thousands, all together? Chocolate lamingtons into castles? Yuk!' And she turned up her nose in supposed disgust!

Laughing, Peter had said, 'Yes! Even if I am the only one to eat them!'

Mrs Mulligan had pulled herself up from her chair. It was clear that she had not finished yet. 'What about the chocolate fish? Do I go down to the village shop and buy a quantity?'

He asked sweetly, 'Will that quantity be enough?'

Mrs Mulligan said, 'Get away!' and 'Fancy that!' and 'I don't know what to do with you!'

Peter looked at the clock. It was time for school and time to stop wondering about these exciting things. Picking up his satchel, he went down the outer metal steps two at a time. Dangerous, but he made it!

Chapter 49

ALL MORNING, MRS Mulligan worked on the birthday celebrations. She arranged the tables and chairs. Then she put the square sandwiches of Vegemite sprinkled with hundreds-and-thousands on the table. She made chocolate lamingtons into castles.

She added four dozen chocolate fish from the village shop, placed in a round circle just in front of the lamingtons. To top it all off, she made a large chocolate birthday cake with seven tall candles. This stood in prime position, ready for Peter to blow out.

She provided glasses ready for lemonade and orange squash, while drink containers were waiting on the side. Cups of tea and coffee were also ready for the adults.

Then she blew up multi-coloured balloons and put them up all round the conservatory. After all this, she was an exhausted woman!

Later, when the jollifications were over and seven year old Peter had received presents from everybody, the blown-out candles were removed and, after the chocolate birthday cake was quickly devoured, his parents presented him with what they called a *special book*.

On the left-hand pages, his mother had written the words, and the right-hand pages his father had illustrated with coloured-pencil pictures. Then a skilled craftsman had bound the book, with the title inscribed on the leather cover.

With a fanfare of love, they gave it to Peter, and the Colonel suggested to Peter that he might like to show the book to everyone.

Returning to his seat, Peter took the book and started to read out loud:

THE BIRTHDAY BOY

The Birthday Boy waited at the gate for the postman, whose name was, according to his mother, Postman Pete.

Postman Pete delivered letters most days about mid-morning. A tall man with a kindly nature, Postman Pete wore a light grey uniform with a whistle attached to his jacket. Walking at a steady pace, he delivered the mail to each letterbox, and occasionally blew hard on the whistle. Into one he delivered an important bill; into another, letters from overseas with strange stamps on them; or maybe a love letter or two, with kisses on the envelopes!

The boy had already told Postman Pete that on this great day he was expecting all sorts of gifts at his party, and maybe by post too.

Well, the day had arrived, and the postman was here. Of course, the boy certainly wouldn't expect a special gift from the postman himself, would he?

But the lad received a big surprise! After the mailman had given him several boring-looking letters, and two parcels that felt like a jigsaw (and made rattling sounds) and a book, Postman Pete pulled out a giant colouring book from his bag and gave it to the youngster.

With wide open eyes the boy said rather breathlessly, 'Thank you!'

Clutching his bounty (and the boring letters) to his chest so as not to drop them, he ran back inside the house and shouted out very loudly to his mother, 'I've got a giant colouring book from Postman Pete!'

Some days later, Postman Pete knocked on the door and introduced himself to the boy's mother, who invited him in.

The Birthday Boy was still working on a picture, using coloured pencils, crayons and even paints.

Postman Pete noted that it would take him some time to finish all the pictures! Then he went on his way, whistling, for seeing how the Birthday Boy appreciated the colouring book had made his heart glad.

The End

Peter gave his parents a great big smile, many kisses of thanks and, finally, grinning, remarked to his mother, 'I'm glad that you didn't say anything about me dealing with horrible cicadas!'

Sophie laughed and, shaking her head, looked at the Colonel, but said quietly to Peter, 'No. I wouldn't have dared!'

Chapter 50

I T WAS SUMMERTIME. Christchurch's dry nor'west winds were blowing strongly, driving out all moisture and leaving tired, dry air.

This particular day, Adam was completely drained of energy. Having been in business meetings all day he was very weary, and during the evening rush hour he drove the car home despondently.

Polly took one look at him and hurried him to bed. She said, fluttering around, 'I imagine you are feeling as you are looking. When you are settled, I'll bring you a drink of hot chocolate.'

Whispering to her, 'I love you, Polly,' Adam sank thankfully between the welcome sheets.

However, the next day Adam remained the same, so Polly called the doctor. After examining Adam, he questioned him about his daily programme. Adam told him that in the early hours of the morning, or very late at night when there was nobody around, he stayed in the office doing extra work that required quiet research. He found himself unable to sleep properly, and severe headaches had begun again.

'In fact,' Adam was forced to admit, 'I was doing all this work, but it was keeping me away from normal family life.'

The doctor gave a hollow laugh. 'You have given yourself your own diagnosis!' With knowing eyes, for he had so often heard these same excuses from others, he packed away his stethoscope and put it into his case. 'I'm afraid that you are suffering from burnout and extreme stress.'

He prescribed some pills to help Adam sleep and went on his way.

The next day was special for Adam – he was allowed to spend it in bed! That night, as Polly joined him under the duvet, he said, 'Do you know, I remember what the Colonel said about stress – that when I work too hard something has to give. The Bible speaks of quite a few people who suffered stress in their lives, like King Saul.' As he put the scriptures away on a side table, he told his tired wife, 'Like the king, I've got a soul out of sync.'

Weary herself from a full day, Polly thought Adam wanted to carry on speaking but instead he started drifting off to sleep, muttering, 'I am so wound up – I feel as if I can't breathe...' His voice tailed off into silence, and then he gave a gentle snore, and slept.

Polly however was wide-awake and thinking about all the implications.

Although he did not like to admit it, Adam was indeed carrying inside himself a hidden burden. It was something that he had never felt before. Something that clung to him and would not let go. However, despite the ongoing poor health, he carried on! He managed it well, but it only took a difficult situation to crop up, to bring out again the feelings of extreme stress.

Legal Affairs was going to be very busy. With Alison's valuable help, Adam was ready to present the vital document *Reconciliation between Prisoners on Parole and Victims of Crime* to the rest of the directors. It had taken Adam such a lot of time and energy to get it to this stage.

There were many outside legal opinions on this subject. Some said, 'The prison population is going to be reduced when you have a decent system of parole in place,' but others reacted, 'Who is going to look after these released prisoners?' Some succinctly said, 'Life means life!' and, 'Can you have a system of parole working when there is much anger in the families, or indeed the rest of society, against the prisoner?'

The same arguments were now applying at *Legal Affairs*. The Colonel, Sophie, Miss Marchant, Alfred P Stroud, even Polly thought differently to Adam. They all wanted to achieve what was good and proper, yes, but they seemed to be saying there was very little that appeared feasible at this stage. As Adam's jaw dropped, the Colonel felt they should try again for a just and equitable solution. He nearly gave Adam a hug, but didn't. Instead, he gave him a friendly, lasting smile.

Clutching at straws, Adam had the bright idea of bringing two other eminent retired lawyers into the discussions. All they did was to sit quietly until the lively discussion was nearly ended, and then they only offered some minute points of legal twaddle – no, sorry, legal jurisprudence!

It didn't do much for Adam – in fact, he was extremely angry. Didn't these people realise that they were actually discussing things that were of the utmost importance – the judicial system versus human morality?

Adam's sleep problems and fatigue returned to the fore and it left him frustrated and fearful. Between two and four o'clock in the morning, the smallest issue grew into almost overwhelming proportions of distress and outstanding confusion. Of course, he told no one that he felt as if he was falling into a deepening void.

Instead, a few days later he phoned Dr Wilke, a psychologist friend, to make an appointment. The doctor would help him to unravel himself and would put in place whatever treatment was necessary to allow him to continue his work at *Legal Affairs*.

Chapter 51

ONCE ADAM STARTED telling Dr Wilke about his inner frustrations and feelings of fear and anger, the situation quickly disentangled itself. He said that although he often read numerous solid books each month, this had diminished to virtually no recreational reading at all. He told him of his increase in weight. He remembered (luckily!) the short-term memory loss. Suicidal thoughts also sometimes occurred, and he explained that he only had short sleeps and occasional palpitations. Rest was neither satisfying nor replenishing. Intermittent stomach and chest pains, dizziness, headaches, and a pervasive unhappiness, were filling his life... It all came tumbling out.

After hearing the sad litany, Dr Wilke said gently but firmly, 'You have clinical depression. I will refer you to Dr Robinson, an eminent psychiatrist.'

A few days later, after reading the full notes that Dr Wilke had sent him, Dr Robinson told Adam, 'You have to stop work immediately.'

Adam was shocked! How could he give up the necessary tasks at *Legal Affairs?* How would *Reconciliation between Prisoners on Parole and Victims of Crime* be satisfied if he wasn't around? He realised that the ramifications of continuing work while he was unable to function properly would not help the judicial system at all and, if he didn't stop work, he would soon become a cot-case.

Dr Robinson responded readily to Adam's questions, stressing that this judgement was made because of the severity of his condition.

Adam's illness was brought home more significantly when, the following day, a gracious lady from the local church who had a small legal problem came to see him.

Meeting in the quiet, tranquil conservatory in the middle of the afternoon, they sat together in the gentle sunlight. Adam became anxious as he realised that he couldn't remember her name, even though she had been his friend for some time. When she spoke, he was unable to give a relevant answer. On looking into his eyes, she found that they were blank and unresponsive. She recognised that something was seriously wrong, but did not realise the full nature of Adam's condition.

Again, Polly was increasingly frightened. She didn't know what to do. Going to the Colonel, she agitatedly said, 'Dr Wilke and Dr Robinson are doing what is right as far as Adam's mental health is concerned, but I wonder if there isn't something more practical that we can do for him?'

'Leave it with me,' the Colonel kindly said.

He went to see Adam, who was now literally trapped in his office, and suggested that he write down how his clinical depression was affecting him. 'It will not only help you, but will certainly help us to understand how you are feeling,' he said.

Adam thought that it would be a waste of time, but the Colonel still insisted he give it a try. So, reluctantly, Adam got out pen and paper and tentatively began to write:

People don't know how much they annoy me! I am finding it very hard to communicate. I always thought that the word 'depression' meant very little and it only happened to other people. The doctors say that it is caused by a chemical imbalance in the brain, but that is no help to me. Yet it is, in fact, the best expression to be used. Hundreds of thousands of neurons, the brain's nerve cells that conduct the energy, collapse, leaving a deep, black hole in the brain – a depression.

Because the brain has to be rebuilt, the recovery takes a long time. The memory has to be re-established to its rightful order. Lost language skills have to be relearned. The daily tasks need to be reconquered. Fear of everyday things all need to be overcome.

In other words, I can safely say that this ailment is not a nice place to be! As one who had always been busy in life, attacking projects with enthusiastic energy, I am totally overwhelmed by this force that has depleted not only my strength, but my 'self' as well.

Adam found that he was totally exhausted after writing these few words, so now he sat in his office doing nothing but staring into his painful self. He was too nervous to go outside – an unusual circumstance for him. If he ventured out, he would flee from people who knew of him as a friend. They wanted to help, but they didn't quite know how. If they tried, Adam would respond angrily.

Miss Marchant was a case in point. She organised his appointment book, took shorthand notes at multitudinous legal meetings and then neatly typed them in half an hour or less. She was very efficient at filing legal documents into the folders marked *Private*. She sent the advice that important people required urgently by first-class post or fast courier.

Adam acknowledged all that, but during their conversations he had begun to feel a rising anger towards her If he didn't watch his Ps and Qs, he would offend Miss Marchant by saying the wrong thing.

At that moment, Miss Marchant came quietly into his office and proceeded to enter items for the following week into Adam's diary. Even though he had no way of coping with this, he wanted to know what was going on. She had already put a stop to any phone calls, as they would be too much for him. Adam didn't notice her, and so she quietly exited again. It slowly dawned on him that she had been into his office.

This brought a sad flood of memories. The Colonel had previously spoken of Miss Marchant's past days.

'When Sophie and I arrived in Christchurch,' he had explained to Adam, 'we met Miss Marchant in a city restaurant. We began chatting and eventually told her about our needy situation for accommodation. She told us that this restaurant was owned by an older cousin of hers, explaining that up above this floor, there were three floors of apartments. "I live in one and my cousin lives in another. The third one is vacant. If you like, you could use it as your base. That will give you time until you purchase a suitable property for yourselves."

'Then, with our permission, Miss Marchant sat in the adjacent seat. Looking at us for a moment and with keen interest on her face, she promoted herself, saying that she was an excellent secretary but was unemployed at present. "I am just serving customers to fill in time," she said. So of course I offered her work at *Judicial Incorporated*.

'Sophie and I settled into the vacant apartment. This was very practical. It had lovely views that looked out towards the Southern Alps.

'One week later, Miss Marchant was out searching for accommodation. She had discovered two large furnished working rooms which were vacant, adjacent to the High Court. Having done all the necessary paperwork with the friendly landlord, Sophie, Miss Marchant and I crossed over the bridge of the gentle Avon River to the magnificent brick building. We all laughed at the *minute accoutrements!* – a tiny hidden toilet and a poky kitchen.

'We did our legal work there quite happily. Miss Marchant did all that an excellent secretary would do. Sophie and I would be on the phone to prospective clients, arranging future court cases, calling on prisoners to represent them in court, plus anything else that would increase our business. Then Sophie became pregnant. Adam – don't say anything to her or to Miss Marchant, who knows the situation, but as far as my wife was concerned, when she had Peter that was to be the first and only pregnancy. The other child was forgotten – well, as much as Sophie could forget. She didn't come out of her misery for a long time. I had been heartbroken over this tragedy too.'

The Colonel paused for a moment. 'I think you should know that, in conversations between us, Miss Marchant revealed that her father was very violent towards her.'

Then he considered whether these facts of Miss Marchant's life should be expanded, but decided he had said enough. *There are some things that are beyond words*, he thought reflectively, so he concluded, 'Sophie and I can cuddle up when we want to share the pain of our little baby being taken from us, but Miss Marchant is still a single woman who is too frightened to let a man get too close to her.'

Adam was glad that the Colonel had made things clear to him. However, there was one point he needed to clear up. 'What is Miss Marchant's Christian name?' he asked.

Grinning, the Colonel responded. 'I don't know! She has never revealed that name to anyone. Given her history, I suspect she never will!'

Coming out of his reverie about Miss Marchant's history, Adam sighed. These days he didn't worry about tomorrow or next week. Instead, he worried about each hour.

Chapter 52

THOSE CLOSEST TO Adam had been informed that he had clinical depression, but very few had any real idea about the complaint, or even of its consequences. They only knew that he was not himself.

One day, Adam received a visit from three members of the Canterbury Legal Association to assess his situation. Polly reluctantly welcomed them into *Honeysuckle House* and, on taking them into the warm conservatory, she told them of Adam's continuing health problems.

Slowly Adam came down the main stairs, one step at a time, to stand outside the conservatory doors. He wanted the occasion to be over. On hearing muted voices from within, he took a deep breath, opened the door, and quickly sat down on his favourite sunlit chair. Giving a little look of thanks to Polly for keeping it vacant, he entered into conversation with his concerned visitors. Although it only took twenty minutes, it drained his mind and tired his body. Afterwards, he went back to his comfortable bed and slept for ages.

The local church people were different. They also wanted to visit, for they really cared, but if they had done so, they would have found that Adam couldn't follow the threads of their conversation or cope with the visits, even when short.

The congregational members were confused, saying to Polly, 'We never knew the illness was *that* serious. One moment he seemed fine and the next he has what you say is clinical depression!'

Polly would wearily explain again. 'Adam managed to hold himself steady until the doctors insisted that he rested. When he heard the word *rest*, he virtually gave in. Complete quiet. Plenty of sleep. No visitors for at least three months. That's what the doctors ordered.'

And then there was worried Iris and concerned Douglas to deal with. They blamed themselves for Adam's strange illness. 'Although we have been good parents, we feel very responsible for Adam's mental health,' Douglas said somewhat righteously.

'Somewhere in the hidden past, there must have been something that we did to cause all this,' said Iris searching through her mind.

Polly cried. Through her tears she said that this affliction could affect *anyone!* At any age! In all circumstances!

Nevertheless, his parents insisted on going up to his bedroom. Silently they observed Adam. They hardly recognised him, lying in bed with his hair and beard all awry and his eyes staring up and seeing no one. They realised then what a very sick son he was. They knew that they couldn't cure him – only support him, and Polly and the family.

Usually, at *Honeysuckle House* many radios blasted out their various stations. Polly had one in their lounge that was tuned into the National or the Concert programme. Now she turned it off.

Mrs Mulligan had a small portable radio in the kitchen tuned to the local stations. This meant lots of jolly and loud advertisements, accompanied by noisy music. She too turned it off.

Jack objected to being told to be quiet as a mouse. Didn't everyone realise how important it was to have his sound system blasting out the latest pop music? Were the sounds really reaching his father below him? However, in accordance with his worried mother's request, Jack began to listen with his earphones while he did his computing work, instead of blasting everyone else's ears.

Sophie stopped playing the piano. The Colonel had his radio turned down. Peter took to earphones.

On Adam's weekly visits to his rooms, Dr Robertson

suggested to him that he would eventually be free of clinical depression, but it might take a while. 'There will be a constant need for you to have loving care, lots of assurance and friendly encouragement. You will also find that almost all your energy is taken up with the simplest of tasks. Answering questions may be very difficult.' Then he asked, 'Are you surprised at the suddenness of your collapse?'

Adam was. 'I know you said something about rest, but I didn't realize that the rest you were talking about was to be like this!'

The doctor nodded sadly. 'Do you hate to hear the phone ring?'

Adam nodded again. Recently, he had been constantly on the phone to all manner of people, all over the world. Now, he hated using it.

Smiling, the doctor said, 'I wouldn't worry. It is an instrument which forces people to speak, whereas being with someone doesn't necessarily require verbal chit-chat.'

Adam was reassured through these prophetic words. However, it was Polly who had to silently hold Adam's hand when he was being enveloped by the terrible darkness.

Concerned secretary Alison was worried about the term, *clinical depression*. Taking the large office dictionary off the shelf to see what it said on this subject, she found that it not only gave 'ongoing persistence' as one of the meanings, but it went on to say, 'caused by chemical imbalance in the brain.'

This gave more understanding of Adam's condition to an outsider, such as her. Alison felt that the doctors were doing their best to help him. She would try to be more understanding.

The following week, up in his peaceful bedroom, seated in a comfortable chair by the open window, Adam could see the beautiful scenery. Alison came into view. She was acting strangely, appearing from the woodland and then disappearing again. Finally, she reappeared and sat on one of the wooden seats around the oak tree. He could see her lips moving, in some sort of conversation. Perhaps she was praying, or singing, or even talking to herself. She didn't look upset or down in the dumps, so he was left wondering what it was all about.

That evening, Adam received a mysterious message from Alison in which there was a short poem. 'Oh,' Adam said to himself, 'she was trying out the rhythm of the piece, and not talking to herself after all!'

God sings to me His love songs –
Sharing songs of life with me.
The music can be simple, or
Profound as it can be.
Notes can speak in dying darkness,
Or the deep rejoice in sound,
But the harmony's discovered
When the Loving God is found!

Chapter 53

AS THE DAYS were getting more like winter, Polly would get the car out of the garage each day and leave the motor running. She then prepared a flask of strong tea with milk, two cups, and buttered muffins wrapped in a tea-towel. She would place them in a basket and put them in the back seat of the car.

Adam would be waiting anxiously for her, neatly hidden by the back door. When he was given the signal by Polly that the coast was clear of those imaginary watchers, he slunk quickly down into the car's passenger seat. Inside the offices the staff watched the car disappear along the drive with Adam hidden inside it. They knew he was very fearful.

Each day they made a silent journey to the beach on the other side of town. When they stopped at traffic lights, Adam crouched down further, keeping his eyes lowered just in case the imaginary public saw him.

Half an hour later, Adam caught sight of the sea. He saw wild grass surrounding the estuary and ducks pecking at their food. The regimented line of seagulls stood smartly together on the stone wall, some on one leg, preening themselves. From the car he noted that if a strong easterly wind prevailed, it fluffed up all their fine feathers so that they had to commence preening again. He watched the birds swooping down, cawing away and checking out what they could see.

When the tide was fully in, Adam observed a different scene – choppy seas and windsurfers who directed their brightly coloured sails to accomplish manoeuvres high in the air, shouting out.

When a storm blew over, he sometimes saw the brilliant bows of the bright colours of the rainbow.

Adam occasionally became tired of the estuary, and asked Polly if she would go a short distance further to another long beach. There was a restaurant at each end. With a long esplanade in between, there were sturdy seats tucked in against substantial walls. Adam delighted in watching the hardy swimmers, or the walkers traversing the sandy shore, or others striding out along the pavement.

One day, after a fortnight of clear but cold weather, Adam opened the car door slightly in order to take in some sea air. Later he took a tentative walk a short distance along the esplanade. A few walking steps one day. Then a few more, and so the walk got longer. Eventually they walked right to the end and back again – but he kept his head down and would not smile!

It took Adam three long months to get to that stage. Part of the reason depended on the weather. Stormy rain clouds, a sweeping forceful wind, the sea too rough or the sun too bright for his eyes, would all trigger a dramatic change to his mood. Polly would hear, 'Hurry, let's get home,' from Adam's anxious lips.

Crowds of people were more of a serious matter. Once Polly paid a call to a shopping mall. Adam sat huddled up in the car, but these pedestrians seemed to be coming closer until they could enter the car. Of course, they weren't really! Adam just imagined it, but he locked the door in case it was so.

When Adam returned home, he was exhausted. After a long sleep and a hearty meal, he did some Bible study in his quiet room. He had time now. Later he got a surprising letter from his editor friend, asking him if he would write a short article for the national legal journal.

Adam looked again at the article he had previously written for the Colonel. Liking what he saw, he set to and wrote a larger piece.

No sooner had he sent it than he received back a congratulatory letter from the editor.

Your writing will not only help with your recovery, but help our readers, too. Clinical depression has been hidden in the closet for far too long. It ought to be given much more attention. Keep struggling on!

So, Adam kept struggling on. However, his situation was becoming worse. Before he had become so ill, he occasionally worked at a small downstairs office that was not used by anyone else. If you viewed *Honeysuckle House* from the front, it was on the building's left-hand side. During his illness he had become fearful of the sweeping trees overhanging the door, making it a dark and dingy place. He refused to go into it, although it had previously been a restful and pleasant place to him.

When he gained more confidence, Adam ventured into this office by himself. Then the next month he collected the mail from the delivery box by himself. In the third month he went further, taking walks into the nearby countryside alone. He even ventured to the local village library, but with crowds of people in mind, he took Jack just in case. Due to his illness, Adam's reading ability had become virtually nil, so he chose simple children's illustrated books. Gradually, he changed to teenage books, and finally returned to good-sized novels.

'What a difference from your first visit to Dr Wilke,' said Polly when she saw these books all piled high. She hoped so fervently that he would be alright again!

Then Adam went to church with her, calling it a celebration day! However, during the last hymn he snuck out of the back door so that no one could speak to him.

Adam was finding out that the reality of things that imprisoned him was that they were not things to be afraid of at all.

Writing in triumph to the national legal journal, he said:

There was nothing in my study, the shops, the library or the church that was going to gobble me up. My shackles were of the mind! How easy it is to become afraid of fear itself. Whatever my external circumstances might be, I've discovered that God's freedom, with the medical staff's help and my efforts, and those of my wider family, colleagues and friends, have liberated me.

By this time Adam felt that he was ready to go back to work. But *Legal Affairs* staff only allowed him to work for three hours each morning. Very wise! His main task was being responsible for the mail coming in and the out-going mail, but only after it had been checked first by Miss Marchant.

After a few weeks of doing this repetitive work, Adam was fully convinced that his clinical depression had gone for ever. He and Polly went to Wellington to attend a one-day seminar called *Healing Life's Hurts*. By the time two hours of intense listening had passed, Adam was exhausted, drained and listless, and even had trouble keeping his eyes open. What had gone wrong with his judgement that he was alright? Going to a nearby hotel, he asked if he could have a room just for the afternoon. Almost as soon as his head struck the pillow, he fell into a deep sleep.

Polly wanted to attend the afternoon session, so she went back until afternoon teatime, when she collected Adam. Returning home by plane, Polly was concerned and asked him, 'Do you think that a whole day like this was too much for you?'

Adam gave a shudder! He thought that he would have enjoyed the thrill of returning to work but attending this day seminar had already stymied him. Giving a sigh, he realised that he was not yet ready to return to work... if ever!

Later, some discussion took place about the possibility of leaving all the legal business behind and starting a quiet and peaceful career elsewhere – although neither Adam nor Polly could come up with a solution.

After a troubled sleep, Adam went to see the Colonel and reluctantly handed in his resignation. The Colonel was not surprised. He knew that something eventually was going to give. It was better for Adam to resign his position sooner rather than later. He would find he became less able to cope, rather than getting better.

At the mid-morning break, the Colonel gathered the staff about him and gave them Adam's news. They were left somewhat stunned. Sobbing, Miss Marchant read out what was eventually decided:

It is with sorrow that Adam Fraser is retiring due to ill health, but is invited, if he is able, to be a silent partner. We wish him well.

Chapter 54

LEGAL AFFAIRS DISCUSSED the whole matter. Would Adam, Polly and Jack have to leave their apartment now that Adam had resigned? If *Honeysuckle House* was sold, would the Colonel, Sophie and Peter have to move elsewhere? What would happen to the rest of the permanent staff? Would the company break up?

Even Alfred P Stroud, the wary accountant, asked the Colonel about the financial health of the expanding business. What concerned him most was the state of Adam's finances, and he wondered what measures could be taken to ensure that Adam and his family had sufficient to live on.

The Colonel reminded him that all the five permanent members of staff had been covered by insurance for such a situation as this. This meant that Adam would receive sufficient money to cover his needs.

'Sophie, Peter and I will still have our living quarters upstairs and Adam and Polly will stay in their own apartment,' said the Colonel. 'However, all the normal business activity will be lifted off Adam's shoulders. The lawyer replacing him will be told that Adam *had been a very skilled man who had a wide grasp of litigation matters*. Adam will continue as a silent director, and still be a vital part of the business.'

Later, Adam was reminiscing, and reminded Polly that he had journeyed all over the world. 'In Dunedin I worked in the Religious Book Centre. Then I studied at Concord College and university before travelling to Port Moresby.

There I met and married lovely you. Then we had four strapping sons!'

Giving her a hug, with a gentle smile before continuing, he said, 'In London I worked for *Judicial Books* and after many years we ended up at *Honeysuckle House*, where we have created an excellent establishment, *Legal Affairs*. Oh! I nearly forgot, we have lived in marvellous homes in glorious countries and we met lots of gracious and amazing people.'

Amused, Polly corrected him. 'We had *two* sons, Thomas and James, to take to England. We had Sam and Jack *after* that move.'

Even though the sales of Christian books and cards had been decreasing at *Honeysuckle House*'s small bookshop, Polly was still keen to continue her business. She readily agreed to the Colonel's suggestion that she do a swap of her bright and welcoming shop for the rather dingy study at the other end of the building.

'Of course,' he said, 'the study that you are going to needs doing up to bring it to bookshop standard. We think the other room, the one that you have been using, will be better for Adam. There he can sit and view the gardens.'

The next week Jack and Miss Marchant worked hard to remove things, throwing rubbish from the disused study into a heap to be sorted later. The Colonel and Polly worked at the other end, removing the glass cabinet and books and cards. They cleaned both rooms and used white paint to brighten them up.

The sun filtered into the main entrance of *Honeysuckle House* where the doors were open, so Adam sat in a large armchair watching the proceedings.

Like soldiers in the Lord's army, the scurrying staff paraded their goods. Francis and Jack carried the awkward heavy cabinet and cumbersome till. Into the study room they brought the bed and all its required equipment. Polly and Alison packed, then carried, loads of Christian books and religious cards on trollies that *Legal Affairs* had put there for their use. Stacking them into adequate boxes, Sophie and the Colonel carried the lighter things like the curtains, cushions and other objects.

As they passed, they met outside the entrance to the house, greeting each other with 'Hello', or 'How are you getting on?', or issued grunts of effort as they were carrying things too heavy for conversation. If it wasn't so meaningful it would have been a hilarious sight!

Adam was so fatigued that he couldn't remember closing his *Legal Affairs'* office door for the last time, but he must have. However, later, when all was quiet and scurrying staff were no longer around, Adam saw a clean bright study at the other end of *Honeysuckle House* prepared for him. His easy chair was put just inside the door. His necessary books were put onto freshly painted white shelves. His new computer was arranged on the centre of his practical desk. His valuable papers were placed neatly on either side. He was well satisfied.

He kissed Polly with great love! Throwing open the French doors, they walked out into the gardens, where they sat together on the ornate garden seat in the cool of the evening. The whole experience was bliss.

Amazingly, over the following weeks Adam began to feel much better. After all, there was nothing to do except rest, rest and have more rest! He slept until at least eight o'clock, had a leisurely shower and a pleasant shave, and after that he enjoyed a slow breakfast with *The Press* newspaper before him.

About ten o'clock, he would leave the lounge to saunter downstairs and sit on the easy chair beside the door of his quiet room. Through the open door he could feel the sun shining, warming him. It was an opportunity to enjoy the cheeky warbling wax-eyes, blackbirds and sparrows.

A leisurely stroll around the bountiful blossoming gardens, and enjoying a rest on the garden seat, was sublime.

Polly sometimes went with him, and together they listened to the buzzing bumble bees or the singing cicadas on the cherry trees. Adam remembered the fuss the Colonel had had with his son Peter over cicada shells!

If it was raining, Adam would close the doors and sit inside his room, thinking of all those things that he usually hadn't had time to think of, like his four sons. What were they up to; where were they now?

Sometimes his thoughts would drift back to his days at the Christian bookshop in Port Moresby. Then, before he knew it, these thoughts now had hurried away to London and *Judicial Books* and the experience of the *Project Team.*

However, Polly had a sneaking suspicion that underneath, there were dangerous signs of something else eating away at Adam's soul.

Not knowing what it was troubled her.

Chapter 55

A FEW WEEKS later, after his study's calming influence, Adam suddenly decided to go and stay at the Colonel's country house. This happened to be empty at the time, and he knew that the Colonel would give his permission, so he eagerly told Polly and gave her the supposed reasons for his impulse.

'There is a constant buzz of conversation at *Honeysuckle House*. Church people wanting to know how I am. The noisy traffic around this area. They are all getting to me. I need to go to the country where it is quiet and peaceful!'

Polly, however, suspected that there was a deeper reason.

Adam arrived at the country cottage. Settling down, he started off by ringing Polly two or three times a day, but most terrifying for her was that he mentioned suicide! Nothing more. It was most alarming for Polly. She didn't know what to do, what to say, not even to the Colonel. Her time of keeping a check on Adam would be now finished if she allowed him to continue on this very suspect venture. But as soon as she tried to change his mind, he dug his heels in, so, very reluctantly, Polly let him persevere.

One time, Adam said to her, 'I am writing down relevant things for the editor of the National Legal Journal about my further experience of clinical depression.' He posted the envelope at the mailbox directly opposite the Colonel's country cottage. Polly wasn't sure what was inside the letter. She would have to wait until the journal came out.

When the journal was published, the editor had written an introductory piece, saying that he acknowledged Adam's writing of his journey through a painful experience that no one should ever have to suffer.

Adam started off:

One question that floored me was – HOW are you? I didn't know how to give an honest answer to that. The way I was feeling fluctuated so much, not only day-by-day but moment by moment!

To me, the question was one related to the core of my being, to my inner self.

Clinical depression had so debilitated me that the more correct question would have been: WHO are you?

There is nothing more frightening than being in a place so dark that we don't know who we are, where we are, or have any idea of how to escape it.

The light of life suddenly goes out. We are left with no more sparkle and no more joy. It is a darkness that eats away, crumbling at the soul.

I found that there were some intense suicidal episodes when I was alone in my office at Legal Affairs. All my friends and associates had no idea of the overwhelming disturbances that pounced on me there. I constantly heard loud whispers of insidious words: What say you tie a piece of cord – (there was a lot of strong red ribbon around to tie up the clients' legal papers) – to the ceiling – (the room had a ceiling fan) – and hang yourself? It was suicide speaking!

I couldn't explain my thoughts to anyone. In fact, I was one of many people who experienced increasing suicidal thoughts without any apparent cause.

It seemed to me that, in the darkest moment, there was no sense of self or personal value and suicide seemed to be the only way out.

It was no longer simply a choice to be made but THE LOGICAL END OF THE PATH AVAILABLE!

Because Adam was not driving, each week Polly would drive up to collect Adam from the Colonel's country cottage and take him for his appointment with the psychiatrist, Dr Robinson. One day he asked Adam to take stock of where he thought his clinical depression was. Using the scale of 1 to 10 – 1 being the lowest and 10 being the highest, Adam took a little while, then slowly responded: 'My scale would be about one and a half.'

The psychiatrist then said that he would send him to the psychiatric hospital for Electro Convulsive Therapy. He explained that an electric current applied to the front of the brain was necessary to bring it back into kilter.

By this time Adam was ready to take anything, given the horrendous disturbances that clinical depression had generated, and the loss of his legal work. After all, he had tried everything else and nothing had worked.

Polly drove Adam to the psychiatric hospital. He couldn't remember much of the journey, as he sat looking out of the window to the surrounds of nothingness.

As they turned into the hospital drive, Adam saw the large grey building before him. His first thought was, *why do they make buildings so ugly when the treatment given within is supposed to be so liberating?*

Adam nervously walked into the cramped reception office. Someone gave him a pen to sign the official forms. Someone else escorted him to the room where his ECT would be applied. Someone else put him on a bed and made him comfortable. Someone else told him that the brain's chemical mismatch would come out alright. Someone else gave him sedation, before the doctor applied the electric shock.

The result of the first treatment was neither good nor bad, but it gave Adam a slight sliver of hope. He now felt some relief from the constant ongoing pain.

When they returned to *Honeysuckle House*, everyone saw a slight difference in him. He was more appreciative of Polly. He was talking freely to Jack and also Sam who visited them. He also went to see the *Legal Affairs* staff, talking to them with a degree of freedom.

Adam was ready for his next session of ECT.

Chapter 56

*H*OWEVER, WHILE POLLY was waiting expectantly for the outcome of the second ECT, Adam was suddenly, and without warning, admitted to the city hospital with a severe stroke affecting all of his right-hand side.

As Polly sat beside the hospital bed, she spoke to Adam with a faltering voice, but he didn't react in any way. The doctors were concerned that Adam had lost his ability to respond or to understand speech. They told her that by holding his unaffected left hand, she could start communicating with him. 'He may not be able to speak, but we hope that he will hear your voice.'

So Polly held his hand and told him things he might remember, saying, 'Adam, my love, do you remember what happened to you? Because of your noisy snoring – not your fault, it was caused by your medication – we slept in separate bedrooms. It was the only way I could get any sleep. About midnight you usually got up to go to the toilet, then you got into bed again, but on this particular night I imagine that your muscles must have failed you. You fell awkwardly onto the floor, probably narrowly avoiding the sharp corner of the lampstand. You must have lain unconscious throughout the rest of the night. I brought you a cup of tea at seven o'clock the next morning as usual. The light from the lazy morning sun was sufficient so I didn't put the main light on. I put your cup of tea down on the little table and opened the curtains. That was when I saw you lying there. Bending down, I felt for your pulse and listened to see if you were breathing. You were, thank the Lord! Your eyes were open but unseeing. I was very scared. I called out loudly for Jack to come and keep an eye on you while I rang for the ambulance.

'We journeyed to the hospital. You were admitted immediately to this ward. Seeing you lying there so peacefully, my biggest hope was that the clinical depression was gone. If that was true, it would be a miracle! The doctors explained that you had had a massive stroke. Sadly, that presents me with a new challenge to overcome.'

Polly hoped that Adam understood all that she was saying. Knowing that he would be in the hospital's best care for some time, she went home, alone.

Meanwhile Jack had been telling the Colonel and Sophie about this terrible tragedy. The Colonel said that he had heard the ambulance on the gravel drive and had looked out of the window to see Jack's father being taken out on a stretcher and put into the ambulance. Then worriedly he asked Jack, 'Did the ECT, the supposedly perfect cure, end up causing this?'

Turning to Sophie, he said, 'Adam had a full medical a few months ago. His heart and blood pressure were OK. He doesn't smoke. None of it makes any sense!'

Jack left them discussing the crisis and phoned Sam to tell him the tragic news. Sam was just going to work and said, 'I will make contact with you when I've finished work. Keep me posted if there is any change.'

Then Jack rang up his grandparents – Douglas and Iris. They had just got up. They were shocked when they heard this latest news. Clinical depression? ECT? Now stroke? They wanted to go to the hospital immediately and sit with Adam, but Jack gave a hollow laugh, saying it was far too early.

So it was a few days later, after the immediate scare was over, that Douglas and Iris went to the hospital to sit with Adam.

Meanwhile, Polly sent hurried letters to Adam's sisters, Rose in Fiji, and Violet and her husband Gregg in Dunedin, giving them the devastating news.

Later, some of his friends from *Legal Affairs* called

to see Adam, who was very sleepy – the Colonel and Sophie, then Miss Marchant, followed by Francis, Alison and Rebekah, tiptoeing around, but concerned Penny marched right up to him, took his paralysed hand and whispered, 'It will be alright.'

Although the visitors all saw Adam determined to win back his capabilities, there was no way he could do so unless he, with Polly by his side, worked hard to regain his strength.

Later, when some of the *Legal Affairs* staff gathered at *Honeysuckle House*, the Colonel asked if they had any suggestions about how they could help Polly.

Sophie said that Polly would always be welcome to come across to their place for meals. She said that Peter would remove himself so that Polly was free to talk about matters regarding Adam, things that didn't really concern their son. Peter was not interested in serious chit-chat anyway, so he was quite ready to do this, as long as he could eat his dinner first.

Miss Marchant, knowing that Polly was not in a state to drive herself around safely, kindly offered that any time Polly wanted to go to the shops in the city or the suburban malls, she would take her, whatever the time or circumstance. There, they could sit sipping coffee and watch shoppers buying exorbitant fashionable items while they chatted, and Polly could safely share her worries.

Alison said that she would continue to write little poems for Adam.

Francis said that because Adam was always keenly interested in the goings-on at the property, he would write updates on a postcard so that Polly could read them to him.

Sam and Jack visited Adam in the evenings. Surprised at their father's returning sense of humour, they and Polly had some hilarious times with him, even though his only two words were 'Yes' and 'No'. This always left Adam elated but rather tired.

The Colonel popped in at irregular times and, with his mellifluous voice, repeated the same words to Adam, 'We all love you!'

Polly knew that their two sons overseas also needed to be informed of their father's situation, but had no idea how to contact them immediately. Thomas and Jo were off enjoying camping expeditions around the south of France with their two children – three-year old Zack(ary) and Mim(osa), just ten months old – but who knew where they were at this present time?

Periodically Thomas sent tourist postcards to *Honeysuckle House*. Polly always put them up on the fridge so that she could read them again. The latest one informed them:

Little Mim is fine. When she needs feeding, Jo gives her breast milk and then a few minutes later, changes her nappy. Where she puts the nappy is a mystery! I drive the car and it carries us onwards to another marvellous camping spot.

Very humorous, but still lacking in facts!

However, Polly found it was a nightmare trying to get in touch with him. It was only through the efforts of the London based *Judicial Books,* whom Adam had been occasionally writing to in some sort of business venture, that Polly was at last able to contact their son.

This business colleague began the process with a phone call to a French friend living in that country, who knew another friend who was living in a magnificent mansion. The owner of the mansion had been sitting for Thomas, who was painting his portrait. Knowing where he was camping, he sent out one of his housekeepers to try and stop him before he left. The housekeeper found Thomas, who hurried back to speak with the owner, who offered him the use of his phone, but he had not taken into account the difference in time between the two countries.

It was well after midnight when Thomas heard Polly's voice drowsily answer. Finally realising who it was, Polly was able to calm him down and answer all his questions. 'Is Dad alright? What did the doctors say? What about the depression? How has it affected him?'

Polly was slowly able to tell him the whole situation, but because of the annoying delays and the time lag on the phone line, it took a long time. 'Amazingly,' she said to Thomas, 'although it's too soon to say, the clinical depression seems to have disappeared. However, from the stroke your father has lost his speech and is paralysed on the right side.'

That was the end of the garbled conversation.

James had moved from London to Thursday Island in North Queensland, where he was teaching local Aborigine teenaged students. When paying a visit to his parents at *Honeysuckle House* a few months earlier, James had intimated that this teaching job at Thursday Island was a follow up on all that he had learned during the London Mission course. He had enthused about his wonderful time there and about the students, including one who was very special, who taught alongside him. Indeed, he frequently mentioned 'this special one'!

Polly started asking him pertinent questions like, 'Is this a young lady you are talking about?'

James clammed up!

Polly smiled, thinking to herself that there were no answers yet, but she would keep an eye on him.

On the long verandah seat, Polly saw James reading one of those *special letters*. Slowly walking up to him, she caught a glimpse of a little inscription SWALK (*Sealed with a Loving Kiss*) on the back of the envelope. On seeing her, James hurriedly rose and went past her, up to his bedroom where he could read it in private. Afterwards he went to the lounge to watch TV.

Polly waited until he came out of his bedroom, then went in to search for the letter. She knew she ought not to be in the room without permission, but said to herself that if she was caught, she would say, 'I'm just cleaning!'

She quickly found the letter under the pillow. It was separate from several other letters bundled together with a thick rubber-band. As Polly's hand reached out to pick it up, James caught her and grabbed the letter back.

Polly told him a fancy story about making sure the room was clean. Laughing, James gently told her off, and said, 'You haven't got your pink feather duster so how can you be cleaning without it?'

Going bright red, Polly gave up searching for those letters. She noticed however that every day in the late morning, James would rush up the drive to the post box and collect two, or sometimes three, of these letters that had been written especially for him. (Any other mail was left to be collected by someone else!) Then, proceeding to the garden seat under the oak tree, James read them time and time again.

Polly was left to speculate about the outcome of the young lady's correspondence to him, and vice-versa!

James was now back at his teaching post, and Polly telephoned him. As she was waiting for him to come to the phone, she had a sudden inspiration. She wondered whether this was the same person that James had been writing to when he was at *Honeysuckle House*. He had given no concrete answers to her motherly questions. Occasionally he offered, 'You mean my angel?' Was this a proper name, or the name that James had given this woman because she was absolutely heavenly?

Polly didn't know, but today she had this unwelcome task to do: passing on the information about his stroke-ridden father. James was, of course, devastated and asked that he be kept up to date.

When the call was over, Polly dreamed about when Adam had been well. With God's help she would be ready for what might happen during the following days, if not weeks, or months, or years, even...

Chapter 57

THE DAYS WERE full. Because of her emotional state, the Colonel's main task was driving Polly to and from the hospital. If there was to be an extended visit the Colonel would return to the hospital later to collect her. If Polly's visit wasn't too long, he waited in the car for her, dealing with his legal documents. One of these documents was the *Reconciliation between Prisoners on Parole and Victims of Crime. Legal Affairs* had decided to pursue it.

The Colonel had begun looking through the names of possible barristers to undertake the task. Miss Marchant had insisted that this person must have a listening ear for the prisoners *and* be a powerful advocate in court. At last he had found someone who had all the necessary qualities, Jane Abernethy, a barrister who was thirty-nine and still single. She resided in a large two-bedroomed flat in the central city with her energetic mother.

After an interview with the Colonel, Judith joined the legal team at *Honeysuckle House*. On coming into her new office – the one vacated by Adam – she saw on the noticeboard these words:

The written law is often misinterpreted and misrepresented, and: Much law means poor justice!

The Colonel was delighted she had noticed it. 'Long ago, it was written by Sophie, my wife, who is a barrister of some repute. You will see her by-and-by.'

During Polly's visits to and from the hospital she and the Colonel had conversations while seated on the comfy plush red seats of his old off-white purring Daimler. Well, *she* did! The Colonel kept his mouth shut and only asked the occasional question.

'When I visit Adam,' Polly tearfully said, looking at him with sorrowful eyes, 'I feel *so* shattered! From my nursing experience, I knew immediately that it was a stroke and that he would take a long time to recover. It would be heavy nursing for me. I knew that I would have to be strong for Adam. I had hoped that the ECT would fix the clinical depression. Now I feel both tearful and angry.'

The Colonel stopped the car at the next layby and offered her his neatly wrapped handkerchief, from the top pocket of his jacket. She wiped the tears away but declined to blow her nose on it – that would be too messy. Giving it back with a smile, she murmured grateful thanks.

Polly had phoned Adam's two doctors, the psychiatrist and psychologist, to tell them of his situation. She had also made a call to the psychiatric hospital Head Nurse regarding ECT, explaining what had happened. The nurse was quite shocked when she heard the tragic news.

On another occasion, Polly smiled at the Colonel. 'Your son Peter is interested in Adam's progress. I told him of how the Biblical image of the young eagle being fed by the adult bird is now echoed at his bedside when I give Adam his pureed food. Unfortunately, most of it goes down his chin. I have noticed that Adam has a trace of independence and rebellion, particularly at mealtimes. He wants dessert first, every time!'

Polly went on, reflecting on how the clinical depression had been so debilitating for her husband. 'When Adam first had this complaint, some church members were surprised. "Christians don't get any sort of mental illnesses," they righteously said to me. I asked them somewhat rudely, "Then what about my husband?"'

The Colonel was shocked at the way some Christians could put everybody into one easy basket.

'When Adam had clinical depression, he was terrified

at the slightest sound. He told me that he was not coping with the constant noises in his head. The sensations and sounds were most weird. Wriggling worms, plopping porridge, fizzing sherbet, periodic spot-welding, metal riveting, and draught horses, that became louder and more persistent.'

The Colonel asked how Adam had put up with this everlasting cacophony, expressing his question by saying simply a quiet, 'Why?'

Polly went on to further explain. 'Adam really thought the next downward step was madness, so he kept quiet, not wanting to reveal anything that would cause other people to think that he *was* mad. What Adam thought was rational and sane quickly led to dark and forbidding experiences for him. Yes, I suppose you could call it madness.'

After a minute or so, Polly brightened up. 'Now I'm sure that Adam has a new, quiet and peaceful sound in his head – the sounds of silence!'

The long days for Polly stretched out. One Monday night, she told the Colonel while driving home that she had been receiving some 'pastoral care'. However, giving a slight shudder, she showed what she thought about the 'care'.

'After Sunday morning service, people who are supposed to be praying for me are constantly asking, "How is Adam?" They never ask me a very simple question, "How are *you*?" The intention is kindly, but what do I say?

'When I started to explain the situation so far, I could see a few people in the group turning away. They obviously did not know how to treat my reply. I ended up praying for myself! It made me feel upset and uncared for, although I knew that God heard my anguished cry.'

The Colonel gave Polly a gentle, friendly squeeze on her arm. She felt the intended warmth, and settled a little, turning her mind to all those who truly loved her, and thought how fortunate she really was.

One Friday evening, Polly gave a sad laugh, for as they turned the corner to drive up between the flowering gardens, they found that the whole of *Honeysuckle House* was lit up.

'Oh, look!' Polly said. 'All these twinkling lights illuminating the lawns in front of the house are reflecting on our gorgeous flower display. It looks as if there is going to be a celebration of some sort?'

As Polly was getting out of the car the Colonel reminded her, 'Yes indeed. We are celebrating another anniversary of *Legal Affairs.*'

Then she remembered the past great occasions and offered, 'Will you please put in my apologies? I won't be coming. Until now Adam has been looking after the personal paperwork, but now that he has had a stroke, I have to try and sort them all out.'

The Colonel was about to move off, but hurriedly said, 'Could I help?'

Polly shook her head sadly, saying that she would do it, even though it might take all night; and she went up into her lonely apartment.

Chapter 58

*S*ITTING BESIDE ADAM in the hospital ward, Polly thought to herself, *It is like starting from babyhood again! He can't swallow properly, his vision is affected, his right arm and leg are paralysed; he is very, very sleepy and unable to tell me what he wants...*

All the medical staff had swung into action – doctors, nurses, orderlies and therapists. Adam was taken to the physiotherapy department to work on his right leg and arm. Two hefty male nurses helped him to stand upright while two female nurses stood by to assist. Polly stood nervously in the background. It was very difficult for Adam, as he constantly veered over to the left side.

Once, when Adam and Polly were alone in the physio department, he began to sing an old familiar song: *Daisy, Daisy, give me your answer do; I'm half-crazy, all for the love of you...*

Polly was overwhelmed and began to cry. Adam gave a lopsided grin – well, as much as he could manage! He sang those words so clearly. Where did they come from? From the hidden recesses of his damaged brain? Was there a difference between singing and saying those words? Adam was unable to speak to Polly, yet he sang! It was very frustrating!

Adam was next taken to speech therapy, where he had to look at picture postcards in order find out what he could remember. He couldn't spell his name or recall the date, day, month or year. He could understand some words but not others. He couldn't blow, whistle or puff out his cheeks. or make any concrete sounds, so the messages he wanted to convey were very jumbled. His mouth and the right side of his face would not obey where he wanted them to go.

Then Adam went to the Occupational Therapy department where he made pikelets. Because he was in his wheelchair, his effort to rise a few inches and sit again was a dangerous operation. He held firmly onto the table with his left hand to give him some extra stability. The therapist stood nearby just in case anything went wrong. It didn't. The pikelets tasted excellent, too!

Before the stroke, Adam had been working on his own computer, typing all his correspondence with his right hand. Now the occupational therapist had to teach him how to type with the left hand using the hospital machine. Very slowly he typed out his name in capital letters. Then on the next line, he added his address. He had difficulty in remembering this, and by the time he was finished he was well and truly exhausted.

As it was early summer, Adam's therapist continued to help him by singing quiet gospel songs. She took him into the small garden outside, where he rejoiced in the sun. She asked if he minded if she prayed for him. Having received his ready permission, she prayed along the lines that God would give speed to his recovery.

However, God didn't hurry things up. Instead, Adam had to learn that his progress was to be slow and sure, under God's jurisdiction!

Polly smiled and looked at him from where she was sitting beside the bed in Adam's ward. From the pillows, Adam returned a lopsided smile with one loving eye half-open, his facial muscles drooping on the other side. He always tried to respond to her.

She told him that the *Honeysuckle House* mailbox was full of encouraging cards and letters from friends, colleagues and neighbours, all expressing their concern and love. Some had special verses, short prayers or even an occasional funny picture. 'There have been practical offers of help too,' smiled Polly. 'As Alison has done most days, she has sent you these gorgeous large posies. However, the nurses say that the flowers have built up to quite a collection and soon there will be no room for anything else!' Laughing, Polly went on to say, 'Will it be alright if I tell Alison that it would be much better to concentrate on her little poems instead of sending more posies?'

Adam gave a half-smile in agreement.

'Francis has sent postcards to keep in touch with what has been happening to the property. Would you like me to read them to you?' she asked.

Adam answered this query with a sudden involuntary movement of his right eyebrow. Polly was encouraged by this and continued by saying, 'Do you know what else Francis has done? He found a verse from somewhere and copied it out. It is a really good one,' and reaching into her bag she retrieved it, and read it out:

Do not pray for tasks equal to your powers. Pray for powers equal to your tasks!

Enthusiastically Polly said, 'I think that applies to all of us!'

Adam gave a slight drooling grin and managed a nod.

Although it was for a trial period to see how things worked out, it was an important weekend for Adam when he returned to *Honeysuckle House*. Of course, it was hard work for Polly, taking the wheelchair apart, heaving it into the car, and then doing the same in reverse when they had completed the journey.

Adam was going to be downstairs, where slight changes had been made to the study he had used when he had clinical depression. His desk, chair and all the other equipment were put to one side, allowing space in the middle of the room for a well-made, cushioned bed with an adjustable moving mechanism. Then his old comfortable chair was put on one side of the bed. There was a moveable bed table that could be placed anywhere. Jack had helped Polly to arrange it all.

The hospital had provided a sturdy ramp on the outside. The French windows enabled Adam access to the outside.

When Adam was 'in residence', Miss Marchant and Alison presented him with a new writing journal. He received it with thanks, but Polly reminded them that it was much too soon to record relevant progress.

Mr C and Mrs M went as quietly as mice from the kitchen through the conservatory, before reaching his room. Their anxious faces portrayed their concern about Adam's condition. In fact, they *fussed.* Polly told them that he now enjoyed the peace that he desperately wanted.

Later in the day, practical Mrs Mulligan, with loving care, brought Adam a cup of thick, hot chocolate and then left without a word being spoken. As he slowly drank it, he thought that if anyone had asked him whether he would rather have clinical depression instead of a severe stroke, he would answer, a stroke every time! He felt very loved and coddled, and it helped his spirits and motivation that he needed.

Adam found it good to sit in his comfortable chair again. Using two or three extra cushions for stability, and with Polly sitting on a conservatory chair by his side, they looked out at the small garden full of the peaceful solitude of silence. They observed the birds flying high. They talked about the effects that the strong wind had on the trees.

When there was no one to disturb them, Polly tickled Adam's feet. The feeling in his right foot was now coming back a smidgen, and he gave a few twitches. He could also bend his right leg at the hip, although rather unsteadily. There was definite feeling coming back to the right side of his face. With romance in mind, Polly snuggled closer to Adam and they made love very quickly, wrapped in togetherness!

After seven weeks of outpatient medical care at the central hospital, Adam was transferred by ambulance to another hospital – the Brain Injury Rehabilitation Service, where they could offer him more 'intense repair'. Mechanic Sam chuckled when he heard this.

One day, after his regular treatment at this department, Adam tentatively walked around a small group of medical staff who were blocking the passageway. He slipped and fell, hitting his head on the hard floor. Nothing was broken, but he was shaken up. Until then he had been without the aid of a walking stick. His practical physiotherapist, who had helped him up, quickly ordered a stick for additional stability.

Since then, Adam had taken his stick everywhere with him, although in *Honeysuckle House* he remembered all the hidden outlines of the furniture, so it wasn't always necessary.

One thing Adam really enjoyed was his rehabilitation in the heated hospital pool. When he had slowly and awkwardly taken off his clothes and struggled into some bathing trunks *by himself,* Polly fitted him out with a floaty for his neck.

Placing his walking stick in the communal container, he went down the few steps into the warm water. Moving into position in the shallow end, either with his physio-therapist or with Polly's able help, Adam tried floating, putting his head back in the water. He was somewhat nervous.

Polly said to him, 'Perhaps you need two floaties after all!' And so they equipped him with another floatie, and it helped his confidence.

Six months later, he started insisting that he could manage a length of the pool by himself! It meant that he was beginning to look like a Michelin Man, with a third floaty around his backside. He managed the whole length on his back, propelling his body with one foot.

The one thing that caused Adam considerable frustra-tion was his continuing lack of understandable speech – words that he wanted to say but couldn't yet get out. Polly was getting better at translating his convoluted efforts. Adam, with difficulty, wrote down what he was feeling, but developed a headache when trying. Again, it was most frustrating!

He tried to tell Polly that at the hospital he could hear the speech therapist coming down the corridor with her jolly, jangly jewellery, ready for the task! It was very difficult, particularly with words commencing with a 'j'. There was much laughter when Adam tried to say those words!

The speech therapist gave him three intense sessions every week. Later, Polly read Adam's official report card: *Two separate but interconnected elements of voice and speech normally intertwined, work smoothly together, but Receptive and Expressive Dysphasia is marred with word-finding difficulties.*

In other words, he discovered he was still without perfect enunciation. 'What's new?' he would try to say, but could not be understood when he said it – very frustrating!

Much later Polly asked Adam again, 'Didn't you have some confusion with the word *flu*?'

'Yes. I tried telling a senior nurse that I had woken up with a slight *flu*. This was a simple statement. The nurse should have understood it, but she couldn't! She called another young nurse but neither of them could understand this simple word, *flu*.

'It was not because of my stumbling words, but I couldn't use other words in the dictionary to make my meaning clear, like "influenza" – "fever" – "sick" – "lurgy" – "bug". At that stage, I couldn't yet recall them! The only word that I could use – *flu* – was all that I knew. However, I couldn't even say the letter *f*. It was too hard to get out. It was most frustrating!'

Polly suggested writing these same words down and submitting them to that nice publisher – the editor of the legal journal, to see what he thought of it.

Before that event they set to, making sure that they had all material covered. Polly reckoned it looked like mice scribbling!

Adam looked at the final first draft and, to his horror, found that the words were all jumbled. Polly came to the rescue and was able to correct his awkward spelling, grammar and his convoluted punctuation.

'It is my spidery left hand,' Adam offered.

'I think it's your brain doing things it isn't used to, or sure of,' concluded Polly. However, they called it *Flu Ventures!*

The editor was a close associate of Adam and had watched his recovery with interest. He told him he was very interested in the *Flu Ventures*. He would not only publish this corrected piece, but he wanted more from Adam's spidery pen next month.

So, Adam wrote, and Polly edited another piece that the editor published. 'The editor has an amazing attitude,' Polly murmured.

As an adult, having to learn to speak again after half a century of fluency is the most difficult of tasks. A child learning to speak accumulates ten words when they start to talk, but my words have already been programmed in. Unfortunately, they are unavailable until, just like the computer, the return button is pressed.

I pronounced words well – as – long – as – I – took – things – slowly! I was able to use strategies such as gesture and talking-around-the-word to get my message across, but even this was a massive task!

Youngsters just go to sleep whenever they are tired, but adults are expected to soldier on. No wonder stroke people (and their spouses) get scratchy if they are tired!

Chapter 59

BEING AWARE OF all that spidery writing by Adam, the occupational therapist recalled that he had been using complex computers throughout his legal profession. Because this was quite different than writing with a pen or pencil, as Adam was now doing, she wondered if the time was right to return to the hospital's computer now.

At first, Adam didn't know what to do with the *wily* computer – with this *obtuse* machine. He couldn't fathom the layout of the keyboard, let alone the actual letters that he was typing with one finger on his left hand; those underlined words that he wasn't able to articulate.

After a lot of work, Adam was finally ready to send a typed letter to his father, Douglas. Folding it into three neat pieces (a difficult thing to do with one hand), he placed the letter inside the envelope, wrote the Christchurch address so it could be recognised, applied the correct stamp and put it in the hospital post box.

Triumph!

The therapist couldn't quite get the full meaning of the letter but seeing as Adam was so proud of it, she let it go:

> *I am sorry for this mistake, book-wise, because this is an opportunity to finalise for this expedience.*
> *I can say these, that this matter has considered the really big numbers. This as a judicious a big as a thesaurus. The matter has little as the terrible, similar mystery. I can reiterate it rather than it importantly. It is called an anti-sabbatarian.*

And he signed it: *Adam Fraser* instead of his ordinary, single, Christian name.

Adam recognised all these letters and words individually, but as a collection they all came out jumbled. However, Douglas was very proud that Adam had written to him, even though he couldn't make sense of the words!

Jump now six months. Adam knew that Polly's help was crucial to his recovery. His own computer, the one that he used to do his legal work on, the one that he had been working on in his study, had now mysteriously appeared in his *Honeysuckle House* bedroom. There it sat, on a side table, ready. He passed by the sad computer daily. It looked at him so despondently. So, after ignoring it for months, Adam reluctantly started typing simple things.

After only ten long minutes of hard work he felt so tired that he had to stop. Often severe headaches were the result. Computer concentration took an amazing amount of energy, so Adam dozed off and on for the rest of the day.

For instance, when Adam tried to put down his first twenty years of life, he phoned his mother Iris regularly for the things that he had forgotten. Iris would always begin by saying 'Y-e-s?' Then, a few minutes later she concluded with 'Help!' She realised that the information Adam wanted, of distant relations or valuable family events, had been almost forgotten by her, too!

Adam tried to write these important points down right away on to the computer, but he found that most of them were still not making any sense. It was so frustrating!

Polly, his unpaid editor, tried to find other words that Adam could use. Unfortunately, his ongoing speech impediment was still in charge, so it was a continuing challenge to find the words. Once that had been achieved, when he typed the words, they came out alright in the end.

It took them quite some time – two long years in fact, before they had in front of them a small manuscript, starting like this:

Polly and I were returning from Dunedin on a twelve-seater bus. The bus company had a list of customers who had already booked in. The driver thus had the information as to where they were to be collected.

When we boarded the bus, the only seats available were in the back row. This did not allow for a very comfortable journey, at least, not for me.

There were eleven people so far and there was just one more passenger to pick up. And there he was, a young musician, listening through his earpieces to the sounds of opera. He started talking to some of the women (apart from the driver, I was the only man) and it didn't take long for them to find out that he was an opera singer. They were most interested in all his comments about his profession.

When we got off the bus for lunch, he joined us in a crowded restaurant. Unfortunately, I found his booming voice and loud opera sounds escaping from his small radio throughout the whole area to be very troubling!

When we returned to the bus, the women said, 'Would you sing something to us?' He chose a song that was well known to them, so of course they assisted him by their loud singing.

The cacophony was dreadful to me. I felt like I was going out of my mind. When we finally got to our home, the driver said that I had been very quiet. I didn't say: 'Do you think you could hear me over the sounds of the singing?' I remained silent instead.

No sooner were we in Honeysuckle House, then two of my sons called in to see me. When they had departed, I promised myself that the following few days would be quieter, and more peaceful!

However, the next day, other visitors appeared – three times! Polly was away each time. No wonder it took me ages before I regained my equilibrium.

Then Adam explained how he had found himself in this situation.

Because of work stress, he wrote, *clinical depression and Electro Convulsive Therapy followed. It had unfortunate consequences, and I suffered a severe stroke.*

Adam said to Polly, 'I hope it is suitable for publishing, maybe for the whole world!'

'Then, we had better give it a name,' Polly said. 'How about *Stepping Stones of Faith?*'

Chapter 60

WHILE ADAM WAS absorbed in this stimulating work on the *Stepping Stones* project, with Polly by his side, he was also attending another hospital, again as a day patient. There were two energetic, bossy women – a physiotherapist, and an occupational therapist. They had a no-nonsense approach that implied that they couldn't afford to have their time wasted. In fact, there was a large clock placed above the door to the spacious room, and if the patients were late or delayed, they had to make their apologies to the therapists. Adam was late for one session. He didn't apologise!

The physiotherapist told him off. 'My time is valuable,' she said, 'so if you don't want to take this opportunity then it doesn't worry me. There are plenty of others waiting in line for a place. When my husband died and I had three children to look after, I needed work and got a job at this hospital. You should get off your chuff and do some hard work! After all, the future is before you.'

Adam listened sullenly, but he took the situation on board.

Later, the occupational therapist told him, 'I want you to take a bus into town.'

Adam grinned. He could manage it – but not yet, not at that time. But this therapist said, even more strongly, 'I want it done in a fortnight.'

He immediately resisted, and told Polly all about it that night, treating it as a joke. However, she herself was a competent nurse, so she insisted that he give it a try, saying with a grin, 'You *will* take the bus. I will take our car. We can meet in town at the Botanic Gardens.'

The next day, at ten o'clock, the bus drew up outside *Honeysuckle House*. With much difficulty, Adam heaved himself up. He looked at the driver. The driver looked at him. Adam wanted to say, 'Town please,' but of course it all came out differently. After they had sorted it out, and after he paid the right fare, he threw himself into a front seat with his walking stick in his hand, mightily relieved that one of the hurdles was over. Oh, the relief when the bus reached his stop! At every corner Adam was hanging on for dear life! He thought, *Yes! Yes! Yes! I can do it!*

Then there was Adam's speech therapist. She was an organised lady who didn't have the same no-nonsense approach the other therapists had. Instead, she hurriedly put aside the speech therapy on this particular day to listen to a tale of his childhood that he was wanting to get out.

'I was twelve... biking along to the harbour... the long pier before me... I fished over the edge... the line disappeared... it got caught underneath... I went down the ramp... I didn't see the green slime... I went into the cold water... I came up under some supports... I held onto one of them... later, I got to the road... it took a long time for help to come.'

This speech took nearly an hour! Adam was describing what he meant with gestures, or by using words that were opposite, or similar in meaning. He also tried to use a list of aids that the therapist had previously given him – write a word down, draw a sketch, try again later, get someone to ask questions that will trigger a word, or leave it alone! However, he thought that the hour-long session would be well over before he half-finished if he tried any of those.

Adam let out an enormous sigh, but the speech therapist clapped her hands. 'Well done!' she exclaimed. 'Well done!'

Sometime later several visitors came, and Adam told the same story in twenty minutes, proudly saying, 'Just pure hard work in the first instance, but rewarding in the second!'

It wasn't over yet for Adam. He attended the Community Speech Language group. To talk quite freely was proving very difficult for him. The Aphasic Programme seemed to be the answer.

'Why do they have such impossible names for a person like me, who can hardly talk?' Adam said to Polly. She shrugged her shoulders.

The people in charge were very helpful to Adam. One explained to Polly that, 'Adam's understanding of both oral and written material is satisfactory, but he has severe difficulties with verbal expression and mild to moderate problems with regard to writing. He needs to improve on that.'

The classes were conducted for two hours, with pre-prepared morning teas in the middle. There were numerous speakers from outside the hospital. After the break, they set to work to answer the written questions, trying to remember what the speakers had previously said. Then they were required to speak out loud, using their mouths, tongues and lips together to form their individual words, often with extreme difficulty!

It was paramount that while each person was speaking, the others should remain silent, even though they knew the forthcoming words, or thought they did.

During the summer break, one of the women volunteers came to *Honeysuckle House*. Adam took her into the conservatory, where Polly had placed the computer for their use. Choosing short sentences and then lengthy phrases, after a number of weeks the volunteer finally said, 'I think that you are ready to speak clearly to the public.'

With this thought in mind, Adam became *an excellent speaker to the public* – or so he thought! One day, as he was relaxing outside the front door of *Honeysuckle House*, he met an intense man who was coming up the drive to deliver some religious material.

Everybody else had disappeared, so Adam was 'it' to be harangued by this man. He went flat out, but Adam stopped him, saying, 'Please slow down. I can't understand. You're talking too fast.'

The man replied, 'What language was that?'

Adam was taken aback, and said rather angrily, 'English!' He was upset and completely disappointed. It meant that he wasn't speaking as clearly and succinctly as he thought. It was so frustrating!

The following year Adam returned to the speech therapy department. Adam slowly continued to improve as the therapist worked one-to-one with him, saying: 'To achieve the return of your speech has been the longest part of your recovery. You are motivated to continue to press onwards to the goal of talking well, so that others might hear and understand your words.'

It wasn't all doom and gloom! Short, chubby and exuberantly happy, reverent in approach and by title, the single Reverend Geoff Silver was the minister of Honeysuckle Church. Throughout the time of Adam's ailments, he had supported him and Polly.

When she was talking to a group of interested listeners, Polly said of this minister, 'He has been a good friend, coming to see Adam regularly in hospital and serving communion at home. He was very patient and understanding of his difficulties in attending worship. Now that Adam is feeling better in himself, he and the minister meet occasionally for morning tea at their favourite restaurant, *Sweethearts.*'

Chapter 61

ADAM'S SPEECH DIFFICULTIES were *still* confusing to his parents. Iris said anxiously, 'I think Adam is still trying to have a conversation but can't get his words out.'

An older but regrettably no wiser Douglas commented, 'Oh, he's still forgetting his words.' He kept an account of the months of intense speech therapy, but it wasn't long before he realised that Adam did not *forget* his words - he just had difficulty in expressing them.

When Douglas was speaking to the Colonel, he sadly told him, 'I feel badly about treating Adam like that and not waiting before rushing in with a whole lot of words that I thought might be suitable. Usually they weren't.'

The Colonel wondered at Douglas' lack of understanding. He himself *always* spoke to Adam quite normally!

On a bright, sunny morning, having heard of these events with his father, Adam phoned him up and suggested that he might like to visit the downstairs room to have some coffee, gingernut biscuits (Douglas liked those) and a long chat.

Speaking hesitatingly, Adam said, 'I can't always get out the words that are there on the tip of my tongue – they sometimes won't emerge. My memory is not the problem, but getting out my words is!'

On hearing this, Douglas realised that he could learn much from his son, so he queried, 'Does it really take such a long time to concentrate on that one word or small phrase before you speak out?'

Adam emphatically said, 'Yes! Sometimes, it takes

hard work to get out *one* word, let alone other phrases and paragraphs. Take *yes* and *no* for instance. Since I had the stroke, you have heard me say these words constantly.

'But Dad, they are simple and basic words, used by others in normal conversation. In fact, I was left with no words except these. Since then, the speech therapists have helped me to learn both ordinary and slightly harder words that relate to me, like *theologian, computer* and *politics*. They tried *judicious judges,* but I can't get out the first letter. I store these away in my new memory storehouse. However, because the words don't get used so much, they are much harder to bring out than a simple yes or no.'

Adam paused for a moment, then continued, 'In one of my speech therapist classes, I recall trying to make my mouth give the right sounds. What came out was totally wrong and erratic! The therapist gave me a mirror so that I could see what my face, mouth and tongue were all doing. Apart from the unusual sight, it was most helpful. When I understood the *reason* for doing all this, the spoken words became clearer. I could *see* the action of my mouth making those sounds.

'Later on, the therapist gave me a topic and I had to write about this subject on a full-sized page. Once written, my spidery writing had greatly improved. Then I had to read it out to her. This was very difficult. Speech required coordination between brain *and* eyes *and* mouth *and* tongue. They all have to work together to be heard and, most importantly, be understood!'

Adam grinned. 'The therapist then put a challenge to me. "By the time we are finished, you will be speaking slowly, clearly and distinctly!" She was just about right!'

Douglas and Iris had been living at Sea View Cottage for some time. Early each morning, Douglas would put on his coat and a long scarf to keep warm and dry. He always wore a striped cap on his head. He was going around the corner to the dairy; there he collected the daily newspaper, and always had a chat with whoever was behind the counter. Just before he left, he bought a small chocolate bar, a packet of gingernuts or a bag of inevitable lollies, maybe all three.

Meanwhile Iris, still wearing her substantial nightie and brocaded dressing gown, made breakfast – muesli for her, tasty porridge for him. She put the kettle on and, when it was boiled, took out two large mugs and filled them with welcome tea. When Douglas returned they enjoyed their quiet breakfast together. While Douglas read the newspaper, Iris listened to Talkback Radio.

Afterwards, Iris did the washing up and Douglas dried the dishes; then, sitting in his swivel chair, he read the rest of the newspaper while she did the vacuuming throughout the cottage.

After this, Iris dressed in her smart red, or maybe blue, polka dot cotton dress and put on her pearl necklace. About eleven o'clock it was time for the trip in the car to one of the little eateries scattered about the area. Sitting on comfortable chairs, they enjoyed a late morning tea; then, having seen and spoken about everything of interest, they returned home for a substantial lunch. After a snooze until about three-thirty, they got out some simple board games or entertained close friends. At six o'clock they watched the TV news while enjoying a delicious tea with lots of buttered toast. A cup of drinking chocolate finished off the day nicely, and it was time for bed.

Yes, every day was enjoyably busy!

However, ever since Adam became unwell, they thought that they should move closer to their son. During that time Polly usually called on Thursdays at about three-thirty, when they had awoken from their slumber. (She didn't like to upset their routine.) Once, she asked them if they would consider selling their cottage by the sea and moving instead to *Honeysuckle House*. 'The bedrooms are empty now that the three boys have left home,' she said. 'There's only Jack.'

Douglas and Iris looked at each other. The thought of climbing all those stairs to the bedrooms was very daunting, so it would have to be a no.

Polly laughed when she realised the impression she

had given. 'I didn't think that you would want to do any climbing. I was thinking of the self-contained two-bed-room cottage at the back of the house. This would suit you well. Although they will still be working for *Honey-suckle House*, Mr C and Mrs M are investing in their own house. You can take your car and explore all the morning tea establishments. You could even leisurely walk along the road to *Sweethearts Restaurant* anytime you liked.'

They looked again at each other. It did not take them long to decide and eventually they moved into the vacant cottage.

After a fortnight of settling in, they trundled along the gravel path to ask whether there was anything they could do to help, and very soon were sitting down to their morning tea! With a twinkle in his eye, the Colonel asked, 'Do you really want to work on the legal side of the business?'

Adam, who by this time had formed the habit of popping his head around the door for morning tea, quickly said to his parents before they could say anything, 'He's only joking!'

Turning to the Colonel, Adam said to his parents, 'What he means is, is there anything practical that you might be interested in?' Turning back to catch sight of the lawns, he said humorously, 'There's always cleaning up the leaves from under the trees. They leave quite a mess.'

Iris immediately thought of when she was younger and involved in back-breaking bending to keep lawns and gardens in order in Mosgiel. She shuddered and said nervously, 'What do you have in mind that is a little less – ah – onerous?'

Miss Marchant, who had many bright ideas, said helpfully, 'You could always help Polly with her Christian books. She goes out often to small church groups or bigger celebratory affairs and always has a book display. I can see you sitting beside the display, done up in your beautiful clothing, telling people of your impression of the books that you are selling. Simply being a companion to Polly would be a big help.'

Iris gave her a grateful smile. Yes, that's what she would do.

Douglas was waiting to receive his instructions. Thinking of days gone by, when he was doing active work on the home in Mosgiel, painting around the dangerous eaves, or up on the roof to change wooden shingles – perhaps they would offer something like that. He gave a shudder!

Alison now joined in with her comments. 'There are some little things which always need fixing, like electric appliances or lights that have gone *phut* and need attention. Things like that. Because of his other activities, Mr C has not been able to do any of these things for ages. You won't be stepping on his toes. There are a few items already waiting to be repaired. We even have his toolbox for you to use.'

The Colonel looked at them both and said, 'Is this enough? Or do you really want more?'

They both laughed. 'No. It is enough!'

'It allows us to contribute a little bit,' said Iris, thrilled at being accepted by them all.

'It allows us to be part of this community,' Douglas smilingly said.

Chapter 62

POLLY HAD DEALT with all the highs and lows of Adam's ailments, but she wondered if he would remember their wedding anniversary this year. When they had celebrated their first wedding anniversary in England, Adam had told her that he had a lovely surprise for her – staying together in a rather posh country hotel. Another year, Adam gave her luscious individually wrapped chocolates. As he had hidden them throughout *Little Throstle,* she had to find them before she ate them!

In Christchurch, Adam had taken her to one of the flash restaurants in town, and halfway through the meal an enormous bouquet of gorgeous flowers from the top florist was presented to her.

Then, Adam had organised a musical concert given by the City Ensemble beside *Honeysuckle House* lake as a background. Dozens of sparkling lit Chinese lanterns gave the occasion its final lift.

Each year was lovingly different! On this due date however, nothing was forthcoming from Adam.

Polly purposely said, 'Let's just pop into *Sweethearts Restaurant* and have morning tea.' When they were seated, she asked, 'What day is today?'

Adam replied with the supposed date. Reaching down into her handbag and taking out a card, Polly said, 'Happy anniversary!'

Adam was surprised! He felt rather silly, for he had forgotten their wedding anniversary! Adam opened the card, and this is what Polly had written:

When I count my blessings – I start with you.

They were in *Sweethearts,* so Adam didn't feel free to give her a kiss. Later, perhaps! They enjoyed their morning tea instead.

Polly then said to Adam, 'Tomorrow you will be talking to the Christchurch Disability Group. What are you going to talk about?'

Adam said somewhat mysteriously, 'I will speak about you!'

'What on earth are you going to say?' she asked demurely.

He remained silent, then, 'Just you wait and see!'

The next day, they arrived at the venue in plenty of time. Polly sat in the front row. If the speech was about her, she was ready to interrupt Adam if need be!

Adam was introduced to the interested listeners. Taking his position behind a lectern, he commenced.

'My wife is a nurse. She told me that from a nursing point of view, since the stroke, I am no longer ill.'

A few gave a nervous laugh.

'She could see that my temper was rising, so she said that at the time of my stroke I was on the critical list for a week. My life was under threat because of what had happened. That event had caused long-term damage to my brain.'

Adam grinned. A few members of the group did as well.

'By now my temper had settled. "You are not ill," she said again. "You are suffering the consequences of what has happened. You have lost normal function in some areas. That isn't illness; it is a disability."'

Adam looked around at his friendly audience.

'Disablement takes away the core of your being. There is an old tale told about the ordinary oyster shell. Often, there is a beautiful pearl inside.'

Leaning forward, Adam asked, 'How is the pearl made? It is made of an irritating, gritty grain of sand within the shell. The oyster emits a mucus to surround the sand, which causes the pearl to develop and grow into its shining glory.

'Disabled lives can be seen in a similar way. For instance, apart from the stroke-damaged body there is a recognisable fault with my speech. It is slow and doesn't always come out as it should! It can take a lot of effort.

'If I have something to tell an audience I put it into the computer and then print it. Without a script, I am lost! One time I was preaching at a church when I wanted to interject with a small point that I had just thought of, but I couldn't get it out. My wife, who was listening carefully, said what she thought I wanted to say. She was right, in this case!'

Adam then said, 'Cast your eyes around this hall,' and he waited as they looked at each other, bringing some to laughter.

'You will find that disability can come in many different sized packages. You may say that you have never walked tall, or not been endowed with writing skills, or have not communicated sufficiently to be understood, but you have come freely to this place, to listen to another disabled person like me!

'I reckon the effects of many disablements can be overcome with persistence, courage and lots of encouragement. However, it may mean a totally new way of looking at things. Whatever way it is with you, I have found that most disabled people never give up! A woman friend has emphatically said, "I am not a stroke patient, but a person who has had a stroke. There is a difference between the two."'

Smiling, Polly, pleased at the friendly crowd's reaction, mouthed to Adam, 'Well done.'

Chapter 63

*T*HINKING THAT WALKING was absolute freedom, Adam had the idea that he could go on the undulating lawns at *Honeysuckle House*, saunter down to the small lake and gaze at the ducks and swans. After all, he always had his trusty walking stick by his side to give him the required support.

He quickly realised that this walking stick wouldn't keep him from falling over, especially when the lawn's surface was intent on tripping him up. It would be much wiser to walk on the firm paths instead. Going to the outer entrance, Adam viewed the friendly housewives going into the village shops, or purposeful men queuing up for the city buses.

From his cottage Douglas caught sight of Adam doing his daily walk, and asked his son if he might join him.

Adam smiled and said, 'Yes, of course,' and they meandered past *Sweethearts Restaurant*, who had been complaining for years to the city council that the gravel road was destroying their business. It was filled with deep potholes that the cars didn't like, so the customers turned round and visited other, more accessible, restaurants. Recently, the authorities had decided to asphalt the rest of the road up to the real countryside, a short distance away.

Later, Adam wrote an article for the *National Legal Journal* about their walking experiences:

> *My father and I were striding past the restaurant into the real country. More truthfully, we were*

> *walking along the last gravel road in the district. We wouldn't normally walk on this type of surface, but we told ourselves that it helped to keep our feet nice and supple!*
>
> *The road twists and turns, so that we saw different views each time we took a corner. In one field, two large bulls seemed to be permanent residents. We greeted them, naming them Bill and Ted!*
>
> *The first time that we walked that road was rather frightening. We could see the bulls in the distance, but it wasn't until we had actually turned the corner that we discovered that they were no danger to us. Why? We could see the true situation for ourselves – a strong wire fence was protecting us. The bulls could have easily hurt us otherwise. We continued walking back, rejoicing that we were safe!*

Another day, the adventurers tried walking their lawned property. Adam said, 'I've been itching to attempt it but haven't had the nerve. The walking stick doesn't give much confidence to go by myself.'

So, arm-in-arm, they went over the grassy folds. No trouble. They chatted about this or that passing thing. They noticed the birds flying high above, and creeping insects scurrying across the ground in front of them. They stopped to examine the lovely bursting buds on the rhododendrons which had begun to show colour. On rippling water, they watched ducks paddling and regal swans gliding. They considered what to do about the overgrown trees and annoying bushes that seemed to be spreading everywhere. They even walked to the tennis courts and the croquet lawn, where they met up with Francis Delgado. He had his head down, working purposefully on the croquet lawn garden seats and re-anchoring them.

Adam thought it was strange that Francis was so off-hand when they were greeting him, acting as if he didn't want them around. He had a sneaking suspicion that he was waiting for someone else, but who?

They didn't seat themselves there but went back to rest on the verandah at *Honeysuckle House*. Douglas finally said goodbye to Adam, and went to his cottage.

Adam went upstairs slowly to view the painting, *The Quiet Scene*. Adam often looked at the peaceful picture. The dry riverbed with large stones and enormous rocks, and behind them, magnificent snow-capped mountain ranges. He quickly realised, looking at the painting, his difficulty writing and speaking to various outside groups about his illness was alright but, as always, he did wish that he could get back *all* his faculties. Then he could enter into real life again! This, though, he never would.

Then Adam realised he had other visitors; the Colonel, Miss Marchant, and Alison. They had climbed the regal staircase, knocked, and when they had got no reply, had gone into the lounge and found Adam intensely studying the painting.

Adam, with a surprised smile, welcomed them in. As they were sitting down, Adam congratulated Alison on her unexpected engagement, which Polly had told him about the previous night. He asked, 'Who is this fortunate man?'

Alison told him her beloved was Francis, and gave her flash diamond ring a twirl. Adam bent over and examined the precious ring. After letting go of her hand, he asked with incredulity, 'Are you talking about our lawnmower adventurer, Francis Delgado?'

Alison blushed, her eyes twinkling, and replied, 'Yes.'

Harking back to Francis' recalcitrant attitude earlier, Adam laughed. 'How did that happen?'

Alison chuckled at Adam's discomfort, and told them how it all came about.

'Francis and I were standing at the entrance to the croquet green and I tentatively said that I was surprised to see how the strong metal straps of this garden seat were secured. Francis explained that the remaining garden seats scattered throughout the grounds would be repaired in a similar manner.

'I said that it seemed there was no space for being peaceful if we didn't look after our gardens too. Francis heartily agreed. Then I remarked how the long drive was hedged with beautiful roses of all shapes and colours, which were a delight to the senses and filled the air with sweet perfume. Francis agreed even more!'

'The next day Francis was sitting on the mower at the same garden spot. I giggled and said, "I suppose you are waiting for me," telling him how he had made yesterday so much better.'

Francis had smiled at her, a smile that lit up his face and made his eyes shimmer, and suddenly she saw him in a new way. Bronzed body, yes. Dark curling hair, yes. Strong muscles, yes. Startling blue eyes, yes. A quiet Spanish accent spoken with a generous smile, yes. A kind listening ear, oh yes! He was the lawn-mower adventurer supreme!

Taking a small drink bottle hooked onto the mower and having a sip, Francis told Alison about his parents who were still living in their Spanish mansion. 'They look different from other people,' he said hesitantly.

He looked to see what her reaction was, but when she didn't show anything but intense interest, he took another sip before carrying on.

'Our house stands high on a promontory looking out over the sparkling Mediterranean Sea. The ornate lawns sweep away from the house and descend in three tiered levels. There are enormous gardens of exquisite flowers, tall palm trees, and brightly coloured bushes, including a long line of oleanders. Anchored seats are placed in shady spots. Down at the bottom of the narrow steps, a sandy beach lays before us with a choice of two short piers, one for fishing and one for swimming. The whole area is paradise.'

'Just like living here,' Alison said, with her hands indicating the lovely *Honeysuckle House* grounds.

Francis replied that his parents' mansion building was complex, saying, 'Originally, it was a house of worship, having the name, *El Santuario de la Cruz – The Sanctuary of the Cross*. When the Delgados came on the scene, they found the lower floor provided extensive quarters for servants. Directly above them was the large dining room and on the other side, the massive kitchen. Going up the stairs were the opulent staterooms for important guests, and on top of that were numerous bedrooms looking out to the sparkling Mediterranean Sea, so – yes,' Francis gave another gentle laugh, 'it just looks like *Honeysuckle House* and grounds, but with the sea!'

Alison chuckled, and Francis continued his tale. 'My Catholic mother, Aimee, was about twenty. She lived in a very seedy suburb of Paris. She tried to get away from the greed and corruption that surrounded her. She was very tall and skinny with short, wild hair and was the butt of many people's humorous jokes. There was one group that always took pleasure in treating her as a sex object, and of course this left her hurt, upset and angry.

'Finally, one dark sodden night my mother ran away. She made her way to the French coast, where she obtained work as a cook on a large fishing boat. Because of her height she slept on a bedroll in a permanent shelter beside the bridge. Every day she descended to the cook-house a happy woman because, in spite of having to hold her head sideways and slump her shoulders, she could now enjoy her work and her new friends – the rest of the crew.'

Francis then added, 'After many adventurous trips, they eventually came to Southern Spain, near Malaga in the *Costa Del Sol* region. There she said goodbye to the fishermen and climbed up the narrow steep steps to the mansion that she had heard of recently. My mother thought that it would be great to settle and get work there, away from the hurly-burly and sad existence of Paris. The owner employed her as a scullery-maid in the kitchen. She worked hard, overjoyed at the position. A year went by, and then the old cook died. Hurrying to the owner, she told him all about her cooking experience and skills on the fishing boat. Immediately he put her in this position with new responsibilities.'

Francis, pausing for a moment, put his hand gently on Alison's. Squeezing his hand in return, she said, 'Carry on! I suspect your story is not finished yet!'

Again, Francis grinned and continued with his story.

'For the past years, succeeding mansion owners had built up a reputation for having great wealth. When banks came into prominence, none of the owners ever trusted them to look after their money and precious jewels. They each had a secret hiding place somewhere in the surroundings of the mansion – in small narrow caves deep down under the palm trees, or in the bushes, or in the wine cellar, for example. However, the current owner had exhausted his money by throwing wild parties and fashionable balls so that, when he died, he was penniless!

'My father, Abbas Delgado, a Moroccan Jew living on the northern tip of his country, and the same age as my mother, was rather a unique man. He was of short stature with small feet, and – forgive me for saying this, father – an ugly face. Being a Jew, he had ended up working for a seedy political agent. Often, under his breath, my father muttered some very rude names for his new employer, including the regular use of *The Boss*.

'The Boss's status would be elevated by the number of seedy clients that he could "do" on the card tables every night. My father's job was to fill up and keep on filling the glasses of wine and whisky for those men.

'One night, the captain of a luxury yacht called in at the docks to do a secret deal with The Boss. My father overheard the goings-on. Apparently, The Boss was the middleman for smuggling marijuana. My father didn't want to be involved in such matters, so he escaped to Southern Spain, and was eventually employed by the same owner of the mansion where my mother worked. He was put in charge of the wine cellar.

'Aimee and Abbas became close friends. Full of action, busyness and very astute learners, this pair – yes, one a giant, the other a dwarf – were happily married! When the current owner did eventually die, bereft of any riches, my parents knew that they were in a position to take over the tawdry mansion. Ensuring that all the legal papers were signed and sealed, eventually they made it their own. The next thing was to make some very hard decisions of what to do with the property.'

Alison was surprised at the twists and turns of this tale. Francis shifted his position off the mower and sat down next to her. Of course, she felt the warmth of his body beside hers. Putting her hand on top of his, she happily told him to proceed with his tale for as long as he liked.

Chapter 64

HE COLONEL, MISS Marchant and Adam were all amazed and delighted on hearing this story. They knew that Alison was a talker – but wondered at the sudden change that had come over her!

Alison went on to tell them that Francis' parents employed an old man to help clear away the filthy rubbish that had built up over all the grounds. One day, he had found a treasure trove of valuable jewels hidden deep in the roots of a massive bush planted many years before. Guessing it would have come from a much earlier owner, the couple now considered this differently – it was a gift from God!

They employed an excellent cook, various gardeners and two handymen. Eventually, the mansion was ready for whoever came next to its ancient doors. And they came. People of all ages, various awkward shapes and sizes! Two old dwarfs from Eastern Russia were first. Later, an enormous giant from Crete – too old for his circus act. Next came the professor, an escaped prisoner from the island of Corsica who had had his ears and tongue cut away. Then a doctor with a badly scarred face from a fight, and finally, two battered and broken women who had been accused of witchcraft. They had all turned up at this gentle place to be welcomed in by his parents for help, healing and peace.

What did they do there? They were welcome guests. They either worked happily in the gardens under supervision or reclined in sleeping chairs on the mansion's terraces. One tried fishing on the seafront pier, but he had to go down and come back up via the steep steps, which was a lot for him so, joining the others resting, he looked out to the rolling blue sea and recalled his yester-years.

Then Francis' parents discovered that they were having a baby – him, Francis Delgado!

His mother had a difficult and painful birth. The doctor, the one with the badly scarred face, assisted. The two women who had been accused of witchcraft were rushing this way and that with many towels and containers of hot water. In another room, the two old dwarfs, an enormous giant from Crete and the Corsican professor, were keeping his father's spirits up with stories of unusual births, plying him with lots of pleasing drinks.

After the birth was over, his grateful father and the other residents stood behind, looking to see if the child was 'normal'. He was expressing himself with loud cries, so they got their answer!

His parents loved Francis intensely from day one. They not only spoiled him with lots of kisses and cuddles, but also took him out into the extensive gardens, always well wrapped up to keep him warm. When he was mobile, he explored. In fact, he had a most satisfactory childhood, growing up wearing a pair of short shorts, sandals, and a jersey only when it was very cold.

When Francis was a little older, about six or seven, it was decided he would not attend a school as such. They had no transport, and the distance to the next village school would have taken all day to walk there and back, so the professor took on his education. In the library were the most wonderful reference books imaginable, containing magnificent pictures of odd people doing the most amazing things. With sign language, the professor introduced the boy to other library books – mathematics, and science, with problems and experiments that he learned to solve with increasing ease.

At every opportunity however, Francis escaped to the gardens. There, he was under the care of the dwarf, Old Tom, who not only taught him English but also how to look after the precious flowers, weed the vegetables with care, trim awkward trees and shrubs and how to – (and here Francis had looked at Alison with enjoyment in his eyes) – sit on a mower and cut perfectly these lawns.

When he was nineteen, and able to take his abilities elsewhere, he left home to explore the world with a pack on his back and joy in his heart.

Alison continued dreamily: 'Francis spoke to me very quietly, and his hand gently moved through my hair as he whispered, "In this place of contentment where I mow these magnificent lawns, I've found you, the woman of my dreams!"'

Everyone was silent with joy as they pictured the romantic scene.

Changing the subject, Adam cleared his throat and said, 'I see you quite often sitting under the oak tree whiling away your time. I thought perhaps you were writing short poems and songs, when all this time, you have been courting Francis – or he has been courting you!'

They all laughed, then Adam asked, 'When are you getting married?'

Confidently Alison replied, 'In early February.'

'Are you having a large wedding, where people from far and wide come to see the beautiful bride coming down the cathedral aisle?'

She giggled. 'No, it will be a small wedding for only dear friends,' she said.

'And where are you getting married?'

Looking downhearted Alison said, 'We don't know yet. All the wedding places we've tried are full. We haven't really made up our minds.'

Adam remembered how he had previously proclaimed the wonderful aspects of *Honeysuckle House* to everyone, so he said with a smile, 'Well, you could get married here, on the lawns of *Honeysuckle House*, just near the oak trees, on the flat area. With two – no, three large marquees, one for the wedding, one for the reception and a smaller one for the caterers; it would be perfect.'

Alison's face lit up, and she blurted out, 'What about

dancing in the conservatory? Recently, I took up country dancing, and Francis came along. We were instructed by *The Amazing Duo*, who played their music on the mouth organ and fiddle. Perhaps we could have them?'

Adam heartily agreed.

A radiant smile came over Alison's face. 'Do you really mean it? Francis and I thought that it would be too much for you if we suggested this,' thinking that Adam's dislike of extreme noise and excitable crowds would be an ongoing problem.

'No,' said Adam quite firmly. 'If I am worried by the noise, I can remove myself. I think I have it all under control.'

Smiling again, Alison gave Adam a grateful kiss on the cheek. He was mightily embarrassed and delighted, in equal portions!

The Colonel, Miss Marchant and Alison had come to revive his spirits, and indeed, so they had!

Chapter 65

*T*HE SUN ROSE on the clear summer morning, promising a hot wedding day. Just below the tall oak trees, the three large resplendent marquees stood still. The vibrantly coloured bushes near the lake, where agitated ducks and regal swans dwelt, gave the whole scene a wonderful background.

Francis, who was not yet dressed in his wedding gear, was checking the temporary winding path, which would allow guests to walk from *Honeysuckle House* before and after the wedding.

Ensuring that the raised surface was satisfactory, and checking that the protection of the wide path's reinforced wooden edge was still retained, Francis walked over to the marquees to adjust the outside ropes. The coloured flags attached to the sides of the roof were moving in the gentle breeze. He opened up the flaps of each marquee so that fresh air would be gently circulated.

Shortly afterwards, Polly and Mrs M tried out the new path. On seeing Francis in the distance, Mrs M commented dourly, 'Normally at this time of the year Francis only wears a pair of short shorts, so I hope he will make himself more presentable today!'

At the large wedding marquee, they sorted out the best positions for the velvet chairs and corrected them slightly. They wanted to make sure that Alison would have enough room as she went down the middle aisle, with her flower-girl, Penny, in front.

Polly said excitedly, 'With petals on Penny's hair and carrying a full flower basket in front of the bride, she's going to look perfect.'

Mrs M muttered, 'We mustn't forget the Colonel, who is giving Alison away.' Checking the distance with the measuring tape, Mrs M found it was just right.

Having completed these tasks, they hurried away into the second marquee. Polly thought about the seating of the guests. There were six large individual tables, allowing eight people to sit at each table – forty-eight guests. At one end was the seating for the wedding party – Alison and Francis took pride of place, then the Colonel and Sophie, and the officiating minister Geoff Silver on the left, with Adam and herself on the right. Vases of flowers decorated the marquee, so it was now filled with ongoing fragrance.

Mrs M reminded herself to take the wedding cake from the kitchen and put it on a sturdy oval table in front of the wedding party later.

Next, they went into the smaller marquee, where they counted the number of cups, saucers and plates to be used for the expectant, hungry crowd. When they had finished all this work, they decided not to walk on the newly laid path but on the freshly groomed lawns on their way back to the conservatory, which was to serve as a magnificent ballroom. The Colonel and Adam had responsibility for the arrangements. *The Amazing Duo* would play all the music.

The decorated velvet chairs, brought in free-of-charge, had been put there by an exuberant man, Gentleman Steve. He was an interesting character and, as mentioned before, had been saved from prison by a brilliant piece of legal work done by the Colonel, and was found innocent by the court jury with an argument that couldn't be faulted. The Colonel hadn't a clue where Gentleman Steve got the marquees and the velvet chairs from, but he trusted him implicitly.

For Alison and Francis' wedding, the Colonel wore his old military uniform. He hadn't tried it on for years, and dragged it out from a dusty suitcase high on top of the wardrobe.

Sophie came into the room to find him taking off his usual jacket. She remarked that she had never seen him before in his army uniform, so she had better inspect the dusty items. Giving them a judicious sniff, she said that the material definitely had a strong aroma of musty mildew, so she took them outside to catch the summer sun and fresh air. Then she sent them off to the drycleaners for cleaning.

When the uniform was returned the Colonel tried it on again. With his tall frame, sparse white hair and thinning features, he looked very smart and gave the verdict that it was still a comfortable fit. He did however mutter, 'It's a bit tight across the chest and around my rear end but I can manage if I don't go too mad during the dances!'

Sophie responded humorously: 'It offers the possibility of splitting open at the most awkward and unusual places!'

The Colonel gave a wry smile, and patted his stomach.

Unfortunately, Sophie and Peter would miss the wedding service, but they hoped to make the reception and would definitely be there for the dancing. Peter had been booked for his national mathematics competitions a long time ago. It was to be held on this Saturday at three o'clock, the same time as the wedding. They were disappointed, but would get a taxi and rush back to enjoy what was left of the celebrations.

Although they had received invitations, Sam and Jack were unable to be there. The three-week holiday trip around the North Island that they'd booked some months ago only finished the following weekend. They had sent small presents and a wonderful wedding card to the couple.

Thomas and Jo, and James and his lady 'Angel', sent the couple wedding greetings via Polly.

At half past two, the lovely bride Alison was standing before the large mirror in Polly's bedroom. Alison reckoned she had done everything that a bride should do before the nuptials except to have her hair done in one of those fancy salons. She felt that some brides ended up looking like manufactured dolls.

Her white wedding dress was simple in form. She was marrying Francis Delgado, an overseas adventurer and a marvellous lawn-cutter (and landscaper!). More importantly, their upbringing in the Christian faith had impressed on her the need for holiness to God, and Francis agreed with this, hence the white dress as a symbol of purity before God.

Standing to one side, and dressed in her own white outfit, chunky black pearls and thick glasses, Miss Marchant would be Alison's bridesmaid. Tears rose to her eyes as she stood back to look at Alison. However, thinking to herself that this would not do, she surreptitiously dabbed the handkerchief to her eyes and gave her attention solely to the bride. She stopped Alison from fiddling with her veil, for it was beautiful just as it was, falling down the sides of her face and revealing her lovely features. She wouldn't even give her the freedom to go to the toilet – yet again. Four times in the last hour? Really!

At twenty to three Francis, now dressed in his smart wedding suit, sat at the front of the large marquee. He was an overseas adventurer and great lawn-cutter, yes, but he was a nervous wreck as well! The holy vows that he was supposed to say to the minister, plus the sparkling anecdotes he was expected to give at the reception, had been written down on two little pieces of paper, but were being destroyed by his nervous hands.

Adam, who was sitting beside him as his best man, was distracted at Francis' behaviour. He leaned over and said, 'Here, give them to me!' Francis handed them over.

Francis' parents, Abbas and Aimee Delgado, would not be coming all the way from Southern Spain to New Zealand. Instead, they sent a giant wedding card signed by them and all the residents at the *Sanctuary of the Cross.* Inside they placed a short note saying how proud they were of Francis, and the absolute confidence they had in his bride and companion, Alison. With all their love, they included a cheque for a substantial amount.

On receiving this, Francis and Alison decided they would put the money away for now. They would always think of this valuable gift as a gracious and holy present. They had been discussing having children, and the gift of money would come in very useful.

At about the same time, the wedding guests that came from the various Christchurch suburbs, and the out-of-towners too, were making their way to seats inside the marquee. They could enter by two flowered archways.

There was Postman Jim, speaking to Douglas and Iris, who had been the first ones to arrive from the cottage, just behind *Honeysuckle House.*

The Mayor came wearing a rakish top hat and light grey suit. Walking confidently and with much joy in his heart, he had just been elected for another term in the city council. He was talking to Gentleman Steve.

Well, talking wasn't really what Gentleman Steve was doing. He was looking at the quality of the velvet chairs in the magnificent marquee. Through a friend of a friend, he had intercepted the removal truck taking the plush furniture from an artistic venue to a city down south that didn't need to receive them until three days hence. It was alright to *borrow* them at no cost for the wedding at *Honeysuckle House.* The chairs would then be taken to the city down south on the Monday after the wedding. However, Gentleman Steve did not mention these matters to the Mayor!

There was lovely Polly, resplendent in a blue suit and matching open-toed shoes. Her hair was not tinted blue, but fair, and done perfectly. She stood near one of the entrances, looking anxiously at the guests and hoping that there were enough seats.

There were friends and acquaintances of the happy couple exclaiming to each other, 'How are you?' and 'Fancy seeing you!' Their talk became progressively louder, so that they soon had difficulty hearing one another.

At ten minutes to three, the Reverend Geoff Silver arrived. Robed in his ministerial garments, he had a white stole around his neck, worn only for wedding celebrations. He stood at the front by a large cross that was brought from the church to give meaning to the proceedings.

The minister surveyed the scene and remembered that Jane Abernethy, the new person in *Legal Affairs,* was to distribute the wedding service sheets. He thought that the two hymns on the sheets had been chosen by Alison and Francis, but they were not well known to him. *Oh, well, we'll see how the tunes go,* he said to himself.

He was relieved to see that the service sheets were already placed on the chairs by Jane. She had performed her duty well. She had wanted to come to Alison's wedding but her ever-friendly, ever-smiling, ever-cheery, ever-talking mother, who lived with her, was now returning from one of her many trips overseas, at the same time as the wedding. Jane had carried out her duties, then reluctantly slipped away to collect her mother.

The minister glanced down at his little service-book. He saw his collection of extra information garnered from the pre-wedding sessions with the couple, but because of his own scrawled writing he was unable to interpret them! He decided he wouldn't need them, as he knew them well enough to speak off the cuff.

The minister wondered if Adam's walking stick would last the distance, supporting him standing so long. Adam had complained of discomfort in his leg if he didn't take a short walk often.

Then he heard the gusting wind. The weather forecast he had listened to on the car radio had not been good. He also heard the gusts creating some disturbance among the afternoon tea crockery in the smaller marquee. Shuddering, he wondered what would happen to the wedding ceremony if a sudden storm came their way.

At last the bride arrived at the entrance, accompanied by the Colonel. Miss Marchant stood proudly behind. The minister put his worries away and quickly got back to reality.

Rebekah More stood near the front of the marquee, beside one of the side entrances. It had been arranged that way so that her daughter, bespectacled Penny, might be given the firm directions needed for delivering the flowers. According to this young miss, only her mother would do!

At the other side of the marquee the smiling church organist began to play, with full vigour, the first notes of *Give Me Joy In My Heart*. Because of the nature of the old organ, her feet had to work flat out on the foot pedals to get more *oomph* out of it!

The minister gave the nod to Francis and Adam. They stood up and, turning their heads, watched Alison come slowly down the aisle on the arm of a very proud Colonel Henry Ivanov.

They were preceded by an eager flower girl, the lovely and now relaxed and happy Penny, wearing a cornflour blue dress. Penny had been overcome with a childish delight when told that she would be throwing flower petals onto the ground at Alison's wedding. Taking a pile of petals from the basket, she distributed them gaily left and right, right and left all the way to the front. She showed no sign of being nervous.

Penny's mother had been watching her keenly, and then very proudly, and at the due moment whisked her smartly to one side. With her almost empty basket held tight, they sat down on reserved chairs to watch the bride and groom becoming a married couple.

Francis was overcome as Alison joined him. With happy faces and celebrating hearts, and with Francis remembering his vows, all went well. He listened closely to Alison, whose words were joyously perfect and uttered without any prompting from the minister.

The happy couple went through the wedding ceremony – the vows, the prayers and the promises to each other. Afterwards they sang heartily with the congregation the two hymns that everyone knew from the service-sheet (even the Reverend recognised them once singing!).

They were married at last!

Chapter 66

REVEREND GEOFF SILVER was just about to say, 'You may kiss the bride,' when warning sounds were heard. The clouds had grown thicker and darker by the minute. Now, forked lightning suddenly illuminated the whole marquee and was immediately followed by a crack of thunder. Rain poured down and vigorous winds swept through the oak trees, blowing them this way and that. The white clouds and the gentle breeze had been transformed from tranquillity to a chaotic storm! Some of the smaller branches fell to the ground, making scattering sounds. This surprised the guests, especially when there was a loud crack and a tree branch fell right beside one of the marquee entrances. Penny let out an almighty yelp which interrupted the minister's final words.

What had been so enjoyable had suddenly become a dangerous situation just as Alison and Francis, the now married couple, were about to kiss.

The startled minister found that his preaching stole was wrapped around his ears. His service-books, including the register of marriages, had been whipped away to the ground. Even the organist, who had just begun to play the recessional piece – Mendelssohn's Wedding March – was surprised by the suddenness of the storm.

The Mayor's rakish hat blew away. He clasped Postman Jim, only to find that he too was rather scared; he had never come across this type of storm during his postal duties.

Children cried in fear. The only baby issued loud

screams that seemed to go on and on for ages. Her mother tried to comfort her as they moved quickly away from the now drooping marquee.

Gentleman Steve was worried about the borrowed velvet chairs that had been thrown into confusion by panicking guests.

'Quick!' called Francis. Looking across at Alison he shouted into her ear, 'Find Polly!'

However, Polly was already coming through the agitated crowd. Seeing the mother and baby's exit, Francis said to them both, 'Take all the women, the older men and the children to the conservatory. Watch out for falling branches. It is better that we get them there to safety.'

The scared guests followed Alison and Polly to the conservatory. They were shocked at their misfortune. As they moved in, they were confronted by flying branches, some of which struck quite forcefully, causing scratches, bruising and even bleeding.

When they were safely inside, Penny began screaming hysterically, until her mother sharply slapped her cheek. She fell quiet and wept with her mother's arm around her in comfort as they joined the others.

Then a rather frightened elderly man remarked that they needed some welcome refreshments, but with all the chaos this would be some time coming.

When Rebekah heard this, she took Penny home. Making their way carefully around all the fallen branches, they safely reached their little home on the opposite side of the road. After filling herself with chocolate drink and a quickly made hundred-and-thousands sandwich that she insisted on, and after Penny had been congratulated again on her wedding flowers episode, she slept very well all through the night.

Meanwhile, Francis had resumed his instructions to the men. 'Loosen the ropes on all marquees! If the taut ropes get caught up in this storm they will break.'

As if one tree – it wasn't one of the massive oak trees, but one of the tall gum trees planted a few feet from the festivities – was listening, there was a loud groaning and sucking sound as it slowly fell on the edge of the smaller marquee. In falling, it pulled away some of the guy-ropes, leaving a tangled mess. Flags that had been flying proudly were now unrecognisable.

Francis had heard from the smaller marquee a loud clattering of cutlery falling to the ground. He had a bright idea. Crawling under the canvas, he looked for strong serrated knives. Finding three, he gave these to the men, shouting out, 'These are for cutting the main marquee ropes. There is no need to be gentle!'

Just to be sure that there was no one inside, Francis glanced in the front entrance. Finding the Colonel standing alone he shouted out, saying somewhat militarily, 'Will you rescue the minister? He is just there,' pointing to the sorry man standing right inside.

Turning slightly, the Colonel found that the Reverend Geoff Silver was frozen in fear. Taking him gently by his arm the Colonel told him, 'We had better go; the marquee is going to flatten very soon. We don't want to be found underneath the canvas!' They battled their way through the strong wind, fallen branches and pouring rain, and made their way to safety, soaked but safe.

Most of the shocked, shivering people were standing in groups in the warm conservatory, not sure what they were to do or where to go. Seeing that there were only a few practical chairs that had been hurriedly taken from the various *Legal Affairs* offices, the Colonel shook himself and went to the large adjacent room at the far end. There, with Reverend Silver to assist him, he brought out the four-seater seats that were used for film shows and small conferences. Soon everyone was seated around the room's perimeter.

Francis and the men continued working, struggling to get the marquees down. However, this was exhausting work as branches were still falling from the thrashing trees. Francis puffed out, 'That's all we can do for now,' and they ran for the conservatory. 'We can see what the storm has done after the rain and wind have finished venting their fury,' Francis said.

Inside the conservatory, Miss Marchant, who still

wore her storm-soiled cream outfit (which had now been ruined by an accident from a baby she was caring for), returned the infant to her anxious and apologetic mother, who said over and over again, 'I am so sorry!'

Miss Marchant gave the mother a reassuring grin, then joined Alison. Soon they were busy settling people down on the seats that had been brought in by the Colonel and the minister.

Mrs Mulligan was away for a few days visiting her very sick friend, and had prepared as much of the wedding feast as she could. She had left the rest to Mrs M and Mr C's care who were very surprised by the sudden violence of the storm. They didn't for a minute imagine that it would have such an effect on the marquees as it had. Now Mrs M and Mr C worked frantically in the kitchen, slicing up the cake for all those flocking into the conservatory. Its sweet icing and cooked fruit through-out made it a must-eat cake!

Meantime, Polly filled the two kettles and the five-gallon urn. She had to wait some time before the urn came to the boil, so she hurried away to collect the cups, mainly from *Legal Affairs* supplies, although a few came from the offices. She even rescued one from Adam's study/bedroom, but this was coated with some old fluff. He wasn't very good at cleaning cups!

Returning, Polly washed them all, filled them with tea and coffee, and arranged them on metal trays. Using a small sliding affair (Adam took credit for this) operating in the wall between the kitchen and the conservatory, the drinks were delivered.

Kindly Iris and the shoeless organist (she had taken off her shoes while playing the organ and was think-ing, *what will happen to the organ and my shoes in this storm?*) delivered them on trays to the thankful crowd.

Alison placed small cartons of milk and little packets of sugar in prominent places. Douglas opened some packet fruit juices and put them in paper cups that were suitable for the children.

Geoff Silver, holding his now dirty but rescued stole, sat down with a thump on the conservatory step. Rushing into his office, the Colonel poured himself a glass of brandy and then took one to the minister, saying, 'This will take away your shock!'

Then the Colonel cautiously approached the rather rickety chair, thinking that he must remind Douglas of the urgent need for its repair. Using his status of the 'man in charge,' he interrupted the noisy crowd with these words: 'The storm is nearly over but we need to do a count to see that everyone is here.'

Miss Marchant called out, 'I am already doing this.' She said that Rebekah and young Penny had already gone home. Mr C, Mrs M and the *Amazing Duo* were already here in *Honeysuckle House*. 'The results are fifty-two adults, plus three children and one sickly but recovering baby. A total of fifty-six instead of fifty-seven.'

Then someone said Adam was missing. Polly was suddenly afraid.

Chapter 67

STRUGGLING TO HIS feet, the minister said that the fact that Adam was missing might have something to do with his damaged leg. He surmised that if anything happened to his walking stick then Adam wouldn't be able to get along. 'Perhaps he is still trapped in the marquee!'

Francis, his bridegroom outfit now somewhat tattered, jumped to his feet and rushed out to the collapsed remains of the wedding marquee. The strong wind and pouring rain with the thunderclouds had died down. Francis searched and found a narrow entrance to the marquee. Peering underneath, he saw two shapes higher than the rest. Francis thought that one of them could be the church organ, thinking to himself that the organist would be pleased.

The other strange shape was moving slightly, so Francis dived under the canvas and found Adam. He noticed that he was partly trapped by a small table and was clutching a book, but not his walking stick, which had fallen to the ground a short distance away.

Adam's head slowly turned, and he feebly answered Francis' call. 'Ah! I've been calling for rescue for ages!'

Francis realised the air in this place was limited, so he held up a portion of the canvas to allow air to enter.

Adam then said, 'I'll give this to you,' and he handed over the book to Francis. He had been holding on to the marriage register that contained the marriages of the Honeysuckle Parish, including the as yet unsigned one of Francis and Alison.

Adam slowly crawled backwards to freedom, remembering to grab hold of his walking stick along the way. When he was clear of the marquee, he took hold of Francis' arm and stood up.

Francis made sure that Adam didn't fall as he hobbled along to the conservatory. Breathlessly, Adam told him that he had first been rescued by a male guest who didn't fully know of his ailments. In the confusing storm, they had become separated. Adam had stopped and had had the bright but silly idea that the marriage register was still in the marquee, so it must be retrieved. The book was underneath the table. He had bent down and suddenly the marquee collapsed around him, pinning him to the ground. He was well and truly trapped!

The *Amazing Duo* – Alice, who played the mouth organ with enthusiasm, and Fred, who was carrying his marvellous bow and fiddle – arrived at the very moment that the rain, thunder and lightning were doing their best to destroy everything. Thinking that they would be safe inside, they began to practice their pieces before the wedding guests arrived. Suddenly they heard a multitude of shell-shocked people entering through the now-opened conservatory doors, so they put their instruments down and helped the sodden to settle.

Still clothed in her soaking wedding outfit, Alison called out to the *Amazing Duo*, 'I'll get the medical aid kit!'

Polly and the musicians applied plasters and bandages to those with bleeding knees, facial cuts or injured scalps. Meanwhile, the rain got up again and the wind continued to shriek with force around the rafters. There were eerie sounds coming through the chimneys and filtering through cracks in the building, but Polly and the *Amazing Duo* didn't take any notice and got on with the task of helping and comforting the shocked, upset and injured people.

A little later Sophie and Peter returned from their mathematics competition. Taking a taxi west from the city, they had noticed the scudding clouds that were becoming larger and more threatening by the minute. By the time they arrived they saw the whole area covered with debris, the result of the violent storm. Some roofs had been lifted slightly and a few chimneys had collapsed. Electric power lines hung from their poles, and fences had gone down. The hard-hatted electricity repair men would soon arrive with their ladders to do extensive repairs. Bright yellow-coated city council authorities were already assisting the shocked residents.

The taxi man kept muttering, 'Very dangerous,' while driving his vehicle with extreme care to avoid the most hazardous threats. He stopped at the open door of *Honeysuckle House*, and Sophie said when paying him, 'Thank you God!' on seeing the awful damage to the marquees and surroundings. Casting her eyes towards the house, she saw that all the lights were on. 'There hasn't been any power loss here,' Sophie said to Peter, who was looking fearful.

Entering the vestibule, they found a breathless Mrs M, who was coming from the kitchen carrying a tray of wedding cake. Having explained that the damaged marquee had been abandoned, Mrs M went into the conservatory shouting out to the recovering crowd, 'I have sustenance!'

'Thank goodness!' said the still frightened elderly man in the crowd, 'I thought it would never come!'

The noise of the people sounded more animated as they enjoyed their fill of tea, coffee or fruit juice along with generous portions of the wedding cake.

While munching a piece, Douglas suggested to the *Amazing Duo* that they might like to strike up their sparkling melodies. 'The quickest way for us to get warm and dry is by dancing,' he added.

The *Amazing Duo* took up bow and fiddle and mouth organ, and the bright melodies rang out loudly as the crowd's attention was drawn from the catastrophe and spirits began to lift.

The Mayor, who had recovered his rakish but damaged top hat, was standing in a corner and, with a tremendously loud voice, he encouraged the guests to dance.

Gentleman Steve and Postman Jim went around with generous smiles and uplifting voices to persuade the people that they *really* ought to dance. 'You will not get dry unless you try,' they repeatedly proclaimed, turning the ditty in to a melodious melody.

Adding to the merriment was the wine and sherry that Gentleman Steve had provided for the guests. Where he got it was a mystery, but right now it was a blessing!

While the guests were wiping their mouths and cleaning their hands, they heard wonderful music coming from the *Duo*. First, the square-dance, then the *quadrille,* followed with the Eightsome Reel, and finishing with *Put your left foot in, your left foot out... do the hokey-cokey and you turn around, that's what it's all about!*

Soon they were comfortably dry but still dishevelled. With crumpled suits, torn dresses, wild hair, interspersed with bodies decorated with plasters and bandages applied at awkward angles, they were a strange looking lot. But they had a ball!

Instead of being scared, Peter began to have the time of his life. He was quickly on the dance floor holding his new mathematics certificate in his hand. He danced with all and sundry. He caught sight of Francis and Alison in their disreputable clothes, but who seemed to be kissing – a lot!

The heat rose quite dramatically. Even though the doors were fully open, the atmosphere had become rather humid. A slight vapour formed over the heads of those who were sitting down and not dancing. Adam, with his inevitable walking stick, and the Reverend Geoff Silver who, through the effects of brandy that the Colonel had given him earlier, now both looked somewhat glassy-eyed.

Because his old military uniform felt tighter since the rain (or so he imagined), the Colonel moved around on the chair cautiously. A relieved Sophie sidled up to her husband and gave him a gentle kiss. He put his arms around her and returned her kiss more passionately.

Everyone tapped their feet in time to the music, while their faces smiled joyously! In fact, they were glad to be at the revised wedding reception of Alison and Francis Delgado for, in spite of the sudden storm, they were having the time of their lives. Yes, a wonderful celebration!

Adam stood by the open doors of the front porch. The air was fresh and quiet now. The storm, thunder, lightning and intense rain had all passed. The whole area was washed fresh and painted with God's summer glory!

With his strong left arm encircling Polly's shoulder, Adam looked at the damaged garden scene before him. Turning, he saw the Colonel and Sophie with Peter, who was still clutching his certificate. He noticed that Miss Marchant was still trying to sort out the mess left by the small baby.

There were also some admirers waiting for Alison and Francis with their cameras at the ready. At last the married couple came out of the house, wearing their smart new going away clothes. They were looking forward to taking off for their honeymoon.

As the happy couple's taxi appeared around the corner of the drive, the minister suddenly realised that they needed to sign the marriage register before leaving. The church authorities would show great concern when they came to check later that all was well in the parish, only to find the couple's signatures were missing. Grabbing the register from inside the conservatory, he quickly made sure that they signed the vital document. Just in time!

Francis had wanted to help with the clean-up of the storm-ravished marquees, but Adam had said not to worry. 'We will do everything tomorrow, or even the next day.'

Then he realised that Gentleman Steve was looking after the marquees and fallen velvet chairs, so that was something he didn't have to worry about. In fact, Gentleman Steve, who had achieved everything that was required plus a little bit more, was now making plans to rescue the velvet chairs. His intention was to get them cleaned and then trucked to the city down south by Monday night. Whether he could achieve that was unknown. As for the marquees? – he shrugged his shoulders.

Adam then considered the great mess in the conservatory, but not at this moment, not at this time!

After getting Alison and Francis' permission earlier, the Colonel had written to the wealthy Malaysian owner of *Grace Chateau*, asking him to book in the happy couple for a ten-day honeymoon. He explained that Francis was the man who had worked for many months in beautifying the gardens of the mansion. Then he signed it, *Colonel Henry Ivanov, a past occupant of many years ago.*

The owner had promptly written back, saying that while he was exploring the history of the place, he had come across some interesting names, including those of the Colonel and of his parents, Petya Ivanov and Hyan Grace Hough. He was pleased to welcome the two honeymooners, especially as they came at the Colonel's own request.

After seeing Alison and Francis off, Adam gazed with satisfaction at the rest of the people who stood or sat patiently right along the verandah, quietly chatting among themselves.

There were the indomitable parents, Iris and Douglas, who now found that they were just plain tired, so were returning to their cottage to have a well-deserved rest.

The Mayor with his damaged top hat was, amazingly, still smiling. Postman Jim continued to relive the afternoon events, shaking his head in disbelief.

The Reverend Geoff Silver was thinking that he must get on with his sermon for Sunday, but then felt that the events of the storm were a good message for the interested congregation.

The organist finally remembered that until they got their damaged organ back, there was a piano for church use. As for her missing shoes, Polly had the same sized feet, so had lent her a pair.

The *Amazing Duo* were both exhausted, but excited at playing some of their music in unusual circumstances.

Adam put his walking stick to one side, and gently drew

Polly closer. Looking into her lovely face, he proclaimed to all that he was so grateful for her being true, faithful, and long-suffering, and that he was going to give her a lengthy passionate kiss on her lips. He did so, and *Honeysuckle House* smiled!

PART THREE

The Majesty of Love

Chapter 68

FRANCIS AND ALISON Delgado were having the time of their lives as they enjoyed their honeymoon in Malaysia's mountains. Driven from the busy airport of George Town by a cheerful uniformed driver, they had been taken in a quiet limousine through the island's forested range until they reached their destination, *Grace Chateau*. Passing through a welcoming entrance, the two romantics were driven up a steep winding drive until they reached the front of the exclusive hotel.

They walked slowly up the wide steps to the spacious foyer and, inhaling the slightly perfumed air, approached the uncluttered reception counter. After signing in, a staff member conducted them upstairs to their quiet honeymoon suite.

The porter had already brought their luggage up to the room. An elderly maid took a little time to put away the clothes, shaking out the creases and placing them carefully on hangers in the splendid dark wooden wardrobe. After she had left, closing the door with a slight but definite click, Francis and Alison were at last alone.

Suddenly awkward, Alison caressed the fresh laundry pile. 'Exquisite towels', she said laughing. 'I think they must be from a royal establishment!'

Francis smiled and replied, 'And apparently the curtains shut and open very quietly.'

'The instruction book is quite informative', said Alison. Looking through the pages, she found:

Curtains will silently open and you will see the dawning of each glorious day. At the end of the day the shafts of brilliant sunset will finally disappear. The island temperatures range from thirty degrees plus during the day to around twenty-four Celsius at night. No tips please.

As she put the book down and turned, Francis was suddenly right behind her. He quickly took her into his arms. Placing a delicate kiss on her forehead, then her nose, he kissed her gorgeous lips and softly said, 'Thank goodness! I can't find any more money for tips!'

They laughed briefly, but then forgot everything else. Alison shed her loose dress and Francis disposed of his own clothing, before they fell onto the bed to make joyous love. In the morning, they were still wrapped up together in happiness.

A hearty breakfast was delivered to their bedroom to start off the couple's day. The rest of the meals were provided in the small central dining room. Covered in pristine white cloths, eight tables were available for their select guests. On the ceiling, small tinted windows coloured the gentle sunlight which illuminated the whole area around them, and made the dark furnishings appear lighter. When the sun had gone down in the evening, or when the weather was unkind, a few small lighted chandeliers hung low over each table.

After each meal, Alison would take Francis' arm with a loving smile as they went outside and sat under the trees to view the splendour of the stars, to walk slowly around the lush, lighted gardens, or to take one of those comfortable seats placed around the long verandah.

In the evening, they would hurry back to their quiet bedroom, close the door, and enjoy their pleasure. Alison would whisper, 'I love you.' Looking at her beautiful face Francis always murmured back in his gravelly voice, 'I know you do, just as I love you!'

While enjoying the delicate, stunning tropical flowers and wild Malaysian bushes, Francis retold Alison all about his tour of magnificent gardens around the world, starting with his home in Southern Spain and finishing with the lovely garden at *Grace Chateau.*

As they slowly meandered the paths, Francis lovingly looked at the size, beauty and colours of the plants. Alison smiled at his joy, saying, 'God made such beautiful vegetation here, and you and the gardeners have created a lovely place for these flowers and bushes to flourish.'

When their days of honeymooning were over, Francis and Alison returned to Christchurch, where they expected to continue being cooped up in the two small-roomed flat where Francis had been living for some time.

Alison was privately disappointed that they would be returning there. In spite of her anxious queries, Francis hadn't looked for better living quarters. Not that she really minded, she told herself. She was married to her new, dear, loving husband, so she could stay anywhere. Every night she comforted herself that the three-quarter width bed meant they could sleep closer together. She supposed its lumpy mattress would eventually become reasonably comfortable...

What a surprise then, when they were presented with the wedding gift of a new home – *Wisteria Cottage,* next door to *Honeysuckle House!* All they had to do was move their sparse furniture into this much bigger place, and Alison did so with a joyful, grateful heart!

Having had an interest in the vacant properties around the district and thinking of future days when *Honeysuckle House* may be expanded, the canny Colonel had been looking out for bargains in property investment.

Living next door, the aged and recently widowed Gloria Shaw, despite her arthritic gnarled hands, had an active brain. She wanted to sell her house, disused horse stables and tack room, plus all its land, quickly.

But before she advertised it, she approached the Colonel to see if he was interested. He was, but the rest of the *Honeysuckle House* board were unaware of the offer. 'You've got a week!' Gloria succinctly said. 'Then I am going into a retirement home in the city.'

After much discussion, the board said yes. A few weeks later, the property was theirs, and Adam changed the name of the house to *Wisteria Cottage.*

Time was spent visiting the city's second-hand shops to buy some good furniture. Alison insisted they buy a new king-sized bed with a strong mattress, and when they found it, the original one was relegated to the dump.

With purpose, *Wisteria Cottage* became their home. Standing on the porch with the mountains before them and *Honeysuckle House,* just adjacent over the broken-down fence, Francis made a request. 'Can we call the cottage by the Spanish name, *Costa del Sol?* After all, I originally came from that area.'

Alison pointed out that the name was alright if you were in Southern Spain, but suggested that they stick to *Wisteria Cottage.* 'That way', she said, 'anyone who goes past in late spring or early summer will see the name and catch sight of the scented wisteria flowers – it just fits.'

Francis established sweeping lawns, planted roses and rhododendrons and hibiscus and hydrangea and plumbago and jasmine and morning glory, and other flowering shrubs and tall bushes. In his spare time, he started to build a wooden summerhouse. He put two strong seats inside so that there was always a place to rest and enjoy the wonders of creation, whatever the weather.

Over time, the vegetable garden became a sight to behold, with its tidy rows of beans, carrots, peas, cabbages and broccoli. Blackcurrant, redcurrant, gooseberry bushes, and clumps of rhubarb and apple and pear trees, were also established. Also, a few free-range hens that gladly supplied fresh eggs to both *Wisteria Cottage* and *Honeysuckle House.*

Alison had already said that they hoped to have four children. In his mind's eye, he also planned the directions the small paths would go, with square-shaped notices to help keep the children from straying as they had their fun.

Four children would mean that Alison would have to give up some of her secretarial work at *Legal Affairs* in *Honeysuckle House* – unless of course he, Francis, took his fair share of looking after the exciting and exuberant children to come.

At *Wisteria Cottage* he was tidying up the cobbled courtyard to clear it of any debris. The deteriorating stables and the tack room needed to be cleared out for future purposes. Then too, the outbuildings of *Honey-suckle House* were given a spruce up every so often. The tennis court received replacement nets and a new set of hoops were purchased for the croquet lawn. Many people came to enjoy a rest, or hold animated conversations under the two old oak trees, so the surrounding lawns needed to be kept in perfect order.

Yes, Francis was a busy man – but not too busy to show his love to Alison. Over time, they had three lovely daughters who gave them a great deal of fun and pleasure.

Chapter 69

*T*IME WENT BY. At breakfast, Francis was always looking through the pages of the local paper. One day he came across this – a local golf course was advertising a training course for beginners, saying: *Come and Try the Golf Course FOR FREE!*

He had been toying with the idea of learning to play golf. Now he had the wonderful chance to do so. He rang the golf club and made an appointment to receive some instruction. There, he met another golf beginner – Harris Tweed. He was the only one to come on the same free course.

They began well but soon got into golfing trouble. A misty rain might have had something to do with it. On the fairway, they managed to place a succession of balls, using different clubs, into diffident bushes and evil bunkers. Even the patient instructor was shaken. They played so horribly that by the end of the exhausting course they both said to him, 'Sorry! No thanks!' Returning their loaned golfing gear to the golf shop, they received most of their deposit back. They said goodbye to the now puzzled, and perhaps relieved, instructor.

While leaving the building they chatted about what had gone wrong. 'Maybe I wasn't holding the clubs right?' Francis said miserably.

Unhappily Harris replied, 'The ball went all different ways when I was supposed to be aiming at the little holes!'

Taking note that Harris was a reasonable man, in spite of his one day's golfing experience, Francis said, 'I work at *Honeysuckle House* as the gardener. My wife is Alison. We have three young girls, Alice, Emily and Judy.'

Harris replied in congratulatory terms, 'You said you work at *Honeysuckle House*? I live on the opposite side of the road to you. I have just bought an old army house there.'

The conversation was going along fine until it was interrupted by a heavy shower of rain, so they quickly got into their cars. Before Francis started the engine, he rolled the window down a fraction and called out an invitation. 'Why don't you come and enjoy an evening meal with us?'

However, Francis had not cleared it with Alison. When he did, as always, he found that she was pleased. Then he said that Harris Tweed wore a smart tweed suit, an expensive coat, and an over-the-top felt hat but without a feather attached. Alison looked forward to seeing him!

When Harris Tweed arrived on Friday evening for dinner, she found that he was the sort of man who, on removing his hat, bowed and gave Alison a gentle kiss on her hand. He was a tall, slender man with thinning jet-black hair and a narrow face. He had a wide mouth, small neat moustache, and brown eyes, with laughter lines to complete the picture. Alison and Francis found out that Harris was an energetic librarian. Although he said nothing of his age, Alison worked out that he must be around forty.

Harris talked amusingly about his father, Mr Tweed. 'He was a University Bookshop owner in Christchurch,' he said. 'He wore tweed clothing all his life, so he named me, his only child, by the same name – Harris Tweed!'

Harris Tweed commenced coming for evening meals at *Wisteria Cottage* on the last Friday of each month. Walking from his home to Francis and Alison's house, he stopped outside the tool shed, where Francis was always repairing something – perhaps an old mower that had broken down – or rescuing parts that might be useful; or even refilling the oilcans.

Harris peered round the door to greet the cheery worker and, after passing the time of day, Francis told him that his reward was waiting for him at *Wisteria Cottage*.

Smiling, and approaching the open front door, Harris gave the main doorbell a sharp ring. On entering the home, he saw that Alison was preparing the evening roast with all the trimmings. She left these now to attend to the visitor. The dinner would be Harris' reward!

Seated at the lounge table, Harris had remembered that last month, Alice had told him importantly that she was nearly five. Emily had said that though she was small, she was almost four. Lisping, Judy told him happily that she was just three. Giving him big smiles, the girls' bright brown eyes had caught him unawares. They looked so sweet that there was nothing he could do except praise them!

On this visit Alison had told him that Francis had just taken them to see their friends, Rebekah and Penny More, who lived at the house called *SweetSounds*. 'It is the house where I lived before Francis and I were married,' she explained.

Harris nodded. He knew something about it from Rebekah during one of those friendly chats they had over the low fence, but he hadn't realised the connection between the two families.

'When my parents died,' said Alison, 'I was lonely, so my old friend from school days, Rebekah, took me in. Her husband had died on overseas army manoeuvres. Her six-year old daughter Penny was a precious and slightly pernickety child. She had been born with Down Syndrome and had a button nose, a speech impediment, and wore glasses...'

She had to stop, because Alice, Emily and Judy rushed in to asked whether Harris had brought gifts for them. Harris wasn't going to let on just yet!

After Alison's scrumptious roast, Harris said that the gifts might be hidden behind the settee cushions, or perhaps under the chairs that they were sitting on. They searched in the deep pockets of his coat and under his felt hat, but they couldn't find anything. Harris said, 'What about the bookshelves?' There they found three new *Golden Books* hiding right in front of them.

By this time, it was eight o'clock; bedtime. Alison insisted that they must clean their teeth and then she listened to their prayers. When she returned, they took up again their conversation about the girls.

'Alice is always following me,' said Alison. 'She does what I do. She copies my sayings, which she sometimes repeats awkwardly to others, causing great hilarity and sometimes embarrassment. She has been looking forward to going to school for some time. Many of her friends have already started, so I had to sit her on my knee and explain that soon she will be five and able to join them. I said that after the school holidays they would all be starting the new term together. Alice was not too sure, but happy that it only meant that her birthday would make the difference. In the meantime, she returned to following me everywhere, copying what I do, and repeating my sayings.

'Emily enjoys collecting dolls. It doesn't matter what size, shape or age they are, or even however disgusting or amazing are the dresses that they wear. She takes some of them to her pre-school at the local centre three days a week. Francis has the responsibility of taking her there and picking her up on those days. At first, he was afraid of all the mothers arriving with their precious kiddies. They were so confident! They dressed smartly, but perhaps they were going to have coffee with their friends.'

Alison continued: 'There are also the usual pre-school helpers who guide the children in their various activities. The first time, a tall, welcoming lady introduced Emily to the other children, and then to all the exciting equipment. Francis said goodbye, but Emily was so busy with a large collection of rag dolls that she had just found, she never heard him. She was too engrossed. When he went to collect her, she said contentedly with a tired sigh, "I've had a lovely time!"

'Judy is very shy and awkward. A few weeks ago, we discovered that she needed spectacles. She loves them! She is very interested in going out of the house to explore the garden and beyond, so that open doors are an invitation to freedom outside. She travels at full speed along the extensive, narrow paths.

'Francis had not worried about putting up temporary fences where Alice and Emily were concerned as they didn't travel far, but Judy does! He has put fences up as fast as she finds ways of getting out. She only needs a short time to get her bearings, and then she's off!'

Francis interjected, 'Our cunning has become greatly enhanced through necessity!'

Laughing, and with permission readily given, Harris now joined in with his contribution. 'Tucked in behind the university in the town centre,' he explained, 'was my father's bookshop. It sold mostly religious and philosophical literature. The customers presented him with many challenges, requesting the latest titles written by unusual authors and printed by nearly impossible publishers.

'My father told me of the wonderful way that my mother Hannah, when she was still single, came striding into the bookshop through the milling crowd, her beauty and demeanour silencing the public. Leaning over the counter, she would whisper a few outrageous words to Dad. His face would go bright red and he didn't know what to do next. I learned later that my mother had informed him that he was a shy man and therefore he tended to get easily flustered. This meant that he could be curt toward his customers.

'"Don't worry", Hannah had whispered into his ear. "God loves you – and so do I." Then, turning, she left the shop as the silent crowd parted for her. My father resumed serving his customers in a state of euphoria!'

Harris continued. 'Now Dad was perplexed. He wanted to know the name of this woman. Who was she, this one who knew about the awkward dilemma of his shyness? It took some time asking various questions here and there, but eventually he found out her address. Armed with this information he decided that he would go and speak to her, but his courage failed. He returned a disappointed man each time, but eventually, he achieved it. The friendship between them grew into a romance and before they knew it, they were standing before the minister to speak these words: "God loves us – and we love each other!"

'Now, Dad was helped in his bookshop by his beautiful wife Hannah. With quiet, recorded classical music playing in the background and with interested faces, they listened to the customers' stories and requests. Sometimes they answered awkward questions. They searched for strange titles and they queried unusual authors and way-out publishers' names. They wrapped up purchases with happy smiles and, on receiving payment, they said on their departure, "We hope you enjoy what you have bought."

'At the end of the day, they closed the bookshop and returned home to enjoy their dinner that was quietly simmering at a slow cooking temperature. Relaxing, they smiled into each other's eyes, saying together, "God loves you – and so do I."'

Alison quickly said, 'What happened next?'

Taking a sad breath Harris slowly replied, 'She died in childbirth – having me.'

'Oh, I am sorry,' Alison said, reaching out to take his hand. Francis cleared his throat before abruptly rising from his chair to get fresh tea for them all.

Thanking Alison and Francis for their understanding, Harris continued. 'Many years went by. When Dad was thinking about retiring, he had the idea that he could sell the bookshop to me. By this time, I had become tired of selling books. I wanted to become a specialist school librarian instead. This meant going to Wellington to study, so I explained to him that he would have to find someone else.

'Dad did find an excellent buyer for the business. What he received from the sale of the bookshop enabled him to journey around the North Island, taking his time to do the sights, including seeing me in Wellington. Eventually, I came back to Christchurch and now take library books to all primary schools.'

Harris stood up and said to his friendly hosts, 'This was an excellent meal and an interesting time, but I must fly as I have things to do.'

Chapter 70

*A*LISON AND FRANCIS hadn't told anyone that they were expecting their fourth child, but midwife Polly guessed it was so. Alison was putting up with the normal things that most pregnant women suffer – swollen ankles and increasing size, so Polly gently said that she was available if needed. Alison was grateful, saying, 'I'm going to the maternity clinic for another check-up tomorrow.'

The efficient nurse enquired, did Alison want to know the sex of the child? She was thrilled with the news that it was to be a boy. Returning home, she gave Francis an extra kiss for, God willing, their family would be complete with the birth of a son.

Almost from the beginning of *Legal Affairs* Alison had been fully employed as a secretary at *Honeysuckle House*. When she had given birth to each of their three daughters, her hours had become more flexible. However, seeing as she was now expecting a fourth child, she was let off all duties immediately.

Everyone crowded round to say farewell to Alison. As Miss Marchant was responsible for her work, she made a short speech: 'With Alison's forthcoming pregnancy, her excellent work will now be taken over by two eighteen-year-old young women who have just come out of Secretarial College. It is felt, dear Alison, that the care of your children is of the utmost priority.'

Alison was overcome. She asked Miss Marchant whether she needed to inform the two young secretaries of the ins-and-outs of the business. Miss Marchant said,

'No, I'll do that myself! You just need to look after your-self,' giving Alison's tummy a gentle pat.

Alison went into hospital at the due time and her labour was short. They brought home their little boy, whom they named Frank.

Of course, this precious boy meant much more to Francis. He was not treating his dear wife Alison or any of his three daughters any differently, but he was over-joyed to have a son. Francis now insisted that they call a halt to any more pregnancies, and Alison duly underwent surgery for a hysterectomy – although their passionate love-making would continue!

Alice, Emily, Judy and the two-year old Frank, were growing up in leaps and bounds, filling their time and experience with excited enthusiasm!

Harris Tweed still called in most Fridays for evening meals. On one such day, as he called into the machine shop to have a chat, Francis excitedly told him about the small V-shaped piece of spare land just near the back of the house, large enough to create a small swimming pool. 'I have drawn up plans,' he said, 'and taken them to *Honeysuckle House*. The city council has just approved them.'

During the summer, the building of the swimming pool progressed. One day, Alison nattered on to Harris that she had already purchased fashionable swimming costumes for herself and for the children. A one-piece red swimsuit for Alice, a light blue one for Emily, and a pale yellow one for Judy, while multi-coloured swimming trunks would delight Frank.

Later that night, when Alison donned her own swim-ming costume, Francis was amazed at how stunning she looked, even though she was a mother of four!

The children watched as Francis worked on this project. It was hard labour digging it out, water proof-ing, pouring concrete, laying pipes – but at last it was done. Finally, the necessary fence and latched gate were in place to prevent any child from getting near the water unattended. Now, he could fill up the pool.

And then, disaster struck.

While the pool was filling up at a steady rate, Frank, dressed in his multi-coloured togs, escaped the family in the house.

Unfortunately Francis had not secured the top clasp of the gate to the pool properly, so the boy was able to push open the gate quite freely. On venturing in, he fell head over heels into the water.

It had been almost a minute before Francis asked anxiously, 'Where's Frank?' and rushing instinctively to the pool, he pushed the free gate open, and jumping into the water, scooped the child up.

Tilting him to drain the water from his lungs, Francis worked frantically to revive his only son, lying so still and lifeless before him.

Alison also rushed to the pool. She didn't actually cry, but from her mouth issued a long keening wail, as if she was seeing this yet not believing any of it. Then she ran back to the phone and rang for the ambulance.

When she returned the three girls were looking on with shock and horror at their little brother, lying so still and chalky blue before them, with Francis gently cradling the little body in his arms, weeping. The tableau would be etched forever in Alison's mind.

Alison encircled the sobbing girls with her arms, comforting them as best as she could.

After what seemed an age the ambulance arrived, and the paramedics rushed Frank, with his terrified mother, to the hospital. Francis and the girls followed in their car. He drove like a madman and the girls were frightened out of their wits.

Sadly, when Frank was able to return home from hospital, his accident appeared to have caused some brain damage due to a lack of oxygen. 'We will have to wait and see what comes of this,' said the concerned doctors. 'What damage has been done is not clear. It may be for the rest of his life, or maybe the brain has some other aspects which will take over his normal function.'

All life had changed. Whereas there had always been joy and laughter and lots of kissing in the household, there was now a deep sadness, pain, guilt and, regrettably, no kissing. Certainly, no pleasurable lovemaking between the parents.

When Alison was getting Alice, Emily and Judy to sleep, they often had frightening and unhappy dreams. So, every night, she told them that although Frank had had a nasty accident, they would all have to learn to make different plans. 'He is still your brother, and a wonderful, gorgeous boy. Later, we will be surprised and happy when he learns how to do things differently. Let's ask God to make it so!' And so they all closed their eyes, joining in the short prayer of faith.

As Alison cleaned up the lounge, she had a sudden thought about Frank's nappies. There would be time for him to wear more fashionable boys' trousers, but at present he had trouble controlling himself. She knew that he would need nappies for some time to come.

She collected some of Frank's plastic balls and soft toys, and put them away in the cupboard. She imagined that they would still get plenty of use.

As she put his highchair back in the corner, she knew that it would be necessary for every meal.

Alison felt very alone.

Where was Francis? Probably moping in the workshop...

Chapter 71

REBEKAH AND PENNY had heard the siren of the ambulance as it was leaving *Wisteria Cottage* on its way to the hospital. Looking at each other, they rushed across the road to see if they could do anything. They saw only confusion.

Rebekah thought that Alison had gone in the ambulance, so where was Francis? Then she saw him hurrying the three girls into the car and heard him call out to her that Frank had had a serious accident.

Rebekah was not too sure how Francis would react to Frank's accident. They had spent many happy times together. Francis always came home early in order to bath Frank. They both got very wet and soap bubbles brought much laughter! He was quite happy for Alison to bath the girls and put perfumed powder on them as long as he bathed Frank.

Often Francis took Frank out in his pushchair, talking to him *man-to-man* and lovingly showing him things that he considered of vital interest. Frank always chuckled and smiled in enjoyment to his pleased father.

Occasionally Francis took him from *Wisteria Cottage* the short distance out to the entrance to the *Legal Affairs* offices at *Honeysuckle House*. There he explained to Frank what the Colonel or Sophie or Miss Marchant or even the new barrister, Jane Abernethy, were doing. In turn, in spite of increasing work, they took time to return Frank's keen interest with some generous waves.

Rebekah also knew that when Frank was at the age of understanding, Francis intended to take him to the workshop where he could sit on the lower workman's bench. On it was a junior oilcan, ready for Frank to use on his own small plastic lawn mower. Beside it, there was an old piece of cloth to wipe off any excess oil.

Rebekah cried out now, her heart breaking for them, 'Oh, Francis! Oh, Frank!'

A few weeks went by, and then Rebekah called with a purpose to *Wisteria Cottage*. Alison was still in tears, so Rebekah briskly told her, 'I understand your situation,' leaving the *understanding* there.

'We have been through similar challenges before. My husband died in a plane explosion. Your parents' deaths were from a cruel accident. Penny has Down Syndrome. Frank's accident is outside our understanding for now. Wipe your tears. We are going out for *you*.'

The next day, while Francis was given the responsibility of looking after Frank, who was playing with his toys, Rebekah went out with Alison on what they named *girl adventures*. They went for an expensive hairdressing appointment. There they were able to talk for ages while the attentive stylists stood behind them, doing their hair with flair.

Then, seated at small crowded café tables, they indulged in generous sips of exotic coffees while watching avidly (and talking eagerly about) the many earnest shoppers who bought racks of diminishing sale stock.

The following week, on another bright, clear day, Rebekah and Alison walked arm in arm the short distance to *Sweethearts Restaurant*. Sitting down inside on the comfortable seats by the open windows, they basked in the sunshine and enjoyed a late morning tea. This took them right through to lunchtime. Then they had bacon fritters and fresh salad, followed by luscious fruits. To accompany this, each had an expensive glass of white wine to finish off with style.

Alison said wistfully to her friend, 'I know what you are up to. You have been very kind and generous.' Looking down at the sparse remains of the lunch they had just consumed, she continued, 'You are trying to get me to look beyond Frank's troubles.'

Rebekah smiled. Wiping her mouth clean of any crumbs, she took her troubled friend's hand and started to say what was really on her mind.

'You know I grew up in an Anglican Orphanage', she reminded Alison. 'One of the counsellors once said, "Love is the key to any relationship," but my first experience of a loving relationship was when you and I met at school. The friendship between us was good and pure, well grounded by the time we left school.'

Alison smiled weakly in acknowledgement, and her best friend went on to say, 'You remember when I met Hugh? I was head over heels in love! He was a soldier, so handsome in his uniform!' Alison put her hand on Rebekah's in sympathy; she remembered the deep pain her friend had gone through.

Then Rebekah shook her shoulders, and continued: 'We were married so quickly! And then Penny came along; our honeymoon baby. Before she was born my Hugh was sent to somewhere in the Middle East. Sadly, there was something wrong with Penny – Trisomy 21, they said; Down Syndrome. She had a button nose and poor eyesight. They said that later she might have a slight speech impediment.'

Alison's concentration was now on Rebekah, and she squeezed her cold hand. Rebekah's grief was something she still lived every day, though she had learned to hide it well.

'I was so scared! I immediately contacted Hugh about getting leave to come home. This took time to arrange, but when he got here I was immediately comforted. He took over, establishing that everything that could be done for our daughter was being done right. Then he had to return to his army station. That left me and Penny all alone, except for you, my sweet friend! A few years later, you had your own tragedy with your parents' deaths, so you moved in with us, and we were able to give comfort to each other.'

The two women hugged each other, and Rebekah continued. 'Penny absolutely loved you; she sensed your grief. She often put her arms around you and burst into simple songs which she had learned from the TV.'

Alison wistfully smiled. She could remember this so clearly. 'Penny would take my hands as she sang. It always made such a difference to me to see her act in such a happy way. Inevitably, I had to eventually smile back at her. When I began to walk outside in winter, Penny made sure that I put on my winter coat and pompom hat and thick gloves, and those ridiculous furry boots. With a serious voice she always told me, "The weather is alright now, but it may be different when you come back."'

They both laughed at this, and Rebekah resumed her tale.

'Hugh died in a plane explosion. "Lots of deaths. Numerous tragedies. Sad outcomes..." – that was what the officious officer said to me. Silly man! After your tragedy and after Hugh's death, I named the house *SweetSounds*.'

Rebekah hesitated for a moment. Then, looking into Alison's deep brown eyes, she slowly said, 'Do you think those *sweet sounds* are here, my friend?'

Alison looked back at her. With God's help, they had been through difficult times, but both had survived. They had forged firm and everlasting friendships which would never end.

'Yes,' she triumphantly said, with rising excitement, 'I think they are!' Slightly altering her posture, she said something even more meaningful, for at that moment she was making a new decision. 'I am not going to mollycoddle Frank. I have looked at a few people who have had similar tragedies, and what they have done is pretty poor.' Giving a shudder, Alison said firmly, 'Rather, I will work with him. Over time, and I hope with much humour and, yes, silly games, we will reach new heights not only with his body, but with his mind and even his personality.'

'That's a pretty tall order,' Rebekah said cautiously. 'Have you set your standards a little too high?'

Alison smiled again. 'Oh, I can recognise some of the pitfalls, but if I don't attempt to do this task, and of course include dear Francis, my friends and you, then I will be too scared to do anything and end up being a miserable mother to an unhappy child.'

Rebekah was greatly relieved. At the city's *Special Needs School* there were children, including Penny, who were practising precisely what Alison had been saying.

Chapter 72

A LISON RETURNED FROM the restaurant a very determined woman. In fact, she informed Francis what *they* were going to do.

Francis was surprised, but they began to tell Frank simple but well-constructed stories. Whether Frank 'heard' them they didn't know.

That was something that the principal of the *Special Needs School* had recommended when Alison had rung him up. With copious tears, she had begun her story but didn't get far. The friendly principal interrupted, saying, 'What about coming along to our school and seeing for yourself what has been done for these eager and interesting pupils?'

Alison ceased crying. She thought that his attitude was so unlike some other educationalists who said that such children should be put in an institution and not be seen.

The next day, Alison sat listening to the principal as he spoke to her in his relatively quiet office, whilst the children were all outside playing in the well-constructed tree-lined school grounds.

'Lots of things,' he said, 'like examining trees, looking at colourful flowers, or playing the latest simple game, all help to involve them and gain their interest. It also helps them to relate to other children.'

Alison listened to what he had to say. She looked around the office and noticed many highly thought-of volumes placed on shelves in a higgledy-piggledy manner. She imagined how some of the books had fallen into the principal's eager hands. Delving into the pages, he would rejoice to find answers to some children's problems.

'Of course, Frank is still quite young', the enthusiastic principal continued. 'He has not got to the age where we can really work with him. If you and your husband, not forgetting the rest of your family, pitch in, he can do all those things I have told you about.'

Suddenly the principal's chair went back so far that he nearly went over, but he continued. 'When he comes here, he will have made a good start. Now,' bringing his chair upright, 'here are the details of one of our essential ladies, Mrs Winifred Warberton. With your permission, she will come to your home and assess the boy and his individual needs.'

Mrs Warberton duly arrived to observe Frank in his home environment. Of a comfortable size both in stature and in spirit, she had a heavily jowled neck. Knowing that children would be drawn to it like moths to a light, she had hidden it by wearing a light scarf. When she spoke, the tones came out like those of a glorious blackbird.

She listened to Frank as he tried to articulate. She had eyes that focussed on 'her' children for a long time, and they were always captivated by this process. She looked deeply into the eyes of Frank now for a clue as to what was going on, saying, 'The deepest expression of a soul is there.'

Smiling at his hopeful parents she said, 'We will all be amazed at his capabilities, his hidden intelligence, and his ability to function, but we need to give him incredibly supportive assistance first.'

Kind Mrs Warberton came in once a week and soon began to appreciate the potential, astuteness and capabilities of Frank. With her support, Francis became more involved. Making a small simple structure out of timber, he put in sturdy thick dowels to build a climbing frame for Frank to use.

They had a long wait while Frank examined the structure.

Francis whispered to Alison, 'For a small boy, this

climbing frame is a bit frightening.' Then he thought of making this into a game. He carefully placed in full sight, at the top of the ladder, one of Frank's favourite soft toys, to lure him up.

Frank now approached the new structure with considerable interest. He put his foot onto the first dowelled rung, then when he had succeeded, he put the other foot on the second rung. Then he tried the next one, and the next one, until he reached the stuffed toy placed firmly at the top.

Frank had succeeded! With joyous drooling, he had achieved his goal! What amazing things he had accomplished – he had used all his limbs, body and hands as well as feet!

Alison and Francis were overcome. Laughing, they threw their arms around each other, danced a merry dance, and then danced again with great excitement, holding Frank in the middle of their embrace! Later, with a smile on his face, Frank thoroughly enjoyed his sleep.

It didn't take long to tell Mrs Warberton the results of the delightful game. She also danced, but briefly, as she became breathless. Instead, she rejoiced that they had found one of the keys to Frank's development. She said, 'Alison and Francis – you are not people who cried *help* but rather, you declared *hope*!'

Chapter 73

ADVENTUROUS PENNY SET off on her bicycle to travel the short distance between her home and *Wisteria Cottage*. Leaving her bike by the outer door and entering, Penny found Alison and asked her to leave the humdrum things of everyday life and take a short walk with her instead.

Alison was surprised, but it meant that Frank would need to be looked after by Francis, who gladly said, 'Frank and I will have a great time together!'

Once they were on their way, and because their expedition was a Penny and Alison thing, Penny firmly said, 'Let's go closer to the mountains, where we can see the snow.'

Stopping to see the gentle stream while watching the ripples on the water and the tall wispy grasses bowing in heavenly recognition, their eyes were drawn to the glorious mountains covered in snow and bathed in winter sunlight. This was a tremendous sight and, with this glorious vision before them – God's wonderful creation – Alison's thoughts turned to her precious son, and her eyes filled with tears.

Of course, as she had been taught, Penny looked away when Alison started to cry. But first, she drew out a hanky and gave it to her. Alison wiped away her tears and when they returned to *Wisteria Cottage*, she suddenly felt a new woman.

Alison gave Penny a hug, and then kissed her on the nose. Thrilled that she had found Alison such a delight, and having done everything right, Penny raced home on her bike and excitedly told her mother all about it.

In Southern Spain, Aimee and Abbas Delgado hadn't heard from their son Francis for ages. They were getting worried, even discussing whether they should phone him, but the following day they received an airmail letter from Alison, their daughter-in-law. They stopped what they were doing and sat down in a cool area, and Aimee read out the unexpected letter.

> *Dearest Aimee and Abbas,*
> *I am sorry that Francis hasn't written, but he was too busy doing things on the property. I have reminded him numerous times that he must let you know about Frank's troubles.*

Abbas looked at Aimee and asked, 'What troubles?' Aimee read the rest of the letter.

> *I want to give you an explanation about Frank. He had been looking forward to going into the swimming pool that Francis had constructed outside, but Frank had decided to be the first one in the water, without us. The result was disastrous. He nearly drowned and was rushed to hospital, but unfortunately serious brain damage had occurred. We have all had to learn how to help our new precious boy.*
> *I'm sure that you will take this letter to the other residents to tell them about Frank. However, Francis is still very upset by this and says to you, 'I have so much to tell you, but I can't get my head around it. Perhaps another time.'*
> *I'm afraid that another time will be a long time coming.*
> *With much love,*
> *Alison*

Aimee and Abbas were shocked at this news but immediately wrote back a loving and sympathetic letter; one that told Francis that they and the other concerned residents would pray for Frank, for Francis and Alison and their precious daughters, that they all might have God's hope, come what may. They sent it to *Wisteria Cottage* with all their love.

Francis could not get Frank's situation out of his mind. He knew that the swimming pool incident was an accident, but nevertheless he still felt responsible for it, and worried constantly that there may be another tragedy like it.

One day he decided that the action of destroying the pool would help him to feel better. Going into the workshop, he collected a long crowbar and set to work. He disposed of the concrete slabs, the wire fence and the heavy gate, plus the hidden pipes. It all took a long and exhausting time, but eventually he achieved his aim and the pool was demolished. As he went back into the house every night, he would be so exhausted that after having had his tea, he fell into his bed for a good sleep.

Maybe that was a good thing, but over time, despite all this hard work, Francis *still* found himself feeling restless. Something else was disturbing him. He felt guilty but couldn't put the guiltiness into words. He felt that God – whether true or not – was punishing him for not having had the sense to secure the pool gate properly, thus allowing Frank to fall into the pool.

Nothing would change his mind.

He was to blame.

He alone.

Sorrowfully, Francis looked at family or close friends who always wanted to ask whether they could do anything for this precious boy, Frank. Though they were wanting to be kind, he withdrew even further into himself. He certainly didn't feel like giving friendly waves to others as he mowed around the two massive oak trees.

Alison missed him, as he refused to call in for morning or afternoon teas, and he no longer chatted to Judy as he transported his daughter to play-school. The moment that Francis had completed his day's work, like necessary repairs, or cutting the grass around the croquet lawn, or seeing to the tennis nets, or checking the waterfowl on the lake, he was off to hide in his workshop. There, the machinery would comfort him.

The underlying problem was that together they had decided that Alison would have her hysterectomy. Therefore, it was now impossible for them to have another child. This was another heavy burden for Francis to bear.

In spite of Frank's accident, Alice, Emily and Judy were growing up with their own individual expressions of *good choices* and *lasting values*.

Now it was school holidays again and they looked after Frank in another way, taking him out for walks in the nearby countryside. They saw tree-lined swampy woodlands, and cows grazing in the field. Frank demanded to stop to taste the delicious wild blackberries. Of course, the girls always wanted some berries too, so they joined Frank and stopped for a while, slobbering over the ripe fruit until their stomachs were full.

Sometimes they knocked on the door of Penny's home and she joined them on these jaunts. They always returned with their faces stained purple!

Through this unsettling period, the Reverend Geoff Silver, the resident minister, visited the Delgado family many times. Francis didn't give him much time, embarrassed that he might say something expressive, which was not like him. He gave a short greeting and then went off on another venture.

Alison and the minister knew that Francis was running away. They chatted for a while, and then Alison asked Geoff, 'You won't forget to pray for Frank, will you?'

The minister kindly answered, 'We *always* pray for Frank.' Then he told her that there were many possibilities when you had a handicapped child like Frank.

'I remember reading a little book, *A Grief Observed* written by CS Lewis. In it, he attempts to look for *any* reason for his wife's sudden death. You might have heard of him through the *Narnia* children's books? He was the author. He also wrote a trilogy of science fiction books and other religious books. He was a professor at both

Cambridge and Oxford Universities.'

Alison said, 'Oh, *Narnia!* I read and re-read the seven books throughout my life. There they are,' she said pointing; 'on the bottom shelves, just over there. Fancy that, writing a book about his wife's death. It probably helped many people.'

The minister continued. 'Yes, it did. CS Lewis said that:

> *Long ago, she was haunted all one morning as she went about her work with the obscure sense of God at her elbow, demanding her attention. And of course, not being a perfected saint, she had the feeling that it would be a question, as it usually is, of some unrepented sin or tedious duty. At last she gave in and faced Him. But it was, 'I want to give you something,' and instantly, she entered into joy.*

At hearing this, Alison burst again into tears, but not of joy. This would come sometime in her and her families' future. However, she had the feeling that all of a sudden her Holy God was in this room with her. Everything was going to be alright, even though she didn't have any idea what could be considered 'alright'.

The minister waited for Alison to quieten her tears and wisely said, 'You never know what plans God has for Frank, and for you, and for the girls, and for Francis. Watch out, and you will be surprised at the outcome.'

Chapter 74

ADAM RECALLED HOW proud Francis was when Frank was born. 'This will change everything,' he cheerily had said. 'Not that I'm not grateful for my daughters. Don't get me wrong! But you see, at last I have my son! Our family is complete.'

Now, Adam didn't know what to say regarding Frank's accident.

Polly suggested to him, 'How about starting to collect donations for Frank from the legal profession, maybe nationally. That would be enough for you to do.'

Adam smiled; it was a good idea. He determined to begin at once.

Douglas had become known for always being in the right place at the right time. Fixing awkward light bulbs, or retrieving fallen objects from behind a wall heater, that sort of thing.

Although Douglas wouldn't admit it, when he'd been feeling down, he would put on his cheery cap and bright red scarf and call on Alice, Emily, Judy and Frank. They would listen in fascination to his made-up stories. Maybe the children would be in the tales, doing wonderful but unimaginable things.

However, Douglas could now not work out how he was going to cope with Frank's terrible accident. Iris said that his family needed some normality, so suggested that they invite the girls to their cheerful cottage for afternoon tea. This would give the children something to look forward to, and also the opportunity to receive some special attention. If you agree, I will have to check with Alison.'

Douglas did agree, so Iris put the suggestion to a frazzled Alison, who gratefully accepted, replying, 'What a lovely thought!'

Iris and Douglas got busy with their preparations. Alice was coming on Tuesday, Emily on Wednesday and Judy on Thursday the following week after school at three-thirty precisely.

'Then there will be a repeat after this,' said well-meaning Iris.

'Oh, good!' said grateful Douglas.

And Polly? She remembered that she needed to let James, and Thomas and his wife, Jo, know of Frank's accident. She began to write them both a short letter, but didn't get far.

As she wrote, she thought back to the time that James returned from his missionary course in London. He was looking at new ways to promote the gospel. He was a schoolteacher and had heard that a teacher was needed on Thursday Island, in Northern Queensland, to teach Aborigine students. He made preparations for going there.

Polly and Adam were thrilled at this. However, before James departed, Polly asked more pertinent questions. A young, very beautiful woman who was also a teacher lived on Thursday Island. She had been on the same missionary course as James.

However, James gave no concrete answers. He just said, 'Oh, my Angel.' The term *angel* was repeated often by him, so that Polly wondered whether it was the proper name, or was the name that James gave to her because she was absolutely heavenly. Whether James met with his 'angel' there, she didn't know.

Polly knew that James, like many sons or even men in general, was not good at letter writing, certainly not on tropical Thursday Island. James had only sent illustrated tourist postcards accompanied by his large scrawling writing on the other side. One day his parents received a postcard on which he had written,

Angel and I are alright. We are on holiday near this local scene.

But he never told them any real news.

Three weeks later another postcard arrived that took Polly and Adam's real interest:

Angel and I are married!

Then, ten months later:

Angel and I are having a child!

Then, when the child was born, they received another.

Her name is Maria!

... and that was all the details offered. However, James sent them a few photos of Maria, smiling, crying or kicking, but never showing her parents, James, or even his Angel!

Polly reckoned that she could make plans for a trip to Thursday Island, but this meant leaving ailing Adam at home. Adam had spent a considerable time in various Christchurch hospitals. With good hospital carers, Adam was independent with almost everything, but Polly still had the main responsibility of ongoing care for him. The only way that Polly could reach the happy couple and their daughter Maria, was to pray to the Lord each day.

Polly wrote to them, telling them of Frank's troubles. A week went by and although they had never met Frank, James and his Angel and Maria sent him a small Aboriginal carved boomerang to cheer him up.

Polly let out a sigh as her thoughts moved to Thomas and Jo. They had bought an old Combi van, first to explore England and then France, Portugal and finally Southern Spain. During this time, they produced two delightful children, quiet Zack(ary) and bubbly Mim(osa).

They lived at camping grounds, either in hired large tents during summer, or small cabins when it was cold winter weather. Thomas was a good artist and, whenever they were feeling desperate for money, the paints and brushes that were stored under one of the vehicle seats would come out and he would go to the marketplace and paint portraits of the local people.

In Southern Spain, the family were captivated by the sparkling Mediterranean Sea. Deciding to spend some time exploring the coastal region, they started at Gibraltar and travelled slowly along the stunning coast to the city of Malaga. They looked out for the magnificent mansion that Francis Delgado had described to them at *Honeysuckle House*, saying, 'If you ever go to Spain, look my parents up. They will always welcome you at the *Sanctuary of the Cross.*'

They found the mansion standing there, magnificently alone. Leaving their van on the road, well secured (they learned later there was a wide area to park cars which was hidden to one side), they hoped to meet Abbas and Aimee Delgado.

Once inside the welcoming gates, they walked past numerous older residents relaxing on comfortable chairs underneath palm trees while looking out to the sea, or snoozing.

In the shade of another large tree, young Zack found an open door. Walking through the entrance, the family found themselves in a grand hall with a high ceiling and large windows. Four tiered rows of tropical and exotic flowers – golden hibiscus, vibrant red poinsettias and white carnations – filled the place with amazing colour and a heady perfume.

At once, they saw Abbas and Aimee, who were relaxing after finishing their leisurely lunch. They recognised them from Francis' photograph that they carried just in case they met.

After Thomas hurriedly explained to them, 'We are the Frasers from *Honeysuckle House* in New Zealand,' Abbas and Aimee stood up and exclaimed that they had been praying for someone knowledgeable to appear. Now their prayer had been granted, just like that!

Abbas fetched some more chairs for them, and they all sat down. Zach and Mim sat perfectly still at the strange sight of the older Spanish couple. Aimee asked if they had had a meal. When they said no, they were invited to eat whatever was left on the table. It was such a lot!

While the children were still eating, Aimee told them that her grandson Frank had had a terrible accident.

Thomas said, 'What?'

Jo said, 'An accident?'

Abbas then told them it was a swimming pool accident and that Frank had some brain damage.

That night in a hurried letter to his parents, Thomas wrote:

Jo and I are very sorry to hear about young Frank having an accident in the swimming pool. We hope that he will recover quickly. Abbas and Aimee Delgado were beside themselves as Francis has not written. They told us that it was Alison who had to take up her pen and let them know.

A week later, Thomas hurriedly wrote again.

I can't get over the fact that Aimee has massive wrinkles which go down both sides of her pleasant face. Abbas is extremely bald and has dark hairs sprouting out of his ears. They have both made us feel at home, saying we are to stay with them in the house, even though we have all our camping gear here. We were made so welcome that we are staying here... forever!

When she got the letter, Polly was surprised. Were they really staying there... forever? Confused, she wrote back saying,

How can you stay there when all you have done is to drive around four countries in an old car, camping with two young children?

Thomas wrote back:

Jo and I have talked at length about the pros and cons of staying here and what it would mean to us. The Delgados are getting past all the practicalities of running this massive place.

Aimee has told us that she was known for being a big woman and that she always had to bend her neck and shoulders to get through doors or passageways, which has become increasingly difficult. Now her eyesight is getting poor. In spite of new spectacles, she struggles to cope with all the extra calls made upon her time and energy.

For some time Abbas has been struggling to keep things going. The nature of his dwarfism as well as his ageing means that he has extra difficulty with his walking. Their bedroom used to be on the mansion's top floor, but they are now living and sleeping downstairs. It turns out that they have difficulty managing the stairs to the first-floor bedrooms to deal with the residents' needs.

They thought about selling the mansion, but wondered where these permanent residents could go, as they have peculiar ailments and look rather strange. Their main concern has always been for the residents; it would be absolutely cruel to send them out into the world.

So now Jo and I look after the business side of things. I went first to see all the mansion residents, who said that they had no complaints with the care that Aimee and Abbas were offering. Between them Aimee and Abbas speak at least four different languages, so they can translate when needed.

One of the residents said that the seats upholstered with bright coloured fabric in the garden were getting faded, worn and one or two were torn. If they were fixed then they could have a snooze, a chat or a long look at the sea, aware that they would be attended to by someone if something went wrong. A third said, maybe even employing a physiotherapist and a nurse who was up to date with the latest care would meet their needs. They were getting to the stage of wondering what their future held. Would they need hospital care, a hospice, or perhaps something different? These ordinary things of life could become insurmountable problems, yet everything is running very smoothly now that we are here.

Where are we living? In the top rooms of the mansion. They look out to the sparkling sea. When not doing schoolwork, Zack, who is starting to speak Spanish, is joined by some of the local children for never-ending computer games. Although Mim is quite young she has village friends playing around the shrubs, bushes and trees. She too is learning the Spanish language.

Older residents of the Sanctuary of the Cross smile with pleasure as they watch us. They have learned that our children are not as intimidating as they had thought. They find that they forget their ailments for an hour or so and, instead, enjoy all the children at play.

Aimee and Abbas spend a lot of time remem-bering their past activities, while also looking content-edly at the wonderful sea.

With lots of love,
from all of us!

Francis and Alison also received a letter from Thomas and Jo.

Very sorry to hear of Frank's troubles. Our children Zack and Mim have coloured in some large draw-ings. Frank might like them. We certainly hope they will make him feel better.

Zack had drawn dogs looking out of the Spanish mansion at the still sea, and Mim had done some pussy-cats, drinking milk. Alison put them on the lounge wall. Whether it was looking at the still sea or drinking milk she wasn't sure, but Frank enjoyed them.

Chapter 75

THE COLONEL, SOPHIE and Peter, all dressed smartly, called in once at *Wisteria Cottage*. The visitors sat in the lounge with the saddened family for about half-an-hour, not saying a word. They just were *being there*. Then, while silently making their exit, Sophie left a small note which said,

Our prayers are for everyone. Frank is in God's tender loving care.

Every week the Colonel arranged for some wonderful orchids to be delivered to Alison and Francis from a Christchurch florist. These lovely blooms were to remind the family of the care of Jesus in their ongoing difficulties.

Miss Marchant didn't normally go to church. However, she went into one of the city's cathedrals to remember Frank. She went into the shadowy church and was very surprised to experience such a feeling of peace in this quiet place. Without words, she prayed to the Lord Jesus for the damaged boy and asked God to be present with the rest of the family in their anxiety and fear.

At the retirement home, when Gloria Shaw heard of Frank's tragic accident, she arranged something that was quite unexpected by the family. She offered to pay any taxi fares to the hospital and for any prescriptions – no questions asked.

Alison broke down in tears when she received the letter. It was typed by someone on the staff but, despite the awkwardness of her hand, Gloria had managed to sign it with difficulty: *With much love, Mrs Gloria Shaw.*

When Alison visited her some weeks later to thank her, Gloria took hold of her hands in her own damaged fingers and gave some valuable advice.

'Frank has had a terrible time, but the boy won't have any idea of the trouble he has caused. He is locked away in his own pleasure dome and will not recognise the pain and sorrow in the rest of the family's hearts. That's why I'm keen to be on board with some practical things, like payment for taxi fares and for any prescriptions.'

Alison listened in wonder at such kindness.

Harris Tweed stopped calling in for a friendly chat with Francis in his machine shop. Nor did he go for Friday's evening meals with the family. Instead, he wanted to give them space to work through those difficult days.

A suitable time went by before he drove the car up to the front door of *Wisteria Cottage.* Harris got out and said to Frank, who was sitting in the sunshine peaceably, 'I have a surprise for you.' Three blue T-shirts were brought out – each one emblazoned with the words: *My Name is Frank and I'm Special!*

Frank look intently at Harris with his deep brown eyes. Harris imagined that Frank was saying some words of thanks. He could never tell, but hoped that the gift meant something special to him.

Harris did something else, too. Having numerous poems on his kitchen fridge, he took one that was put into an ornate frame and gave it to the family. Alison put the poem up on the kitchen mantle-piece:

> *If you hem in both ends of each day with prayer, it won't be so difficult to unravel in the middle.*

A reminder for all to see.

Alison, coming in from outside, would be casting an eye on the framed prayer, reminding herself of other prayers that were just welling up inside her, like, *O Lord of mercy,*

Lord of grace, be very kind to Frank.

When Francis came into the kitchen from his grass-mowing at lunchtime (a flask of tea and a few chicken sandwiches with salad lovingly made by Alison that morning) he took notice of the prayer up above. It would comfort him to reflect on the simple words.

Alice, Emily and Judy were growing up fast and doing whatever young girls do. On seeing the words of this prayer, they would join in.

Gradually, day by day, week by week, month after month, things improved and the situation became less critical.

Francis and Alison discovered that they were now able to enjoy kisses and cuddles again. Strengthened by a greater love for each other, they were now able to think concretely, take advice happily and be with each other unashamedly!

Alison knew that Francis' real problem was not being able to have any more children, a son perhaps. But after many tearful discussions with him, they concluded that God in His wonderful mercy had given a child called Frank *into their care!*

Alison lovingly said, 'Frank needs our love, and that is the end of it.'

Chapter 76

E MUSTN'T FORGET Sam or Jack Fraser. Sam knew that Francis Delgado came from some magnificent mansion in Southern Spain, that his father was a dwarf and his mother, a giant. He also knew that Francis had been a worldwide wanderer, gaining gardening expertise before coming to New Zealand.

Sam had been thinking about his future prospects, as well. Working in the garage repairing cars and trucks was not so satisfying now. The job was more mundane and repetitive every week. It was time to explore other opportunities.

As he drove to *Wisteria Cottage* to express his belated sympathy, he also wondered whether he could be employed by Francis. Standing now at the entrance of the machine-shop Sam suddenly cried out, 'I want a change from repairing cars!' And then asked, 'Can I work here with you?'

Francis jumped with surprise at Sam's voice. He was in somewhat of a trance. There was a quiet sound of radio music playing in the background. Francis turned around and, holding out his rather grubby hand, said, 'Welcome to my hidey-hole.'

Sam grasped Francis' hand and there followed a short man-to-man conversation. They agreed that Sam leave the garage if he really wanted to. He did, and they fixed a time when he could start work.

The following week at half-past eight, Francis showed Sam how to carry out certain fundamental tasks. This included how to clean each machine by taking them down to the bare essentials, removing grass or dirt from the smallest parts before putting them back together again.

He showed Sam how to keep the shed clean, and how to oil each machine. He instructed Sam on the correct use of each individual gardening tool and how to use a rake to collect the cut grass. He told him about the awkward way the hedge clippers could suddenly have a fit and refuse to work. He told him about the chainsaw that normally ran smoothly but sometimes was difficult when used on thicker branches.

'You can come and get my help any time!' Francis said.

Francis gave Sam a demonstration of how to mow around the flower gardens and bushes. He went carefully around the two glorious oak trees, saying proudly, 'I do this regularly once or twice a week. All sorts of interesting people sit here, including children. Always stop the machine before you do anything else, and pick up the fallen leaves or branches, and of course any toys or rubbish. The fallen acorns can be collected and given to Polly for safekeeping. Put the grass cuttings in the compost bin around the back,' and he took Sam behind the house to show him where the neat row of wheelie-bins were placed.

Of course, Sam knew most of these things, but didn't get upset. He could see that Francis wanted to tell him everything on his working agenda. Sam was also helping Francis to move slowly on from his concerns about Frank.

They soon became a team.

Jack did things a little differently. He certainly knew that he had grown tired of being stuck on the upper floor at *Honeysuckle House*.

When Adam became aware of Jack's disquiet, he discussed this with Polly. They agreed that they approach a sheep farmer whom Adam had helped on some legal matters. 'We want to get Jack away from his normal environment,' Adam said to the farmer, who agreed that Jack could work on his farm for three months over summer.

Once Jack had been received into the homestead, the

farmer taught him many things, including, 'Our local sheep are chosen for slaughter, whereas the sheep in Biblical times were kept for their wool and milk. They were also given individual names.'

Jack had not known that before. Indeed, he had been taken into the countryside on weekend jaunts in the car and, like most town people, been annoyed at the flocks of sheep upsetting the right-of-way. Now he could learn a lot about farming first-hand.

Working on the old oil-powered tractor, Jack wore a dusty singlet, oil-splattered trousers, enormous lace-up boots and an old racing cap, to give him protection from the elements. He was a farmer, so he ought to look like one!

One of the first tasks was searching for lost sheep on this large farm. Before him lay the huge expanse of the dry riverbed. In the distance, he saw gigantic rocks with creepers that clung tenaciously around the solid edges. Sitting on the top were very strange, almost prehistoric creatures; lizards, sunning themselves.

Jack thought the sheep would be very thirsty, so he proceeded to look further in the riverbed for water. Their tongues would be very dry and their weight low without water, so he looked inside tree stumps or other places to see if any moisture had collected. He then gave loud hollers, but it was deathly quiet. There were no sheep.

Over the distant side of the river were the snow-covered mountains, looking lethargic. Above them were some wispy clouds. Then Jack felt a gentle breeze caressing his legs, softly blowing over his body, and then across his face. He saw a magnificent falcon launch into the now stronger, windy air. As the bird flew in unimaginable flight, dark rain clouds formed in the distance. The falcon swooped down over him and seemed to be squawking out, *rain is coming!* before it returned to the glorious heights.

When he finished working on the farm, Jack returned to Christchurch a different man. He decided that farming was not for him, but his attitude to everything had radically changed. Instead of being a man tucked away with a computer, he became involved in a new intimacy with God that made a subtle yet mind-blowing change to his life.

So, following the same direction as his English grandfather Albert Williams, who had often recited short poems and told interesting stories, and his other grandfather Douglas, who also composed well-structured stories, plus Sophie, who wrote articles for a legal journal, Jack too began to write.

He decided to start with stories about Alice, Emily, Judy and possibly Frank. (He still continued his work on the computer, for it was his only means of income.)

Alison was glad that Jack wanted to read his story to the girls, giving her permission happily, on condition that they first were washed and in clean nightclothes.

Jack then asked about Frank. Alison said, 'Frank will be having an enjoyable time in the bath with his father standing by, ready to dry him.'

Jack came over to *Wisteria Cottage* lounge at the appropriate time. Snuggling together on the large settee, Alice, Emily and Judy quietly listened to the new story.

Said the proud author, 'I have called this story GOODNESS. Once Upon a Time – all good stories have this at the start – there was a little girl who lost her name. In fact, she couldn't remember what it was. If anybody asked her, "What is your name?" she said, "Um!" She said, "Ah!" She even said, "Oh, bother!" and stamped her foot in frustration. She didn't know her name. It had disappeared.

'She searched everywhere for the name. She looked under the bed, but there was only thick dust there. She searched in the laundry basket, but only found some dirty socks. She looked in the biscuit tin, but there was no name in there. *Where* was her name?

'She asked her parents if they had seen her name anywhere. They shook their heads and said, "No." She asked her little brother if he had seen her name anywhere. He just gave his shoulders a shrug. She asked the dog, but he only jumped up and barked loudly. She even asked the budgie, but it just cheeped and looked the other way. She couldn't find her name – anywhere!

'The little girl's mother was always cleaning the house, or changing the newspaper in the bird cage, or making sure the dog had enough water, or washing the little girl's dirty socks, or baking biscuits for the tin. She was too busy to worry that the little girl had not found her name.

'However, her father saw that the little girl was getting rather upset. After all, it is a bit frightening not knowing who you are, isn't it? He took her on his knee and cleared his throat.

'When her father did this, the little girl who had lost her name knew that he was going to be serious. So, she put on her serious face too, waiting for him to speak. He asked her, "Do you remember how the Bible tells us about God making the world and everything in it?"

'The little girl nodded. Her father said, "Well, when God made the light, He named it, Day. When He made the darkness, He named it, Night, and when He made the sky it was named, The Heavens. Everything that God made, He gave it a name."

'The little girl looked at her father. She was still rather grumpy, but she said, "I still don't know what *my* name is. It is still lost!"

'Her father gave a sigh. Then he said, "Whatever your name is, it is given by God. When you do find it, it will be a name that is full of goodness."

'She thought for a while about what her father had told her – God gave everything a name that is full of goodness. And then she knew what her name was! She smiled to herself. She became excited. She laughed aloud. She told her parents. They beamed with happiness. Then she told her brother, but all he said was, "Great!"

'She told her dog, who barked even more loudly. She told the budgie, who burst out into more song, chirping madly. She shouted in the biscuit tin and her name echoed back. She gave the dirty socks a miss, because by this time they were a bit smelly. She blew under her bed when she shouted out her name. Then, opening the bedroom windows, she called out to people walking to-and-fro, "I've found my name. It is Good!"

'So, the little girl – who now knew her name was Good

– went out every day and did good things! Maybe you've seen her. Or even met her!

'Now the little girl shares her name with other people. She tells them they are good, too! And the little girl – whose name is now Good – dusts her room once a week, even under the bed; taking out the laundry, even those dirty socks. The little girl even gives her things away to others, so that there is nothing left for her. The little girl now not only talks to and feeds the budgie, but even takes the bird outside for a bit of a flap.

'First, she did this for herself. Then, she did it for her family. Finally, she did it for everyone. Being full of goodness means being good to all people, everywhere.

'What can *you* do to be good? Maybe you can be good to your mother. Maybe you can be good to your father, even your brother, but that might take a real effort! Even be nice to those animals. Even be nice to the neighbours as well. You could be good for God too!

'All of us can be good in all sorts of ways – just like the little girl who lost her name, but found out she was full of Goodness.'

Alice, Emily and Judy clapped their hands, satisfied. Getting off the settee, they nearly forgot to say thank you to Jack. Remembering at the last moment, they gave him delightful lip-pecks all over his face making him rather embarrassed. They went off to bed, thinking of things that were full of goodness.

Chapter 77

AN EAGER FRANK and anxious Alison arrived at the city's friendly school, *Children with Special Needs.* The principal proudly introduced Frank to the other pupils. Frank was so pleased with this that he gave them all a toothy grin.

Alison was overwhelmed with the welcome that Frank had that day. 'You never know,' she said animatedly to Rebekah, standing alongside with her daughter Penny, 'how all the children will relate. We've got to have faith in God.'

'Yes,' Rebekah agreed. 'We've got to have faith. You never know what God is going to do when you place any problem in His hands!'

Francis had already built a small stool for easier access when Frank washed himself in front of the bathroom mirror. As well, Alison made sure that he also had the practical things, like a Flash Bag with a Velcro fastener containing his lunch portions, plus a large hanky for wiping his drooling mouth.

Three months went by. Alison and Francis saw Frank's results in the interim school report card, which read:

Frank appears to be interested in everything, particularly if it has moving parts. He has uttered some large words, although the teachers have had to listen carefully if they want to understand them! His eyes have an intensity which is fixed firmly on us when we speak to him. Sometimes, as we speak to others around him, he has that same intensity, only we are not sure which person he is listening to. Occasionally we are left wondering what he is saying or what he has understood, but we have no doubt that words are being absorbed by this growing lad.

The kindly, still single, but now bearded Reverend Geoff Silver launched into inspiring talks for the children with great gusto. The adults were amused at various meanings that could be drawn from his scriptural speeches.

Once, he gave the children some wheat seeds, instructing them to put a little water in a glass and add a few seeds. He told them that in a few days, they would sprout. Bending down, he held some of the seeds in his hand. 'Look how small these seeds are,' he said to the awed little ones. 'Some people might think that nothing large could grow from them. They are wrong! Why don't you try it at home for two weeks? Then bring them to church and we will see what the wheat seeds have done.'

Unfortunately, Frank thought that the minister was saying that he had to *eat* the seeds, so after ten days had gone by, he did so. They tasted ghastly!

There were many other important aspects of Frank's growing up, one being the annual exhibition: *The Children's Event!* Held at Christchurch's beautiful tree-filled central park, all the large pennants flying high on the tall pavilion could be seen by all around.

Inside, at the front desk, was friendly Mrs Warberton. She was carefully instructing two young people from the school on how to make the visitors feel welcome. There were only a few seats – mainly for the older adults – but there was a large grassy area for the rest of the milling crowd. Some of the children were in wheelchairs, so there were adult carers to look after them.

This year, Earnest and Earnestine Waller were the special guests. He was a rather stout man with friendly eyes and a pointed beard. His attractive sister was dressed in summery fashion. When one learned that they were famous throughout Australia, and particularly in Melbourne, where they had their own permanent exhibition, one could understand not only their outstanding enthusiasm, but also the serious nature of their work for children with all sorts of learning difficulties.

All the children of this *The Children's Event!* had watched with interest the erection of the massive pavilion. Then they had *helped* to construct similar, smaller models out of cardboard pieces, using lots of glue. Their constructions were based on *their* own proper plans.

Naturally, the principal was very excited about the whole process. He bounced along with a delightful smile, looking at these constructions and congratulating his pupils profusely! Excitedly, Frank told him that the exhibition was *mar-vell-ous*, rolling this new word around in his mouth. Again, the principal smiled with delight.

Later, there were the children's competitions in various categories. Frank wanted to enter one that would show his limited skill – the *Most Amazing Boy*.

'This is certainly one that he could win,' said a very proud Francis before the event. 'He is quite a performer.'

It was true, for Frank came out with hidden meanings of words that were really expressive.

Being older and perhaps more mature, Penny chose to enter another category – *Helping Parents*. She was able to say confidently to the judges, 'I've done the baking for my mother,' and, 'I've been cleaning my bike all year,' and even more self-righteously, 'I've been to church and listened to the sermons every week!'

However, there was no way that judges Earnest and Earnestine Waller could verify these examples. They gave Penny a small gift just in case their final choice was misguided. Over the years, they had learned this the hard way.

Frank was thriving at his special school, partly nurtured by his own outgoing personality. That meant that he could use a lot of new, long and difficult words.

One day, Adam heard him trying to get these words out perfectly. He said to Frank, 'I can see the effort involved in speaking! Well done young man. We are in the same boat, both learning more and more.'

It is a wonderful thing that a loving God looked after them all – Alison and Francis, Alice, Emily and Judy. Aimee and Abbas. Iris and Douglas. Polly and Adam and their sons, Thomas and Jo and their children Zackary and Mimosa. James and his Angel and Maria. Sam and Jack. Then there were the Colonel and Sophie and their son Peter, Rebekah and her daughter Penny, Miss Marchant, Harris Tweed and Gloria Shaw, as well as the principal and Mrs Warberton of the Special School, the Reverend Geoff Silver and other sincere people – rallying around Frank.

With much love, concern, prayer, gifts, good advice and of course, a listening ear, they all contributed their support in different ways for him.

A miracle, in fact!

Chapter 78

IRIS WAS EXCEEDINGLY edgy as she waited at Christchurch airport for their youngest daughter, Rose, to arrive from Port Moresby. As for Douglas, when he was nervous he had the annoying habit of quietly humming a sonorous tune, again and again. Now, he was humming this flat tune to such a degree that it annoyed Iris – so much so, that she said irritably, 'For goodness sake, stop it!'

Douglas was surprised that the humming caused her such a problem. He told her that it might be her imagination. Naturally, this further riled Iris.

They weren't in such a state because of Rose, but because she was bringing with her a young woman named Mira Wood, whom they didn't know.

Three weeks ago, Rose had written to tell them about Mira, explaining that she was working through some difficult circumstances.

Accommodation had already been arranged for them at the new Village Motel, just down the road from *Honeysuckle House;* this would take the pressure off Mira of having all those loving people asking her questions too soon, or inappropriately.

Rose had also written to Adam and the Colonel, seeking their permission to make sure all of *Legal Affairs* staff were aware that Mira would be coming to this quiet place to deal with her problems regarding past sad events. She suggested that under the two magnificent oak trees would be a good place to listen to her story.

Adam knew what his sister was like, speaking with

almost always short and succinct sentences. Rose's greater knowledge of Mira's situation gave her a perspective on the problem at hand.

Seeing as Adam knew Rose well, the Colonel agreed to all this.

Iris and Douglas were left wondering what all these sad circumstances were. Iris had already told Douglas that they mustn't judge, for they hadn't yet heard the full story, but they were still edgy when they went to the airport.

They certainly didn't take any notice of the extreme weather on this day, but it was hot and muggy inside the airport, where the air conditioning wasn't working well. Outside, the hot nor'wester wind blew short blasts of debilitating air.

Seated in uncomfortable airport seats, Iris thought back to the days when Rose was much younger.

Rose had studied at Concord College, the same Bible college as Adam, where she gained her degree with honours. She spent time working in a laboratory at a Dunedin Hospital, studying haemophilia, leukaemia and a whole lot of other blood-related ailments. Years went by and, with all this experience behind her, she went to work at a medical college in Fiji as a senior staff member. *Quite an important position,* Iris thought proudly.

At the start of the 1990s, Rose commenced working with single girls who found themselves pregnant. She found that some of them had HIV/AIDS – a disease that was becoming quite prevalent. Rose had selected a team of doctors and nurses from the Pacific area who could provide much needed education, support and care for patients who had contracted the illness. Working closely with others and tailoring their responses according to each country's situation, her responsibilities grew.

While she was travelling around the Pacific, she had given some good news to Iris and Douglas. 'I have been offered a position by the churches in Papua New Guinea, in both medical and social needs.'

After settling in Port Moresby, Rose wrote again to

her parents, saying that the country had a wide range of customs that challenged how this new disease, HIV/AIDS, could be dealt with.

> *During my travels, I stay in local houses in various parts of the country. There are always key people to look after things, and their job includes finding out where single girls were "sleeping" (what a ridiculous term, they weren't actually sleeping) with amorous, sex starved men working away from their homes.*

Iris and Douglas had been writing friendly letters to Rose, but the AIDS problems in Papua New Guinea and the greater Pacific area were now suddenly becoming more widespread.

Iris drew herself together. Rose was nearly here, and, of course, young Mira Woods also.

They came through customs and Rose beamed when she saw her mother. She said, 'I love you, Mum,' giving her a kiss followed by a big hug.

Turning to Mira, Iris welcomed her with open arms. Smiling, the shy young girl responded.

Douglas followed with a manly kiss and hug for Rose, and a small kiss on the hand for Mira. Although she didn't show it, she was embarrassed.

As they were vying for a taxi, Iris looked at Rose. She was dressed in stylish but practical clothing – a straight, unadorned outfit. Her eyelids were lightly pencilled with a startling bluish shade, bringing out the whole of her freckled face. She usually used Max Factor lipstick, which enhanced her looks. Rose had the same appearance as before, but Iris noticed that she had aged. She realised that getting older applied to everyone, including herself.

As they journeyed to *Honeysuckle House*, Mira, wearing a summer dress, was seated in the front passenger seat. Taking in the wonderful Kiwi greenery and early summer flowers of suburban Christchurch, she listened to the rather garrulous taxi driver.

Seated in the rear seat, Rose whispered that Mira was nineteen, a truly charming and amazing young woman with a warm personality. 'Look at her glorious jet-black hair!'

Iris had another look at Mira's hair and felt the desire to feel the lovely tresses, but at the last moment refrained from touching her.

On reaching *Honeysuckle House* they went their separate ways – Rose and Mira going in their taxi to the motel, and Iris and Douglas walking to their two-bedroom cottage to relax.

Chapter 79

IRIS HAD ENJOYED her time under the oak trees, but now her arthritic knees were very painful. She could no longer bear to walk on the undulating grassy surface to the anchored seats. The thought of Mira and her long tale had left Iris disappointed but, thinking outside the box now, she reminded the relevant staff at *Honeysuckle House* and *Wisteria Cottage* that *they* must come and hear Mira's story.

Those assembled received Mira with open arms, telling each other that Rose wouldn't have brought the young Australian girl without good reason.

The day was perfect – not too hot, not too cold, with a gentle breeze. The sun provided shade under the oak tree's branches. This peaceful spot – with its structured seats and green grounds around – was a very pleasant place to be.

Rose looked around at her family and friends while Mira was getting herself together. Rose's older brother, Adam, was gaining weight. He had told her that the results of the stroke could be seen for what it was. 'The whole right side is getting more stooped, and I can't help it.'

Her sister-in-law, Polly, a strong supportive wife to Adam, was wearing fancy glasses and an ornate pearl necklace. She looked serene under the oak trees.

Rose's father, Douglas, was wiry and balding. When Rose made mental calculations, she realised he was now eighty-nine.

Rose looked around at the others present. There was

resplendently smart Colonel Ivanov, who had a slight bend to his shoulders now, thinning but riotous long white hair, a fading moustache, and thick, long eyebrows that danced in the breeze. He was a friend to all.

A slightly younger but still beautiful Sophie, the Colonel's wife, sat beside him. All-over whiteness was Rose's quick summary of her – white hair, flowing white dress and smart white shoes. She exuded grace and serenity.

Miss Marchant was very prim and proper. She had complained to Rose yesterday that she had a back injury which was getting more uncomfortable, but there was no complaint from her lips today. This was Mira's time.

While seated separately in garden chairs, Alison and Francis were relaxing, looking as fresh as daisies. The children were all at school, so their parents could relax and would be listening with interest to Mira.

Mira looked around at them all, at their encouraging, loving faces, then, surprising them all, her face crumpled and she began to weep. Getting her small handkerchief out, she said very quietly in a choked voice, 'How good it is at this peaceful *Honeysuckle House*. You have welcomed me so warmly – and I am very grateful.'

Rose wondered if Mira would cope as she told her long tale to people whom she barely knew, when she was already so emotional. Putting an arm around Mira's shoulders in a sympathetic manner, Rose asked her, 'Would you like to start now? All these people are agog to hear what you have to say.'

They all gave her encouraging, smiling reassurances.

Mira sniffled one last time, put away her soggy handkerchief and began to recount her story.

'A few words at the start. Our father, Jack Early who was part Aborigine, was an exciting man – well, to us, he was. Employed as a mining consultant by a company in West Queensland, he had a serious accident and died of a heart attack. Dad hadn't told the company about his heart condition, which had only been diagnosed by his doctor the previous week. We found that there was an insurance clause that he must inform the insurance company of any changes in his health, like heart disease. He didn't do so, and there was no pay-out for my mother. We still miss him very much.

'My mother, Claire, had trained as a teacher, and found work on Thursday Island. So, I, my younger sister Evie and our mother set off on a voyage, sailing through the Great Barrier Reef on our way from Cairns to Thursday Island.'

The old wooden vessel, with its very efficient crew, had several elegant rooms, occupied mostly by retired people. The ship's lounge had a bright, festive, celebratory feel to it. Most passengers were formally attired, with the older ladies wearing elegant dresses. They had just been given commemorative bouquets. The men, some ex-military, were in yesteryear suits, wearing bow ties, and were about to have their cigars lit by an elderly steward.

Evie was nearly thirteen, a cuddly sort of girl, who insisted on having a very short haircut, and Mira was aged fifteen, with very small, angular features; vivacious and cheerful, she always enjoyed life to the full.

The captain addressed the passengers, but he seemed a little drunk; certainly he slurred his words. 'I have an announcement to make. The Violin Trio will play through the evening!'

The Trio were resting. Their violin, viola and cello had been put away for the journey. They were not expecting to play; however, under the captain's persuasion, the Trio eventually got out their instruments and commenced to play beautifully. Their small audience was rapt.

Suddenly the ship stopped, violently and terrifyingly. The mast came crashing down amid the rumble of wooden structures. The boat had struck something!

Then the first mate shouted down to the passengers: 'Get out! Get out, to the lifeboats, or we'll all drown!'

The terrified voyagers hurried up onto the deck. Normally there were gentle winds and slight swells, and the temperatures were about thirty degrees Celcius, but now the wind had suddenly come up with terrific force;

a black squall, the first mate said. Rain descended upon them, and everyone put lifejackets over their now very wet clothing. The jackets were adult size, too big for the young girls, but they managed awkwardly to keep them on.

The crew prepared the lifeboats and, as they steadied the two craft, the passengers hurriedly slithered in. Then, slowly, the boats were lowered into the troubled sea. The crewmen remaining jumped into the water and were taken on board the lifeboats.

In the fading darkness, Mira could see her scared mother huddling with all the other bewildered people on their lifeboat. Nobody spoke, but they all held hard onto the sides of the vessel.

Evie whispered, 'Mira, we won't drown now. We've done what the first mate said.'

Looking up at their mother's face for any reaction to Evie's troubled words, the ever-practical Mira said very quickly, 'I'm afraid that the first mate is scared too. We still have to get to shore and away from this storm. Once there, we'll have to keep a look out for crocodiles and snakes. We'll need to make a fire to keep ourselves warm. Then, somehow we'll have to make contact with other people there, and they might be miles away. No, I'm afraid it's not over yet.'

Evie snuggled up to her even more, and Mira snuggled up to their mother. It appeared that Claire needed warmth, for her wet underclothing was showing through her lovely but now ruined dress. Mira could feel her shivering violently, obviously in shock.

Straining at the oars, the crew took up the challenge and rowed to the shore. Mira never knew what happened to the drunken captain. Perhaps he drowned, as so many captains do. She looked back at the foundering ship; it suddenly gave a shudder and a loud whining scream, as though crying out for help, before it tiredly listed onto its side. Water was pouring into what she thought was the lounge, before the whole hull broke up and disappeared into the ocean.

The passengers were in awe of Mother Nature's power,

and aghast at their fate. A few of the women began to sob quietly, but the crewmen heaved on their oars, working with the water to take them to shore.

All of a sudden the wind and rain stopped, and the clouds dispersed as quickly as they had come. The bright moon came through with its magnificent light shining all over the area, like a promise.

At last on the beach, the crew hastily fastened both lifeboats firmly to a strong mangrove tree. These trees went all along the shore. The first mate had already taken a strong flashlight from the lifeboat's emergency pack and shone it onto the shore. There were some sparse bushes and wispy tall grasses close by and, in the distance, towering palm trees, while further inland was the canopy of a luxuriant rainforest. There was no sign of crocodiles, dangerous snakes, or anything else nasty, so the first mate made the decision to camp the rest of the night there on the sandy beach.

The passengers all scrambled out of the boat and made themselves as comfortable as possible. What a circle of very tired adventurers! The old steward who had been offering cigars to the men earlier, gave a shout when he found a lighter in his pocket. The first mate quickly arranged parties of men to gather firewood, while he coaxed flames from still-damp grasses and twigs. Soon they all bathed in the glow of a warm, comforting fire. They had no food, so the first mate, though exhausted himself, persuaded the others to sleep, saying he would keep watch over them. The motley group settled down on the sandy ground around the fire.

Claire still hadn't said anything, and Mira worried that the shock had made her mute. A short distance away was a deep sandy hollow, sheltered by a low sand dune, providing more privacy, so Evie and Mira led the silent, acquiescent Claire there. It was near enough to be able to hear the low conversation that wafted over their heads, but they quickly fell into a deep sleep, curled against each other for warmth.

The cold night gradually turned into a glorious day. When the girls awoke, small geckos near their faces proudly preened themselves. The sun rose, strong and reassuring. Mira sat up and looked over the sand dune, to find they were totally alone, for the rest of the people – including their mother – had disappeared!

The girls were terrified. Where could they have gone? What time did they disappear? Why did their mother not wake them up?

Suddenly they saw the reason. A large saltwater crocodile rose up from the mangroves, moving toward the shaking girls, coming right for them! The water shattered into explosions of droplets as it moved from side to side, slumping forth on its awkward but adequate feet.

Evie and Mira were scared out of their wits. They didn't know which way to flee in order to escape the monster. It opened its mouth wide, showing its giant teeth, but Mira had no idea that it was blind in both ancient eyes due to an accident. It couldn't see them, but moved by the power of its nose, scenting food.

The girls hunkered down further into the deep sandy hole. It wasn't enough. The crocodile waddled closer – close enough that Mira, shielding Evie, could have reached out and touched its scaly armour.

Then suddenly a strange sound came from the trees surrounding the beach. Mother!

Heroically, Claire raised her now-croaking voice and shouted out horrible insults to the crocodile, luring it toward herself. Surprised at the unusual sounds, the beast changed course to investigate, which instantly encouraged the rest of the people to charge toward it, shouting at the tops of their voices. Confused, but sensing danger, the croc changed course again and ran for the safety of the water, where it swiftly sank below the waves.

Chapter 80

CLAIRE WAS THRILLED when she realised what her emotions and her croaking voice had achieved. With much rejoicing and hugging, the whole relieved group were together again.

The first mate had the responsibility of looking after the sleeping passengers and crew, but his own exhaustion had overtaken him, and he'd nodded off. Waking first in the early morning sunshine, he'd seen that they were resting in crocodile territory. He could see the imprints from their feet, and was just about to warn his charges when one of the crocodiles suddenly appeared. He called out, rousing his charges and sending them into the trees, which they hastily climbed to reach safety.

Puzzling over why the girls hadn't heard the alarm, they came to the conclusion that the gusts of wind, and the dune the girls slept behind, had all combined to dull the shouts.

Unfortunately, the sniffling and shivering that Claire had had earlier was turning into a full-blown cold. This had kept her waking up so often that, hearing the first mate's warning cry, she escaped in panic, unwittingly leaving her daughters behind.

The first mate burrowed about in the lifeboat for supplies, but found only a few hard biscuits and a little water. 'If my memory is correct,' he said, pointing, 'I think there's a sugar mill some miles away in that direction.'

So they dutifully trekked through sparse bush and crossed streams, until they came to the welcome sight of a homestead. The first mate muttered to himself, 'Our wreck happened near the Low Isles. That means we're near Rocky Point, about Ayton.' He then explained that it was named after Captain Cook's own house in England.

Some of the women had lost their shoes in the sea, so they had wrapped tough grass around their feet to give them some protection. By the time they reached the homestead, their feet were scratched and bruised, and some were even bleeding.

The large farmhouse was named *Bungendore,* proclaimed a notice attached to the gate. The first mate jokingly said as they made their way through it, and climbed the steps, 'I bet there's no greater honour than being visited by a sorry group of *MV Valour* wanderers!'

A muscular man was relaxing on the verandah. Resting on the small table beside him was a large plate of toast covered in chunky marmalade, and an enormous mug of tea. He was surprised to see them, but introduced himself as Fred Woods. Following the first mate's explanations, he gave orders to an Aborigine woman who had come silently out of the house, to make tea, and then asked the group about what sort of breakfast they would like. 'Bacon? Sausages? Eggs? Followed by sweetened porridge?'

Somehow a huge breakfast spread was produced, enough for them all, but their host made no comment on supplying food for so many. After breakfast, 'Mrs Mops', the friendly but enormous Aborigine woman with dark curly hair, and her ten-year-old daughter (who was the spitting image of her parent), showed the ladies how to operate the awkward shower.

Gratefully, they scrubbed themselves until they were positively fragrant. Mrs Mops supplied plenty of lovely perfumed talcum powder, left over by the mistress of the homestead who had died the previous year. They all agreed that it was a pity to have the lovely talc in the cabinet unused. Mrs Mops said further that Mr Woods had yet to remove his wife's clothing from her enormous, over-crowded wardrobe, and opening the wardrobe she revealed many lovely garments, telling them that Mr Woods had said to let the ladies help themselves.

'This is wonderful!' the excited women exclaimed, examining the different colours and fabrics. Sadly, the two girls missed out, as the clothes were far too big. Once they had been washed and dried, Evie and Mira put their old clothes on again.

Mr Woods was in his mid-forties. Mira found this out later from her mother who, having dressed first, came out of the room and was suddenly mesmerised by this friendly man. In spite of her miserable cold, she managed to hear him say he had lost his wife a year ago. Eagerly, sympathetically, she told him that her husband had died as well, in the same month, in a mining accident.

After chatting to Mr Woods for some time, she learned that he was in charge of a sugar-cane business and had an outside staff of four as well as Mrs Mops and her daughter. He had no children.

Mira said, laughing at the thought, 'I can imagine how mother's heart went thump, thump, thump, whenever she saw Mr Woods! In my opinion, they must have become pretty friendly while the rest of the women were still trying on the beautiful clothes.'

Meanwhile, the men were shown the single outside shower. This was adjacent to the full forty-gallon water tank standing under the now blazing sun. When the clean men returned, Mr Woods said that he would radio Ayton, the next town. The first mate smiled to himself at this; he'd been spot-on. Mr Woods radioed that the *MV Valour* was broken on rocks, and the captain was missing, feared drowned, but most of the group staying at his homestead wanted to go to Cairns. He said that his transport would take them to Ayton the next day.

It wasn't long before evening was upon them. The women chatted together about fashions, families and the like, before getting some sleep on the old but sturdy chairs and two couches on the verandah. The men slept in an open shed on wooden bunks.

The following day, after another bracing breakfast, the two open trucks from Ayton arrived at the door, carrying more supplies for the farm. All the rescued people thanked Fred Woods profusely before clambering in and being driven away.

However Claire, who had been outside throughout the night with the rest of the women, looked and sounded terrible. Her throat was now very sore. After getting little sleep the previous night on the beach, she now only managed a restless dreaming through the dark hours of this night. Her cold had become a fully-fledged fever, so she was unable to travel. Evie and Mira stayed with her.

Mr Woods was very worried. He insisted that Claire wrap up with lots of blankets and an expensive quilt – his wife's. He gave instructions to the now anxious Mrs Mop to put Claire in one of the spare beds inside. Evie and Mira were to be put in a second small adjacent bedroom, which unfortunately had only a single bed. Mr Woods would move to the outside sleeping quarters, for the sake of propriety.

The next few days saw Mr Woods sitting by Claire's bedside, chatting about this and that. Her recovery took some time, so he had plenty of quality time to talk with her.

Evie and Mira gave their mother's face and hands a wash every day, and fresh water was kept in a jug beside her, changed twice a day. There were plenty of hand towels for the rest of her body whenever she wanted to use them. When she needed to pee, the girls were ready to put the pot in position and then empty it.

After ten days or so, Claire was able to sit up and give instructions to the girls, and not just suggestions. After all, she was a very proper schoolteacher!

Claire said that Mr Woods would go into town and send a message of cancellation to the Thursday Island school authorities. Smiling, 'Our address is now c/o *Bungendore Homestead*, via Ayton.' She said further that they both needed new sandals, summer dresses and more pretty underwear as well.

However, Mr Woods excitedly interjected, 'But before you do anything like that, we have an announcement.' Turning to Claire, giving a slight signal to her that everything was going to be alright, he softly said, 'Mira. Evie. Your mother and I are in love!' and, taking her hands, added, 'We are getting married!'

The girls' mouths flew open and their eyes grew huge with surprise. Then they were happy for their mother – for both of them. Suddenly, romance was in the air! It meant the coming together of two very lonely people. Together they would be a happy twosome.

Some weeks later, after the quiet wedding was over and the few friendly guests and the earnest priest had gone, the happy couple, Mr Frederick and Mrs Claire Woods, had a few days of honeymoon bliss at one of Queensland's tropical islands. When she was departing, Claire said to her daughters, 'You have a new stepfather, so can decide what surname you would like to be called by. Whether you would like to keep using the Early surname, the one that you grew up with, or the new one, Woods. Think about it and give us your answer when we get back.'

When the happy couple had returned from their honeymoon, Claire came into the girls' room, closed the door and said that she had some things to discuss. Sitting on Evie's springy bed, which Mr Woods had bought her from Cairns, their mother explained that she had decided to send Evie and Mira to an excellent boarding school close by.

Their faces crumpled, but Claire hurriedly said they would be home for holidays, and that she would take them to visit the Cairns shops each month on a spending spree. Fred would be coming regularly into town on sugar cane business too, so both of them would visit.

Then she asked what the girls wanted to call Fred. 'Mr Woods?' she suggested.

'Too formal.'

'Fred?'

'Much too friendly.'

'Stepfather?'

'Too much like in the films.'

'Well, how about Dad?'

Mira explained that their second father was quite different to their first. 'Maybe we can call him Uncle Frederick?'

Claire was quiet for a moment. Then, smiling, she

said, 'Yes. I think that name will be suitable. What do you think, Evie?'

Evie nodded and smiled back. 'Yes,' she agreed.

They all trooped into the lounge to find their step-father marching nervously back and forth, his hands knotted behind him. Reaching up – he was much taller than they were – each gave him a kiss, a peck on each side of his face. His worries lifted when he heard them call him simply, Uncle Frederick.

Chapter 81

WITH EYEBROWS RAISED, the Colonel interrupted Mira with a smile and said, 'What a terrific story. Can I suggest we take a break for tea before continuing? You must be parched, my dear!'

He had just seen Mr C trundling up with a giant basket of excellent goodies. Some time ago Adam had decided that the morning teas could be brought out under the two oak trees, rather than journeying back to the house to have their sustenance. The cook would put into the giant hamper milk, sugar, tea, coffee, cups, spoons, napkins, small bottles of fruit juice, jam-filled muffins, petite sandwiches, maybe a small chocolate cake, and send the muscular Mr C to the starving crowd with it at about eleven o'clock. Someone else would take the empty hamper back afterwards.

Mira laughed when she heard of this scheme. Nodding, she said, 'I think I would like a drink of fruit juice, and – yes, one of those amazing-looking muffins, please?'

Wiping the crumbs from her lips, she at last began the next part of her story.

Claire, Evie and Mira had enjoyed life to the full. This made Uncle Frederick very happy. His happy smiles were far greater than the worried frowns that he had given before. Mira supposed he had been thinking about his first deceased wife, and guessed that he was also worried about the year's poor sugar crop.

The girls spent many hours helping their mother to

apply a fresh coat of white paint to the outside of the house. They stripped old wallpaper away from two rooms inside, replacing it with gorgeous coloured paint and, once it was dried, hung up fashionable artistic prints. The sunshine streamed relentlessly down on the homestead and, even though they were inside, they wore shorts and skimpy tops bought in Cairns. Their good moods were further bolstered as they sang along to the latest songs on the portable radio and made teenage jokes that they thought were hilarious!

Claire just smiled, saying that she was a teenager once too.

Occasionally, they went out to the sugar fields with Uncle Frederick and he told them the history of the property. In the nineteen-hundreds Josiah Pinkerton, the owner, started to plant sugar cane. Each year the crops were safely harvested and taken to Cairns by railway, until the time they were destroyed when the train left the rails and tumbled down to the snaking river.

There was nothing left worth salvaging. Josiah Pinkerton certainly didn't have any sort of insurance. At first he was angry, and then despondent, moping around the property day after day, until eventually he sold the place for a pittance to a land agent. The property lay unused for years until Uncle Frederick came along. He was working part-time in the Townsville Town Hall while completing a university degree, and found a government survey of the place. He quickly purchased the property for a song, and he and his first wife moved in. They had a happy marriage, but then suddenly she became very ill, and a year later, she died.

The time came for Evie and Mira to be at boarding school. The holiday was over. Claire took them to a Cairns department store, one of those large old-fashioned haberdasheries. Seeing as they were to go to a girls' private school just outside Cairns, they had to buy what were, to the girls, ghastly uniforms that the school imagined its pupils would like; enormous broad brown hats, which would protect from the sun, thick brown stockings, and practical underwear. Next they went to the photographer's rooms to have some photos taken to put in their lounge and, of course, to take to school.

Uncle Frederick drove them in the car, past tall palm trees on each side of a gravel road, until they reached the school. Two enormous turrets stood at each end of the building. In the middle, wide steps swept up to two open wooden doors, where they were received by the principals, the Misses Kettle, spinster sisters. They both wore voluminous black gowns. They were in the business of educating girls, so they *correctly and demurely* greeted their newest pupils.

Evie and Mira didn't feel very correct or demure, but forgot their initial nervousness and offered broad smiles. Immediately the principals returned the smiles. Then two senior girls showed them around, saying that girls were only punished by being given demerits, and no one was ever caned, even if they were very naughty.

The senior girls explained that there were two divisions, the upper school and the junior school, with one principal for each. There were also six other teachers, who were all pleasant but very strict. Mealtimes would be shared together in the large dining hall, to create a better atmosphere.

Mira studied hard in all subjects, getting top marks. Evie worked hard too, and it wasn't long before they were together at the upper school.

By now, Mira was showing signs of exhaustion. She quickly said, 'I'm sorry, I feel drained... may I tell the rest of my story tomorrow, or on another day?'

The interested crowd were disappointed, but said that they would come back and listen to her again – but only when she was ready.

Of course, agitated Iris was waiting for Douglas to tell her the latest about Mira. She then turned it into prayer for the forlorn Australian girl.

Chapter 82

URING THE NEXT two days, although warm, it began to rain heavily. Mira and Rose had various shopping and doctor's appointments to attend to, so it was the following week before they managed to get together again.

However, this time there were only four ready listeners – the Colonel, Douglas, Adam, and of course, Rose.

At breakfast time that day, Mira told Rose that she had some hesitation in how she would present the next stage of her journey. 'I know you say the telling of my story is necessary for my healing, but this next part has more... um... you know... intimate pieces!'

Rose told her not to worry. 'I've been thinking. I'm glad that only these three older men are here. They are very gracious, so if you tell them honestly and truthfully, they will understand what you have been through.'

So, beneath the shadows of the two oak trees, Mira told them the next long chapter of her life.

She was still one of those irascible teenagers. Though quite small, her cheekiness grew. Perhaps she thought she was ready to take on more in life than she actually was...

Then Rick Strait came into her life.

Rick was the only child of the school caretaker. He had no mother alive, as far as Mira knew. His father, who was rather fussy in his caretaking duties, was extremely tough on Rick when it came to doing all his jobs, both at home and his (different) school. Rick was also being watched by the local authorities; in other words he had had a run-in with the law some time before.

Rick became interested in Mira, suggesting that they do some... *er,* other things together. Excited, the silly girl wholeheartedly agreed – this was far more exciting than studying!

He took her a little way from the school property, where no one could see them. He pulled her into his arms and kissed her, first on the cheeks, then on the lips. Mira had to admit to herself that she enjoyed it. She had never been kissed before, apart from by her mother and sister, and Uncle Frederick, who gave her little pecks on the cheeks, but this was different; it stirred up butterflies in her stomach. She was soon looking forward to more of Rick's thrilling kisses.

The following week, the kissing stories about them started to circulate around the school. Rick would have been the only other person who knew what they were up to, so Mira was disappointed that he was telling other people. Some of her friends started to say rather stupid and unkind things.

Then the two principals' suspicions were aroused. Scared of the consequences if they found out the truth, Rick and Mira simply disappeared, and the headmistresses had no choice but to call the police.

Mira fell silent for a long time; then, raising her face, she said now to Rose, 'I know you are wondering if I can continue,' giving her arm a slight nudge, 'but I would like to tell the rest of my tale as much as I am able.'

Rose gave a slight inclination of agreement, and the men smiled kindly at her.

'Have you ever been afraid? Not just frightened by some passing event, like a person jumping out of the bushes at you, but a fear that percolates into your soul, trickling down to the very marrow of your being; so afraid that the hairs on your head stand up and your mouth is so dry that you cannot speak, when your heart is beating at twice its normal rate and when your skin goes goose-bump cold? That sort of fear?'

Her listeners all agreed that they did understand.

'My disappearance from school meant that a few pupils had the stupid idea that I had been kidnapped, or even murdered. However, the truth was that Rick and I had taken a sailing cruiser and were travelling through Australian waters, and then later, along the shores of Papua New Guinea.'

Rick and Mira had hurriedly walked down very early one morning to the Cairns Marina, where there were a whole lot of large vessels tied up in neat rows. Confidently, Rick had climbed into a flash sailing cruiser and opened the hatch. Of course, Mira followed him. She didn't know where he got the keys from, but he easily started the motor and they went out into the wide, open horizon to enjoy the calm sea.

Mira examined the equipment down below. There were two narrow beds, made up. In the small galley provisions had been packed away neatly into tiny cupboards. She looked inside to find they were full of tinned fish and peaches. Also, there were matches for a small primus stove tucked away. There was a long narrow metal chain made of steel, but she didn't have any idea of its purpose.

Returning to the deck, Mira made herself comfortable. A few minutes later, sweating in the heat, she went below, where she took off her outer clothing and settled on a bunk for a sleep, in just her underwear.

Meanwhile, Rick just continued to sail the boat. Mira woke up only when it seemed to have stopped, and the change in movement disturbed her. The sea was very calm, and the boat gently rocked to and fro.

The cabin darkened, and Mira could see Rick, now fully undressed and aroused, standing in the hatchway. She froze, not knowing what to do. Suddenly he dropped into the cabin, a strange look on his face that frightened her. She was afraid, yet aroused, when he lay down with her and they – well, made love, she supposed?

When it ended she found herself disappointed, and wary of this new Rick, who *did* seem to find the experience hugely enjoyable.

It was only half an hour before he wanted to do it again, but by then Mira was sore and didn't want to. But he wasn't taking no for an answer; he turned her to face him and began again, this time much more forcefully, hurting her. She was terrified!

He took her three more times that afternoon, ignoring her weeping pleas, and when he finally seemed satiated she dared to ask, 'When are we going back?'

But Rick knew by then that she had become a danger to him if they returned and she told anyone what he'd done to her. He gave her a strange look, and said, 'Go back? Are you mad? This boat is stolen. The owner is probably even now contacting the police. I've got enough fuel to go for miles, and we can sail too. We'll go to those distant northern islands where only a few people live. When the coast is clear we'll journey to the shores of Papua. Don't you want an adventure? We'll have the time of our lives!'

Mira was shocked at this turn of events. As she hurriedly pulled on her clothes, she told him that she didn't have any others, and no money to buy new ones if they got anywhere near shops.

Rick smiled slyly. Reaching into a cupboard, he pulled out a selection of bank notes and flapped them trium-phantly at her. He told her he was collecting money from some pupils who had wanted items that were not allowed by the school authorities, so he'd arranged a higher price than the norm. It seemed that he had been planning this trip for quite a while.

Giving a long sigh, Mira fiercely wiped tears from her face and said, 'I was a miserable fool. An idiot!'

The Colonel leant over, took both her hands firmly, and gently said, 'I think we all know how you feel; I'm afraid he didn't have any idea of rape or its consequences.'

Mira looked at him for a long moment, then very hesi-tantly choked out, 'I wish I had known too, *before* it all happened.'

Suddenly Rose said, 'I think Mira has told you enough for one day. She needs to rest, and so do you gentlemen

403

– I can see it on your faces.'

Rose gently took Mira by the arm and, with the men slowly following, they all went back into *Honeysuckle House* for a welcome respite.

Iris was waiting for the latest update from Mira via Douglas. When she heard of the sexual shenanigans, she immediately took it to the Lord, praying earnestly for Mira, that the telling might be sufficient to bring peace.

Chapter 83

TWO DAYS WENT by. The Colonel, Douglas and Adam were becoming increasingly worried about Mira. They remarked that perhaps after all, she may feel she had said enough.

Rose put them at their ease. She said that Mira was ready to tell the rest of her story, but only to them. Even though there were cruel and nasty aspects that had to be dealt with, she had to go on and finish her tale.

'Mira has said that telling the events to you three understanding men was like going to a friendly and venerable priest and confessing all!'. Rose added, 'Forgiveness *has* now come into the picture. Mira is feeling that the telling is just like disposing of old clothing. You take one layer off before you take the next off. When she is finally finished, she reckons that she will be absolutely free.'

The three men thanked Rose and, going on their way, they discussed proudly how they were now being compared to a friendly and understanding priest!

Later, when Mira was more settled and the weather was still as a millpond, they all went out under the oak trees again to listen to the next stage of her story.

Douglas took Mira's hand in his, because he was feeling his age and required someone else to be close to him. He was holding the small morning tea hamper with one hand and Mira with the other. She was his anchor.

Well, that's what he told his wife later that day, for, from the cottage window, Iris had seen Douglas walking slowly, hand in hand, with this young lady!

Crossing over the well-cut lawns, Douglas chatted about all sorts of subjects – like the increase in the number of waterfowl, gesturing towards the lake with the hand that was carrying the hamper – most awkward. When they drew up to one of the garden seats, Douglas asked Mira if she would mind sitting with him so that they could enjoy a view of the faraway mountains. Then they moved on and took their time as they strolled to the ridge, where they relaxed under the oak trees and waited for the others to arrive.

The Colonel, Adam and Rose followed them. Adam told them, 'My right foot has been turning inwards for some time. Do you mind if we have a rest on one of those seats, over there?'

As he was resting, Adam noticed that on top of the ridge, Mira had already set out morning tea. He thought it was a very long way to go to get to his cuppa!

Then the Colonel humorously said, 'Mira is looking at us, wondering what the hold-up is.'

Smiling grimly, Adam said, 'Yes! We mustn't keep them waiting,' and they slowly made their way to the ridge, where Adam and the Colonel collapsed into portable deck chairs. Rose and Mira hugged each other.

The righteous Douglas proudly said to the others, 'Eat up! Look, there are lovely cakes and flasks of drink for the weary!'

Soon, having enjoyed her morning tea, Mira carried on with the next stage of her tale.

Over two long, miserable and unhappy years, she and Rick sailed to and from many of the Torres Strait Islands. He was always convinced that the Cairns owner of the vessel was still chasing them, so that when close to the shore, Mira was kept securely bound in the cabin. She had learned what the steel chain was for!

When they occasionally ran out of food, Rick fished, but without much success. Somehow, he always managed to get hold of some bananas, coconuts and even tinned meat – stolen no doubt.

It was hot and clammy, so Mira dressed in very little.

Her clothes were used for other practical purposes, such as cleaning engine parts. Rick always had some beer; she supposed he got it from other sinister blokes who, like himself, were escaping the law.

One evening, as the sun was going down, Mira saw through the small porthole (Rick had closed and locked the wooden slats in the hatch overhead) some children playing freely. She wished she could be like them, enjoying life without a care in the world, and the thought made her cry, again. She was doing a lot of that, these days.

Rick often had sex with her, sometimes very roughly and other times more gently, then sneeringly described it to her as 'deep lovemaking.' Mira was by now disgusted at his behaviour but had to do what he wanted; he had a very quick temper and was not afraid to raise his hand to her. It was a very fragile existence, and she lived in dread of one day finding herself pregnant.

Then one night they were caught in a sudden electrical storm. There was no rain, but some amazing lightning and thunder. The sea grew more and more wild and tipped the vessel from side to side, and from bow to stern.

Suddenly Rick disappeared overboard, to Mira's shocked, terrified, delighted surprise! Leaning and struggling over the bow, his feet had slipped on the wet deck and, with a loud cry, he disappeared into the angry sea. As she wasn't tied up with the metal chain just then, she tried to steer the boat. She had no idea where they were or where to head for, but she most certainly wasn't going to turn around to rescue Rick – even if she knew how to!

Just as quickly the storm was over. The sea became quieter; the clouds raced away; the gracious moon came out. The twinkling stars, well – twinkled. Mira felt, but wasn't sure, that the boat was going in an easterly direction. She secured the wheel with the metal chain – yes, the same one that Rick had used to secure her – and settled down for a much-needed sleep. By then she had no choice, but to trust herself to God.

There was still a little food on board, and some ghastly brackish water left in the damaged pantry. Mira ate and slept, and slept and ate. She saw no one.

Then another sudden storm arose, this time with rain – so again, she hunkered down adjacent to the wheel with the chain wrapped around herself and the pedestal.

The weather was atrocious. Mira was thrown this way and that, but it wasn't long before she came to Hood Point, west of Port Moresby, near the Coral Sea – though she only knew this when Rose told her. She had reached the Hula peninsula.

She cried out to God. If He was in control, then He would surely look after her for this final spurt! Immediately, she was thrown off the boat, and she started dogpaddling her way the short distance to the beach. There she lay in the shallow water, too exhausted to go any further, or to care what had happened to the boat, and that is how Rose found her.

Rose took over the story here, but explained it from her own point of view.

'I was inside the small Hula house that the church authorities had supplied for my periodic visits,' said Rose. 'The village itself had suffered a good deal from regular storms in the past. One was so fierce that they lost quite a few people, crops were washed away, and fishing was stopped. When they began to reconstruct the village, they had to relocate it much further from the shore. However, in their wisdom the church author-ities had put my renovated house just a short way from the shore, so that I was unfortunately still exposed to storms, like this one.

'It felt very vulnerable to be so near to the sea in storms. However, this time I increasingly felt that I should go outside. It wasn't one of those things like being so afraid that the hairs on my head stood up on end, but I felt strongly that something wasn't right, someone was needing me.

'Putting on my large raincoat, I lit my Tilley-lamp and went out into the storm, which still had some *oomph* to it! Just as I came down the steps of the house, a large flash of lightning lit up the area and I could see someone in the shallows, struggling to reach shore. I ran down and rescued her,' Rose said simply, with a smile.

Mira picked up the tale. This time though, it was with a very flat, distant voice, as if she was not telling the story herself.

'Rose took me back into her house and we warmed up. I was given some food and a lot of sweet tea. Very shyly, I started to tell her about my leaving school and sailing from Northern Queensland with a cruel companion. On the shores of Papua, a terrible storm made him fall overboard, never to be seen again. I went on struggling with the boat until I fell overboard, and Rose rescued me.'

Rose went on to say, 'Tau Rebu – remember him, Adam?'

Smiling, Adam enthusiastically nodded. 'Tau, my faithful companion in the Port Moresby Christian bookshop!'

Rose continued, 'Well, Tau was a key person in Hula village. I took Mira to Tau and Para's house. One of their daughters, Ari, along with her husband and two children, helped Mira move on from her miserable experiences.'

Douglas softly said into the silence that followed, 'I think forgiveness is the key here – of Rick, but especially of yourself, Mira. You know, a long time ago, I had the opportunity of standing in the memorial gardens at Belgium's battlefield, where I could imagine the death and destruction of war. I realised that I needed to forgive my father, not for being a soldier, but for disappearing when I needed him most, when I was only two. Now, my dear, you have been telling us a very sad story in a totally different situation, but I am sure that forgiveness is necessary to gain your own healing. Even though Rick may never know, or might or might not accept it, you have to forgive – so that *you* can move on.'

Mira thought about what he had said, here in this beautiful, peaceful garden that seemed to wrap itself around her like a warm hug.

Rose got up and said, 'I think that the story telling is over for now. I know you will all be praying for Mira.'

And so Mira and her 'friendly statesmen' walked slowly back to *Honeysuckle House*, surrounded by sunshine and goodness that curled around her heart and began the work of warming up Mira's frozen soul.

Chapter 84

*M*IRA AND ROSE were away in the city on urgent business, so they couldn't be there at a celebration at *Sweethearts Restaurant*.

Sophie was unwell. Her left arm, wrist and fingers had a tingly feeling that she couldn't get rid of, making her very anxious. She snapped at the Colonel. She didn't mean to, but the words came out with such a rush, and so often, that she was always saying sorry to him.

When the Colonel had had enough of this, he said, 'I think we will go to the doctor.'

Sophie responded, 'There is *nothing* wrong with me,' even though she knew that the tingling was getting worse.

The Colonel insisted, 'We *will* go to see the doctor.'

So they did. They found out that Sophie's tingly feeling was caused by angina, so a bed at a private hospital was arranged for the ongoing tests that were required. The Colonel insisted on nothing but the best for his Sophie! He (and of course, son Peter) went regularly to visit. The Colonel even sent her gifts of beautiful flowers from *Honeysuckle House* gardens, inscribed with small, personal, loving messages.

It meant that Sophie would miss out on all the elating company of Iris, Violet, Polly, Miss Marchant, Alison and Rebekah as they walked along the road to *Sweethearts Restaurant* for lunch. They were celebrating Miss Marchant's birthday – though her actual age was very much kept a sacrosanct mystery, and no one ever probed.

This fashionable woman presented herself wearing

her summer dress, lovely chiffon scarf and flat shoes in the latest style. Miss Marchant had exchanged her chunky necklace for something that she considered a more mature person such as herself would wear – an elegant pearl rope. Although the lenses remained the same, her glasses now had more attractive frames.

When they were all seated and had intently studied the menu, they selected whatever took their fancy. While waiting, they took note of the short pithy sayings inscribed on the restaurant's wall. One read, *Relive one forgotten joy from your childhood,* and another, *Meander barefoot across soft, damp grass.*

Then bespectacled Violet told them amusing stories from her work and life experiences.

'One night I was walking around the hospital and found that the task of cleaning a bedpan had not been done properly. A junior nurse was responsible. I took her to the sluice room and showed her how to clean the dirty pan. The light there was quite bright, and when I came out into the dim corridor, I was shocked to see a pair of pyjama trousers walking towards me. I think my face must have shown my fear for a gentle voice said, "Nurse, it's only me." I realised that it was only a very dark-skinned patient. When he smiled, his teeth gleamed!'

This story brought forth some laughter, so Violet carried on.

'One day I was bouncing around my husband Gregg's computer room, cleaning it with my pink feather duster, looking for dust and spider webs that I could bring down with glee. Gregg remarked that he never sees the dirt and dust accruing.

'"Well, it's there," I said, "only you need to attack with a pink feather duster to find it!"

'Sitting in his comfortable computer chair, Gregg replied succinctly, "You know, you will never need a pink feather duster when you are in heaven."

'Innocently, I asked the eternal question, "Why not?"

'He replied, "We will be in a pristine clean heaven where there is no dirt or dust, ever!"

'I replied, "So a pink feather duster will be redundant?"

Bringing forth mock tears, I said, "What will I do instead?"

"'Apply for another heavenly job," was his answer.

"'Suggest some then," I said.

"'Well, ironing. You like that, getting all the crinkles out of your blouses and my trousers. Yes, great satisfaction from ironing."

"'But," I said, "if you are right and it is a pristine clean heaven, the clothes that we wear will also be without any crinkles."

"'Well, what about car cleaning? You always take a bucket of warm water with great joy, pouring it over the car and then drying it with a chamois until it is bright and shiny."

"'Oh, grow up! There will be no cars in heaven. And heavenly water will *be not too hot and not too cold, but just right for us.*" With a broad smile, I looked at Gregg's desk asking, "Do you think that in heaven they have retailers selling computers? And what happens to the computers when they are redundant? Think again. God will make us afresh and so we will be interested in other things, like God, and not computers!"

"'Or pink feather dusters," he exclaimed under his breath.

'We smiled. After having a good round of hugs, we continued doing pink feather dusting and computer writing while waiting for the day when we will be together in heaven.'

Everyone enjoyed that story. By this time the waitress had arrived with their substantial meals and selected drinks, and all talk ceased for the time being. They celebrated Miss Marchant's cryptic birthday with a special iced chocolate cake, with one lit candle on top, giving it celebration class!

Going bright red, Miss Marchant said quietly, 'Thank you all for celebrating this occasion with me.'

While she carefully and skilfully cut the cake, they all broke into singing, 'Happy Birthday to you, wonderful lady!'

'Hip hip hurrah! Hip hip hurrah! Hip hip hurrah!'

Chapter 85

ORKING WITH THE staff at the Young People's Association in Dunedin, the bluff giant, Gregg McKenzie, when confronted with the staff's own personal tragedies, or if they had more general things they wanted to talk about, listened carefully, for they always came to him with their thoughts, or seeking solace.

Maybe it was Gregg's quiet voice and honest demeanour that drew them in. He would use comforting, uplifting words that he thought would be suitable just for them. They found that Gregg was a considerate man, who was not concerned with the fripperies of life.

Now, however, Gregg was looking for more meaningful discussions when he and his wife, Violet, paid short visits to *Honeysuckle House*. Maybe his brother-in-law Adam, certainly his father-in-law Douglas, conceivably the Colonel, possibly Francis, or even outdoors Sam, would be willing to discuss some of these important matters with Gregg.

On this occasion, the sparkling sunshine streamed through the sheltering oak trees. The men were relaxing after enjoying the lunch prepared by Mrs Mulligan. Gregg made a meaningful comment: 'I get the feeling that we are members of the Christian Sceptics' Club.'

Raising his eyebrows, the Colonel asked, 'Why?'

Francis queried, 'How?'

Adam and Douglas were surprised. 'Sceptics' Club?' they said. 'How do you mean?'

'We talk about why Jesus died on the cross, but surely

it can't cover *my* situation! People say that surely there is a limit to God's forgiveness,' explained Gregg.

Putting down his cup on the garden table, the Colonel wryly offered, 'Oh, I get what you're trying to say. What about *my* guilt? – that sort of thing. Surely the sacrifice of Jesus won't cover *that!* We offer acts of penance, we visit counsellors who advertise their wares in the daily newspapers, and we have to do something to earn our forgiveness. I suppose Christian Sceptics' Club is right.'

Having been brought up as a Spanish Catholic, Francis was used to priests offering forgiveness at the sacrament of confession. Over time, his understanding of this rite became much broader. There was confession in church in all its ritual and holy aspects, yes, but there was also forgiveness for sin, at all times and at every occasion between God and himself – between God and the world.

Francis offered these thoughts, then continued: 'The sacrifice of Jesus has been offered once and for all. It has already been paid. God bangs down his everlasting gavel, declaring that He won't remember our sins again. End of story!'

Francis went on to give a personal illustration. 'Once, when I was returning home, my little boy, Frank – he would have been two, just before the accident anyway – I saw him take up a hard plastic ball and throw it with force at my three daughters as they were talking to each other. They were taken by surprise and one started to cry. The other two were most upset and approached Frank angrily.

'I was also very surprised. I had never seen him behave like that before. His naughtiness was going to be dealt with by my strong discipline! Wrapping his right hand in mine, I proceeded to punish him. Well, I should say that the *expectancy* of punishment was there, amidst the screams and footwork, but his hands were not touched. Why? The punishment was delivered to my own hand and he was left with a few tears and moments later, a mumbled apology!'

Francis concluded. 'In the same way, people are shown love when a merciful God has taken the punishment

Himself. After all, it is the loving essence of who God is.'

They all agreed that this was what Jesus had done on the Cross of Calvary.

That evening, while out walking around in the garden under the sparkling stars, Douglas mentioned to Gregg about Francis living in *Wisteria Cottage* next door, as he pointed in that direction.

Douglas described Francis's lovely wife, Alison, and the family of four children – three girls; Alice, Judy and Emily – and Frank, the boy whom Francis had previously mentioned to Gregg, who had nearly drowned in a swimming pool accident.

'Frank has recovered,' Douglas said, 'but has permanent brain damage. The whole family has been through a lot of sorrow, but he now goes to a school for disabled pupils, which he enjoys immensely.'

Gregg was silent, but not because of anything that Douglas had said about Francis or Alison or any of the children. For many years he and Violet had tried for children. Much sorrow followed, and they had finally concluded that there would be no children.

Gregg explained to Douglas that it had put quite a strain on their love life and, indeed, on their marriage. 'I'm afraid our situation didn't stop other people coming up with good advice, saying things about the joy of adoption, or propounding IVF. We have always turned them down with a gracious and sad smile, saying, "We don't think that's for us."'

So, Gregg thought it would be a good idea to be introduced to the children at *Wisteria Cottage*, and he asked Douglas if he could arrange this.

Douglas and Gregg called in at the cottage at morning teatime, about ten-thirty. Alison had just taken an enormous batch of muffins out of the oven. She said sweetly, 'The muffins will soon be cool if you want to wait a few minutes!'

When he came in from lawn-mowing, Francis was starving, but had to clean up before he was able to share in the buttered muffins and strawberry jam. While they were all munching, Douglas told them something about Gregg's life.

'He is linked with *Honeysuckle House* through Violet, his wife. Gregg is my son-in-law,' he explained, spluttering somewhat. 'He married my daughter, Violet.'

Gregg smiled. Increasingly Douglas was getting into quite a confusing muddle. Taking over, he gently said, 'I don't want to be a nuisance, and please say no if you want to, but Violet and I discussed the matter last night and we would like to take all your children out. Purely as a Christmas gift, you understand. Maybe join with the council's stupendous picnic in the botanical gardens, or visit the city to see the Christmas decorations. Something like that.'

Francis was a bit taken aback. *What reason does Gregg have for wanting to take our children out? Is it because he doesn't think we have sufficient funds to provide treats for the children? Should we accept this generous gift, or not?*

Sensing this, Gregg added: 'I'm sorry, I should have made my reasons clear. My wife and I are unable to have children of our own, and it's heartbreaking. Spending time with children who are virtually family already would be a blessing for us.'

Abandoning his thoughts, Francis directed this situation to Alison.

However, Alison was promptly pleased. She thought that this kindness offered by Gregg and Violet meant that she would have some time for extra things. Perhaps a visit to the old dears. Gloria Shaw's arthritic hands had become so painful that she couldn't use them much at all, making her extremely grouchy.

Alison gratefully said yes to Gregg's offer, expecting Francis to do the same. Smiling, and following Alison's lead, Francis extended his hand to shake Gregg's. 'We had better see what our children think about this.'

Sitting on a large blanket on the grass next to the house, the children were watching shirtless Sam. At last, he was removing straw racks, folding saddle-stands, horseshoe bridle-brackets and the like from the stables and tack-room that had been left over from Gloria Shaw's residency.

Sam put them on the cobblestone area to be taken away during the afternoon. His instructions were to paint the whole place inside and out with white paint. He would then put in some basic furniture to make it presentable. The Colonel had told him a while ago that it would be for *Legal Affairs'* new staff to use. However, they had already found other places. Sam wondered if it would ever be occupied.

Douglas and Francis sat on two garden seats close by. The children turned their heads and looked intently at Gregg. Getting down on his haunches to be on the same level with them, he said, 'I am amazed at what I've heard,' leaving it to their imagination as to what he had heard.

Emily asked, 'Is it the skill with the knuckle-bones that I have been practising?' – showing off her ingenuity in her cupped hands.

Alice enquired, 'Is it the cleaning out of all this rubbish?' – pointing to the pile that Sam was collecting.

Judy said practically, 'I know, you have gifts for us!'

Although his mother told him it was rude to stare at visitors, Frank was becoming famous for staring at everybody. Frank had tried it on Harris Tweed, and it seemed to have worked. This time he stared long and hard at Gregg.

Gregg laughed at all these strange answers and, returning Frank's stare (there was no way that he could be fooled by the boy), he said, 'No! I haven't got any of these things. As you know, we're approaching Christmas, so how would it be if you came with my wife and me to a wonderful display of the celebration? You can either choose between the city council's marvellous picnic, or seeing the Christmas decorations in the city centre. This will include Father Christmas in his grotto!'

Of course, they chose to see Father Christmas in his grotto.

The next day, right on the dot of ten o'clock, a large hired limousine, with a smiling chauffeur wearing a peaked cap, drew up outside. With their faces shiny clean, their hair neatly done, and their nails trimmed on all digits, they climbed into the limousine. With large smiles, they sank down into the comfortable seats. Gregg and Violet were already in the vehicle, and welcomed the children with wide, warm smiles.

The limousine cruised along at a leisurely rate. They were fascinated by the city's splendours. At last they reached one of the large decorated department stores right in the heart of the city. A very efficient but kind lady from the store took them first to the shop window. There, on display, was the *Babe of Bethlehem, Gentle Mary, Wondering Joseph, Awesome Shepherds* and the stately *Three Kings with their Gifts*.

Once they had had their enchantment, the children were escorted inside to Santa's grotto. They enjoyed sitting on his knee as much as Santa enjoyed listening to the children's excitable chatter, particularly Frank. They were then taken downstairs to have an overly-rich morning tea, before a hurried visit to the toilets (matron Violet looked after Frank). At the prescribed time, they were taken back to their home, very happy.

Thus the celebration mode of friendship between the children and Gregg and Violet commenced. Every Christmas, they looked forward to their coming up from Dunedin, wondering what the 'gifts' would be this time. They could be taken to an outside music extravaganza where children listened to wonderful songs of joy; or visit a real farmyard full of old vehicles and wagons, where the farmer and his wife put on a children's stupendous meal. This year though, the children had the task of decorating the *Honeysuckle House* Christmas tree in the conservatory.

Gregg had already written to Alison, saying he wouldn't be at *Wisteria Cottage* or *Honeysuckle House* as early as he'd hoped, explaining that work was keeping him until just before Christmas.

That done, Gregg wrote individually to the children, saying that the gift for this year would be doing the decoration of the massive Christmas tree at *Honeysuckle*

House. He drew crazy pictures of him being sorry, which made everyone laugh.

Violet then wrote four individual notes that she put inside Gregg's envelopes, saying that she was really looking forward to having time with her sister Rose.

Just before Christmas, Rose will join me to attend the unveiling of the new statue of Nurse Hickson. In 1886 she founded the first midwifery house in Factory Road, Mosgiel. When I was a student nurse in Dunedin, the matron told us of her meeting Nurse Hickson just before she died, in 1930! How about that! Then Rose and I go back in time for Christmas celebrations, including a look at the wonderful tree that you've been decorating in the conservatory. I will see you then!'

(Violet had already been given detailed instructions by Iris that when she and Rose were in Mosgiel, they must go and see the houses where their past family members had lived. 'Apart from the house where Adam, you and Rose grew up, opposite the Presbyterian Church in Church Street, there is Ayr Street, where my parents David and Lilian used to live and where I grew up; the house at Forfar Street, where my grandparents Alec and Emma lived with Auntie Madge: and your father, Douglas, lived with his mother Janet in Glasgow Street. You will have a busy time.')

Seeing the poor Christmas decorations in the boxes, Alison took an urgent request to the Colonel, who said, 'Yes. I'm afraid the decorations are getting a bit old and tatty now. Go ahead and buy some new ones from the city shop, and charge it to *Legal Affairs'* account.'

Having bought them, under Alison and Polly's direction, and with Sam's help, the children were now *in charge of operations.* They worked for some time on the massive Christmas tree that stood in pride of place, just where you came through the conservatory door entrance.

Fussing, Miss Marchant made sure that any ladder climbing was safely done. She had already seen that the base of the tree was secure. She calculated the safe distance required before Judy or Alice climbed up the tree to attach new lights and coloured streamers.

Although she shouldn't have, Judy extended herself, reaching quite high to place the haloed angel on top of the tree. However, it was slightly crooked, so that night, Sam returned and fixed it securely.

Judy and Frank, with Polly and Adam's help, worked on the tree's lower branches. Using loads of bunting, baubles and bangles, and ornamental paperchains, they hung them around the Christmas tree.

To finish off, they added various-sized stars and brightly multi-coloured tinsel. Stiff red paper was used to cut out jolly Father Christmas, in several different shapes, as it happened! Judy had learned how to do this at school. With her face showing absolute concentration, she taught the others how to put together the intricate pieces. (They were alright, but no prizes were won!)

Sophie, who had been recovering from her illness, now seated herself on a window-seat and watched, amused by the children's noisy activity.

Frank was most insistent that they left room for the expected presents which Father Christmas would deliver later.

To the children, it was a perfect, gloriously bright and stunningly beautiful room, enhanced by the glorious Christmas Tree!

Chapter 86

*J*ACK WAS FEELING miserable. He said that he had picked up a dangerous flu bug, or some dreaded lurgy that totally exhausted him. Well, that's what it felt like! However, he didn't retire to a sickbed on the upper *Honeysuckle House* floor, where he had been living and working for many years now. No! After his time on the farm, Jack had decided that he would move to the recently renovated and still vacant stable-hands residence that Sam had just finished doing up at *Wisteria Cottage*.

Of course, he arranged this first with the Colonel and Adam, and then with Francis and Alison. Jack paid a minimal amount of board to Francis. Now that independence was his goal, Jack was wanting to live a new life, because God was now in control of *every* aspect, including his board.

Hearing the friendly sounds of the Delgado family's activities from the open cottage windows, he saw the children playing on the clean cobble-stone yard. Large round wooden containers filled with pansies brought colour to the area.

Jack noticed the wonderful way Sam had renovated the stables and tack room. At the far end of the building was a small study housing a computer, with all its equipment. Next to that was a small bedroom containing a single bed, a wooden cabinet, and a chest of drawers. Lastly, there was a comfortable lounge/kitchen with its mini-table, one chair, microwave and small fridge. The room was heated by a tiny gas fire, so by opening the door through, the lounge and bedroom would receive some warm air. A TV was mounted high on the wall, and he could sit and watch the programmes while he ate his meals. Perfect!

As Jack was snuggling down into his comfortable bed, he thought the only thing he needed was the help of a few people to look after him during his illness. Nurse Polly had already said to him that, 'If you have flu, the only thing to do is to drink lots of water and get plenty of rest!'

There was Alison, but she was far too busy with her children, or making muffins, these days. Francis also was busy, so he only looked in at the end of the long day. The children were not allowed to visit Jack, as they were warned that they would get the dreaded lurgy from him. There was Sam, too, but he always had some excuse that his girlfriends were waiting for him when he finished work. Then there was his father, also forbidden to visit due to his own dubious health.

However, Mira came into Jack's mind quite a lot. He had first seen her walking around the gardens from his upper room at *Honeysuckle House*. Strikingly beautiful, she had the most wonderful smile that lit up all the surroundings! He hoped to get to know her more.

Well, at eleven o'clock one morning, after several miserable days of the flu-type bug, Jack heard a soft knock and then a lovely voice said sweetly, 'Can I come in?'

Mira!

Jack hastily croaked, 'Just a moment,' and hurriedly straightened out the bed's duvet, then put the used tissues into one of the plastic bags on the floor. He pulled on the top half of his pyjamas and, a few seconds later, invited Mira in.

Some people would prefer to open the sick door a smidgen, or even half-come in, putting their face around the door, but brave Mira confidently walked in and immediately said, 'Hi! How are you feeling?' without a care in the world.

It is like being in heaven, Jack thought. *This bright,*

open smile for only me to see!

The bedroom didn't have any chairs, so without a second thought Mira sat on the end of his rumpled bed and asked again, 'How are you?'

Jack said, 'I think I'm getting better!' Then, not having anything else to say, he grinned. Unfortunately, when he did this, his whole face, full of cold, became sore and uncomfortable.

Mira guessed at Jack's discomfort and said quickly, 'Rose and I have just been to see the girls and Frank at *Wisteria Cottage*. Did you know that the children have the responsibility of the Christmas tree this year?'

He nodded.

'Alison said you were here, feeling miserable.' Then, she asked if she could bring anything with her the next day.

Jack was overwhelmed. She was coming to see him the next day! Bliss! Croaking again, he asked, 'Can you bring another writing pad and two pens, one black and one red? I want something to write down any ideas for the stories that I have.'

He received a good deal of satisfaction from writing for the Delgado children. The tools of the trade, he felt, were the smell of ink that he put on thick creamy paper.

'Oh, you write stories, do you? How many have you written?'

'I've just published my first story.'

'Are you able to tell it to Alison's children?'

'Yes. I've read it to the girls when Frank was in bed,' he said proudly. 'My grandfather and my father were both writers, so I have followed in their footsteps.'

Mira stood up. Still with a radiant smile, she said that she would remember to bring the writing pad, and two pens – one red, one black. Softly she closed the door, leaving Jack amazed and a little giddy at what had happened.

The following day he woke up still with a very sore throat. His voice, throat and sinuses were still in a terrible state. He remembered his mother's advice of lots of water, but he didn't think that the water was doing him any good. Alone and sneezing, Jack fetched a chair from the lounge/dining room, went back to bed and waited for Mira.

Later in the morning, Mira's lovely face still held that magnificent smile. She had been down to the village centre and found some artist's materials there. She had bought a giant writing pad and lots of different coloured pens. 'This ought to keep you going for quite a while!' she said, dropping them onto the bed with delighted anticipation of his reaction. Jack did not let her down; his own smile spread broadly across his face, making her smile even more.

Jack asked if Mira would like to read one of the stories from his grandfather. As she said yes, he retrieved, from the small cabinet by his bed, a bound volume of *Short Articles and Pithy Poems* written by his English grandfather, Albert Williams, all those years ago.

Mira settled herself more comfortably as she began to read.

Jack took the opportunity to look at Mira in all her beauty. Her lovely eyes moved side to side. Her rosy lips and mouth moved together as she read this small book. Her dusky arms were smooth and golden. He thrilled with the pleasure of her loveliness...

Jack quickly came to the realisation that he was absolutely in love with her! *How did this happen so quickly?* he thought; further, *What does all this mean?* And when Mira had finished reading, she gave him another wonderful smile. *It's like the sun coming out*, Jack thought. *That's what it means!*

Putting the bound book down on the bed, Mira said very reluctantly, 'Well, I'd better be on my way. I hesitate to give you a kiss because you might give me your germs,' and she closed the door quietly behind her.

Jack was thrilled. She had promised him a kiss! He settled down into the bed for a delightful Mira-dream-filled sleep.

Mira and Jack's friendship grew by leaps and bounds into something more meaningful. When he recovered from the flu – rather quickly – they began taking walks around *Honeysuckle House* gardens. While listening to each other's serious concerns or over-the-top funny events, they often found themselves in each other's arms, and it was only natural then that they would stop to, rather awkwardly at first, enjoy a kiss or two.

But that was all. Jack knew from somewhere that kissing is given in all sorts of ways: a peck on the lips, a slight whisper on both sides of the face, or a long full and sloppy kiss that stops observers in their tracks. It was not, as his mother had humorously said when he asked her about it, *The Osculation of the Orbicularis Oris muscle!* Although he was an adult, he had not yet mastered the skill of kissing perfectly; nor had he really been motivated to. Until now.

Mira too was most reluctant to move too rapidly, after her past experiences with Rick Strait.

Whenever they were seated on one of *Wisteria Cottage*'s hidden bower-seats, or walking together around *Honey-suckle House* lake, or sitting on the grass relaxing under the welcoming oak trees, their hands were clasped together – a sign that greater things were in the offing. In fact, they knew their futures were to be together.

Mira told Jack about some of her past with Rick and of her sorry self. 'He destroyed all of my girlhood fancies,' she said sadly. 'Because of that I don't want to go any further yet, Jack,' she whispered to him. 'It is early days, so don't get too excited, will you?'

Jack told her that he was quite content to wait for something more, no matter his feelings or desires.

One hot and glorious day they had enjoyed a game of tennis. Jack had won, but he accorded Mira the overall title because, 'You light up the courts with your radiance!'

She returned one such of her radiant smiles. 'Thank you,' she whispered.

Later, sitting on the *Honeysuckle House* verandah with cold lemonades, Jack said, 'What do you think of when you go into a bookshop which is very busy and full of hesitant customers? They might have stacks of books piled high, and harassed assistants working under great strain. You feel that it's chaotic, and you may decide to poke around on your own for any hidden treasures!'

Mira laughed. She and Rose had just been to a large city bookshop while its annual sale was on. They'd had to deal with a similar scene.

'I've often dreamed of my ideal bookshop,' Jack continued. 'One that is self-supporting, where I wouldn't need to worry about profit and loss, ordering new stock, or even about the customers – a place for those prepared to spend time searching, delving, investigating, until they find the treasure themselves, and where the secret life of words is all you need.'

Then he added slightly hesitantly, 'Next Monday I have an appointment with the manager of a large second-hand bookshop, about working there as his assistant. If I get this position it will start just before Christmas. Do I look scholarly enough?' – giving her a learned wise man look from under his brows.

Mira laughed, and Jack said more seriously, 'Do you think that you could come into the shop and give it a once-over glance before I go for my interview?'

'I think I can do that,' Mira graciously smiled.

They went into the city and found the bookshop. It was pouring down with rain, so Jack remarked, 'Today there won't be many people around, so you can take plenty of time when you're giving the bookshop its once-over.'

There was nothing in the narrow front windows of the shop – just a small, brown, crumpled-at-the-edges notice saying *Antiquarian Books*. Only once people came through the door did they behold the beautiful and bountiful literature inside. The first thing they noticed was a rather large, ancient till; not some fancy machine that did most of the money calculations. Behind it was a scholarly man, his spectacles placed awkwardly on a leathery nose, reading.

In a confusing way, spread over three rambling and slightly musty storeys, the shop was crammed full of a plethora of volumes in all shapes and sizes. Ranging from ancient literature to more modern publications, they were produced by out-of-the-way publishers, or written by scholarly but unknown dons.

Jack and Mira slowly walked up a creaking staircase to the next floor. There they were confronted by sporting manuals, unusual biographies and scholarly works, on every topic imaginable. There were memoirs from each and every war and, of course, plenty of children's fiction.

Then they climbed the stairs to the creaking, narrow, and somewhat eerie top floor, where they found a wide selection of old philosophical and religious titles, presenting various ardent arguments on serious subjects.

On a dusty top shelf, Mira found some musty folio pamphlets, arranged in a series of cardboard containers featuring long-forgotten authors. She picked one at random and, flicking over its pages, she said with all seriousness, 'Do you really want to work here?'

Jack explained to Mira, 'You could say that I wouldn't get too much excitement selling second-hand books. However, if I get the position, I know there will be more modern second-hand books from the general public, the universities and libraries. Sorting them out into various categories, then putting them together in the right section over the three floors, before finally presenting them for sale to the general public, will be wonderful!'

They laughed at his explanation. Not knowing if some energetic person might come up the stairs to this eerie room, Mira tenderly wrapped her arms around Jack and gently kissed him.

After releasing him she said breathlessly, 'As long as I know you are settled in one spot, I will marry you, if that is your intention!'

Taken by surprise, a thrilled Jack hurriedly went down on one knee on the ancient floor and asked her, more properly, to marry him.

'Yes,' she said, 'as soon as you like!' They kissed again more urgently, this time in agreement.

Jack indeed started work for *Antiquarian Books*. He bought an engagement ring for Mira with his very first earnings.

Chapter 87

CHRISTMAS CELEBRATIONS WERE upon Christ-church. From large retail stores to small earnest businesses, and dinky little shops, crowds of people were opening their hearts, wallets and generosity for the festivities.

The city council had added its touches as well, for on each lamp post and hanging from every shop verandah were various coloured decorations and bunting, adding sparkle and shine to the burgeoning summer.

In front of one of the most famous retail shops in town, Mira and Rose stood in wonder and amazement as they gazed at a Christmas window. The display was packed with small doll-like characters demonstrating a host of activities and interests, always on a Christmas theme. In the middle was the real reason for the season – the nativity scene.

The excitable crowds, with their heavy gifts wrapped in all sorts of coloured paper and neatly tied with enormous bows of ribbons, stood outside the window.

Mira viewed all the scenes and figures through the now sticky-fingered windows. Then, in the reflective glass, she caught a glimpse of a well-dressed young man standing on the other side of the road. Her heart did a double flip. She thought that she was seeing a ghost, for there was – *Rick Strait!*

His face was slightly changed, but it was undoubtedly him. Questions flooded her mind. Wasn't he dead? All the facts had pointed to it; however, he was obviously still alive! What was he doing, following her after all this time?

How did he know I was here? What do I tell Rose?

Mira slowly turned to have a better look at him. Standing with hands in his trouser pockets, he showed no concern, anger or frustration, but simply stared at her with a hidden expression that said very little.

Grabbing hold of Rose's arm Mira quickly said, 'Let's have some coffee.' She hurried into the store and descended the steps to the lower floor, arriving at the restaurant very flustered.

'Whatever is the matter?' asked a surprised Rose when she caught up with Mira. Concerned at her pale and shocked expression, Rose hurriedly added, 'You look as though you've seen a ghost. I'll fetch some extra strong coffee!' She placed their order at the counter.

When the steaming coffee arrived, Mira quickly gulped some of hers and, flushed now, said agitatedly, 'I think I have just seen Rick Strait!'

'What! Where?' Rose questioned, looking around.

'Just over the road. I saw him reflected in a shop window.'

Rose waited for a moment, pondering this news. When they had finished the coffee (rather hot in Rose's opinion, though Mira drank hers in one or two gulps), they took the lift to the top floor: *Women's Garments.*

Rushing across to the windows, they looked out to see if Rick was still there. Mira grabbed hold of Rose's arm and pointed him out.

Rick stood quite still among the crowd, but had moved slightly so he could keep his eyes on both entrances – Colombo Street and Cashel Mall, both busy thoroughfares.

Rick slowly raised his eyes to the top floor staring for a moment at each window. He caught a glimpse of Mira, who immediately jumped back. She was really frightened. 'What will I do now?' she said, bursting into tears.

The mature assistant, who had been watching them, was patiently waiting. Knowing that young girls were often easily upset for all sorts of reasons, she came over and softly asked if she could be of any help.

A concerned Rose whispered to her, 'We are having

young man problems! He is down in the street. Can you phone for a taxi so that we can escape through a back entrance?'

'Just one moment please.' The woman hurried to the phone and ordered a taxi, telling them where to come. Then she told the two worried ladies to go to the back of the store, where they would find another lift for the staff. 'This will take you down to a lane and a taxi should be waiting for you.'

They thanked her profusely.

Meanwhile Rick realised that Mira might do something crazy so, rushing into the store, he hastened past the menswear and the furniture department to find a narrow back door. It was an exit, he presumed, that led to a delivery lane.

Rick was too late. He had observed that the agitated Mira and an older lady were getting into a taxi. Just before they left, he heard this lady say in a clear voice to the driver, '*Honeysuckle House* please.'

Rick now knew where Mira was staying.

Chapter 88

*F*OR ANYONE GOING to *Honeysuckle House*, it would involve starting off at the road entrance and following a winding, meandering driveway before arriving at the pristine dwelling. However, the approach to *Wisteria Cottage* was a much shorter distance from the road.

In between the two properties there was a dilapidated old fence. In the early 1950s, a tall hedge had been planted beside it, so it was impossible to cross over.

For a long time, Francis had been discussing with the Colonel about removing the groaning barrier and building a decent path between the two properties. Having been given permission, Francis had never got around to it, but at last, he did. Hopefully, he would get the pathway done before Christmas.

When he heard about this project, Frank was thrilled that his father was working on the path. Each day Frank sat on his trike watching what progress had been made. He even followed Francis to see him tip the rubbish into the destroyed swimming pool.

Another day, his father used new weatherproofed timber to put in a short, arched bridge between the two properties. The following week, Francis put strong pliable wood edging on each side of the twisting path. He then laid down some medium-sized grey river stones, and hundreds of small multi-coloured round pebbles on top, to strengthen the surface. Finally, he put in numerous garden lights, with sensors that came on automatically when someone walked along the path at night.

Francis was pleased with what he had done. Frank was pleased for another reason!

When the work was finished, and because Frank was an adventurer himself, he got off his trike and enjoyed playing with the coloured round pebbles on the path. They fitted into his hands so neatly as he turned them over and examined them, with a concentration that was very telling.

Frank focused on one colour at a time, and after a while the path looked like it had been painted by an artist – pinks to one side, blues in the middle, whites on the other side. It was not as his father had created it – a veritable mismatch of colours.

The next day, when there was no Francis (there had been a mix-up between Alison and himself as to who was looking after their son), Frank grew braver. He went over the bridge and all the way to *Honeysuckle House*, holding the precious coloured pebbles from yesterday. Out of the corner of his eye, Frank noticed Mira standing idly by the *Honeysuckle House* front door. Because she was looking out to the wonderful gardens, he drew closer to her; it may be that she had seen something interesting, and Frank wanted to see what it was.

Because it was so still and quiet, Mira heard faintly, and then more loudly, the sound of approaching visitors. Yes, she thought, a woman... then a man... and a small child, walking slowly up the drive. She supposed that the taxi they had been travelling in had stopped at the entrance on their instructions so that they could look at all the lovely gardens lining the driveway.

When the visitors had finished looking, they came around a bend and were delighted to see the smart white Edwardian house, decorated outside in silver tinsel and green and red foliage, ready for Christmas.

When Mira looked more closely at the visitors, she gave a sudden start and moved forward, to the edge of the verandah. She stood very still, her heart pounding, mouth open. Could it be...?

And as one of those visitors turned her head and stared into Mira's eyes, she too gasped, wide-eyed.

Slowly, Mira came down the verandah steps and, catching her breath, asked hesitantly, 'Evie? Is it really you?' Then more strongly, 'What are you doing here?'

Evie's expression was one of thrilled joy. 'Mira!' she breathlessly responded.

The two women rushed joyously into each others' arms, hugging and jumping and laughing in disbelief.

With Evie was James, her husband. He was holding the hand of Maria, their daughter.

Letting go of Mira, Evie knelt down to explain to the astonished child, 'This is my sister, from long ago. My name back then was Evie, but Daddy changed it to Angel. He thought that I was an angel sent from heaven – and, I suppose, still does!'

Then Frank, who didn't have a care in the world, as fast as his limbs would allow, rushed up to Mira and, taking hold of one of her hands, put a pink pebble in it. He then went over to Evie and put a blue pebble in her hand. Then he loudly lisped, 'Join – t... two!... Join – t... two!'

Both Angel and Mira looked at Frank, not comprehending what he was saying, but James had guessed, and realised this must be young Frank.

He quietly said, 'He wants you to put your hands with your pebbles together!'

The long-lost sisters, still holding their pink and blue pebbles, and with tears running down their faces, did as requested, then embraced and kissed again.

Frank looked at them with a drooling grin, knowing he had done something remarkable!

Hearing all these unusual voices and laughter, Polly hurried out onto the verandah. Before her stood her son, and two young women. She didn't quite get the connection between them, but she threw her arms around James, saying excitedly, 'At last, you have come home, and for Christmas!'

Laughing, he said proudly, 'We flew in quite early today – at three o'clock in the morning to be precise. We stayed at an airport motel to have a sleep as we didn't want to disturb you or Dad too soon.'

Standing back, Polly took a good look at the two women, arms wound round each other, looking thoroughly delighted! Of course, she already knew Mira, and James had indicated Angel, but how did the two girls know each other?

James saw her puzzled look, and said, 'They're sisters, Mum!' He suddenly remembered that this was the first time his mother had seen Angel, or Maria. James lifted his daughter into his arms and pulled Angel to him, and hurriedly said, 'This is Angel, Mum. And this delightful little person is Maria.'

Polly was so overcome that she burst into tears. At long last her prayers had been realised! She gave Maria a double hug, which the smiling youngster returned.

James explained to Maria, 'This is your grandmother. Oh, correction. Here are both your grandparents.' He had just seen Adam slowly coming through the entranceway, so raising his voice, he said to his father, 'Hello Dad! Do you know that Mira and Angel are sisters?'

Adam was thrilled at this. 'Sisters!' he said succinctly. 'So... Angel, you are Mira's younger sister, Evie?'

The two girls nodded happily, and Polly hugged each of the new-found sisters.

'Come inside Maria,' Polly said tearfully to her granddaughter, trying her name for the first time; 'You will want something to eat, or... is the Australian term *tucker?* Let me look at you again!' She gave a laugh, 'All well-tanned Queenslanders!' Maria's skin, like Angel's and Mira's, was a rich brown.

Taking Maria by the hand, and with Angel and Mira right behind her, Polly went into *Honeysuckle House,* where the whole of the main entrance was decorated for the Christmas season. Polly directed them all to go upstairs into the lounge. 'Yes, that's right, the door standing open, just up there.'

However, before they went upstairs, they were all met by a querying Mrs Mulligan. She had opened the kitchen door to see what the fuss was about. Over the years she had been trying out all her own cooking creations, and was now a dumpling of a woman! Mrs Mulligan told them that she was just taking another batch of raisin scones out of the oven, and a rich chocolate cake was cooling down, so she beckoned the little girl (James whispered, 'Her name is Maria'), and asked, 'Would you like to come into my kitchen?'

Maria would, and the kitchen door closed firmly behind them.

James correctly commented that the seemingly starving child wouldn't be seen for at least an hour or so!

Meanwhile, Alison was speeding along the new path to catch up with Frank. Thinking it would be nice to go into Mrs Mulligan's kitchen and try out some delicious food too, Frank was just about to do so.

Alison stopped him, her hand resting purposefully on his shoulder. 'Come along,' she insisted. 'You can see that they have guests. You can come here another time.'

She hadn't realised that Frank had been instrumental in arranging two of the guests' reunion, but looking again at the visitors, Alison realised that she knew the man's sunburnt face and exclaimed, 'Oh! You're James!'

'Yes, Alison,' James said smiling. 'I have come back home with my lovely wife Angel, and my daughter, Maria.' And as he was telling her all about it, they found their way up the stairs and into the lounge. Distracted, Alison forgot all about taking Frank home.

And Frank? Knowing that's where the raisin scones and rich chocolate cake would be, he slid away into the cook's domain.

Chapter 89

*M*IRA AND ANGEL smiled and smiled at each other. Settling down into the comfortable lounge chairs, they enjoyed their chit-chat, until Angel introduced a rather sad note.

'Mother was in deepest despair. Having just got over another bout of flu, your disappearance was an absolute shock. I imagine this made her open to all sorts of infection. She was certainly unwell, and so in bed for many weeks.'

Angel continued. 'I was shocked too, but in a different way. I became listless in my studies, and at the start of the following term I decided to leave school to do nothing worthwhile. It might have been the worry of your disappearance that did this, I don't know. Uncle Frederick looked after both of us. He made plans to move mother into a hospital in Cairns, but no sooner had he got her into the car than she suddenly collapsed, and shortly after died.'

Mira wept. 'Mother!' she said, sobbing inconsolably. 'Being like that, all because of me! But I was so frightened as to what could happen that I took the easy way out - not saying anything.'

James got a clean hanky from his pocket and gave it to her. Angel closed her hands over Mira's, murmuring kind things. The rest made sympathetic noises.

'The funeral was on the *Bungendore* property,' she said very quietly, 'and the burial was in the small country graveyard, a few miles away. Much sadness.' Then both broke down and cried again.

Very quietly, Polly got a fresh box of tissues out of the cupboard, just in case it would be needed.

Angel remembered sadly all the details that had stayed with her.

Accompanied by the school principals, the Misses Kettle, and sad Mrs Mop and her daughter, who stood on the verandah, Uncle Frederick slowly came down the steps of the house. Two weeks before, he and Claire had discussed a funeral, just in case, and decided on a horse-and-carriage burial in a local area. The undertakers would do everything required.

Walking slowly to the carriage, Uncle Frederick's shoes kicked up small whiffs of dust that made the horse whinny nervously. Seated high on the carriage, holding the horse's reins in one hand, the undertaker reached down and helped Uncle Frederick climb up the high steps to join him. He didn't acknowledge the undertaker's kindness, but instead sat on the hard boards staring unseeingly ahead.

The simple coffin lay in the back of the carriage. There were flowers around the bier, but even these looked wilted in the sun, almost as if they too were bowed down with grief. Slowly, progress was made to the burial grounds. The other undertaker and Evie were following in a car. The black-robed parson spoke briefly about Claire's life, and then the two undertakers uncoiled the strong ropes and gently lowered the coffin into the freshly dug grave. The old silent gravedigger waited patiently for them to be finished, then filled it in with his shovel.

Uncle Frederick, having buried a second wife, immediately returned to work, leaving Evie to grieve alone. Mrs Mop wasn't quite sure how to deal with her, except to ask time and time again if she would like another cup of strong tea.

The Misses Kettle tried to persuade her to come back to school as soon as might be convenient, so she slowly picked herself up and continued her studies. Uncle Frederick sank into a depression, but each month he remembered the occasion of Claire's death.

Grinning through her tears, Angel said then, 'On

completion of my school education, I went to a college in Cairns, where I graduated as a teacher.' Then she told of how she went on an adventure, leaving the small almost unknown *Bungendore Homestead* for cosmopolitan London.

James smiled. He knew all about this but recognised that most of it would be new to the others, so he didn't interrupt.

'Each year the Protestant churches provide opportunities for twelve selected young people, representing various countries, to attend a London course to get to know the ins-and-outs of missionary life. I applied and was accepted. On my arrival, I was introduced to other members of the group.

'We stayed in a large church house in London for six months, studying the Bible and what the scriptures said on missionary life. In between studies, James and I clicked,' she said, lovingly taking his hand. 'Before we knew it, we were engaged. We had little cash to spend on an engagement ring. James told me that we would pick up a cheap ring from one of the market stalls, until we could afford a better one.

'We might be engaged but we had to toe the line during the intensive course, meaning, at the end of six months, we were split into two groups for an extra six months – me going to India, and James to Jamaica. We still wrote to each other,' she laughed, 'and we got to know one another quite well. This was the time when James gave me the name *Angel.*'

Here, James did interrupt. 'I thought that here was a special angel who came down from heaven to dwell on earth, to be loved only by me!'

The delightful name stuck! When they sent a postcard to James' parents to give them the good news, he automatically said Angel instead of her proper name, Evie. Incredible, but there it was!

All the budding young missionaries went back to their own individual countries, telling the churches what fascinating and ghastly things they had learned from the trip. When James came back alone to *Honeysuckle House* for a short time, he would say only Angel, never Evie.

James had been teaching English in Christchurch, and he had been saving up enough to make the trip to Australia the following year. He had already been in discussion with the teaching authorities, explaining that he was looking for some work in North Queensland. He didn't tell them that this was where his lovely fiancé was living!

Angel went on: 'In one of the letters to James, I had told him that first we needed to go to Cairns, where Uncle Frederick was by now living in a retirement home. He had moved there shortly after our mother had died. Of course, Uncle Frederick said we could get married there. He was still fit enough to walk me down the church aisle to my groom. He had some debilitating complaint affecting his body, which stopped him from walking long distances. I said that a sturdy wheelchair would be fine.

'Uncle Frederick then told me that he preferred the name Evie to Angel, as this was the name given by her mother, and he would always think of me as Evie.

'"Here is a small gift for you," he added, and he gave me a lovely ring. "I gave that ring to your mother when we became engaged. When she died, I kept it for you."

'I gave Uncle Frederick a big hug and then a kiss on his cheek, wondering what James would say to this generous gift. James was most reticent about accepting the engagement ring. After all, the ring that he gave me was specially chosen by him. It was a love gift of promise! Then having thought about it, James decided that he was being too proud. If I was quite happy to have the engagement ring that Uncle Frederick had given Mother, then that was okay. However, this London engagement ring was ours alone, so he took me in his arms and said I could wear *two* engagement rings on my finger.'

James then gave her another short but delightful kiss, smiling at the two engagement rings sitting comfortably on her finger.

'Uncle Frederick never made it to the wedding. He suddenly had a stroke and became too ill to be moved, and three days later he died. After his burial in the Cairns cemetery, we married at the registry office.'

James comforted her with, 'My parents never made it to Australia either.'

Polly gave a hurried contribution. 'What with all this confusion in our minds, and the situation here with Adam being in and out of hospital so frequently –'

Adam pompously interrupted, 'We never got out of this place.'

Polly hurriedly finished with, 'But now we've seen the outcome in the lovely form of Angel, which is what we will call her rather than Evie, since we have always thought of her that way. And besides – it fits!'

Chapter 90

S GREGG WAS getting out of a taxi at the front gate of *Honeysuckle House*, his intention was to smell the perfume from all the wonderful flowers that were blooming before entering the house. However, on the opposite side of the road was an agitated but smartly dressed young man.

Observing him more closely, Gregg felt that he was having an argument with himself. He obviously couldn't decide whether to flee this place or to stay, so Gregg asked him, 'Is there anything wrong?'

The young man replied, 'Is anything wrong? I should say so!' Then, he asked, 'Are you going to *Honeysuckle House*?' pointing in that direction.

Gregg said, 'Yes. I usually take a look at all these flowers before I go and talk with my relatives and friends. Do you want to come in? I can be with you if that will be of any help,' beckoning him with a welcome gesture.

The young man came over the road to ask, 'What is your name?'

'I'm Gregg. This place,' referring to *Honeysuckle House,* 'is always a sanctuary of peace.' Looking at the young man's troubled face, he said very quietly, 'It doesn't look like you have had much peace.'

At this, the young man's face crumpled, followed by a few tears which he forcefully wiped away. 'I've done a hideous deed, to a young lady who is in there. I have such fear of confronting her with my apologies. I am too scared to even move – hence the argument with myself.'

Gregg took this young man's trembling hands and

said firmly, 'Well, in my experience you have two choices. You either take the bull by the horns, confronting your devils, no matter what they are, or you skulk away and do nothing. Remember though, those lasting things on your mind will be there forever. They will never go away unless you attempt to deal with them now.'

Then he waited for a moment and said slowly, 'Now what do you want to do? Go to this young lady, expressing your sorrow? Or go away, never having had the opportunity that this woman may forgive you?'

Gregg was extremely patient. He didn't ask for names, either this young man or the lady he had apparently treated so abominably, or what had occurred. All would be revealed if this young man would consider the first circumstance – whether he would go in or not.

Waiting a long moment, the young man then gave, in sudden gulps, some of his tale.

'My name is Rick Strait. I'm from Queensland. I raped Mira many times on a stolen boat. We were wrecked and separated on the shores of Papua. Someone rescued me, and I suppose her. My circumstances changed so much that I need to confess to her and ask for forgiveness... but I am frightened of her reaction.' Then he spoke very softly, 'I have seen her once in Christchurch at one of the city shops – but she ran off before I could speak to her.'

Gregg, inwardly shocked, remained outwardly calm, and firmly said, 'Give those same words you've just spoken to me, to Mira. Remember, I will be by your side.'

Together they walked slowly down the drive, their feet echoing on the gravel beneath. Gregg held Rick's arm tightly, for he wasn't going to have the young man escaping at the last minute!

There was no one on the shady verandah, so they went inside, where Gregg said firmly to Rick, 'Sit down on this chair, and I'll –'

At that moment, Alison hurried down the stairs from the lounge to 'rescue' Frank from Mrs Mulligan's 'clutches' in the kitchen. Her son would otherwise be encouraged to devour lots of scones and maybe two or three slivers of chocolate cake – Alison knew what the cook was like! 'Try another piece!' Mrs Mulligan would say. 'Wouldn't you like to try another scone?' – pressing him to finish up the everlasting supplies! 'Would you like a drink of lemonade?' would follow.

Alison, mid-stride, saw Gregg along with the seated Rick and said, 'Hello, Gregg, fancy seeing you! Where is your lovely wife, Violet? Oh, I remember, she is with Rose down south at Mosgiel.'

Shaking Alison's hand, Gregg quickly said, 'This is Rick Strait. He is from Queensland. Is Mira here? He wants to say something to her.'

'Yes, I'll get her,' Alison said, climbing the stairs again.

Rick was sitting very still, all the time wondering whether the words that he would say to Mira were suitable.

When Mira heard the news, her rosy, animated face suddenly changed to an expression of panic. She exclaimed to Angel, 'Rick Strait is *here!* Rose and I saw him in town, but we got a taxi and managed to avoid him. What do I do now?'

Angel shrugged her shoulders in a kindly way. Though she had known Rick Strait from the boarding school, she had no idea yet of the atrocious activities that he had imposed on Mira on the boat.

Although he didn't know Rick, James cleared his throat and said, 'If we all go down to see him, then presumably he won't be able to do anything except talk.'

They all went down – Mira and Alison, followed by Polly and Adam and, behind them, James and Angel.

Rick stood up and, coming forward, met Mira at the bottom of the carpeted stairs. He looked sorrowfully at her. Then he cast his eyes over the rest of the group who were standing behind Mira. He did a double gulp. There was Mira's sister, Evie too! What was she doing here? His nerves were at a breaking point. He thought, *I've got her people standing in front of me. I've got Gregg holding my shoulder behind me. Help!*

Gregg now whispered what they had just agreed. Rick gulped again. He knew the whole crowd had come down to hear what he had to say!

Breathing deeply, he said in a rush, 'My name is

Rick Strait. I'm from Queensland.' He looked directly at Mira now. 'I acknowledge that I raped you many times, Mira, on that stolen boat... until I fell overboard on the shores of Papua. Someone rescued me – and you, too, I presume?'

Mira nodded her head gently, though she was shaking.

'My circumstances have changed so much, and so have I. I want to say how sorry I am for having kidnapped and raped you, for those whole two years... but I'm so afraid of your reaction! I have come to tell you that I'm very, *very* sorry for what I did to you.' His voice was choked, and tears filled his eyes. ' I can't expect you to forgive me, but I had to confess this to you. To let you know how terrible I feel now about the whole misadventure.'

Mira waited for a very long time. She remembered all of those occasions when Rick had violated and mistreated her so despicably. Throwing his confession around in her mind, she asked silently the perpetual question: *does he really mean it?*

She recalled how Douglas had said that forgiveness might be on the agenda. Mira shook her head in some disbelief that this idea had now become real to her. Quick! What was the thing that she found when reading about forgiveness?

It is 'a powerful attribute, so use it wisely.' If I am to forgive him, she further thought, *which one of us is going to be better? Is there any 'better' in forgiveness? If I don't forgive him, will he be a useless soul, forever? By my talking so freely here at Honeysuckle House, I have nearly emerged from all my anger and frustration. How else will I take this situation without forgiving him?*

Mira thought some more but this time about Jack.

I have a future now; I am in love with Jack. (Jack was at work in the bookshop at that moment.)

She heaved a great big sigh, moving her deep brown eyes to look into Rick's worried ones; his shaking hands and shoulders, the tears on his cheeks. *I do believe,* she thought, *he really meant what he said. There had clearly been a considerable amount of activity deep down in his soul. He had obviously been thinking of asking for forgiveness for some time, and had come here for this one purpose. It would have taken him a lot of courage to give his confession of such terrible things before people who didn't know him. It showed that he was indeed, very sorry!*

Aware of the silence as everyone around held their breath, Mira decided that she *would* forgive Rick. Didn't Jesus say, *For if you forgive other people when they sin against you, your heavenly Father will also forgive you?*

She took Rick's trembling, sweating hands into hers, looked into his tears and gently said, 'I forgive you, Rick!'

Rick fell to his knees, sobbing and crying out, 'I am forgiven! Oh, thank God, I am forgiven!'

Mira felt something soft and warm stir in her heart, and knew that she too was forgiven. She said softly, 'We are both forgiven. Stand up with me. Together, we will face the world.'

Chapter 91

REGG KNEW THAT, having received Mira's forgiveness, Rick ought to allow her some space to work out the repercussions. Stepping into what was quickly becoming an awkward situation, he said to Rick, 'Where are you staying?'

'The Young Peoples' Association Hostel in the heart of Christchurch,' said Rick.

Then Gregg wisely advised, 'Maybe tomorrow or the next day you could come back, and we have a conversation about the next steps you could take.'

Relief all round. They thought this was a good idea and decided that tomorrow would be a suitable time. But who would come?

Polly said that she would be going to a Christmas celebration at the *Home for Gentlefolks* with Douglas and Iris. They had been struggling through the past year, and had just seen an advertisement for the retirement home at their favourite spot by the sparkling sea. Making their application, they were accepted if they could come in right away.

Alison explained that she and the four children would be wrapping up their Christmas gifts, asking if Maria would like to join them. Angel smiled and quickly agreed to Alison's suggestion – anything to keep her daughter occupied, as she realised she must be with her sister for this discussion.

Gregg spoke firmly, 'I will pick up Rick from the hostel. James, Angel, Adam, the Colonel, Mira, Rick and I will gather underneath the two oak trees at ten-thirty. I believe sharing these stories will be very relevant; it will help the ongoing healing process.'

Personally, Mira thought that the fewer people who would attend to hear more about these hidden events, the better!

Frank happily smiled as he rode on his trike beside his mother back to *Wisteria Cottage*, telling her wisely that this was a day for *re-joic-ing!* He had worked out a new word!

That evening, as they sat on the *Honeysuckle House* verandah, Mira discussed her situation with Jack. Taking her into his arms, he gently offered, 'Do you want me to be here? I could take some hours off work.'

'No!' said Mira firmly, resting her head on Jack's shoulder. 'I wish I could have you by my side, but it is not fair to the bookshop. If you pray for me – and I suppose for Rick – that I will have the strength needed; that will be enough.'

The following day, Gregg collected Rick from the hostel and together they met with the invited people in the shade of the two grand oak trees, to hear, but not judge, Rick's story and then, Mira's.

When she had heard of yet another oak tree meeting, Mrs Mulligan started preparing morning tea for them, but Adam told her that this meeting was too important for distractions, so morning tea wouldn't be needed; 'But thank you. However, if you can you supply bottled water for those who want it, that will be very helpful.'

Mrs Mulligan sniffed and clacked her teeth. She didn't like this one bit, preferring to supply tea, coffee and a selection of freshly made sandwiches and cakes to the listeners. Nevertheless, she sent a cold-box with recently bottled cool water that was stored away in the back of the larder.

Rick was a bit hesitant at first. After all, there was only one person that he really knew – Mira. Apart from Evie (who for reasons he didn't understand was now called Angel), all the rest were comparative strangers.

He began by telling them how he was nearly drowned when he fell out of the boat. He'd been thrashing around in the rough Papuan seas, never thinking it would come to this – falling overboard with no means of getting back. The vessel was moving away at a terrific rate. He thought about Mira – would she survive without his sailing skills? He gave a shudder, thinking that if he hadn't been so stupid and had secured his feet in a better place, he wouldn't have gone overboard anyway. At least he was wearing a lifejacket, which kept him afloat through the roiling foam-topped waves... He wondered about sharks and salt-water crocodiles, but by then was too tired to fear them. He drifted on and on until early dawn, by this time very cold. Suddenly, in the distance, he finally spotted land – he could hardly believe it!

He didn't know how long he'd floated like that, but at last the waves were getting smaller and less wild, and he realised he was being gently drawn into Port Moresby harbour. He could just see the native houses standing like soldiers on stilts on the shore; the children just coming out to play; women preparing food on outside fires, and the men making their boats ready for fishing. *Just a few more minutes,* he thought, *then I'll be able to give them a shout...*

Because the storm had done such terrible damage to the fishing boats, the keen fishermen had decided they wouldn't go out, not just yet. Instead, they were repairing their boats, so didn't see Rick.

Bereft of those strapping men who could come to his rescue, he was however eventually washed up onto the shore. He didn't do any shouting, but the children looked at him in surprise, then shouted out to the men that there was a stranger on the shore.

A large Papuan man came rushing through the crowd to squat down and remove his life-jacket. Then he shouted out, 'Get some water and some clothes!'

One cackling woman rushed for the cold water from the deep well beside the school, just outside a memorial hall. Another went inside for a set of dry clothes, returning with a new T-shirt with the letters CWM on it

(City Wide Mission, Rick had learned later on) and some rather large shorts that came down over his knees.

The smiling, over-sized giant himself took off all Rick's wet-through clothing and replaced them with the dry ones. Then, throwing Rick over his shoulder, he carried him back to his large house. On the way he shouted to his anxious wife, 'Prepare a bed for this man to sleep!'

But Rick was soon as right as rain. He didn't need any sleep just then, but found he was ravenous. Hurriedly the woman plated two bananas and some of the morning's leftover fish, a mug of well-brewed tea with lots of sugar, no milk.

Sitting as he watched this man wolf down the food, the host was wondering where his guest had come from, but his patience and manners won out, and he waited for this man's own time.

Rick ate both bananas and finished all the remaining fish, washing it down with three cups of the sweet black tea. Finally satiated, he looked worriedly at the giant and said, 'Where am I?'

The man smiled. Rick learned later that he was living in one of Port Moresby's most important villages. He had received education in one of the town's technical schools, and had then gone on to the university. He spoke excellent English, plus the local tongues of *Police Motu* and *Pidgin English.*

But for now, he said simply, 'I work for the City Wide Mission. See, I'm wearing a T-shirt with our logo. We reach out to people who have been drinking to excess, bringing them back to a sober state. We also rescue young people, girls mostly, who have got AIDS. We tell them all about Jesus Christ, who can save them from their horrible mess.'

Rick looked at him and said, 'So what should I call you?'

'Solomon Henau.' Reaching over, he gave Rick a strong handshake. 'And this is my wife, Nuala.' He turned to the woman who had prepared the bed and food; she said nothing, but smiled expressively at her husband's never-ending talk.

'And what is your name?' Solomon asked. 'Was there a vessel somewhere? Was it destroyed in the storm?'

'I'm Rick Strait. I sailed from North Queensland, but I fell off my boat.'

This caused Nuala and Solomon to shake with laughter, till they saw his embarrassment, and stopped.

'You know,' Solomon said, 'I have rescued you the same way as Jesus Christ rescued people throughout his ministry.' He gave another raucous laugh that disturbed Rick even more; he found out later that the whole village were inured to the *Praising the Lord* stuff. People came in and out of Solomon's home far into the night and prayed with vigorous force that people would be saved. Indeed, later, one old scholarly man who had been to the Papuan Bible College told me, 'Satan and all his minions had better remove themselves when Solomon is around!'

Now Solomon said earnestly, 'Well, I must get on! It is time for a few of us to be going into town for a conference. Rose Fraser from the National Church is going to address us on the dangers of HIV/AIDS. If you like you could come along with us and we could drop you off at the police station to get your situation sorted out.' He gave a chuckle. 'I presume you don't have a passport hidden in your shorts?'

Rick returned Solomon's humour. 'No,' he said, 'nothing like that.' Actually, he had never had a passport and certainly didn't have any clearance from the Papuan authorities. The thrill of being rescued and clothed in dry clothes and having his fill of food suddenly dropped away. He was very wary, particularly of the local villagers, who were so interested in him. The news had spread quickly that a young man had been shipwrecked, was from Queensland, had little clothing and no possessions, but he was going to the police to fix him up with all of these things.

Leaning forward, Adam interrupted Rick. 'Do you know where Rose Fraser is from?'

Rick shook his head. 'No. Should I?'

Adam broke in to Rick's story; 'Rose is one of my sisters! Fancy her being the speaker Solomon was going to see! She will come back to us for Christmas.'

Rick looked at Adam, surprised. If Rose was the mature lady who had taken a taxi with Mira that day... but he didn't say anything to Adam, just continued with his tale.

They had driven into the city and drawn up at the large police station. Solomon said, 'When you're finished, you could come back to my place,' and proceeded to give him directions.

Rick gave a shudder; he really didn't want to return to the village. Then he realised that if he didn't get any joy at the police station, and as he hadn't got a passport, money or possessions, Solomon's home would be somewhere to stay, for a few nights, anyway.

Outside the police station, there were many policemen talking among themselves. Inside, there was a barn-like room with a few struggling electric fans. There was also a large duty desk dealing with people who were arrested following some friction, such as an argument over a few measly hens, or the latest fight in Port Moresby's bars; plus the lost and forlorn who didn't know and didn't care about themselves.

Rick joined this long queue, waiting very patiently in the growing heat. Finally, a policeman gave him his full attention. All the local people stopped what they were doing and became interested in his story. He told the man all the pertinent points and he wrote them down, very slowly. Rick was getting upset by then, and suggested that someone higher up should deal with this problem, so he reluctantly fetched a senior officer and Rick was forced to tell his story again.

In a separate room, Rick didn't have all the local people listening in, but wasn't aware that by now those same people in the queue were spreading an exaggerated tale around the area like wildfire: *Rick Strait, the dangerous criminal, who came from Queensland on a cruise-liner with a beautiful girl, has been arrested for removing valuable clothing from Chief Solomon's house.*

Soon Port Moresby was abuzz.

Chapter 92

SOLOMON HENAU CAUGHT the gist of this sorry tale during his conference's lunch break. Excusing himself, he raced back in his truck to the police station, demanding to see someone who was knowledgeable of all the facts concerning Rick Strait. While he was waiting, he turned to see Rick sitting behind him, lonely and despondent.

'What have they done to you?' Solomon asked sadly. Turning around and seeing a new desk sergeant scurrying to the front, one who hadn't heard the sorry tale, Solomon emphatically said, 'This chap has been through dangerous waters. His Queensland boat was destroyed in the storm and his partner was washed away. He was saved by me. I gave him food and clothing. I brought him to this station, to get another passport and legal documents – yet you treat him like a common criminal!'

Solomon was a little bit off in his explanation, but the matter was now sorted out by a top senior inspector. Through his efforts, Rick was referred to the relevant authorities. However, it turned out that it would take up to a week, maybe a fortnight, or possibly three weeks or so, to sort the situation out.

'What is your local place of residence?' the inspector finally asked.

Solomon kindly said, 'You can stay with me, as long as you won't be too disturbed by my bias for holy living.'

By now Rick had come to realise that Solomon was really a decent man, coming back to the police station to sort out the whole matter. He took his chance and quickly said to the police, 'Yes. I'll be staying with Solomon Henau.'

Taking him by the arm, Solomon said, 'I've got to return to the conference. This will only be on today. Rose Fraser has just returned from America with the latest information on these diseases. If you like you can come with me and listen. You never know, you might pick up some valuable tips.'

Rick gave a bitter laugh. If Solomon really knew of his recent circumstances, he might not be too keen on having him to stay!

Returning to Solomon's village, Rick had got into the swing of things. He did plenty of back-breaking practical work repairing the fishing boats, but refused to go out in them. He had had enough of the sea. Next, he worked on some old cars that were scattered around the village, but found that only a few were salvageable.

Later on, Solomon invited him to yet another religious meeting (all refused so far), but this time the speaker was to be Solomon Henau himself, at the Sir Hubert Murray Stadium. There would be a jazz band.

'You must have heard them?' Solomon asked. 'They practise in the memorial hall, adjacent to where you are staying.' Solomon explained that the band attracted a wandering crowd of locals and encouraged them to go into the venue. He said that large choirs from various churches were coming together on the three Sundays beforehand to practise modern gospel songs.

So along with others, Rick agreed to go out to inform the villages scattered around Port Moresby. 'Of course, we'll come,' they earnestly said. But on the night itself, most people found excuses for not going.

Prayer! You couldn't go anywhere without finding people praying at meetings all over Port Moresby, particularly prayers for Solomon. They all said, 'He is an excellent gospel preacher. Of course, we will pray for him.'

The great day arrived – it was evening, six o'clock, and though the night was already pitch dark, the blazing stadium and whole electrified city lit up the skies. There were a lot of Europeans scattered throughout the crowd, but the majority were local people from Port Moresby and the outlying areas. Rick sat on one side of the stage with his new, enthusiastic friends from the village.

Speaking softly, Mira interrupted Rick. 'Rose Fraser and I were there too. We were seated high up, right at the back of the stadium.'

Again, Rick was silent, thinking about how she had been so close, so near. He gave a wry smile and carried on with his tale.

It all began with some very wild gospel tunes played by the jazz band. Then they had the combined choir singing for all they were worth. The old scholarly man – the one Rick had met in the village – came up and prayed; not for long, but it was still a very exhausting prayer to Rick, for whom all this was so new!

Then Solomon commenced by shouting out, '*Changing Directions.* Listen!' and the crowd was almost silent. 'Many times, Jesus had told His disciples that He would be nailed to a cross to die like a thief.' Then, 'Listen!' he shouted out again. (Solomon told Rick the next day, 'I just say Listen! numerous times. It keeps the crowd on their toes!')

'Jesus told how God had a special plan for Him. However, one night He was arrested and taken before the Jewish court, and the Roman court, and sentenced to death.' Solomon then asked a pertinent question: 'Was the death of Jesus really necessary? Did it have to happen?'

Some people in the crowd threw their answers back: 'No! We don't think so!' and 'There are things that He said that were foolish and dangerous, but he never deserved death.'

'Good answers,' said Solomon, and he repeated the words for anyone that didn't hear them.

By now, a steady stream of perspiration trickled down Solomon's neatly pressed white shirt. 'Just look at some of the things Jesus said: *I will be handed over to be condemned to death. They will make fun of me, spit on me, whip me and kill me. After three days, though, I will be raised to life!* You see, Jesus knew what He was doing. He was doing God's work! Now how about that!'

Solomon thumped his thick Bible down numerous times, but this action didn't interrupt his message. 'Yes! Jesus died for us to take away our sin. He died for you, and for me,' his finger going right and left around the stadium. 'He took the punishment that should have been ours.'

Then Solomon literally *changed direction*. Turning around, his back to the crowd, and the twisted microphone doing its task, he cried out, 'If Jesus died on the cross so long ago, how can He save us *now*? Can a dead man save us from our sins and from our punishment? But Jesus came alive again! He rose three days later from the grave in which He was buried!'

Solomon's voice grew quieter as he finally said, 'We can only have this life because Jesus died *in our place.*'

He turned round to face the crowd again, saying in triumph, 'Come to Jesus, if you desire Him to save YOU!'

Then he put his Bible down gently on the lectern and stood there, waiting, waiting, and waiting some more, before people started to come forward. Just a trickle, then a continuing flood of people, some already weeping in penitence.

Rick gave a grin as he said, 'The preaching was quite a new experience for me. I examined my thoughts. Was this talk of a Saviour really *personal?* I was unsure. Did I accept Jesus as my saviour? No, I'm afraid I did not. I was waiting on forgiveness that might come from Mira. Knowing her strength and fortitude, I reckoned that she might still be alive.

'The next day, I went into the Port Moresby newspaper office and a kind reporter read out one cutting that said, "In Hula, on the south-eastern coast, a vessel from Queensland was destroyed in a violent storm. Miss Mira Woods was the only soul saved."

'I just *had* to find out where she was. Searching for ages, I discovered her on the day after she flew to New Zealand.'

Chapter 93

OW MIRA TOOK up her bleak story. This time she directed the events towards Rick. She didn't look at him, but he still needed to hear these sad words. 'At the village of Hula, I stayed in Ari's home, feeling deeply depressed. Ari was very kind, but she got the idea that there must have been a man involved, wondering how I had got pregnant when I had said I was on the boat for such a long time. Anyway, I had to recognise that I *was* pregnant when I felt movements inside!'

Rick's head came up in a start. Mira was *pregnant?*

'I stayed indoors, only going outside to wash and for my toilet needs. The second-hand clothes came from Ari's large collection. They were far better than the rags I had been wearing all that time at sea.

'Some local men had dragged the damaged boat to shore. Rose had been in contact with the Port Moresby police, telling them all about it. A fortnight later, a CIB inspector came to examine the damage. When he had finished, he came to us – Ari and me – where we sat near the waving palm trees, enjoying the gentle sea.'

I won't take much of your time,' the inspector had said to them. 'The stolen vessel was taken from the Cairns marina some time ago. The owner circulated all the details to the Australian and Papuan authorities. However, I reckon that its broken-down condition will mean an insurance claim for the owner.'

His voice changed. 'How come you are here? What can

you tell me about the damaged vessel? Just so I can put it into my report to the insurance company,' he reassured Mira.

She didn't have to say anything too painful, so she told him how she was kidnapped, and held by the young man who stole the boat. She told him about being chained up whenever Rick went ashore, but avoided more detail, finishing with the wreck and being rescued by Rose Fraser.

Then he very cautiously asked, 'Did this young man do anything to you? Did he hurt you?'

Reluctantly, Mira told him that there was a child in her belly. She added softly, 'He raped me, many times,' and then she suddenly burst into tears.

The inspector kindly said, 'You don't have to tell me anything more. I get the picture. Best of luck with the baby.'

Sobered and saddened, he quietly got into his vehicle and was driven back to Port Moresby, where he filed his report. Mira received a copy later, titled, *MISSING VESSEL, DESTINY:*

> *The perpetrator was a young man, name unknown. He took this vessel, the* Destiny, *out to the islands, just near to the Northern Queensland and Port Moresby outlying shores. He was accompanied by a kidnapped female who is now being looked after by the people of Hula, east of Port Moresby. The boat was effectively destroyed in a storm. The man went overboard, presumably drowned. I recommend that the damaged vessel is an insurance matter, to be taken up by the owner should he so wish. I am closing this case.*

The troublesome days slowly now became lazy weeks. Mira enjoyed all the activities of the Hula villages – for instance, after school, all the children played around the villages, quite free from restraint.

Grinning with pleasure, they told her all about how the sago was made, why bunches of bananas were so prolific and why the large coconuts fell down for eating, and you had to be careful not to be struck by a falling coconut. They also told her about the comings-and-goings of the friendly school staff, whom they seemed to treat as additional parents.

On one of his quiet visits the pastor said to Mira: 'You have been shipwrecked, but Jesus has brought you here and saved you through these wonderful people.' She hadn't told him that she had called out for the Lord's help while struggling in the sea. How did he know? He must have been a truly wise man!

Mira liked the way that the Hula people had their Sunday services. She often sat outside the church and listened to their melodious singing. One older gentleman came when they were having Communion, and he sensitively served Mira. It wasn't as she had been used to back in Queensland, but it was very meaningful all the same.

A few weeks later, Mira woke up in the middle of the night in terrible pain, sure that there was something wrong with the baby. She didn't want to disturb Ari, so she grabbed a lamp and quietly went out to the toilet, where she sat for some time. Then the pain grew worse. She had had this off and on occasionally, but this time, it became overwhelming.

Suddenly, the silent baby fell between her legs, followed rapidly by what looked like a piece of raw meat. Confused, Mira grabbed the baby and found that the child was still attached to the afterbirth by the umbilical cord, but Mira's bloodied hands could not hold it. Slipping down the long drop toilet, the baby was captured by the oozing mess below.

She tried to scream, but no sound came out. Mira, in body shock and mental horror, was on the edge of despair. As she was wiping the tears away, blood from her hands smeared her face.

Ari woke, sensing Mira needed her, and by now could follow the sounds of weeping out to the toilet. She flung open the toilet door to find Mira in severe pain, so she woke her husband and he went to fetch Rose, who had just returned from Port Moresby, and Tau, Ari's father, to start up the lorry. Ari helped her back to the house, where she enclosed a by-now hysterical Mira in her arms, saying soothing things to comfort her. Taking off her bloodied nightshirt, she washed and dried and clothed Mira, and wrapped her in a blanket while they waited.

Now, unheeding and unknowing, as she told her listeners what had happened, Mira began to rock, back and forth, back and forth, incessantly. Hesitating, guessing that he would never fully know what she was going through, Rick placed one of his hands gently on her shoulder to steady her.

Mira looked up and gave him a startled look, but she didn't say anything. However, it was sufficient to stop her falling into the great chasm that lay before her. After a few moments, she was able to continue.

Rose came quickly to Ari's home and took Mira's hands, the ones that had been covered in blood. Just the fact that she was near gave Mira great comfort.

Whispering, Ari explained to Rose, 'Part of the afterbirth is still in there, I think.'

Mira was hurriedly taken in the lorry to Hula's small hospital, where the nurses took great care of her and a midwife and doctor ensured the afterbirth was safely removed, and then Mira was made comfortable in a hospital bed. Rose had stayed by her side through it all.

Months went by. Mira was fully recovered when Rose said to her, 'I think that we're going to have a trip of holiday bliss – that's you! – combined with specialist work – that's me! How would it be if you came with me on my New Guinea island travels, not doing anything at all, while you think about what you'll do in the future?' Then she offered gently, 'I suppose you are not ready to go back to Queensland?'

Mira shook her head slowly, ashamed at her sudden disappearance from school and family, afraid to face them ever again. They would be mortified; they would surely hate her!

When they came back from this wonderful trip around

the New Guinea islands, Mira was still wondering what to do with her life. Then she met Elise Steinbeck.

Elise was an extraordinary artist, employed by Port Moresby University. Rose and Mira went to her art festival there. The display was in the airy, central quadrangle, made up of strong upright pieces of concrete slabs. In amongst the artistic crowd, Rose and Mira were introduced to her.

Elise was a slight woman with a beautiful smile that lit up the whole place. Brought up in Jewish orthodoxy in Melbourne, her Polish father was cruel. Earlier on he had lived through the Second World War, and so held heart-rending memories. By the time he came to Australia he had met and married a young Jewish woman and soon they had a daughter, Elise. He expected the child to be perfect, but instead there was sorrow and despair when she didn't or couldn't live up to his extreme expectations.

When she was of an age to escape her father, Elise went to Port Moresby, alone. She was soon influenced by Doctor Rowe, an older man who was the university's Chaplain; he had happened to visit the Christian bookshop at the same time she did. They started to talk and before she knew it, the chaplain had arranged for a small room at the university campus to be available, where she would be able to paint. He supplied her with brushes, paints and old paintings that she could paint over to re-use the canvases.

At first Elise painted dark and cruel images, getting rid of all the hard memories of her cruel father. About a year later, her paintings began to draw on fresh God-like inspirational themes. These were very good to look at, but right out of Mira's price range!

Informed of Mira's recent history, she encouraged her to paint too. Mira still had memories of Rick Strait and his cruelty, and the loss of the small semi-formed child. Painting like this allowed her to work through those terrible times.

Then there came that occasion which Rick had spoken of – the preacher, Solomon Henau. Rose and Mira, with

Elise, went along to listen to him. Mira had made her first commitment to Jesus when she was confirmed. This time she was in quieter circumstances, inspired by Solomon, and she accepted Christ as a dear Friend who would now wrap her in His wonderful care.

Mira was wistful now, her face glowing as she spoke to her listeners. 'Remember the old hymn, *Tell Me the Old, Old Story?* Well, that one phrase: *Lord Jesus, make me whole?* That was what I needed – and that was what Jesus gave to me that night.'

They were all silent, in awe of a wonderful, forgiving Comforter whose healing is always there on offer for us to take. Then Mira went on:

'The middle of November meant that the Christmas season was arriving soon. Rose surprised me one day saying, "I have decided to go to New Zealand and see all my relatives and friends. Do you want to come?"

'I eagerly replied, "Yes, please!" And that's how I came to be here, at this very welcoming *Honeysuckle House*, among my new friends – all of you!' She waited a moment and then she quietly said, 'That now includes you, Rick Strait!'

Surprisingly, Mira and Rick embraced. It is amazing what forgiveness will do.

Epilogue

*A*T *HONEYSUCKLE HOUSE,* Polly and Adam snuggled up to one another on a garden seat near to his study. They had developed the habit of doing this on most summer evenings. This time, he was suddenly disturbed by his mobile phone interrupting the peace and tranquillity.

On answering it, he heard Sam speaking in an excited but garbled way. It took a few minutes for Adam to realise that he was talking about his soon-to-be baby son.

Polly, worried at Adam's strange expressions, said, 'Well, what is it?' and unsuccessfully grabbed at the phone.

Adam smiled. 'Hang on a moment,' he said to his proud son. Speaking to Polly, 'Last year Sam married delightful Fleur. You said that being forty-five, he will be sixty when the baby reaches fifteen. Now Sam and Fleur are going to have a boy, and they have already given him a name – Eli Fraser.'

'What fun!' said Polly. She was going to be a grandmother again! She must get out her knitting and create some garments for the baby. She wondered how Jack and Mira were getting on but, having this fleeting thought, she tucked it away for another day.

Adam didn't have to worry, just be an accepting grandfather yet again. And remembering to pick up the phone, he now told Sam all about his experiences with *him* as a baby.

Adam and Polly were thoroughly blessed with joy!

The Author

Robert Simpson is a Presbyterian minister now resident in New Zealand's Christchurch. In 1969, he went to Port Moresby as a literature missionary. There he met and married his English wife Margaret, an excellent nurse and midwife. They have four strapping sons who between them have produced eight grandchildren, the latest in the photograph on the inside back cover.

Robert has worked in bookselling, publishing and insurance as well as serving the ecumenical church in Australia, Papua New Guinea, England and New Zealand. He is a graduate of the Bible College of NZ and, twenty years later, the United Theological College in Sydney, Australia.

Twenty-five years ago, Robert retired through ill health. Following Clinical Depression and Electro-Convulsive Therapy, he had a severe Stroke, after which he had to learn to talk, walk and write again. This took a long, long time but gradually, he has authored devotional books and novels.

A PHOTOGRAPGH OF THE AUTHOR AND HIS LATEST GRANDSON CAN BE SEEN INSIDE THE BACK COVER.